Cal's grin broadened.
He couldn't help it.

"Why, Miz Livy, could it be you're *jealous?*"

"Jealous?" Livy repeated incredulously, going pale, and then her blue eyes blazed up at him. "Why, you have your nerve, you—you conceited polecat! If we weren't on a public street, I'd—I'd slap your face, Caleb Devlin!"

He raised an eyebrow and hooked his thumbs in his frock coat pockets. *"Again?* My, you are becomin' a violent woman, aren't you, Livy?" he drawled. He saw her hands clench into fists at her sides. "If the urge is really overpowering, we could just duck in here, so you could get it out of your system in private," he added, nodding toward the jail they were standing by.

He felt his grin widening. Her face was flushed—like a woman in the throes of passion. She really would slap his face if he told her *that!*

Dear Reader,

Laurie Grant fans rejoice, the Readers' Choice Award-winning author is back this month with her new Western, *Lawman*. In this fast-paced sequel to her 1996 release, *Devil's Dare*, a lonely lawman rediscovers love in the arms of his childhood sweetheart. Don't miss this wonderful tale from an author whom *Affaire de Coeur* calls "an unbelievably gifted writer."

For those of you who enjoy the Regency era, Taylor Ryan's *The Essential Wife* is the delightful story of a dashing nobleman who suddenly finds himself in love with the penniless heiress whom he has arranged to marry out of pity.

Nevada Territory is the setting for *All But the Queen of Hearts*, Rae Muir's heartwarming Western about a shy farm widow and the handsome stranger who was swindled in a poker game by her late husband. And we are very pleased this month to be able to bring you Silhouette Yours Truly and Special Edition author Beth Henderson's first historical for Harlequin, *Reckless*, in which a young woman accused of being a jewel thief is rescued by a mysterious baron intent on clearing her name.

We hope you keep a lookout for all four titles wherever Harlequin Historicals are sold.

Sincerely,

Tracy Farrell
Senior Editor

Please address questions and book requests to:
Harlequin Reader Service
U.S.: 3010 Walden Ave., P.O. Box 1325, Buffalo, NY 14269
Canadian: P.O. Box 609, Fort Erie, Ont. L2A 5X3

Lawman
Laurie Grant

Harlequin Books

TORONTO • NEW YORK • LONDON
AMSTERDAM • PARIS • SYDNEY • HAMBURG
STOCKHOLM • ATHENS • TOKYO • MILAN
MADRID • WARSAW • BUDAPEST • AUCKLAND

In grateful acknowledgment to

Helen Wade, who helped with details regarding the
Episcopal Church, and Paul Becerra
and Mr. and Mrs. Sergio Egea,
who helped me with my Spanish.

ISBN 0-373-28967-7

LAWMAN

Copyright © 1997 by Laurie A. Miller

Books by Laurie Grant

Harlequin Historicals

Beloved Deceiver #170
The Raven and the Swan #205
Lord Liar #257
Devil's Dare #300
My Lady Midnight #340
Lawman #367

LAURIE GRANT

combines a career as a trauma center emergency room nurse with that of historical romance author; she says the writing helps keep her sane. Passionately enthusiastic about the history of both England and Texas, she divides her travel time between these two spots. She is married to her own real-life hero, and has two teenage daughters, two dogs and a cat.

If you would like to write to Laurie, please use the address below:

Laurie Grant
P.O. Box 307274
Gahana, OH 43230

To Deb and Mary, Hussies both

And always, to Michael

Chapter One

Brazos County, Texas
1868

"Oh, son, I still can't believe you're here, and *alive*," Sarah Devlin said. Her voice was choked with tears, but her face was beaming as she stared across the table at him.

His brother Sam, seeing that Cal was in the midst of chewing some of their mother's famous pecan pie, said, "Aw, Ma, Cal sent me home ahead of him just so you *could* get used to the idea." Sam grinned in delight, for it had been he who had found Cal, whom they'd all thought dead, when he'd herded some cattle north to Abilene on a trail drive. Sam had his arm around Mercy, his new bride, whom he'd also found in Abilene and brought home with him to Texas.

"Sorry I'm not the same beautiful boy you sent away, Ma," Cal said with self-deprecating humor, referring to the black patch that now covered his sightless right eye, the two scars that radiated over his cheek from beneath the patch and the black hair that was now mixed with silver. The middle child of the Devlin brood, he was only four years older than Sam, but he looked ten years older.

"You're still a beautiful sight to me, Caleb Travis Devlin," his mother replied stoutly, her gaze still adoring. "I'd gotten so used to thinking of you as dead, you could have come back with both eyes patched and no arms and legs and I'd still think you were a beautiful sight."

"That's all we need on this place—one more cripple." Garrick's sour voice came from the far end of the table.

Cal winced inwardly as he glanced at his eldest brother, who'd had a leg amputated above the knee after a minié ball had shattered both bones in his shin. It was obvious Garrick still hadn't gotten over the depression that often came with such a loss. Cal knew what such a morass of despair could be like because he'd gone through it himself.

"Now, Garrick, we all think you do very well, especially now that you've gotten that artificial limb," Sarah Devlin declared. "Why, you keep this family together, Garrick. And you quite put me in mind of your father, sitting at the head of the table like that."

"Yeah, I do real well for a cripple, lurching around the farm like a drunken pirate, telling the hands what to do. But it's been Sam who's been putting the Devlin stud farm back together, with the cash he brought back from Abilene."

Cal watched as Sam tightened his jaw and stared down at his hands. Then Mercy took his brother's hand and squeezed it, and Sam smiled slightly at her. Thank God for Mercy Fairweather Devlin, who had made his brother so happy and who was going to give Sam a baby in the spring.

It hadn't escaped Cal's notice that Annie, their widowed sister, had been twisting her napkin while Garrick was talking. Now she spoke up. "Oh, Garrick, not tonight," she said, her voice anguished. "Not when Cal's just been restored to us. We've all lost *something* in the war, and I think we should be thankful he's back, not dwell on what will never be the same again."

Garrick said nothing, just stared morosely down at the food he'd been picking at.

He was probably in pain, Cal guessed, for his brother had already let slip the fact that he suffered a good deal of chronic pain from the way the Confederate army surgeons—"butchers," he called them—had "repaired" his leg. And it was likely he was in a good deal of emotional pain, as well. He'd probably have been able to adjust fairly well to the loss of his limb if Cecilia, his flighty wife, hadn't run off the day after Garrick had come home minus a leg. Cal figured he'd have to get Garrick alone soon and see if there was any way he could encourage him. Cal was an ordained minister, after all. Surely that was a part of his job.

He cleared his throat in the awkward silence that followed Annie's outburst. "Who's pastoring the Bryan Episcopal Church these days? I'm sure they didn't leave the pulpit empty all those years I was away, especially after I came up missing."

"No, I'm afraid they filled that position with indecent haste, right after folks in Bryan found out you had gone away to wear blue, not gray. The fellow that's preaching now, Josiah Maxwell, is the same man who took over when you left."

"You don't say that as if you like him very well,"

Cal said, noting the way his mother's lips had pursed when she said the man's name.

"I don't, and God forgive me for that," she admitted quickly, her eyes troubled. "And it's not just that he isn't *you*, Caleb. Maxwell doesn't have your gift with people, son. He's self-righteous and proud, and as far as I'm concerned, during the war he was hiding behind the cloth as an excuse not to go and fight—for one side or the other. He could have at least gone as a chaplain, seems to me."

Cal sighed. He'd known the pastorate wouldn't have remained empty all those years he was gone, but he'd had this dream of coming home to find his congregation ready and waiting for him.

"Do you suppose he'd be at all amenable to my offering myself as associate pastor, or as some sort of a helper? The congregation had grown to the point that I was thinking of suggesting hiring an assistant myself before I left."

Garrick let out an inelegant snort. "He'll let you help him when there are snowball fights in hell, brother."

"Son, I do wish you'd mind your language at the table!" Sarah Devlin snapped. "I didn't raise you to talk like that!"

"Sorry, Ma. But it's best he knows what his reception's apt to be like. And it ain't only the preacher, Cal. Folks in Bryan still haven't forgotten the war—how could they, when they lost so many sons and husbands and brothers, and we've still got a provisional federal government? Folks haven't forgotten you fought your own kind."

"I had to do what I thought was right," Cal said, trying to keep his voice even. He could feel himself flushing with anger.

"Garrick, I absolutely *will not tolerate* the War Between the States being fought over again at this dinner table, do you hear me?" their mother said quickly, smacking the scarred old table to emphasize her point.

Garrick had the grace to look ashamed. "I'm sorry again. I just thought Cal ought to be warned how it's going to be. Cal, if I were you I'd tread real softly when I go into town, and don't be real surprised that no one else is killing the fatted calf over your return."

"I appreciate the warning," Cal made himself say, as soon as he could master his temper. "I suppose it's only natural people would feel that way, even though the war's been over a good three years."

Then Sam spoke up, a mischievous grin on his face. "Say, brother, I've got somethin' I've been waitin' to ask you ever since we left you in Abilene, and my curiosity's been plaguin' me all those weeks we traveled and while we waited for you to come home."

"And what might that be, Sam? Dare I ask?" retorted Cal with good-humored wariness. Thank God for his amiable younger brother, who could always be depended upon to defuse a tense moment with something funny. The devilish glint in Sam's eyes promised just such a moment.

"Who's the girl you planned to look up once you got back, Cal?"

"Oh, she's probably already married," Cal said casually, looking down so his face wouldn't betray the longing he'd felt ever since he'd regained his memory of who he really was—and of the girl he'd left behind when he'd gone off to war. Whether she was married or not, she'd probably succeeded in forgetting him just as thoroughly as he'd forgotten that he was Caleb Devlin.

"Maybe, but you never know, brother," Sam said, his grin and his drawl broadening. "Now, if you were to tell me it was Lucy Snow, for example, why, I've got good news for you. She's been wearin' black for some poor boy ever since Second Manassas, Ma tells me—"

"Sam! Lucy Snow is a wrinkled-up prune of a woman!" chided Annie, obviously trying to hold back a giggle. "Cal has better taste than that! Uh...it *isn't* Lucy Snow you were going to look up, was it?" she added with a sudden anxiety.

Cal chuckled. "No, Annie, it wasn't Lucy Snow. If memory serves, she was a wrinkled-up prune of a woman even before the war, wasn't she? She never wore her bonnet out in the sun. But I believe she was sweet on the Tetersall boy, not me."

Annie sighed in exaggerated relief. "Oh, Cal, they were all sweet on you! Everyone wanted to marry the bachelor preacher," she said, with a fond smile at her brother.

"So who is it, Cal?" Sam persisted. "Come on, brother, you aren't going to get out of telling us."

"All right, all right!" Cal said, holding up his hands in mock surrender. "I can see you won't give me any peace till I tell you. But remember, it was just someone I thought about once I recalled who I was. I know she's probably already married. You've all got to promise me this won't go beyond the Devlin supper table."

They all raised their right hands, an old family ritual that suddenly had all of them smiling, even Garrick. They felt like a family once again.

"All right, I'll tell you. It was Olivia Childress."

Silence hung over the table like a cloak for several heartbeats. Sam looked at their mother. Sarah looked at

Garrick. Garrick looked at Annie. It was Annie who found her voice at last.

"Oh, Cal. I'm sorry. Olivia Childress married, all right. She married a man named Dan Gillespie, over at Gillespie Springs."

Cal shrugged. That was that, then. The woman he'd dreamed about when he'd been in the Union army, right up until he'd been injured, and had started to dream about again these past two months, was taken. He'd just have to forget her.

"Don't be sorry. It's probably just as well," he said with forced lightness. "She told me she hated me when she found out my uniform was going to be blue, not gray. She probably cusses every time she thinks of me, if she thinks of me at all. And if we never meet again, at least she'll remember me as that *handsome* Devlin boy she hated," he said, pointing to his eye patch.

But something in his sister's face warned him there was more. "Annie, is there something you're not telling me?"

His sister looked uneasy. "He's dead. Dan Gillespie, that is. He died just last month."

Hope flared anew. Gillespie Springs wasn't that far from Bryan—just an hour away. He could ride over some fine day and pay his respects to the widow—with Annie along to make it respectable and all—and maybe, after a decent time passed...

"He—he killed himself, Cal," Annie added, her face anguished.

Cal's jaw fell. "How awful! Poor Livy—how hard it must have been on her!"

"Poor Livy, hell!" growled Garrick. "They say he put a bullet through his head 'cause Livy was cheatin' on him!"

Chapter Two

The silence in the room was deafening. Out of the corner of his eye, Cal saw his mother shoot a disapproving glare at Garrick, but even she, apparently, could not find any words to say.

"Best shut yer mouth, brother. You'll draw flies," Garrick commented sardonically after an endless moment.

Cal did so, feeling foolish. "I—I don't believe it," he said at last, smothering a very unministerial urge to sink a fist in Garrick's mocking face. "Livy wouldn't do such a thing—not the Livy *I* knew, at least. She's the kind of girl to honor any commitments she made. Especially the bonds of matrimony."

"People can change, Cal," Sam offered mildly, "and not always for the better. What's it been—seven years since you last saw her?"

Cal said nothing, his mind filled with remembered images of Livy dancing with him at a local ball, her lovely face upturned to his, her eyes alight, the touch of her as smooth as silk as they whirled around the dance floor.... Livy kissing him in the garden later that same night, the scent of her perfume mingling with the honeysuckle, her eyes now dark with a woman's se-crets…and later, her scornful blue eyes as she told him never to darken her door again.

"They say she's carryin' the other man's baby," Garrick said, just as Cal was searching for some topic, *any* topic, to change the subject to.

"Garrick, sometimes you don't have the good sense God gave a jackass," Annie hissed. "Why didn't you just keep your mouth shut? There was no need to bur-den Cal with such—such gossip!"

"He'd find out soon enough, I reckon," said Garrick, unruffled. "I just thought I'd better tell him before he gets a notion to ride over an' comfort the widow."

"I had no intention of doing that," Cal insisted, though he wasn't at all sure he was telling the truth. "And just how do 'they' know these things, Garrick, whoever 'they' are?"

He wondered why he was torturing himself with the questions, when his brain screamed that he didn't want to know the answers.

"Dan Gillespie put it in the letter he left near his body for his brother to find."

"Oh? And did he also put in the name of the man who—" Cal glanced uneasily at his mother, his sister and sister-in-law, and rephrased what he was about to ask "—stole his wife's affections?"

"Didn't need to," Garrick answered bluntly.

Cal raised an inquiring brow and waited.

"Everyone around knew who it was—a Mexican va-quero who'd been workin' for 'em for a spell. He'd been acting way too familiar with the missus. Dan shot him when he found out it was more'n that. Then he killed himself."

Cal closed his eyes, feeling a familiar headache de-

scending over him like a black cloak. He'd had headaches at intervals ever since the battle that had robbed
him of one of his eyes, though of course he hadn't remembered the cause of his loss until he'd regained his
memory. Headaches hadn't come often, in recent years,
but he could always count on one arriving whenever he
was unduly tired or upset. And now he was both. He
rubbed his forehead.

"I assume," he said wearily, "that no one doubted
Dan Gillespie's say-so?"

"I've had enough of this conversation," their mother
said, and stalked from the room. Annie and Mercy followed, after giving the men at the table uneasy glances.

Garrick snorted as he lit a cheroot. "Of course not!
The man shot his wife's defiler, a greaser at that! A
man has a perfect right to avenge his honor, doesn't
he?"

Yes, especially when the accused 'defiler' was a
Mexican, Cal thought, sick at heart. No white man in
Texas was going to stop and get a Mexican's side of
the story first. Nothing had changed.

"And just how is everyone so sure that the baby
couldn't be Dan Gillespie's?" Cal found himself asking, just when he wanted nothing so much as to go
upstairs and lie down in the dark.

"Gillespie said it wasn't, in the note he left. Not that
he needed to.... He an' Livy didn't have any children
in six years of marriage—"

"But the war," Cal protested. "From what you're
telling me, they got married during the war. Wasn't Dan
in the army during the war?"

Sam nodded. "Terry's Rangers."

"Well, I can understand why they might not have

had a child during the war, especially if he didn't get home on leave much. But after—?''

''When he came home,'' Sam said heavily, his eyes on the table, ''it was pretty much common knowledge that Dan couldn't...um, he wasn't able...''

''Oh, Sam, just *say* it, damn it!'' Garrick said with a snicker. ''The ladies've gone out on the porch—they cain't hear you! Dan had a war injury that caused him not t'be able to get his pecker up no more! That's what our little brother's trying to say, Cal!''

So Dan Gillespie had killed his wife's lover and then killed himself, leaving Livy to face the consequences.

''What's happened to Livy after all this?''

Garrick's shrug of the shoulders was eloquent. He didn't have to say, *Who cares?* ''How am I supposed to know?'' he muttered at last.

''You were remarkably informed up to this point,'' retorted Cal. ''Don't stop now! You mean the gossip stopped with the sinful woman's lover getting killed?''

''Now don't try t'make me sound like some tale-bearin' ol' biddy,'' Garrick growled. ''Some of th' scandal was in the newspaper, seein' as how the Gillespie boys' father founded that town an' all, and you know how people talk. It sure beats jawin' about the carpetbaggers still crawlin' all over Texas. All right, if you must know, I heard tell that in Gillespie Springs, Livy Gillespie's about as welcome as fire ants at a picnic.''

''Why doesn't she just leave?'' Cal wondered aloud.

Garrick snorted again. ''Who knows? It ain't like their little farm's prime acreage or nothin', though Dan did manage to keep the taxes paid on the place. Some say she's just stayin' so as not to give Robert Gillespie, her brother-in-law, the satisfaction. He wants her gone bad, ol' Bob does, so he can add their land to his hold-ings, but Dan didn't change his will before he died. His old will specified that the land went wholly to Livy 'and their issue.'"

"Isn't that a little inconsistent?"

His brother looked puzzled.

"Not to change the will, I mean, after going to the trouble of killing the man who'd cuckolded him and of leaving a note and all."

Garrick shrugged again. "Damnation, Cal, the man had to have been out of his mind, after findin' out some Mexican had taken his place in her bed, and killin' him. He must have just forgot!" His voice took on a scornful edge. "And now the 'issue' that's gonna be livin' there is some other man's bastard."

"Garrick—" began Sam.

"Oh, shut up, little brother. You think just 'cause you married the preacher's daughter that every woman is as innocent and pure as they'd like you to believe! Well, if my wife skeedaddlin' at the sight of my chopped-off leg ain't enough proof that women ain't t'be trusted, then the likes a' Livy Gillespie surely oughta be!"

Ignoring Garrick's bitter remark, Cal met Sam's gaze in a moment of shared amusement, both remembering the circumstances of Sam's hasty wedding to Mercy, which had come *after* their wedding night rather than before. Yes, Garrick supposed a lot of things that weren't necessarily so. Maybe this was another of them.

In any case, however, it wasn't going to matter to Cal. By now his head was throbbing unmercifully, the pain settling behind his eyes like red-hot needles, so that even the flickering light of the lamp caused agony when he looked at it.

"I hope y'all will excuse me, but I'm gonna turn in," he said, rising to his feet. "It's been a long day."

Once he had reached the sanctuary of his room, he had a moment of indecision. Should he dig into the old carpetbag he kept under the bed and bring out the bottle of laudanum he hadn't used in months? Was it weak to seek relief from this pain in a bottle of strong medicine? He didn't want to start craving it, the way he'd seen some wounded men do during the war. Yet he knew he wouldn't be able to sleep when the pain got to be this intense, so at last he reached under the bed and brought it out, unstoppering it and taking a couple of sips. He knew its euphoric effects would banish his headache and then bring a healing sleep. And maybe the narcotic-induced euphoria would keep him from thinking about Livy Gillespie.

He'd think about Lizabeth, the woman who'd taken him in when he'd finally fallen off his horse at her isolated farmhouse, wounded, shivering with fever and having no idea of who he was. Even though he'd been wearing a blue uniform in the midst of rebel territory, Lizabeth had hidden him and nursed him until he was well. When he'd gotten better he'd just never gotten around to leaving. He didn't know what regiment to return to anyway.

Eventually love had grown between him and the widowed Lizabeth and he had married her, only to lose her to pneumonia later. From there he'd drifted on to Abilene, where Sam had found him tending bar as "Deacon Paxton."

Yes, Cal would think of Lizabeth. Now there had been a good woman, a trustworthy woman. As he lay in the comforting darkness of the bedroom, waiting for the laudanum to take effect, he tried to remember her face. She'd been a blonde, her hair a reddish-gold shade she called strawberry. She'd had big green eyes and a determined chin...but somehow, every time he tried to picture her, Livy's face intruded instead.

Walking up the steps of the Bryan Episcopal Church was like coming home. Built of freestone in hues of mellow gold and gray, the exterior of the building was in harmony with the golden autumn morning.

Entering the sanctuary through the short narthex, Cal lifted his eyes with pleasure to the stained-glass window behind the altar, which portrayed Jesus as the Good Shepherd, surrounded by sheep and tenderly holding a lamb. It had been purchased at some considerable sacrifice by the parishioners when the church was still newly built, a couple of years before the war, and Cal, just ordained, had taken over as the rector. That window reminded him of why he wanted to minister to God's people. He'd often write his sermons while sitting in the front pew, looking up at that window for inspiration.

"So it's true—you're back. What are you doing here?" demanded a raspy voice behind him.

Cal knew who it was before he turned around. "Hello, Josiah," he said, extending his hand as he faced the man who'd taken his place as rector. "Yes, I'm back, and not dead after all, it seems." He smiled pleasantly at the portly man, who was five years his senior. "It's nice to be home."

Josiah Maxwell just breathed heavily, his dark eyes suspicious. "I *said*, what're you doing here?" He jerked his head around to indicate that he meant the interior of the church.

Cal sighed inwardly. So Maxwell wasn't going to make it easy. "Why, I just came to look at my favorite picture. It sustained me, thinking about that picture during the war. I even remembered it after the shell hit—" he gestured toward his patch and the scars "—and I couldn't remember anything else. I just couldn't remember where I'd seen it."

He knew as soon as he'd said it that mentioning the war had been the wrong thing to do. It gave Maxwell an excuse to object to him sooner.

"You mean when you were wearing a blue coat and killing other Texas boys?" Maxwell asked with a sneer.

Cal took a deep breath. If he'd thought his appearance would appeal to Maxwell's sense of compassion, he'd been deluding himself. "Josiah, that's all over now. It's been over for three years. I'd hoped by now folks would be willing to let bygones be bygones, and live for today and the future, not dwell in the past, however tragic it's been for all of us. I—I'd even hoped maybe you might have some work for me to do to help you here."

Maxwell's flush had risen up his neck, past his muttonchop-whiskered jowls to the top of his thinning brown hair.

"Work? For you? I'm the rector here—I don't need any help."

"I know you're the rector, Josiah," Cal said patiently. "I'm not trying to take your place, merely to offer assistance. I'd be happy to do anything, as a deacon or in whatever capacity you'd like. When I left, this place was crying out for an assistant rector."

Maxwell's arms folded over his ample belly. "I got nothing for you to do here," he insisted. "I reckon I'd sooner work with the devil himself."

"You wouldn't consider consulting the vestry first, before giving me your final answer?" Cal asked, referring to the lay governing board of the church. "I'm willing to wait until they can meet."

"I'll just bet you are," said Maxwell with an ugly laugh. "You waited three years after the war was over to come home, didn't you? I guess that makes you a patient man. But the vestry isn't going to vote any different, so you may as well forget it."

Cal thought about explaining his loss of memory, then dismissed the idea. Chances were Maxwell had already heard that part, too, and didn't believe it. "I'm sorry to hear that," Cal made himself say in a calm tone. "Well, I'll see you on Sunday, then, Josiah."

"I wouldn't bother, if I were you. Folks see you come in, they're apt to leave. They don't hold with worshippin' alongside a' traitors."

Cal just stared at him for a moment before turning on his heel to go. Back in the narthex, he encountered a drawn, haggard woman dressed in mourning black, who looked faintly familiar.

"Good mornin', ma'am. Aren't you Miss Lucy Snow? Cal Devlin," he explained, when the woman just stared, gaping, at his eye patch. "It's nice to see you again," he said politely, while thinking inwardly that Annie had spoken the truth when she'd said Lucy was a wrinkled-up prune.

The woman's blank stare turned to narrow-eyed outrage. "Don't you even speak to me, you blue-bellied *devil!*" she snarled, and swept on past him with a swish of black bombazine.

So he wasn't even welcome in his own church, he thought. Perhaps it was just a matter of time, of being patient while people he'd ministered to learned to trust him all over again. Perhaps he'd have to work on the Devlin farm for a spell, training and selling horses with

Sam. Cal liked horses well enough, he guessed, and
Sam would welcome his help, though he didn't actually
need it. But even as Cal considered the appealing prospect he knew it wasn't for him. He wanted something
of his *own* to do.

He mounted Goliad outside the stone church and
headed down to the post office. He'd promised Mercy
he'd see if there was a letter from Abilene from her
father, the Reverend Fairweather. And Annie wanted
some yellow thread from the mercantile. Now there
were two good places to determine if his reception at
the church was going to be typical of the whole town.

The post office was just a small frame building,
hardly big enough for the clerk and three chattering ladies who occupied it, two of whom were enormously
fat and identical in all respects, including the number
of chins they possessed. The Goodlet twins? Sam had
told him back in Abilene how the twins were no longer
the buxom charmers who'd once competed for his attention.

Conversation ceased as he entered the post office.
"Good morning, ladies," he said, bowing before stepping up to the counter, where the clerk favored him with
a basilisk glare.

The third woman put a net-gloved hand up to her
mouth as if Beelzebub had just spoken to her.

"Well, I never," murmured one of the twins.

"The nerve of some people!" sputtered the other,
setting her chins wagging.

Cal smiled grimly at the Wanted poster on the wall,
suppressing the urge to ask Leticia what she'd "never"
and Alicia whether she meant he'd had a lot of nerve
not to be dead.

"What do you want, mister?" demanded the goggle-eyed clerk, his Adam's apple bobbing up and down. It was as if he hadn't been the prize pupil in Cal's catechism class before the war.

"Nothing much," he said pleasantly. "Just wanted to see if my sister-in-law, Mercy Devlin, had any mail waiting."

The clerk looked through a stack of letters. "Yup. Here," he said, shoving one of them across the counter at him, then staring pointedly toward the door.

Cal took the hint, feeling the women's eyes on him all the way out the door and hearing the buzz of talk begin once he was safely out of the building. On to the mercantile, then. Since it was just three short blocks, he left Goliad tied to the post-office hitching post.

He passed the Bonny Blue Flag Saloon, remembering that it had been merely the Bryan Saloon before the war. He was thirsty, but kept on walking. Maybe he'd stop in after he was done with his errand. Stepping off the plank sidewalk and into the dusty street to allow two more ladies to pass, he tipped his hat, but they merely stuck their noses in the air and sailed on, their bustles sending their skirts billowing in their wakes.

Sitting on a weathered bench outside the Bryan Mercantile and Emporium was a trio of idlers.

"Well, if it ain't the prodigal son, returned from the dead," began one, whom Cal recognized as the livery owner, a man who had never darkened the door of the Episcopal church, nor, it was well known, of the Baptist church, either.

"Eww, I *thought* I smelled somethin'!" jeered another man, stopping his whittling to eye Cal.

"You did, Asa. A no-good skunk," the third man chimed in.

"Good day, gentlemen," Cal said evenly, and went

on in. He heard the creak of the boardwalk as they rose to follow him. Apparently he wasn't even going to be allowed to purchase Annie's thread in peace.

As his sight adjusted to the dim interior of the mercantile, he noticed a pair of ladies studying a bolt of blue calico. He nodded to them, hearing one of them gasp as he turned toward the proprietor. The latter was standing behind the counter, favoring him with the glare Cal was now becoming all too familiar with.

"What do *you* want?" the man said.

"Just some yellow thread for my sister, Mr. Ames."

"Yella? He wants *yella* thread, did you hear that, Asa? Ain't that the appropriate color fer him t'buy?" chortled one of the idlers behind him.

"What kind of yellow, Devlin? We got two-three shades here," the proprietor said, fishing around in a case and holding out several hanks of thread.

"Oh, I expect he'll take *coward* yella!" the liveryman announced, before Cal could say anything.

Cal felt his temper fraying. He didn't want to raise a ruckus, not in a store or in front of ladies, but he didn't think this trio of no-goods was going to be content to let him go without one. He knew as a man of the cloth, even an unemployed one, he ought to just continue to ignore them, but he wasn't sure how long he could. Turning his cheek had never been his strong suit.

"I'll take that one," he said, pointing at random to a hank of thread the color of the daffodils that came up in February here. He laid a five-cent piece on the counter, not even waiting to see if he had paid too much. He just wanted to get out of there before these idlers made him do something ugly in the confines of the store.

"Bill, I guess he's too yella to say anythin' to ya," jeered Asa, just as Cal was turning around.

"No, I'm not," he countered. "I've just been raised not to call you what you are in the presence of ladies," he said, jerking his head in the direction of the two women, who were already shrinking back against the far wall, watching them.

They let him get all the way out of the store and halfway down the street before they challenged him again, but Cal could feel them following him, like a pack of wild dogs waiting for the right moment to attack. He kept walking, his head held high, his back straight. He had never been a coward, and he wasn't now—he just thought the fight that was going to result was going to be so...*useless.*

He heard one of them clomp up onto the sidewalk and shout through the bat-wing doors of the Bonny Blue Flag, "Hey, boys, guess who's back in town? Traitor Devlin, that's who! Why don't ya all come out fer a second and give him a rousin' welcome like he deserves!"

Three or four cowboys heeded the summons and came running out.

Cal wasn't armed, hadn't thought it appropriate for a preacher to strap on a six-gun. That was both a blessing and a curse, for although no one could pull a gun on him fairly if he wasn't armed, wearing one himself might have kept the beating he was about to receive to merely verbal abuse. But damnation, if he was going to receive some bruises he was going to mete out some, too.

"Hey, blue belly! Devlin! Reckon I'll be the first t'show ya how welcome ya are here!"

Cal heard the thudding of the cowboy's boot heels as

he ran up from behind, intending to jump him, and met the man's advance with his fist instead. He was pleased to see the cowboy fall like a rock, a crimson stream spurting from his nose.

So much for turning the other cheek. Lord, what he wouldn't give to have Sam at his side right now. There'd still be a fight—likely it would have happened sooner, but it would have been a little less lopsided.

After that it was chaos, with the other six men all jumping him at once, fists flying, calling out to every loitering male within earshot to join them. Cal fought desperately, landing punches on every body part of anyone he could reach, and receiving curses and blows in return. A cacophony of noise filled the dusty air.

He never saw the blow that felled him, for it came from the right, on his blind side. All he knew was that suddenly the struggle was over and he was cloaked in a cloud of velvet black.

The woman just mounting the buckboard to begin her drive home had seen the scarred man with the eye patch go down and had wondered what he had done to incur the enmity of so many men at once. To say he was outnumbered in the situation was putting it mildly.

She knew what being the underdog felt like, right enough, and she hated the feeling. Still, she wasn't inclined to intervene; she'd been on the receiving end of male wrath entirely too much lately.

Probably the man *had* done something to deserve the drubbing he was getting, like welshing on a poker debt or cheating another man on a horse trade, so she probably shouldn't let it trouble her conscience. And yet... She paused, about to cluck "giddap" to the horse, when she heard one of the ruffians yell something about getting tar and feathers.

She wasn't going to let that happen—wasn't going to let her reluctance to confront any more angry males extend so far that she would meekly allow them to do such a barbarous, painful thing. Not while she had breath in her body. She had been unable to save Francisco, but perhaps she could help this man, at least until she could find out what he had done.

Setting the brake and securing the reins, she picked up her shotgun and aimed it into the air, letting go with one barrel. She hoped she wouldn't have to use the other one. Then she pointed it at the stunned attackers, who were still bent over their unconscious quarry. The man who'd started to run to fetch the tar and feathers froze in his tracks.

"Y'all ought to be ashamed of yourselves, all of you pickin' on one man!" she shouted in the sudden silence, jumping down from her buckboard and stalking over to the fallen man. "Go on, get out of here! I'm sure you got better things to be doin'!" She kept her shotgun aimed at the half-dozen men, who obediently backed away. A couple of them slipped back into the saloon.

"You know this man?" one of them asked.

She darted a glance at the crumpled form, but he was lying facedown. "No, but that doesn't mean I'm going to let you bullies kill him. He was unarmed," she said with a calmness she was far from feeling.

"Ma'am, I'm sure you mean well, and I shorely do honor yore sense a' fair play," one of them began with an ingratiating smile, "but I think you oughta know this here yella-bellied coward fought for the Yanks, and then hid out for the rest of the war."

No, it couldn't be....

"So?" she asked belligerently, not lowering the shotgun or letting herself think about who it was she was protecting.

"So we was jest treatin' him like such traitors deserve t'be treated," the dusty, sweaty ruffian answered. "So perhaps you oughta get back up on yer buckboard, ma'am, and ride on t'wherever you was goin' and don't worry yore purdy little head—"

Were they going to rush her and try to take away her shotgun? Was she going to have to shoot one of them to prove she meant what she said? *Could* she shoot one of them?

"You heard the lady," said a voice from behind her. "Now get on outa here."

Olivia Gillespie turned to see a man behind her, his Colt drawn and aimed at the four who still remained. He touched the brim of his hat to her, then his eyes went back to the other men.

There was a long silence as they eyed each other, and finally the liveryman said, "Well, all right, Devlin, we'll let him go this time. But mebbe ya better tell yore brother we don't like his kind in Bryan no more."

"I reckon you've more than made your point," retorted Sam Devlin, with a meaningful glance at his brother's still form. "But if you ever lay a hand on him again it's gonna be you lyin' there, not my brother. Now get on outa here, like I said before."

He watched the four until they had slunk into the saloon, then turned back to Livy.

"Miz Gillespie, I'm much obliged," he said as he walked over to see to his brother. She watched as he gently turned him over onto his back, and winced as she heard Cal groan.

If she hadn't been told it was Caleb Devlin, she never

would have been able to guess. The eye that wasn't patched was rapidly swelling shut, and he was covered with scrapes and bruises. There was a laceration on his unscarred cheek that would likely make a new scar, and another over his lip. The hair she remembered as being black as a crow's wing was now streaked with gray. The patch had been shoved out of place, and she gently pulled it back in place over the closed lid.

"Cal, it's all right. They're gone now," the younger Devlin said softly, but the injured man didn't react further. He was still unconscious.

"It's a good thing you came along," she said, glancing briefly at the tall, dark-haired cowboy, who looked like a younger version of Cal. "I'm not sure I could've held them off forever, even with old Betsy here," she said, with a nod toward the ancient shotgun.

"Oh, they probably wouldn't've had the gumption to try anythin' else," he said with a reassuring grin. "They're just braggarts and bullies. I had a feelin' that things might not go right the first time my brother showed his face in Bryan, though, so I thought I'd better check and see how it was goin'. Looks like I shoulda come a mite sooner."

She didn't want to add to his self-reproach, and so she changed the subject. "You're Sam, aren't you? Last time I saw you you were just a skinny boy flirting with the little girls at the annual church picnic on the river."

Sam smiled. "I reckon I've grown a little since then. Now, I think I spotted Cal's horse down the street a piece. If you could just wait with my brother, I'll bring him up, but I reckon my Buck would mind less than his stallion about carryin' Cal home over his saddle," he said, nodding toward the placid buckskin gelding that stood at the hitching post, switching at flies with his black tail.

"Nonsense," replied Livy. "There's no need to do that when I've got my buckboard. I'll help you load him onto the bed of my wagon, and you can tie his horse on the back."

at the kitchen post, watching at Ben with the
his index...

"Nonsense," replied Lucy. "There's no need to do
that way. I'm not any Sock said. I'll help you load
him onto the be... or gas, suppose she... you will do all... ...
those on the bed...

Chapter Three

Cal woke to the bite of a needle piercing his cheek.
"*Ow!* Damnation! What do you think you're you doing,
Annie?" he growled, opening his eye as far as the
swelling would allow. His sister was poised over him
with a needle and black thread.

"Land sakes, Cal, is that any way for a minister to
talk? And I should think it would be obvious what I'm
doing, though I'd hoped to finish this while you were
still passed out," Annie responded tartly. "I'm stitching
up your cheek, brother dear. Now hold still while I do
just one more."

Cal set his teeth and gripped the edge of the table,
trying his best to focus on his mother, whom he could
see hovering anxiously behind Annie. Not a sound escaped his lips as the needle flashed past his eye and bit
him twice, once on either side of the laceration. He felt
the odd sensation of the thread tugging at his skin as
Annie's nimble fingers knotted the stitch and then
snipped it with some sewing scissors she took from the
table. "Now hold on, this is going to sting," she cau-
tioned, and dribbled whiskey from a bottle over the
stitched cut.

The resultant fire on his cheek felt like a foretaste of hell. "Annie, who'd have thought you were so good at piling on the agony?" he groaned. "I already hurt right smart in muscles I didn't even know I had."

"You're very welcome, I'm sure," Annie retorted. "Maybe I should have just left you with another couple of scars after those no-accounts settled your hash in town."

His head was pounding again, but he managed to say, "Thanks. I didn't mean to sound ungrateful. How'd I get home, anyway?"

"In Olivia Gillespie's buckboard. It was God's own mercy she happened to be in town buying supplies and saw those men whaling on you just as they got the notion to get out the tar and feathers. She stopped them with a blast from her shotgun."

"Livy Gillespie is the one who saved me?"

Annie nodded. "Her an' Sam, who'd started feelin' uneasy a little while after you rode away from here. Then she was kind enough to offer her buckboard to haul you home. You didn't even rouse when Sam an' one of the hands carried you upstairs an' laid you in bed."

"Is she—is she still here? I suppose I ought to thank her," he said, his mind still reeling at the thought of his rescuer's identity. He hated the idea of her seeing him like this, broken and battered. His face was probably more black-and-blue than white.

"No, she left as soon as we had you safely in bed," said Annie, to his relief. "Said she had to get back to her farm before it got too late. Land sakes, but that's one independent woman. She wouldn't even hear of Sam riding along to make sure those rowdies wouldn't bother her again when she went back through town— she just made sure her shotgun was loaded again."

"How'd she...was she..." He couldn't find the words to ask if she was still the prettiest girl in Brazos County.

"Is she showing yet, is that what you're tryin' to ask? No, I can't really say she was, though she was wearing a wrapper, not a dress, and Lord knows a woman can hide a thick waist in one a' those for a long while."

"Oh." His head ached too severely for him to hear any more about the intricacies of female garments. He wished Annie hadn't mistaken his meaning, for in his astonishment at hearing that Olivia Gillespie had helped rescue him he had forgotten all about the scandal that clouded her name.

Cal closed his eyes, and Annie took the hint. He heard her chair scrape against the floorboard. "You get some rest now, you hear? I'll bring up some soup at suppertime."

He'd have to go and thank Livy for saving his hide, Cal thought. It was only the polite thing to do. But not until he looked a little less fearsome.

However, it was a good fortnight before Cal felt well enough to venture beyond the boundaries of the Devlin farm. The pain from the beating he had endured had diminished within a week, for nothing had been broken except his nose—and perhaps his confidence. He hadn't expected to be welcomed like the prodigal son, but he had to admit he hadn't figured on the amount of hostility that had greeted him the day he'd ventured into town. The pain of the community's rejection had hurt him every bit as much as his bruises had—maybe more so, for this pain hurt in his soul.

He strapped on the gun belt that Garrick had found for him, and shoved Annie's late husband's Colt into it. He wasn't going to ever let himself get caught in the same helpless position he had been in a fortnight ago.

But how was he ever going to make a place for himself around here, where only his family accepted him? Should he have stayed in Abilene, where he had been liked, and helped Mercy's father get a church built in that wild cow town?

Maybe he should just concentrate on the task he had set himself for the day, he decided as he got dressed. Today he was going to ride over to Gillespie Springs and thank Livy for her role in saving his life. There would be time enough tomorrow to figure out what he was going to do with the rest of his life.

All in all, he didn't look *too* frightening, he decided as he took a last look in the small mirror that hung over his dressing table. The bruises had faded. He had a slight bump at the top of his nose that hadn't been there before. His left cheek, which had been unmarked, now bore a pink slash that would in time lighten into a pale scar, but he was growing a mustache to cover the small scar over his lip. Already the mustache didn't look half-bad, he thought. Maybe it would give Livy something to look at besides the patch over his right eye—not that it mattered. He was only going to deliver his thanks, nothing more, he reminded himself as he went downstairs and out the kitchen door, pausing to kiss Annie, who was churning butter on the porch.

"You're goin' to see *that woman*, aren't you?" she asked with narrowed eyes.

Cal paused. "'That woman?'" he repeated, raising an eyebrow at her tone. "I'm going to pay a thank-you call on Olivia Gillespie, who saved my worthless hide."

Annie looked back down at the churn, her mouth tightening. "Well, just be careful."

He didn't know if she meant for him to be careful around Livy, as if she was some dangerous female who might corrupt him merely by breathing the same air, or to be careful in general, after what had happened in Bryan, and he didn't ask.

He saddled Blue, a roan gelding. Sam had taken Goliad, his stallion, to breed a mare who had come into season late, which would help them get a jump on getting the Devlin stud farm back to its former position of prominence.

It was a pleasant hour's ride southeast to Gillespie Springs, over rolling farmland that paralleled the Brazos River. In the spring some of these fields would be flooded for rice growing. In others, on higher ground, cotton would be grown, but now desiccated rows of the dried plants stood minus their white bolls, except for a few dirty white puffs scattered around. Cattle and horses grazed in some of the fields. A mockingbird sang from its perch in a gnarled live oak.

Reaching the little town of Gillespie Springs, which stood where the road bent to accommodate the wide red expanse of the Brazos, Cal stopped when he saw a sign on a building that said Jail. He didn't know where else to inquire about the way to Livy's place, and in view of recent events, he figured the sheriff would know.

He did, though the puzzled frown on his weathered old face made it clear he couldn't understand why the decent-looking stranger in the black frock coat would want to know.

"Miz Gillespie's place? Down there at the end a' town, across from where the springs is," he replied curtly to Cal's inquiry, and then went back to the dinner he'd been eating at his desk when Cal came in.

Cal got back on Blue and rode the half mile back in the direction from which he had just come, where a stand of cottonwoods revealed the existence of the springs the town had been named for. A sign proclaimed the shady grove Gillespie Springs Park, but across the road a fence much in need of mending enclosed a white frame, two-story house with a dried-up front lawn. A windmill creaked in back next to a barn. In the pasture beyond the barn a cow bawled mournfully once or twice.

Then it was utterly quiet except for the clucking of some pullets looking for bugs among the sad-looking, wilted roses. No one answered his knock.

Perhaps she wasn't home, but did she have no one to help her with the house or the livestock? Had the Mexican alleged to be her lover been the only employee the Gillespies had?

Could she be in the barn, gathering eggs or doing some similar chore? He walked around the side of the house.

Was the ache of regret never going to get any easier to bear? Olivia wondered, standing in the shade of the big cottonwood tree that stood in the backyard between the house and the barn. She stared down at the makeshift grave marker, which was actually a hunk of limestone she'd waded into the spring to get. Smoothed and rounded by centuries of running water, it had been as heavy as her heart felt now. Behind it, she'd lashed two sticks together to form a cross. Someone—one of his Mexican friends or relatives, she assumed—had hung a rosary on the cross and left three roses in an earthen jar. She never saw these offerings left; she assumed whoever brought them came at dawn or after dark, or during the rare times she went to the stores in town.

Francisco, you deserve better than this, she thought, feeling the familiar stinging of tears in her eyes. *You deserve better than a makeshift marker and a grave in the yard of the woman whose lover they say you were.* But the sheriff had had a vicious sense of humor and had insisted Francisco be buried here—"so you don't ever forget what you done, Miz Gillespie."

Livy had half expected the Mexicans in the community to move Luna's body in the dark of night to someplace else—to one of their yards over on North Street, perhaps, for there was no Catholic church in Gillespie Springs. But maybe they felt Francisco had already suffered enough, for the grave had not been disturbed.

Rest in peace, Francisco. You know and I know it was all a lie.

Something—a rustling in the grass, a snapping of some tiny twig—warned her she was no longer alone.

She whirled, already wondering what she could use for a weapon, for she hadn't had one the last time she'd been taken by surprise.

The man standing at the edge of the tree's shade was a stranger to her, yet not a stranger—tall and lean, his hair streaked with gray, a patch over his right eye. It was the latter detail that caused the hand that had curved instinctively over her abdomen to relax.

"Cal?" she breathed. "What are you doing here? Are you...are you all right?" she asked, remembering the day she'd seen him in Bryan, beaten senseless to within an inch of his life. "You—you're growing a mustache...." she babbled, as he came closer.

He smoothed long fingers over it self-consciously. "Yeah, I thought it might cover up one of my new scars, at least. But I've mended, thanks to you. Sam told me what you did that day, and I—I just came to thank you. I reckon I might be singin' with the angels now—or worse—if you hadn't shot off that gun."

"I—I didn't even know who you were when I stepped forward," she said, staring at him, seeing a new scar on his cheek. Even in the shadows she could see the faint discoloration that remained around his left eye.

"Or you wouldn't have helped me?" His mouth curved into an ironic smile, a smile that transformed the scarred face into one that still had the power to make her heart pound.

"No! Yes! I meant I…well, I would have helped anyone in your position," she said, feeling flustered. "I—I just didn't find out it was you until one of those rowdies said you deserved it because of fighting for the Yankees," she added, but when she saw his face cloud over at the mention of the war, she wished she could unsay it.

"And what do *you* say, Livy?" he asked, in that husky drawl that had always wreaked havoc with her resistance. "Are you still mad at me for wearing blue?"

No, Livy wanted to say. *Oh, no, Cal. I've had thousands of hours to regret not telling you to do what you had to do, then return to me safely.* She heard the unspoken question in the tone of his voice, saw in his face his desire to recapture what they once had. She had but to say the right words and he would reach out and they would begin to bridge the enormous gap between them.

"Cal," Livy began, "it was a long time ago. Years. A lot has happened," she said, and was about to ask if he still wanted to be her friend in spite of what was being said about her when his eye fell on what lay behind her.

She saw when he grasped the fact that she was standing in front of a grave, then noticed his gaze narrow and realized he must have glimpsed the roses.

"Your husband?" he asked, staring at her. "They buried Daniel Gillespie here?"

"No, it's not Dan," she said. "Dan's buried in the cemetery next to the church, at the other end of town. No, that's…it's Francisco Luna." She saw his confusion. "He's—he's the one Dan killed…before he killed himself."

The puzzled expression was transformed into one of understanding, and then he frowned. "Livy, you had him buried *here?* You put flowers on his grave? Then—then it's true, isn't it?"

She saw him take an involuntary step back, even as her brain screamed with disappointment. *Then it's true he was your lover*—that's what Cal meant. And then her disappointment changed to anger, anger that he was just like everyone else in Gillespie Springs who had judged her based on what was said, without giving her a chance to defend herself.

He added, "But…was that wise? After what happened?"

Livy saw his gaze shift to her belly, and knew that he'd seen the slight thickening there. She crossed her arms protectively over her abdomen in that age-old, unconscious gesture of a pregnant woman, feeling the anger rise and surround her like flames.

"You think what you want to think, Caleb Devlin, it doesn't make any difference to me. And yes, I *am* still angry at you, you—you traitor! One of my brothers was killed, and the other one never bothered to come home. My husband came back a broken, bitter shell of a man. Daddy died of a broken heart when we couldn't pay the taxes on the plantation. And you think I shouldn't be angry at you? And what business is it of yours if I gave six feet of earth in my own yard to Francisco Luna?''

She watched as a muscle worked in Cal's jaw. "Livy, I'm sorry. You're right, it's none of my business. I was just—''

"I don't want to hear it," she told him. "I'd have thought after your beating you'd have a little compassion for other outcasts, but as that doesn't appear to be the case, you can just get out of here!''

"Livy, please—''

"No! Get *out!*''

But he just stood there, and with a little cry, she ran for the house, slamming the door. She headed for the stairs, intending to run up to the sanctuary of her room, where she could give in to the tears that threatened to overwhelm her, safe from his probing gaze.

She had reached the second-to-last step when she slipped.

Even outside, he heard her scream, and with the scream, the curious paralysis that had made him stand there while she denounced him vanished. In a few short strides he'd reached the door and wrenched it open. Thank God she hadn't taken time to lock it.

"Olivia?" he called, striding into the kitchen. "Where are you?" And then he almost stepped on her, lying in a crumpled heap at the bottom of the stairs that led up from the kitchen.

"*Olivia?*''

She lay on her side, her knees drawn up against her

abdomen, her skirts twisted around her ankles. Her eyes were closed, her face pasty white, like a poorly bleached muslin sheet. Moisture beaded her upper lip.

Her eyelids fluttered at the sound of his voice, then opened. She blinked once, twice, as if trying to focus.

"Olivia, it's me, Cal," he said, kneeling at her side. "What's happened to you? Did you fall?"

Her eyes drifted shut again. "I guess so...." she murmured. "Slipped..."

"Can you get back up? Does anything seem like it's broken?" he asked, feeling the delicate bones of her wrists and wondering if she even realized who he was.

"Can't... Dizzy, bleeding..." she said, and then some spasm seemed to seize her and she clutched her abdomen and moaned.

Cal hadn't seen the blood at first because of the black widow's weeds she was wearing, but as he started to scoop her up off the floor he felt the warm dampness on the back of her skirts and saw the crimson stain of blood on his forearm.

"Olivia! What's happening? Are you—are you..." How did one delicately ask a lady if she were losing the baby he wasn't supposed to acknowledge she was carrying?

Her eyelids fluttered open and she gazed at his face as if puzzled for a few seconds. "Yes...I'm miscarrying. And do you know what? I'm...glad...."

Her announcement stunned him. "You're miscarrying? Lord God, Livy, you need a doctor! I'll get him— where is he?"

"Right in town...next to the bank. But he won't come...hates me, too..."

"I don't care. You need help, so he's going to have

to see you," he told her, but then realized she couldn't hear him, for she had passed out.

For a moment he considered what he should do. Livy's pulse was rapid, faint, and her skin felt cool and clammy. The port-wine flood beneath her was growing. He thought about riding hell-for-leather back down the road to the doctor's, but did he dare leave her for so long while he went to persuade some stiff-necked hypocrite to do his medical duty? Deciding the answer was no, he strode back down the hall, grabbed an afghan he'd seen folded up on the back of a horsehair sofa and wrapped it around Livy, then lifted her and carried her to where Blue stood tied under a tree.

Galloping back into town with her cradled in his arms, he found the bank at the center of town and the doctor's office in the building that stood just next to it, as Livy had said.

The chairs in the small waiting room were fully occupied by a woman and her handful of children, all of whom gaped at the sight of the stranger who strode in carrying the town's most notorious female.

"Mama! That man's got a patch on his eye like a pirate, and the lady's *bleedin'!*" one boy cried. He pointed at the trail of blood behind Cal, causing his mother to gasp and pull him against her ample bosom.

"The doctor—where is he?" Cal demanded curtly, when it seemed the woman was only going to stare in horror.

She pointed to the door at the other end of the waiting room. "In there. But you'll have to wait, just like we are. He—he has a patient—"

Cal didn't wait. He strode over to the door and called through it, "Doc, I got a sick woman here—she needs help now."

"Be with you in a few minutes," a raspy voice answered in a disinterested fashion.

That wasn't going to be good enough. Cal steadied his unconscious burden, then kicked the door open, surprising the elderly sawbones and his "patient," another elderly gent who sat opposite the doctor across the examining table, on which lay a checkerboard and checkers.

Cal kicked the game off the table, sending the wooden disks flying.

"Now wait just a minute, stranger. You can't—" began the doctor, putting down a bottle of whiskey.

"This woman needs your help *now*," he told the astonished sawbones as he laid Livy gently down on the now-empty examining table. "I think she's losing her baby."

Recovering his professional poise, the doctor bustled over to his patient, while the other old man continued to stare with undisguised curiosity.

"But that's Miz Gillespie!" the doctor said in consternation after he saw her face. He seemed to freeze in place.

"You got a problem with her name, Doc?" snapped Cal, allowing his hand to hover suggestively near the gun on his hip. "Seems to me it doesn't matter who she is right now, just that she needs your help. And I'll pay your fee, if that's the problem."

The doctor stared at the gun, then back at Cal's face. "I guess you're right, Mr.—?"

"Caleb Devlin."

"Mr. Devlin. Very well, then, I'll see what's to be done. Hap, we'll finish our, uh, business later," he said to the other old man. "Why don't you show Mr. Devlin back out to the waiting room?"

"I don't think—" began Cal.

But the doctor was very much in command now. "Go on, you can't wait in here, even if you was this woman's husband, which I believe you ain't. Go on out to the waiting room. And you tell that Ginny Petree an' her endless brood a' brats with sore throats that it's gonna be awhile."

Chapter Four

Cal retreated, but he knew he wasn't going to be able to remain in the tiny waiting room with half a dozen children studying his eye patch while their mama stared pointedly at the dried blood on his arm and the dark red splotches on the floor. He went on outside and stood stroking Blue's nose at the hitching post, wishing there was something he could do while he waited.

As if in answer, a shot rang out inside the bank building next door, and a heartbeat later, a woman screamed. Then her screams blended with shouting, just as three masked men dashed out of the bank, one of them carrying an obviously full, heavy gunnysack.

Even as Cal tensed to respond, the sheriff came running out of his office opposite the bank, drawing his gun. He aimed, fired, and one of the bandits, the one carrying the gunnysack, went down with a hoarse cry. But then one of his partners fired, even as the other one snatched up the gunnysack, and Cal saw the weathered old face of the sheriff go rigid with agony as he clutched his chest and fell, measuring his length in the dusty street.

Everyone else who had been on the street had taken

cover, Cal noted as he took aim over the withers of his horse. Good, then his shot wouldn't be apt to hit an innocent person. He fired, and his shot dropped the man who had gunned down the sheriff.

Cal hadn't shot at a man since the first half of the war, but evidently his practice had paid off, he thought grimly as the outlaw fell.

Now the only one alive, the third bandit looked wildly in Cal's direction before yanking his mount's reins from the hitching post. He aimed a wild shot that whistled harmlessly past Cal, then vaulted into the saddle, still clutching the gunnysack by its drawstrings, and spurred his horse. *"Hyaaah! Giddap!"*

The world narrowed to the back of that fleeing outlaw as Cal took aim again. He fired as the horse hit a full gallop, and saw the bloody hole appear in the outlaw's upper back. The man's arms flailed wide, dropping the gunnysack. Coins spilled out the loose top and into the dirt. Boneless as a rag doll, the man fell from the saddle, landing with a thud. The horse galloped on.

In the momentary silence that followed, punctuated only by the pounding hoofbeats, Cal was barely aware of the faces plastered at every window as he holstered his gun. It was over. The outlaws were all dead.

A moment later there was an explosion of noise as people shoved and elbowed their way out of the bank, the general store, the saloon and into the street, hollering back and forth to one another about what had just taken place. A couple of men went to the fallen sheriff, turned him gently over, and when they saw there was nothing to be done, closed his eyes. They did likewise for the bandits who had died just outside the bank. But the rest of the townspeople started to clap and cheer.

"That was some shooting, mister!" someone cried out.

"He can see to shoot better with just one eye than most men can with both a' theirs!" Cal heard an excited youth say. The boy ran the few yards to the body of the bandit who had fallen from his horse.

He turned the man over with his foot. "He's dead, all right! Shot right through the heart!" he called. He ran a few feet back and snatched up the bag, stuffing in the coins that had spilled out. "An' here's the money, all safe an' sound!"

Cal ignored the praise. Oh, he'd done the right thing. But he had killed two men in little more than the time it had taken to blink twice, and even though one of them had murdered the sheriff, he couldn't rejoice in the fact that he had taken two human lives. He felt sick inside. He wanted to flee from the sight of the exultant faces he saw around him; he even turned to mount Blue, forgetting all about Livy being inside the doctor's office. But as he was loosening the gelding's reins, someone clapped him on the back.

"That was quick thinking, mister, and excellent shooting, like the boy said."

Cal turned, intending to tell whoever it was to just leave him the hell alone, but before he could get the words out, the prosperously dressed man wearing a handlebar mustache extended his hand.

"James Long, mayor of Gillespie Springs. I'm also the owner of the hotel." He beamed at Cal.

In spite of himself, Cal found himself returning the handshake, though he couldn't return his smile. "Cal Devlin."

"Well, Mr. Devlin, you have the town's thanks for

your quick actions, which saved their hard-earned funds on deposit in the bank."

"Too bad I wasn't fast enough to save the sheriff," Cal muttered. "Now, if you'll excuse me—"

"All in good time, sir," Long persisted, keeping a hand on Cal's arm. "As you pointed out, the town has been tragically deprived of its peace officer. And I'm repeating myself, but I'm impressed with your quick action and accurate shooting. Might you be interested in the job?"

"I'm no lawman, I'm a minister," Cal replied.

"Oh?" Long was surprised, of course. "And where is your pulpit, if I may ask?"

"Well..." Cal hesitated, not knowing if the man had heard of the notorious minister in Bryan who had fought for the Union. While he wasn't exactly *reveling* in the mayor's praise, he didn't want that praise to turn to disgust, either. "I guess you could say I'm not exactly employed as a man of the cloth right now. But—"

"Doing anything else you can't leave?" interrupted another well-dressed gentleman, who had just joined the mustachioed mayor.

"No, I can't honestly say that I am."

"Mr. Devlin, this here is Mr. Robert Gillespie, the bank president," Long informed him, and the stocky man extended his hand.

So this was the brother of Livy's late husband, the man who coveted the small farm left to Livy. He wasn't at all thin, but somehow Cal had the impression that if Robert Gillespie had been an animal, he'd have been a weasel. Maybe it was the utter coldness of his gray eyes.

"Well, Mr. Devlin, I can only add my urgings," Gillespie said in a rich, cultured voice. "We have a preacher here in Gillespie Springs, and we *had* a sheriff, but God rest Olin Watts's soul, we don't have a sheriff anymore.''

"Now the way I see it," Long added in his earnest manner, "bein' a lawman is just as much servin' the Lord an' your fellow man as bein' a minister is. In both jobs, you stand up for what's right, am I correct?''

Cal couldn't argue with that. "I reckon so. But surely there's a better choice than a one-eyed man," he said, with a gesture toward his eye patch.

Long's gaze went to the bodies of the three dead bandits, and then he lifted an eyebrow. "Those fellows wouldn't agree with you, I think.''

"But—"

"By the power vested in me as mayor, I'm offerin' you the job, son.''

"And I concur," added Robert Gillespie.

"But you don't know anything about me. I could be a murderer or a thief myself," Cal protested. *Or a man who served with the Yankees.* He particularly wondered if Gillespie would be so hearty in his urgings if he knew that Cal had just aided his sister-in-law. And then he remembered Livy, whom he had left bleeding in the doctor's office, and suddenly he was anxious to be done with this interview and see about her.

"I don't have to know anything," Long insisted. "What I saw was a man who didn't have any reason to mix himself up in our troubles—you didn't know the sheriff, you didn't have any money in this bank, but you did the right thing anyway. In my book that makes you the right man for the job. Say you'll at least give it a try. You get your quarters above the sheriff's office gratis of course, free dinner every day from the saloon, supper from the hotel, and forty dollars a month, too. It's a good deal, I'd say.''

Forty dollars a month—not much more than what the average ranch hand earned. Cal eyed the townspeople, who were staring back at him, some smiling, some solemn—but in none of the faces did he see the hatred he had seen in the faces of the folks in Bryan. Of course, none of these people knew what color his uniform had been in the war, or that he had spent the last half of that war fighting for neither side. They might not be so quick to grin at him if they knew.

But in the meantime, until they found out, he could try being sheriff. Maybe before the gossip spread from Bryan, he could do such a good job that it wouldn't matter which side he had taken in the war. Hadn't he been looking for something he could do, something he could call his own?

"All right," he said. "I'll give it a try."

Several of the onlookers cheered and clapped again. Gillespie bent over the fallen sheriff and unpinned his badge. He handed it to Long, who wiped it with a handkerchief before holding it out to Cal.

Cal took it, breathed deeply and pinned it to his shirt.

The mayor extended his hand again, and Cal shook it, unsmiling, but that didn't dampen the mayor's sense of ceremony. "Ladies and gentlemen, I'd like to present the new sheriff of Gillespie Springs, Cal Devlin!"

The cheers and clapping began all over again, and the throng was just rushing toward Cal when, from behind him, someone cleared his throat.

"Mr. Devlin!" the doctor called from his open doorway.

Cal watched as the doctor caught sight of the bodies by the bank, saw his eyes widen as he realized that one of them was the sheriff. Then the sawbones turned back to Cal and Cal knew he had spotted the badge he had just pinned on.

"All dead?"

Cal nodded.

"Hmmph. Heard the shots, but I was busy with—with the lady you brought in. If I could just have a word with you?"

Cal nodded again and, grateful for the doctor's timely interruption and for the fact that he hadn't mentioned Olivia's name, left the townspeople who had just been about to surround him.

He followed the sawbones back into the office, past Ginny Petree, who glared at him, and her children, who stared at him goggle-eyed. No doubt she would spread the news soon enough that just before he became the new sheriff, Cal had carried Olivia Gillespie into the doctor's office. He wondered what the president of the Gillespie Springs Bank would make of the gossip.

The doctor didn't take him into the examining room, however, but into a small room adjacent to that.

"Is she—is she going to be all right?" Cal asked.

The doctor folded his arms across his barrel chest. "She is, though she'll need someone to watch her close overnight—she lost a lot of blood, you know."

Cal knew. "The—the…" He couldn't bring himself to say the word.

"The baby?" the doctor filled in briskly, his gaze piercing. "She lost it. Ordinarily I'd say 'unfortunately,' but under the circumstances…"

Cal looked down at his boots, not knowing what to say. Livy's words, when he'd found her at the bottom of the stairs, echoed in his ears. *Yes, I'm miscarrying…and I'm glad.…*

Had she been rejoicing that she would no longer have

to bear the child who had been the evidence of her sin? As understandable as that was, Cal found it hard to believe the Livy he had known could think that way. Had she cared so little for her slain lover that she would only be relieved to lose his baby? But perhaps she had changed since he had left for the war. Perhaps he had never really known her at all.

The doctor's raspy voice intruded into his thoughts. "I hope you'll pardon me fer askin', but I'm just wonderin' how you come into this? How'd you happen to be, uh....were you—were you *with* Miz Gillespie... when the miscarriage began?"

Cal started to say yes, for it was the truth, and then he realized what the doctor had meant by "with" and he felt fury rising in him at the implication. He met the old man's inquisitive gaze. "I was just payin' a call on Mrs. Gillespie to thank her for a kindness she did me recently," he nearly growled, fighting the urge to punch the sawbones in the nose for what he was implying. "She fell down the stairs, and I'm the one who found her."

The doctor must have realized he'd offended him, for he took another look at the badge on Cal's chest. "I meant no offense," he said quickly. "Just curious, is all...."

"Can I see her?" Cal wanted to see Livy, but he also wanted to escape the questions he knew the doctor was dying to ask.

The man nodded. "She was asleep when I left her, but I imagine she'll rouse when you talk to her." He gestured for Cal to follow him.

"Why, Cal, you waltz divinely!" she said, laughing up at the handsome young rector of the Bryan Episcopal Church, who released her with obvious reluctance as

the music died. She glanced around, and just as she'd suspected, the eyes of almost all the ladies at the ball were on them, and they were envious eyes. And why shouldn't they be? She'd been dancing with the catch of Brazos County, and he looked as if he couldn't bear to give her up to her next partner. She didn't want him to, either. There was a way she could keep him with her, but would he think her fast? He might...but if she didn't try she'd never know.

"Cal..." she said, allowing her lashes to flutter as she looked up at him over her fan, "would you like to take a turn in the garden? I think I'm...a little too warm...."

He smiled down at her, enthusiasm dancing in his wonderful gray-blue eyes. "Miss Livy, I can't think of anything on this earth I'd like better...."

"Livy..." murmured a voice.

Was it the same voice she'd been hearing in her dream? "Mmm, yes..." she answered.

She extended her hand to Cal and together they stepped through the French windows and out into the rose garden, lit only by the light from the Childress ballroom.

"Livy," the voice said again. "Livy, can you hear me? Open your eyes."

Obediently, she did so, but it seemed like such an effort. Her lids seemed weighted down with rocks.

A face, bending low over her, swam into focus. It was the same face she'd seen just moments ago—surely it was just moments ago—under the cottonwood in her backyard.

"Ah, you're awake," he said. "How are you feeling?"

How was she feeling? How *should* she be feeling?

she wondered as she studied his solemn face, and then she became aware of the insistent cramping within her belly.

And then she remembered the fall, the sudden sharp pain that had seized her as she struggled to regain her senses at the foot of her stairs and the gushing wet warmth between her legs. She had miscarried the baby, she remembered, and for a moment, sorrow for the loss of that innocent life flooded over her as she lay there looking up into Cal's concerned face.

But where am I? she wondered as she took her eyes from his face and looked around the tiny room. She recognized at last that she was in Doc Broughton's examining room—the same room in which he'd told her, just weeks ago, that she was with child. A fact she had already suspected, but the confirmation of that fact had filled her with horror. And the same fact had left the doctor's face stern with disapproval, for it was, unfortunately, well-known that Dan Gillespie had come back from the war unable to perform his husbandly duties.

But now she was no longer going to bear the baby whose brief existence within her had brought about her disgrace. Sorrow became mingled with a regretful relief. As much as she had longed for a child, this one would have been born into a world of ugliness, and her love for it would have had to exist side by side with her hatred for its father.

"I'm tired," she managed to whisper at last. "So tired…"

"The doctor says you're going to be all right," Cal said, nodding toward the door he'd closed behind him. "But you lost the baby."

"I—I guessed," she admitted.

"I'm sorry," he murmured, his gaze leaving hers, but not before she had seen the question in his eye.

Then she remembered the way he had found her, and how she had told him she was miscarrying, and that she was *glad.* Heavens above, what a heartless monster she must have sounded—to have admitted to a man she had once known so well that she was glad to be losing a baby, whatever the circumstances of its conception! What must he think of her?

"It's for the best," she told him.

His penetrating gaze returned to her face. She had forgotten he could study her that way and see to the depths of her soul, and the ability seemed undiminished by the patch that now covered one eye.

She was unable to stop the tears that belied her words.

He reached out and caught a tear with a finger. "You rest now, Livy. I'll talk to the doctor and see what's to be done."

Just then she caught sight of the shiny, five-pointed star pinned to his chest, and she grabbed at his wrist before he could leave.

"Why are you wearing that?" she asked, puzzled.

His face grew guarded. "Don't worry about that right now, Livy."

He started to gently disengage his hand, but she tightened her grasp. "No, please tell me. I—I thought I heard shots earlier...."

"Seems there was a bank robbery taking place just about the time I was layin' you down there," he said, indicating the examining table she was still lying on. "The sheriff was killed. I stopped them and...well, seems I'm the sheriff of Gillespie Springs now."

It was a lot of news to digest on top of what had

happened to her today. In addition, the doctor had given her something to drink and it was making her feel so muzzy-headed....

"So...you're the new sheriff...." she murmured, and then she let her too-heavy lids drift shut again.

He found the doctor waiting for him in the hallway. The old coot had probably been listening at the keyhole, Cal thought with irritation.

"You were saying that Mrs. Gillespie was going to need someone to be with her," Cal began.

"Just a few days, till she gets her strength back," the doctor said. "She an' Dan used ta have some widow woman to help with the cleanin' and such, but she high-tailed it outa there when—when Dan Gillespie died, and I can tell you she wouldn't come back."

"You know some woman who might be willing to take the job?" Cal asked the doctor. "Some woman who needs the money more than she worries about what people think?"

The sawbones looked doubtful. "I dunno. Folks is pretty disapprovin' a' what they say Miz Gillespie did."

Cal felt a surge of anger. Livy needed another female with her at such a time, damn it. There were things she'd need done, questions she'd have—and only another woman would do. He'd stay with her himself if there was no other choice—he wouldn't let her be alone—but he knew that was the last thing Olivia Gillespie would want and the last thing her reputation needed, especially right now.

"You might ask around town," the sawbones said. "Mebbe they'd listen, since it was *you* askin'. You're ridin' pretty high in folks' opinions right now. But meanwhile, I gotta get back to my patients. And I'm gonna have to see them in my waiting room,'' he added, as if it were somehow Cal's fault that his sole examining room was occupied.

"Give me an hour," Cal said shortly. "I'll see if I can find someone, then I'll locate a wagon and take her home."

"Good luck," Broughton said, a skeptical note in his voice as he headed into his waiting room to see Ginny Petree's restless brats.

As he left the doctor's office, Cal was hailed by Mayor Long from the steps of the Gillespie Springs Bank.

"Devlin? Everything all right?"

Perhaps Long would know of a woman who could stay with Olivia, he thought, striding over the planking that led to the bank next door.

"Oh, everything's fine," he said. "I was…just checking on a friend."

Too late, Cal saw Gillespie standing in the shadows, just inside the bank door. *Hellfire,* Cal thought, borrowing one of Sam's favorite expressions. He couldn't very well ask Long if he knew a woman who could help Livy for a few days right in front of the brother-in-law who hated her.

"We were concerned when we saw you go into the doctor's office," Gillespie said, his voice purring. "I trust you were not injured in the fray? I assure you, the town will pay all bills incurred in the line of duty."

"No, I wasn't, Mr. Gillespie."

"Oh please, call me Bob. All my friends do," said Gillespie, slapping Cal on the back. "And I'll call you Cal, if that's agreeable?"

Cal hoped the fact that he detested Gillespie's familiarity and overhearty voice didn't show as he nodded.

"Bob, I won't keep you from your duties," he said. "I was just hoping the mayor would be kind enough to show me around the jail—you know, where the keys are kept and so forth?"

As he'd hoped, Gillespie either took the hint or wasn't interested in such mundane details, and said he was sure he'd be seeing Cal around town. But Cal was aware of the bank president's eyes boring into his back as he and Long crossed the street to the jail.

Was it only a couple of hours ago that Cal had entered this office to ask where he might find Olivia? How ironic that he was now returning as its new sheriff. He didn't mention his previous visit to Long, though. Instead he listened and watched patiently as Long showed him around inside, pointing with pride at the two cells—fortunately empty, Cal noted.

Long *tsked* as he observed that the sheriff's desk still bore the remains of his dinner—a meal Cal had so recently seen the sheriff eating.

"As I said, your quarters are up above," the mayor explained. "You reach it by a stairway out back. Come on, I'll show you," he said, reaching inside the desk for a ring of keys. "But I'll warn you, Olin Watts, the old sheriff, wasn't known for bein' neat. Every so often he'd have this Mexican woman come and tidy up, but Watts was kinda stingy with a coin, so she only did it once in a blue moon."

Cal followed him back outside and up the weathered steps.

The mayor hadn't exaggerated the late sheriff's lack of tidiness, and apparently there hadn't been a blue moon lately, for clothes lay haphazardly piled over the room's only chair. The bed was unmade, the wrinkled sheets yellowed with age and lack of washing. Half-empty cans of beans and cups with coffee rings took up half of the table. The other half was littered with yellowed newspapers. A daguerreotype was nailed to the cracked plaster wall, and as Cal bent to study it he saw that it had been taken at a hanging, for it featured three dangling bodies with hoods over their heads, their necks bent at unnatural angles.

"The Galtry brothers, horse thieves," read the scrawled notation on the plaster wall, "hanged March 8, 1868."

"He certainly had an odd sense of the artistic," Cal said, straightening and turning from the picture.

Long chuckled, then looked dismayed as he surveyed the clutter. "That Mexican woman'll come and clean this for you. I'm really sorry, Cal. Why don't we put you up at the hotel tonight—at the town's expense, of course? I'll have Jovita Mendez come and set it all to rights this evening."

Cal had been conscious of the quickly passing minutes and had wondered how he was going to bring up the subject of the woman he needed to find for Olivia, but perhaps James Long had just supplied the opening he needed.

"Aw, don't worry about this mess, it won't take long to straighten up in here. But I do need to find a woman, now that you mention it—"

James Long grinned. "Right behind the saloon there's a brothel of sorts. There's two-three sportin' women that live there—I imagine they can cure what ails you."

Cal couldn't help but smile at the way the mayor had mistaken his meaning. "No, I don't mean that kind of female. You mentioned a woman who'd come and clean? Mrs. Daniel Gillespie just happens to be…an old acquaintance of mine, and she's, uh…been real ill," he said, praying Long wouldn't press him for details. The full story would be spread soon enough, by that nosy mother in the waiting room. "The doctor said she was gonna need someone to stay with her for a few days, and I was just wonderin' if perhaps this woman you mentioned would be willing? I'd pay her."

He saw the mayor's sunny expression become clouded. "Miz Gillespie's…a friend a' yours?" There was a world of insinuated meaning in the way he said *friend.*

"An old friend, from my growin' up days in Bryan," Cal said, careful to keep his voice casual. "I'm just tryin' to help her out.…"

"Yes, of course," Long said quickly, not meeting Cal's eye. "Sure, I imagine Jovita Mendez'd be glad to earn some money takin' care a' Miz Gillespie. She probably doesn't earn much takin' in mendin' and cleanin' houses and such. Come on, I know where we can find her."

By the time the sun was setting, Cal had hired the middle-aged Mexican woman, who was pathetically grateful for the job, and together they had brought Livy back to her own house in the buckboard Cal had found behind the barn, pulled by Blue.

Jovita Mendez insisted on fixing him supper after she'd tucked a sleepy Olivia into bed, and with her new employer's permission, sent some clean sheets with him when he at last took his leave.

"That Señor Watts, he was a peeg, *Dios* rest his soul," she said, crossing herself as she handed him the sheets at the door. "Don't you worry, Señor Devleen. I weel take good care of the *señora* for you."

He started to tell her that it wasn't for him, exactly,

but he guessed that this plump woman, unlike the rest of the town, was not an inveterate gossip. And that the shrewd eyes saw more than he might have wished. "Thank you, Jovita," he said simply. He went to the barn to collect his horse, knowing he'd have to settle him at the livery stable before seeking his own rest.

He hoped his mama and Annie weren't going to worry when he didn't show up back at the farm tonight. In the summer, he could have ridden Blue home before it had gotten fully dark, but he wasn't about to chance the roan breaking a leg loping over the road on this moonless autumn night. He'd get up early the next morning and ride home in time for breakfast, tell his family about his new job as sheriff and be back in Gillespie Springs before noon.

At the same time as Cal was struggling to make the room over the jail fit for human occupation—at least fit enough so he could get some sleep without worrying about roaches carrying him off—a conversation was taking place at Gillespie's habitual table at the Last Chance Saloon.

"Thought you'd want to know I was takin' care a' your sister-in-law this mornin', just about the time Olin Watts was gettin' gunned down," Doc Broughton said, then took a sip of his whiskey.

Robert Gillespie raised a brow at the cold-blooded way Broughton had mentioned the killing of the sheriff, then growled, "What makes you think I'd care about that murdering bitch?"

"Oh, I think you'll care," murmured the sawbones smugly. He puffed on his cigar until Gillespie was about ready to strangle him, but the banker would be damned if he'd ask and thereby show too much interest.

"She lost that baby. Had a fall down the stairs, she told me, an' started bleedin'. She was hemorrhagin' by the time she was brought in t'me. If our fine new sheriff hadn't found her, she mighta bled to death."

"Why didn't you just let the bitch die?" Gillespie growled.

"Aw, Bob, you know I cain't do that," protested Broughton. "I had a waitin' room fulla people, and that sorta thing ain't good for business. Ain't it good enough that now the woman ain't gonna give birth to no half-greaser bastard to inherit your brother's land?"

Gillespie was still examining his mixed emotions about his sister-in-law's miscarriage. "Yes, I reckon that's one good thing," he finally said.

"And besides," the sawbone continued, "Devlin was appearin' t'take an interest. Seems he *knew* the woman...."

By then the rest of what Broughton had said earlier had sunk in. "You say Devlin *found* her? How'd that happen?" Gillespie demanded, chewing on the end of his own cigar.

The sawbones shrugged. "He said he was just payin' a call. He'd been real insistent that I drop everythin' to treat her, and he got real defensive when I, uh, kinda probed around as to how well he an' your sister-in-law was acquainted."

Gillespie studied the rotund physician. "Hmm. Now isn't that interesting? This one-eyed fellow shows up just in time to stop a bank robbery, and he just happens to know Olivia. And he just happens to find her losing her baby. I call that an interesting bunch of coincidences, indeed I do."

Chapter Five

Predictably, Sarah Devlin wasn't pleased to hear that her son had taken on the hazardous profession of sheriff.

"Honest to Pete, Caleb Travis Devlin, I just get you back from the dead, and now you've taken up the most dangerous profession there is," she complained as she dished up his second helping of flapjacks. "You might just as well tell me now what hymns you want played at your funeral," she added tartly.

Cal grinned. "I expect you'd have to hold a funeral here, and you ladies'd have to sing any hymns without accompaniment, 'cause I don't reckon Mr. Maxwell would countenance preachin' my funeral service," he drawled. Of the three women present, only Mercy returned his smile.

"Cal, you stop teasin' Mama," snapped Annie. "You 'bout worried her to death not showin' up last night. She's already imagined you murdered somewhere on the road, and now you come in and tell her you've hung a star on your shirt because the last sheriff was killed right in front of you?"

"I already said I was sorry for not returning last night, and why I didn't," Cal said evenly. "And you know there isn't much chance of anything interesting happening in Gillespie Springs again for about another hundred years, so you can stop frettin'. I was hoping *someone* in this family would wish me good luck, at least.''

"I do, brother," Sam said from across the table, extending his hand over a plate that had been piled twice as high with flapjacks as Cal's had. "I think it's right fine we have a lawman in the family now."

"You haven't said why your other arm's in a sling," Cal commented.

Now it was Sam's turn to grin. "That Goliad a' yours took exception to pullin' up after he beat Johnson's stud in a race from their barn to Bryan. That was *after* he bred their mare, mind you. But don't worry about me—nothin's broke, I'm just a little sore."

"He won't do that if you give him a treat before he runs—an apple or a lump of sugar or something," Cal said.

"Now you tell me," Sam said ruefully, but the twinkle in his eyes showed he didn't blame Cal. "I think ol' Goliad's gonna win us as much money racing as he is in stud fees. Not bad for an old warhorse."

But Garrick, who'd been sitting silently, pushing his breakfast around on his plate, didn't let the talk drift to Sam's favorite topic, horse racing.

"Did you meet up with the Widow Gillespie before you played hero in front a' the whole town?" he inquired.

Cal finished chewing before he replied. "I did."

"Is she still, um, in a 'delicate condition'?"

"Garrick! I'm sure Cal did not bring up the subject to her!" Annie scolded.

"Annie, you're becoming a prissy old woman!" Garrick retorted sourly.

Annie gasped and seemed about to reply in kind when Sarah intervened. "Garrick Devlin, you will apologize. I will not have you speaking to your sister in this fashion."

"Mama, it's just the truth. Ever since her husband died she's been as fussy as an old hen."

Annie sniffed and pulled a lacy handkerchief out of her pocket.

"Sweep your own doorstep first, mister," came their mother's firm reply. "You haven't exactly been sweet as pie yourself these days."

Annie looked mollified, Garrick sullen.

Cal spoke up before anything else could be said. "As much as I'd love to stay and chat, I've got to be getting back. They'll be expecting to see my face around Gillespie Springs."

"But Cal, you never told us anything more about Olivia," protested Annie.

He'd hoped he was going to get by without doing so, but that hope died as he saw the curiosity written all over Annie's face. He might as well get it over with; the gossip would get back this way before long, anyway.

"Olivia miscarried yesterday," he said, rising. "Thanks for breakfast, Mama."

Annie's mouth dropped, then she clucked sympathetically. "She must have been in town and saw it all?" she guessed.

Cal didn't bother to set her straight. His inquisitive sister didn't need to know his role in the matter.

"I expect it was the excitement—the bank robbery

and all," she said knowingly. "Still, it's probably for the best that she—"

"*Goodbye*, Mama, everyone," said Cal firmly, reaching for his hat on the peg by the door. He did not want to discuss the matter any further. He'd spent too much of last night tossing on the lumpy mattress and wondering if Livy's losing the baby was for the best or not.

"Now you be real careful, Caleb, you hear?" his mother added, just before he shut the door.

"I will, Mama. Don't you worry," he told her gently.

He arrived back in Gillespie Springs to find one of his jail cells occupied by a scared-looking lad perhaps ten years old, while an angry, balding man paced in front of the cell.

The man stopped pacing as Cal entered. "Oh, there you are, Sheriff Devlin. I took the liberty of arresting this young hooligan until you returned."

"Oh? And what law did he break?" Cal inquired, studying the white-faced boy huddled on the cell's cot. The boy stared back, looking more frightened than before as his eyes rested on the black eye patch Cal wore.

"I'm Fred Tyler, and I own the general store. I caught him red-handed, filchin' the licorice sticks!"

Cal stepped over to the barred alcove, and the boy cringed. "What's your name, son?"

"D-Davy. Davy Richardson," the lad quavered, his eyes big as saucers as he gazed up at him. Cal knew he was frightened all the more by the patch and the scars on his face, and felt a rush of sympathy for the boy. But he steeled himself to remain impassive.

"We haven't met, but I'm Sheriff Devlin," he told him. "You know how long a jail sentence a thief usually gets?"

The boy hung his head. "No, sir."

"It's about five years," Cal announced, though he had no idea if this was true. "Did you take the licorice?"

The boy was silent.

"Ask him to stick out his tongue, and you'll see what the little thief's been up to," Tyler suggested from behind him.

Cal felt a flash of irritation at the proprietor's self-righteous tone, but he didn't turn around. "Well?" he asked, raising an eyebrow.

The boy looked at him for a second, then defiantly stuck out his black tongue—at the storekeeper.

Cal had to struggle not to laugh. "I guess that's all the proof I need. Davy Richardson," he said in a stern voice, "I hereby sentence you to five years."

The boy blanched still further and gulped. "Don't I get a trial or nothin'? I'm sorry, really I am!"

Cal allowed his face to relax slightly and let himself appear to consider the question. "Nope, no trial. A black tongue is pretty much all the evidence I need to convict you in this case. But I'd consider commuting the sentence..."

"C-commuting? What does that mean?"

"That means I'll change your sentence to sweeping out the general store, then the jail office here, and when you've done so, I'll declare you've paid your debt to society."

Tyler huffed, "He won't stick around five minutes to sweep. You're lettin' him off too easy, Devlin."

"Oh, yes he will," Cal said with certainty. "You know what happens if you don't finish the job, Davy?"

Davy shook his head warily.

"I'll form a posse and hunt you down, and then

you'll get *ten* years, in addition to the hidin' your father'll probably give you when he finds out.''

"I ain't got no father. He's dead," the boy informed him matter-of-factly. "But don't worry, I'll finish the job. Now let me outa here—*please?*"

"All right," Cal said, removing the keys from the desk with an appropriate flourish. He unlocked the cell, and the boy sprang out as if he'd been there five years already.

"Now hold up there," Cal said, when the boy would have followed the proprietor out the door. "On your way over to the general store, drop this off at the saloon," he said, handing him the dirty plate and silverware that had been there ever since yesterday, when Sheriff Watts had been eating what turned out to be his last meal. "Tell them the new sheriff is ready for his dinner whenever it's convenient, please."

"Yes, sir!"

Cal waited until the merchant had taken his leave before grinning with satisfaction. He'd just settled the first case of lawbreaking since his term as sheriff had begun. Then he began to go through the desk drawers, which were as messy as the old sheriff's room had been. He supposed he was going to have to hire a deputy, too, for times when he had a prisoner to guard and his duties took him elsewhere.

That task completed, he figured it would be a while before dinner would be delivered from the Last Chance Saloon. He had time to explore a little.

He knew the buildings on Main Street already—the bank, the jail, the doctor's office, the general store, the livery stable, the Baptist church, the saloon, the hotel, the millinery, the bathhouse and barbershop, and at the

far end, across from Livy's house, Gillespie Springs
Park.

He strode down the side street between the bank and
the hotel and came to South Street, or so the painted
sign proclaimed it. He had already learned that South
Street was deemed the more desirable of Gillespie
Springs's two residential streets. The prosperous townspeople—the doctor, the owner of the general store, the
mayor, the saloonkeeper and their like—lived in modest
but well-built stone-and-frame houses there, the lots
separated by picket fences, most of them freshly whitewashed.

At the west end of South Street, up on a little rise,
stood an antebellum mansion of red brick on a lawn
shaded by ancient live oaks. A brass plate on the black,
wrought-iron fence that surrounded the grounds proclaimed that Robert Gillespie lived there. Behind the
house stood a circle of frame cabins, which probably
had been slave quarters before the war.

So this was Robert Gillespie's place. He apparently
hadn't believed in sharing his wealth with his younger
brother, Cal mused, for the house Livy lived in, while
comfortable, was nothing like this.

Leaving the Gillespie mansion behind, he crossed behind the Baptist church and came to North Street, which
ran parallel, behind the bathhouse-barbershop, saloon
and jail. Here, directly behind the saloon, was the ramshackle row of rooms known as the cribs, where a quar-
tet of whores entertained their customers. The rest of
the houses were mostly rickety affairs, too, little better
than tar-paper shacks with tin roofs.

North Street was where the employees of the hotel
and the bank, and Gillespie Springs's few immigrants
lived, and Long had told him almost all of the humble

dwellings were rented from Robert Gillespie. Here and there Cal saw chickens scratching among the weeds that grew alongside the houses, and behind one unpainted, straggling picket fence a fat pink sow lolled in the sunshine. Down the street, three boys were kicking a ball back and forth.

South and North Streets might have been in different worlds, Cal thought as he cut back up the side street that ran between the saloon and the jail. He was tempted to go down to check on Livy now, but he resolutely put it off till after dinner.

The sounds of Jovita's humming drifted up the stairs to the bedroom, and Olivia smiled. *God bless Cal for finding her for me,* she thought, *and after I spoke the way I did to him, too.* How would she have ever managed alone? She still felt weak as a newborn colt. She could hear the plump, middle-aged Mexican woman down in the kitchen now, rattling pots as she cleaned and straightened. A delicious smell wafted up the stairs, caused by the simmering chicken broth Jovita had promised "Señora Gillespie" for dinner.

Just as soon as she regained her strength, Livy would have to apologize to Cal for the harsh way she'd spoken to him, and thank him for hiring Jovita for her—and for saving her life, too, of course! Well, since he was now the sheriff, it wouldn't be too hard to encounter him casually in town.

Olivia supposed most women would be so overcome with embarrassment at the thought of a man other than their husband having seen them in the midst of such an intimate, *female* crisis that they would be unable to face that man again. But she had never been one for false modesty. To blush and turn away when a man had saved her life would be unforgivable, in Olivia's estimation, particularly when it was doubtful anyone else would have lifted a finger to help her.

She'd thank him politely, and that would be that. As much as her heart had warmed at the sight of him, she must not let on.

Cal Devlin had suffered enough in this life, she thought, remembering how he'd been listed as missing in action in the middle of the war, and later given up for dead by his family. Then, just recently, she'd overheard the gossip that he'd been found in Abilene, and was returning home.

It had been a shock, discovering that the bruised, beaten man lying unconscious in the dust at her feet in Bryan was none other than Cal Devlin, but while she and his brother transported him home in her buckboard, pulled by the horse she'd rented from the livery, Sam had filled in the gaps in the story. She'd learned about Cal losing his memory along with the sight in his right eye during the war.

Olivia had grieved inwardly, thinking how hard it must be to come home scarred and maimed, and find such hatred and intolerance in the very town where he'd once been so loved and respected.

When Cal had told her in the doctor's office that he was now the sheriff, Olivia had heard the reborn pride in his voice even through her laudanum-induced fog. And Jovita, who had gone into town early this morning to purchase a few things from the general store, had returned with the full account of what had taken place outside the bank yesterday. The good folk of Gillespie Springs were apparently quite pleased with their new sheriff.

Which was precisely why he must not associate with

her. The very last thing the new sheriff needed, if he was to continue to have the support of the townspeople of Gillespie Springs, was a friendship with the infamous Olivia Gillespie, whom everyone knew had driven her husband to suicide by her infidelity.

She was *not* going to cry about *that* again, she vowed, staring out the window at the sunshine stealing through her window. It was a warm day for early November, so Jovita had left the window open a couple of inches. Olivia tried to concentrate on the antics of a squirrel cavorting in the branches of the cottonwood tree, clearly visible from where she lay, but it was no good.

"Whore! You took the very last thing I had left to me, didn't you? You took my pride, and gave it to that greaser when you lay down for him! And now you tell me you're gonna have a baby, and you expect me to listen to some crazy tale of some man rapin' you in the barn! I'm no fool, you lyin' slut! Bob's been tellin' me about you and that Luna, an' how y'all been lookin' at one 'nother..."

"But Dan, you have to believe me!" she pleaded. *"Francisco didn't touch me, I swear to you! It was—"*

"'Francisco'? Well, I guess you would be on a first-name basis with your Mex lover!" Dan roared, and swung his fist, catching her squarely in the side of her head.

Everything had gone black, and when she awoke, it was to the news that Dan had killed Francisco Luna and then turned the gun on himself. The sheriff's disgusted face had frightened her—and then he'd read her the note Dan had left, in which Dan had explained that he had killed his wife's lover, the father of the baby she carried, and intended next to shoot himself.

Her reason for silence—the need to protect Dan from

*the truth—was gone, but the sheriff hadn't wanted to
hear her side of the story. Neither had anyone else. Her
brother-in-law, Robert, had seen to it that the contents
of the note had been circulated about town, and before
her husband had even been buried, Olivia had found
herself an outcast.*

Cal was already an outcast in Bryan; it must not happen to him here, too, not when he'd just gained a chance
to build a life for himself. But it would happen if he
was known to be friendly with Olivia Gillespie. She
would be appreciative of the help he'd given her, but
that was all; she'd nip in the bud any further attempts
at friendship.

But perhaps it was assuming too much on her part to
even imagine he'd want to be her friend, especially
when he thought she was the one who'd been putting
roses on Francisco's grave....

All at once she heard the sound of footsteps on the
porch below and then a firm knock at the door. She
heard Jovita's humming cease, and the creak of the
boards as the Mexican woman went to the door. Then,
a moment later, Jovita's voice. "*Buenos tardes,* Señor
Devleen! Yes, the *señora* ees much better today! Yes,
I am sure she would welcome a visitor. Come een! I'll
just go up and see eef she ees awake first!"

It was surprising how fast a woman of Jovita's
plumpness could move when she was excited. "*Señora!*
Eet ees—"

"Yes, I heard," Olivia interrupted. "Tell him I'm
asleep, won't you? I'm in no condition to receive callers, Jovita," she protested, her gesture indicating her
nightgown, her hair loose on her pillow, the fact that
she was in bed.

But Jovita wouldn't listen. "Nonsense, *señora.* Thees

ees the man who helped you, no? He looks so anxious—just let heem see you are better, yes?'' Before Olivia knew what she was about, Jovita had found and draped a lacy shawl about her shoulders, combed her hair and set the room to rights. A minute later, Cal was entering the bedroom.

He was so tall he had to duck to avoid hitting his head on the lintel. For a moment he just stood there holding his hat in his hands, his presence filling the room as he studied her.

''I—I hope I'm not intrudin' at a time when you're not feelin' very well, Livy,'' he began, stroking the brim of his hat self-consciously. ''But after yesterday I thought I'd better come see how you were doin'....''

Could he hear the way her heart was pounding? ''That was very kind of you, Cal,'' she said, being careful to keep her voice coolly polite. ''As you can see, I'm much better. Thanks to you.''

He looked down at his boots. ''Anyone would have done the same.''

No, they wouldn't have, she thought, but did not say so.

''I'm glad you're feeling better,'' he said. His eyes returned to hers. ''You, uh, you have a mite more color in your face than you had yesterday.''

His observation caused even more blood to come rushing up her neck and into her cheeks, heating them. ''Yes, I feel better.... Still weak, of course, but I guess that's to be expected.''

He nodded, still gazing at her in his direct way.

What more was there to say?

''I—I like the mustache,'' she said at last, idiotically, when the silence seemed to stretch on uncomfortably. ''It looks dashing,'' she told him, and meant it.

He gazed at her as if he thought she was loco. "Dashing?" he said with a short, disbelieving laugh, and made a gesture that indicated the scarred right side of his face as he shook his head.

"Yes, *dashing*," she insisted, her heart twisting as she realized he thought the scars and the patch had made him ugly.

She was ambivalent about asking him to sit down, afraid he would misinterpret it, that he would think she wanted him to stay. But no, he would be right. She *did* want him to stay—she just couldn't let him know that.

It seemed rude to keep him standing, though. "Please, won't you sit down?" she said, motioning toward the chair beyond the small bedside table.

He looked uncertain. "I—I shouldn't…can't stay but a minute…." He sat down, nevertheless.

"Jovita tells me you're quite the town hero," she said breezily. "They can't praise you highly enough, after yesterday."

He smiled, and his face lost a little of its tenseness. "I just happened to be in the right place at the right time, that's all."

"So modest," she teased. "I never knew you were such an expert marksman."

His face grew somber again. "I wish I could do it over again, Livy. Two men are dead because of me. I should have just wounded them, so they could have been captured."

His anguished face caught at her heart. "You mustn't blame yourself for their deaths, Cal. One of them murdered our sheriff. The other one could have killed you— I hear he shot at you, but missed. You did what you had to do."

He looked away. "I know…but I just keep thinkin'

about how I might've done it differently...if I'd taken time to think. But I was so angry at seein' that old man gunned down—he was just tryin' to do his job...."

That was what Olin Watts had said to her, Olivia thought, after he'd read her Dan's suicide note. *I'm just doin' my job, Miz Gillespie.* But that had nothing to do with the event that was tormenting Cal's soul now, so she resolutely pushed it aside.

"Look at it this way, Cal. If the robbers had been captured instead, probably both of them would have been hanged for killing the sheriff and for the bank robbery. I'd wager they would rather have died quickly, the way they did, instead of at the end of a rope."

"I suppose you're right," he said, but his expression remained bleak.

"You'll be a good sheriff," she assured him. "Gillespie Springs is lucky you came along." But how was she going to stay away from him if he lived in the same town? They'd never managed to stay away from each other when they'd been growing up, when her family's plantation and the horse farm he'd been raised on had been so temptingly close. She couldn't count the number of times she'd awakened to the rattle of pebbles on her window and had gone out to meet him in the moonlight. They'd never done anything that might have ended in disgrace, but they'd come close sometimes....

He sighed. "I hope so. I'd like to be able to uphold the law here without killing anyone ever again. I'm going to try not to, anyway."

"I know if there's a way you can avoid it, you will," Olivia said. "But you be careful, won't you?" She hoped he wasn't going to be so wary of drawing his gun again that he'd be an easy target for the next troublemaker that came through.

His face lightened. "Don't worry, Livy, I will. Well...maybe I'd better be goin'. I don't want to tire you out." He glanced at the sheet she had pulled up to cover most of her shoulders. "Would it be okay if I came back when you were feeling better—when you're up and around?"

Now was the time, she knew. This was when she had to end it.

She took a deep breath and forced herself to meet his gaze. "That won't be necessary, Cal," she said, keeping her tone brisk. "I'm sure you'll have a great many things to do, settling in as the sheriff, and I—"

He stiffened. "I know it isn't 'necessary,' Livy," he said, his face taking on a wary look. "I asked if I could come back because I *wanted* to."

She couldn't look at him any longer. She couldn't tell him the truth, for she knew Cal, knew him to be chivalrous to a fault. If he thought she was refusing to see him for his own good, he'd be that much more determined to come.

"Cal, I appreciate all you've done, and I thank you, but I think perhaps that better be the end of it," she said. "We've each done the other a favor. Perhaps we should just leave it at that."

His face seemed suddenly set in stone. "So now we're even, is that it?"

She looked away, unable to meet his eye. "I don't mean to be unkind. It's just that...well, I'm a widow, after all. It hasn't even been that long, you know."

"Somehow I don't think that's the reason."

Oh, Lord, why was he making it so hard to do the right thing, to send him away for his own good?

She took a deep breath. "Very well," she said, "you want the truth, and that is that I've learned to live without depending on a man, and I find I like it that way."

Chapter Six

If her words hurt him, it was difficult to tell. The only change she could detect in Cal was a certain stillness, as if he were bracing for the next blow. She waited, her face turned away from him, listening for the sounds of his boot heels thudding down the steps.

The chair creaked, but the only other sound she heard was his intake of breath. She turned back to see him standing by the chair.

"Livy, I…maybe you're readin' somethin' I didn't mean into my wantin' to visit. I know you're recently, uh, bereaved. I—I didn't mean…"

She looked away again. "Oh, I think you did. But don't worry about it, Sheriff. I'm used to men assuming too much about me. They *assume* that since I had a Mexican lover, I'm fair game for any man. Well, I'm not."

"Now it's you who's assuming, *Mrs.* Gillespie," he said, his voice cold as a Texas norther. "I wouldn't dream of interfering with your mourning, no matter *who* it is you're mourning for."

A second later, she heard the door close and the sound of his boots retreating down the steps.

I wouldn't dream of interfering with your mourning, no matter who it is you're mourning for.

Oh, Lord, she had gotten carried away in her defiant pose, and it had succeeded too well. The way she had worded it, it sounded as if she were admitting that the stories about Francisco and her were true. Now Cal believed the gossip—if he hadn't already—and he would despise her for being a treacherous, faithless woman.

It was for the best, she told herself, even as she sank back into the pillows, scalding tears flooding her eyes.

Cal marched back down the road into the heart of town, head erect, but not really seeing anything or anyone he passed. Her words still stung. How could Livy, the woman who had been his sweetheart years ago, praise him as a hero and compliment his mustache, then turn on him again? As if she hated him, as if she suspected him of—of assuming she was a woman of easy virtue, and wanting to sample her favors!

He hadn't given much credence to the story of the supposed Mexican lover, until he'd found her standing by his rose-decorated grave. And now she had come right out and admitted it was true! *They assume that since I had a Mexican lover, I'm fair game for any man....*

Then he thought about what she'd said last—*I've learned to live without depending on a man, and I find I like it that way....*

Well, that was just fine. He was going to be busy being the best sheriff Gillespie Springs ever had. He wasn't going to have time to be paying courtesy calls on an ill-tempered widow, even if she didn't have any other friends. She'd made her choice. He'd found Jovita for her, so she wouldn't be alone and helpless while she regained her strength.

Now, come on, Cal, tell the truth, at least to yourself. Could he honestly say there wasn't a shred of truth in her accusations? Could he put a hand on his worn, well-thumbed Bible and say he didn't still *want* her, that somewhere deep inside he hadn't been hoping that after a decent interval, she and he might begin again what his going off to war had ended?

No, he couldn't, but as God was his witness, he hadn't intended anything dishonorable, anything that would hurt her. But she hadn't hesitated to hurt him—again.

He let himself remember that other time, back in 1861, when he'd ridden over to Childress Hall, her father's cotton plantation, to tell her of his decision and to ask her to wait for him.

She'd been wearing a dress of some sort of flimsy, light blue material sprigged with dark blue flowers, over a hoopskirt that swayed when she'd walked across the veranda to meet him, giving him glimpses of her lace-trimmed pantalettes and neat ankles above kid slippers.

"*Cal, you must be reading my mind! I was just about to send a note asking you to supper! Delilah's cooking chicken and dumplings, and strawberry pie, and...*" *Her voice trailed off for a moment.* "*But you look so serious! You aren't still thinking about that silly quarrel we had the other night after the church picnic, are you?*"

"*Yes. No. That is, not about the quarrel, Livy. You know I can't stay angry with you. But I've come to tell you that I'm leaving tomorrow—to join the army. I've come to say goodbye, and to ask you to wait for me...if you want to, that is.*"

He'd seen her fine eyes narrow into blue storm clouds and the lips he loved to kiss tighten into a furious line. "I might. But it depends. What army are you joining, Cal Devlin?"

"Aw, Livy, don't make this so hard. You already know the answer to that—I haven't changed my mind. How can I, when it would be going against all I believe in?"

She'd looked at him as if he were some species of vermin. "Evidently you don't find it hard to contemplate going against your fellow Southerners, against other Texans, or to think about having to kill them in battle?"

"Livy, I hate the idea. You know I do. But in this instance my fellow Southerners are wrong, and I have to fight on the side I believe to be right. Livy, my family's all fired up at me about this, please don't let it divide us, too! Disagree with me about my choice, but please say you'll wait for me? This awful conflict isn't going to last too long, sweetheart. It can't. The South doesn't have the wherewithal to fight like the North does. And then we'll have the rest of our lives to be together, Livy, if you'll be there waiting for me when I come home to you...."

She'd laughed then, scornfully and without mirth. Her face was that of a stranger, a stranger who smelled a foul odor. "Wait for you? You must be joking, Cal Devlin. Unlike you, I have some loyalty to my country—"

"Your country is the United States of America, Livy," he'd interrupted her to say. "We're trying to preserve the Union—"

"My country is the Confederate States of America now," she'd informed him in lofty tones. "And as a loyal daughter of the South I despise all her enemies— and that includes you, Caleb Travis Devlin." She'd

*turned her back on him before saying, "I suggest you
get back up on that stallion and ride outa here before
my papa takes a bullwhip to your hide."*

*He'd ridden away as ordered then, and left to join
the Union army the next day. A year later, in a letter
from his mother—Sarah Devlin wrote him regularly,
even if she'd deplored his choice—he'd learned that
Olivia had married Dan Gillespie, a captain in the Confederate army, when Dan was home on leave.*

So much of that world was gone now, almost as if it
had never been, Cal thought. He had ridden past Childress Hall on his way to Gillespie Springs. The plantation was a ruin. After Livy's father had died, shortly
after the war ended, the estate had been bought by carpetbaggers at a fraction of its value. Those scoundrels
had had no notion of how to manage such a place, par-
celing it out to sharecroppers and living in just a room
or two of the formerly splendid mansion. The big house
looked as if it would fall down around their Yankee
ears any day now.

Yeah, he'd forgotten Livy could hurt him like that,
but he wasn't going to lie awake at night and ache, as
he had after his long-ago dismissal.

He was so deep in thought that he nearly bowled right
into a plump matron coming out of the general store.

"Oh!"

"I beg your pardon, ma'am!" he said, grabbing hold
of a package that had spilled out of her overladen grasp
right into his hands.

"Oh it's *you*, Sheriff Devlin," said the doughy-faced
matron, her startled face relaxing into a simper as she
recognized him. "You—you frightened me, coming
along so fast out of the sunlight! But I suppose I wasn't
watching where I was going, either!"

"The fault is entirely mine, ma'am. Sorry," he said, tipping his hat as he restored her package to her. As she was still staring expectantly up at him, he added, "Do you need some help carrying your parcels, ma'am?"

"Oh, Sheriff, you're so *gallant!*" She sighed, fluttering her lashes up at him as she unloaded her parcels into his hands. "My husband's waiting just down the street...."

As he trudged down the wood planking in her wake, Cal tuned out the woman's artless chatter, still thinking of her remark about his sudden appearance frightening her.

He couldn't blame Livy for not wanting to be around a man who looked like he did. He imagined the sight of his scarred face and patched eye would frighten most women. It had been stupid to forget that he wasn't the same man he'd been.

Robert Gillespie watched out the window of his office in the bank as the new sheriff handed the parcels up to Ada Gray's husband, who'd been dozing in their wagon until Mrs. Gray had jostled him awake.

"A real Sir Galahad," he muttered to himself.

"Uh, 'scuse me, Mr. Gillespie?" mumbled the startled saddle tramp standing on the other side of the vast mahogany desk.

"Nothing, Leroy," Gillespie said, straightening and turning away from the window. "As I was saying, I want you to ride into Bryan and find out what you can about that Caleb Devlin. Just ask around, quietlike, at the saloon and such. See if you can dig up why he left there, since he's a preacher and all."

"Uh, boss, what d'ya want me to tell 'em if they ask

me what business it is a' mine?'' Leroy Scruggs asked him.

''Just act like you've met him, and you're curious, that's all. Folks love to gossip—and if you can get some ol' biddy talkin', you might find out quite a lot. Or buy some ne'er-do-well a beer. Above all, don't tell anyone *I* want to know—in Bryan *or* Gillespie Springs, understand me?''

''Yes, Mr. Gillespie,'' replied Scruggs quickly, fingering the money in his pocket Gillespie had given him.

''Report back to me as soon as you've found out all you can, and there'll be a bonus for you if you're quick,'' Gillespie told him. ''Now go on, there's no time like the present.''

The cowboy's spurs clinked on the puncheon floor as he left.

Yessirree, thought Gillespie as he turned back to the window and saw Devlin, now free of Mrs. Gray, striding into the jail, *the sooner I solve the mystery of why you're here, mister preacher-turned-lawman, and just how you came to be helping Olivia, the sooner I can breathe easier.*

The news that Olivia had lost the baby had already eased his mind considerably, for he'd imagined how suspicious it was going to look when that little bastard was born and it wasn't the least bit darker than its mother, indicating it could not possibly have been sired by that Mexican the way he'd told those who'd come to the funeral. And what, God forbid, if it had actually looked like *him?*

Yes, it had been a godsend that she was no longer bearing the child, *his* child—though why she couldn't have conveniently died, too, was galling in the extreme.

He liked neat, tidy endings, just as he liked rows of figures that added up just right.

Cal sat at supper in the dining room of the Gillespie Springs Hotel, chewing thoughtfully on his steak. It wasn't bad for a small hotel in a tiny town in the middle of Texas, he mused, though his mother could have taught the cook some things about making tough beef flavorful. James Long, who owned the hotel, had no doubt primed the cook to make him comfortable, but the cook had welcomed him like the prodigal son and pledged to cook him anything he desired, anytime. He'd already been promised apple pie for dessert.

Six o'clock and fully dark already, he mused, staring out the window of the lamplit dining room in which he was the only patron. It was already early November. Before he knew it it'd be Christmas.

The saloon looked to be doing a good business tonight, he thought, as he watched a pair of men stroll through the bat-wing doors across the street. The tinkling sounds of the piano reached his ears faintly, playing a bouncy version of "Camptown Races."

After the promised pie, Cal ambled over to the Last Chance Saloon, figuring it to be the best place to get to know some of the men of the town. He'd once tended bar at the Alamo Saloon in Abilene and had taken pride in knowing every man in town, as well as many of the cowboys who came through on trail drives. Tonight he'd have a beer, chew the fat with some of the locals for a spell, then check the rest of the town before seeking his bed.

The place was small, with only eight tables, but certainly big enough for a town the size of Gillespie Springs. Instead of the usual painting of a plump nude woman over the bar, there was one of a fierce-looking bull.

Cal saw Long and Gillespie sitting in the far corner and nodded to them, but he was hoping Long wouldn't invite him to join them. Cal wanted to get to know some of the other townspeople and to avoid Gillespie when he could.

"Evenin', Sheriff. Hank Whyte's my name. How 'bout if your first whiskey's on the house tonight?" offered the barkeep affably, looking up from the glass he was drying behind the long, polished-wood bar.

"That's mighty kind of you," responded Cal with a smile, perching one booted leg on the low brass rail in front of the bar. "Why is this place called the 'Last Chance'?" he asked. "I used to do your job, and it looks like a prosperous-enough place to me."

The barkeep chuckled. "You did, huh? Well sir, it's named on account of my missus sayin' this was my last chance to make a success of things. You see, I'd failed as a lawyer—couldn't keep enough paying clients 'cause I was always taking on lost causes—failed as a shopkeeper and finally decided to run a saloon. She said it was my last chance. Been here for four years now. So far, it's going pretty well."

He saw Cal glance at the painting of the bull behind the bar. "Oh, and she made me hang that up, too, rather than the kind of painting most fellows expect to see in a saloon. I just tell everyone it's a portrait of my dear wife."

Cal couldn't help laughing.

The barkeep rolled his eyes ruefully, but there was a twinkle in them. "I hear tell you're not married, Sheriff? You couldn't be, or you'd know being married to a woman like that is no laughing matter." He seemed about to say something else, but just then his attention was caught by whoever was coming in the door. "Uh-oh."

Cal turned to see what was bothering him.

A lanky young man with an old Confederate forage cap set askew on his head had just let the bat-wing door swing shut behind him. He came shambling in, his mouth half-agape, a vacuous smile trained on the barkeep.

Cal raised an inquiring brow at Hank Whyte, then looked back toward the young man approaching them with his awkward gait.

"That there's Georgie, and he's a mite...uh, simple," said Whyte softly. "He's all right, he don't misbehave none, but Gillespie don't like it when Georgie comes in when *he's* here. I've told Georgie t'come 'round back for his beer, but he just don't understand, I reckon."

Just then the young man opened his mouth, giving Cal a glimpse of blackened, irregular teeth. "W-wanna *b-b-beer!*" he stuttered, then plunked a nickel down on the counter and stood back, grinning as if enormously pleased with himself.

"Fine, Georgie, you just go on outside and I'll bring it to you," urged Hank in low tones, gesturing toward the back door.

But Georgie had spotted the star on Cal's chest and was grinning at it.

"Don't wanna...g-go outside. T-t-talk to th-th' sheriff."

Out of the corner of his eye, Cal saw Gillespie get to his feet and start walking stiffly toward the bar.

"*Out!*" Gillespie rasped at Georgie, making a sweeping gesture in the direction of the door. Reaching the retarded man's side, the banker shoved at his shoulder.

"Hey! I'm talking to *you*, you idiot! Get out of here and stop bothering the sheriff! He doesn't have time to deal with fools like you," he snarled.

Georgie turned and was regarding the shorter man with puzzlement. "W-wanna talk t-t-to th' sheriff," he informed him, as if that should put an end to the matter.

Gillespie grabbed hold of Georgie's collar. "I said get out of here!"

Cal straightened and put a restraining hand on the banker's forearm. "Now, just a minute, Mr. Gillespie. The man has the money for a beer, and he's mentioned a wish to make my acquaintance. I don't see anything wrong with that. I don't reckon he's going to be bothering you if he's up at the bar talkin' to me. All right, Georgie?"

The retarded man's grin nearly split his face. He nodded vigorously, then winked at Gillespie. "Okay, Sheriff!"

Cal could see from the vein that bulged dangerously in the side of Gillespie's temple that the bank president wasn't pleased to be contradicted, but Cal couldn't help that. He wasn't going to let Gillespie bully Georgie just because he wanted a beer. Whyte looked uneasy, but he poured Georgie a beer all the same as Gillespie sullenly resumed his seat with Long.

Georgie not only drank a beer with Cal, he kept him company while he patroled the town, chattering volubly in his stuttering fashion about everybody and everything. And Georgie, who lived at the boardinghouse, knew quite a lot. He was a fountain of information. By the time he had bid Cal good-night at the steps leading up to his quarters above the jail, Cal knew a whole lot more about Gillespie Springs than Long or anyone else had told him. Gillespie would have been astonished if he could have heard how much Georgie had noticed, Cal thought as he hung his vest and shirt on the hook on the wall and prepared for bed. From Georgie's artless observations, it seemed that most of the town was controlled in one way or another by Gillespie. He held notes on many of the properties and owned several shacks on the street behind the saloon, renting them out at rates that to Cal seemed high. The last sheriff had pretty much been the bank president's puppet.

Cal was going to have trouble with Robert Gillespie sooner or later; he knew it in his bones. He sighed wearily as he sank into the room's one chair. It was unfortunate he'd had to butt heads with him tonight over poor Georgie, but it was good for Gillespie to know now where he stood. Cal Devlin was no man's puppet.

He reached for the well-worn Bible on the table. Just because he was no longer a preacher was no reason he couldn't continue to gain wisdom from the Good Book. He opened it at random.

"Blessed are the meek, for they shall inherit the earth," he read, and thought of Georgie. He'd always failed at meekness, himself. He read down a little farther. "Blessed are the merciful, for they shall obtain mercy.... Blessed are the peacemakers, for they shall be called the children of God...."

Was that showing mercy, being kind to a man like Georgie? Cal hoped it was and not merely an exercise in pride in showing Gillespie he couldn't be pushed around. "Lord, help me to be a peacemaker," he prayed aloud.

But his thoughts, as he lay down on the bed a few minutes later, were not of making peace and showing mercy but of Olivia Gillespie.

Chapter Seven

Gillespie's hired cowboy was back within three days.

"You was right to check up on him, boss," Leroy Scruggs opined after barging into the bank president's office right at noon.

Robert Gillespie slapped the letter he was reading— an important missive from the president of the Houston and Texas Central Railroad—facedown over the map of Texas he had been studying at his polished mahogany desk.

"Didn't anyone ever teach you to *knock,* Leroy?" he snapped.

The cowboy looked surprised and took a tentative step back. "Sorry, Mr. Gillespie, but I reckoned you wanted the information you sent me after powerful bad, so I rushed right back to town. Barely stopped to water my horse, let alone to wet my own whistle." He looked longingly at the pitcher of water Gillespie kept on a small stand behind his desk.

He'd be damned if he'd let this unkempt saddle tramp drink out of *his* glass, the only glass in the room, Gillespie decided, and ignored the look. "Well, spit out what you learned, quick, and you can be on your way

over to the Last Chance with money in your pockets,"
he told the sweaty cowboy, deliberately keeping him
standing.

"Waal, sir, that there Caleb Devlin ain't much liked
in Bryan, not by a long shot he ain't. He used to be the
apple a' their eyes there, the saintly young minister, the
most eligible bachelor in town."

"Used to be?" Gillespie echoed. "What happened?"

Leroy smirked. "I'd a' left town, too, if I was him.
Seems he went off and served in the army—"

"So did thousands of men," Gillespie said, impatient
to get back to the important letter he'd just opened when
Leroy arrived, a letter that could decide his whole future.

"Yeah, but *he* served with the Yankees," Leroy said
triumphantly.

Gillespie, who'd been tilting back in his chair, leaned
forward now, which brought his front chair legs crash-
ing down, causing Leroy to start at the sudden thud.

"Folks around Bryan didn't cotton to their young
minister bein' a traitor. Even his family, though natch-
erly them Devlins faced down anyone who criticized
him," Leroy continued.

"Naturally. Hmm…so our new sheriff was a blue
belly," mused Gillespie, imagining how that was going
to affect the good people of his town. James Long had
been a captain in the Confederate army, Jack Gray a
second lieutenant. Hank Whyte had lost a son. They
weren't going to cotton to this news, either, by God.

"And did he have a distinguished-service record, our
Yankee sheriff? Did he kill lots of good Southern
boys?"

Leroy snorted. "That's where it gets even more interestin', boss. Seems halfway through the war, he just

up and disappeared, right in the middle a' battle. It warn't till just this summer his brother found him in Abilene, tendin' bar. He claimed some shell hit nearby and knocked him silly—that's how come he's wearin' that eye patch, too. Claims he lost his memory a' who he was.''

Gillespie lit a cigar and puffed on it, considering the grinning cowboy through a haze of smoke. ''Go on,'' he commanded. ''I take it he did not get a prodigal son's welcome when he came back to Bryan?''

Scruggs looked confused. Obviously he wasn't a student of the Bible. ''I don't know about no prody-gal son, Mr. Gillespie, but when this Caleb Devlin finally come back t'Texas last month, the folks in Bryan, they ain't forgave nor forgot what he done, ridin' off to join the Yankees. Seems he not only got throwed outa the church he used t'preach at, but a bunch a' good ol' boys in town 'bout beat him t'death. He damn near got tarred an' feathered an' ridden out on a rail.''

Too bad the good ol' boys hadn't succeeded, thought Gillespie. It would have saved him the trouble. ''Well, what about Devlin and Miz Olivia? Her name used to be Childress, I recollect. Were you able to find out anything about a previous relationship between the two of them?'' inquired Gillespie.

Leroy looked sly now. ''Yeah, some ol' biddy I got t'gossipin' said she recollected they was sweethearts before the war. They was gonna marry an' all, and then the war started, an' Miss 'Livia got all riled up 'cause her beau was gonna go be a Yank, and she broke the engagement.''

Gillespie let out the breath he'd been unaware of holding and allowed a smile to curve the corners of his mouth. ''You've done very well, Leroy. Very well indeed." He reached into his pocket and plunked a five-dollar gold piece down on the desk.

Leroy eyed it dubiously. "I thought you said I'd get a bonus if I was quick. I reckon I spent this much in buyin' drinks for them fellas in Bryan."

Gillespie snorted. "Yes, and I very well remember staking you for...ahem! traveling expenses, shall we say? It's not my fault if you chose to drown your profits in drink." The cowboy continued to look sulky, though, and Gillespie reconsidered. He might need this saddle tramp's services again before he was through with Cal Devlin.

"Very well, here's another half eagle," he said, grudgingly tossing the other man a second gold coin. The cowboy caught it, and the grin settled on his face again.

"That's more like it. Say, Mr. Gillespie, for a double eagle I'd consider gunnin' him down for ya," Leroy offered.

Gillespie narrowed his eyes. He'd felt an instant antipathy from Devlin, and it was certain the new sheriff wasn't going to be amenable to control as old Olin Watts had been. Gillespie bitterly resented the way Devlin had interfered the other night in his treatment of Georgie. But as much as he relished the idea of seeing Devlin lying in his blood in the street, he wasn't sure he was going to have to murder him to get rid of him.

"I don't think that's going to be necessary, Leroy," he said, blowing a smoke ring right into the cowboy's eager face. "Feel free to tell whoever's drinkin' in the Last Chance what you told me. It'll spread like wildfire, you'll see. After what you've found out gets spread around, I reckon Devlin's gonna slink outa Gillespie

Springs with his tail between his legs, just like he slunk out of Bryan.''

He saw the saddle tramp's face fall. "Don't be so eager, boy," he counseled. "Devlin's got one behind bars right now who thought he'd come test the new sheriff and shoot up the town. Devlin got tired of him runnin' his horse up and down the street, shootin' at the moon, and ran a rope from the hitchin' post of the saloon to the one in front of the hotel. It tripped the horse as it came runnin' through. Then, while the cowboy was still tryin' to figure out what day it was, Devlin took away his six-guns neat as you please and had the fellow behind bars.''

"Do tell," Leroy responded sourly.

"But hang around, and I'm sure there'll be work for you before long," promised Gillespie. "I frequently need a...let's just say an agent, an enforcer." He paused and considered, then set the cigar down and made a tent of his fingers. "In fact, I might be needin' you tomorrow...."

Leroy brightened.

Olivia had never been one to enjoy being confined to bed or idling around the house, and she was impatient to get her strength back. The waves of weakness and fatigue that plagued her reminded her of the waves she had experienced once when her papa had taken the family on a trip to Galveston. Olivia had been allowed to remove her stockings and wade into the warm water of the Gulf of Mexico. Her strength acted just like the waves that had splashed against her feet in those long-ago days, for she'd feel just like her old self after a night's rest, and then, when she tried to get up and do something, like snapping a bowlfull of the last black-eyed peas from her garden, it would recede just like ebbing seawater.

And her tears seemed to come so easily, especially when the exhaustion swept over her just when it seemed she ought to be up helping Jovita with the household chores. She wept for the baby, even though she had wondered how she was ever going to love it, conceived the way it was. And she wept every time she thought of the way she had sent Cal away, and the hard, set way his face had looked as he had turned to go.

Jovita's constant cheering presence helped, though. "You got to be patient, Señora Gillespie," she said as she pushed the savory chicken dish she had cooked across the table to Livy. "Your strength weel come back, you wait and see. Just have another helping of thees *molé*—eet was the recipe of *mi madre*."

"Why not call me just Livy, Jovita? Señora Gillespie is such a mouthful!" Livy suggested with a smile.

The Mexican woman smiled back. "All right, Leevy. Eet ees easier."

"Good. But maybe you could tell me something. Why do I want to *cry* all the time, Jovita? I've never liked weepy women, and now I've become one, it seems!" she said ruefully, as tears stung her eyes yet again.

The Mexican woman's eyes were liquid with sympathy. "Ah, you grieve for the *bebé,* no? You lost your husband, and now the baby, too. You have much to bear, *es verdad.*"

Olivia noticed she didn't say, "and now *his* baby, too." She figured that Jovita Mendez was as aware as everyone else in Gillespie Springs that the baby Livy had lost was not her husband's posthumous child, but there was no judgment in the woman's sympathetic gaze. It was so tempting to confide in Jovita, to tell her all the things she had kept inside her these last few months....

"A woman loses something of herself when a baby leaves her body. Even when the baby ees born healthy after nine months, many women become *triste,* sad. I deed myself, when my babies were born. Eet weel get better, you weel see. In a few days you weel be good as new, but now you must rest and sleep much, and eat lots of Jovita's good food, yes?"

"Yes," Olivia said with a smile. "You take such good care of me—I'm getting quite spoiled, you know. But I—I wondered something...."

"Yes?"

"How do you feel about working for me, when a Mexican man is dead because he was...friendly to me? Don't you...don't you and the other Mexicans in this town ever think...well, maybe I was responsible? For Francisco Luna's death, I mean?"

"You did not kill heem," Jovita said quietly.

"No, I know I didn't...actually shoot him, but—"

"I do not believe the story that you and my nephew Francisco were lovers, *señora,*" Jovita began, her liquid black eyes locking with Olivia's. "Friends, *sí,* but lovers, eet ees a lie, no?"

"Francisco Luna was your nephew?" echoed Olivia in shocked disbelief. "But why didn't you tell me? It—it must be you who put the rosary on his grave, and the flowers, right?"

The Mexican woman nodded. "Me, and sometimes Rosa, hees *novia.*"

"He was engaged to be married? How tragic!" Olivia said, tears stinging her eyes for the woman who would never be Francisco's wife now. "But—he never said…"

"He was saving money so he could afford to buy some land," Jovita told her. "But Rosa ees why I knew you were not Francisco's lover. He was not a man for two women, my nephew, though I know he liked and respected you. And all of the *tejanos* in town, they know you deed nothing to cause hees death."

Olivia nodded slowly. "I see…thank you for telling me this, Jovita. I'm really glad you've come."

The woman beamed. "And I am glad, too, that Señor Devleen asked me to come. He ees a good man, Caleb Devleen."

Livy looked away, not wanting the Mexican to see how mentioning Cal's name affected her. "Yes, he is." She could feel the woman's bright black eyes studying her.

"Perhaps one night we have heem come for supper for some of Jovita's good cooking, no?"

"No!" Livy said, too quickly. "That is, it's not that I don't want him to eat your good cooking, Jovita, it's just that I don't want Mr. Devlin to…uh, get the wrong idea about me…." She felt herself flushing and started fiddling with her fork in confusion.

"But Señora—I mean, Leevy…" Jovita's brown face was furrowed with concern. "The *señor,* he cares about you! I can see eet in hees face!" When she was agitated, Jovita's accent grew thicker.

Livy reached a hand across the small table and touched her arm. "Jovita, it is true that we…used to be, um, close, but there is nothing more now, believe me. And I think you know how people in town feel about me. If the new sheriff was known to be my friend, well…the people here might…turn against him, don't you see? I don't want that to happen to Cal. He needs a new start in life—and I don't want to be the cause of him not being treated fairly here. Am I making any sense, Jovita?''

''*Sí...*'' the woman said slowly, after taking another bite of the *molé*. ''But forgeeve me for saying thees, Leevy, I do not believe that there ees nothing more now for heem here—'' she pointed to the center of her chest ''—een your heart. You love heem, and because of that, you—how do you say—sacrifice, yes?''

Livy stared back at Jovita. ''Yes...I suppose you could put it that way. I care enough about Cal that I put his well-being ahead of my own selfish needs.'' She felt perilously close to tears as she said it. How did this middle-aged woman see so deeply into her soul?

''To need a man's love ees not selfish, Leevy. Eet ees what God meant us to do, I theenk. But what eef Señor Devleen needs you for hees—what did you call eet—*well-being,* Leevy?'' Jovita asked.

''Well, he doesn't,'' Livy said firmly. ''In time he'll build a new life here, and he'll be able to put our youthful friendship in its proper perspective.'' She was aware that she sounded too prim, and that the simple woman across the table probably didn't understand what a ''perspective'' was. ''That is to say, he'll be able to look at it the right way.''

''But Leevy...a man needs a woman een hees life, no? You would be able to watch Señor Devleen court another woman?''

Livy's fork clattered as she dropped it on the crockery plate.

''Forgeeve me, Leevy. I should not ask thees. I make you angry, yes? Eet ees not my business,'' Jovita said quickly.

Livy swallowed hard. "No, it's all right, Jovita. I'm not angry. It's just...hard to think of. Yes, if Cal started courting another woman, I...would have to—to be happy for him. He deserves some happiness. His brother told me he was married for a while, during the war, but his wife died...."

"And your husband died, too. What of you, Leevy? Eet ees soon, yes, but you are a young woman. Do you not meess a man's arms around you?"

"No," Livy lied. "Do you?" She was curious about what Jovita would say now that she had turned the tables.

"Yes, sometimes. But I have had a good man. When my Manuel died, I thought I must die, too. Now I can remember that happiness with joy, and I have my children, even though they are grown and have families of their own. Eef a good man comes to me again, well..." She winked. "But you are too young to leeve with just memories, Leevy. I theenk you need a good man to love you and give you babies," Jovita asserted.

Livy could only gaze at her openmouthed for a long moment. "No. That's not for me, Jovita. I've tried it once, and now that Dan is gone, I have to stand on my own two feet. Which brings up something else I've been thinking about," she said, deliberately changing the subject. "I want to discuss your wages with you."

"Oh, eet ees not needed," Jovita said with a quiet smile.

"Yes, it is. You get room and board here, Jovita, but I don't expect you to help me out for only that. Dan left me a little money, and if I feel strong enough tomorrow I'm going to walk down to the bank and withdraw a bit of it. I need a couple of things at the general store, anyway. Now why don't we say two dollars a week, plus your room and board? That's what I used to pay the lady who helped me here, before…my husband died.''

Jovita's face looked troubled again. ''But eet ees not needed, Leevy. Señor Devleen, he paid me through the end of the year. He said he wanted me to stay at least that long, and after that we would see, he said.''

''He *paid* you through *December?*'' Livy asked incredulously. ''That's two full months!''

Jovita nodded.

''And after that we'll see,'' Livy repeated. A spark of irritation was soon fanned to a flame within her. What presumption! She squelched the voice inside her that protested it was merely evidence of Cal's thoughtful caring. *We'll see, indeed!* How dare he take it upon himself to pay for her housekeeper, as if she were a *kept* woman! Well, when she went into town tomorrow, she would just have to set Cal Devlin straight!

Chapter Eight

"Now I've got some friendly advice for you," Cal admonished the bleary-eyed cowboy as he opened the door of his jail cell the next morning, "and that is to ride on out of here and don't come back to Gillespie Springs if you're just lookin' to raise hell." He'd been called out of bed after falling asleep last night when this same cowboy, who'd been drunk as a skunk, had decided to shoot down the chandelier in the Last Chance Saloon because Hank Whyte wouldn't sell him any more whiskey. "This is a peaceable town and we aim to keep it that way."

"Mebbe I will ride on," mumbled the cowboy, groaning slightly as the bright rays of the sun struck his eyes.

"And maybe you won't, I know. But the next time—if there is a next time—there's a five-dollar fine or a week in that cell you just left," Cal said pleasantly. "Your horse is at the livery stables," he added. "Didn't seem fair to leave him tied to a hitchin' post all night without food or water. You'll owe the livery four bits for his keep."

The hungover cowboy made no rejoinder as he stumbled in the direction of the livery.

Yessir, he was really beginning to settle in as sheriff of Gillespie Springs, Cal thought as he looked up and down Main Street. He'd already become acquainted with a number of folks, and though it was too soon to call any of them friends, they seemed to like him and approve of the job he was doing. Not that there'd been any *real* crises to handle since the day of the bank robbery—arresting a drunken cowboy sure didn't qualify as one—and Cal frankly hoped there wouldn't be. He was ready for a little peace and quiet, and the chance to grow roots in a peaceful place.

If only Livy Gillespie hadn't made it clear she had no room for him in her heart, he would have to say life was just about perfect, he thought. It had been three days since he had last seen her, and she had as good as told him never to come back. What was it going to be like, living here, seeing her around town, knowing she lived just down the road but didn't want to have anything to do with him? He wanted to believe he had merely erred by rushing her, that it was just too soon after her husband's shocking death, but her words kept coming back with haunting finality: *I've learned to live without depending on a man, and I find I like it that way....*

Just then, as if he had the power to summon her with his thoughts, he caught sight of Livy, accompanied by Jovita Mendez, walking up the road from the direction of her house.

His first thought was what was she doing out of bed? It had only been four days since she'd lost the baby! He was conscious of an overpowering urge to run to her, carry her back to bed and lecture Jovita for failing to properly take care of Livy. But as the distance between them rapidly diminished, he could see the determined set of her chin and the firm resolve in her gait as she made a beeline for him.

She seemed paler than he remembered—or was it merely the black bombazine mourning dress that washed the color from her cheeks and made her skin look so translucent? There was nothing pale about the twin blue storm clouds in her eyes, however. Olivia Gillespie was mad as a wet hen about something, and it looked as if she was going to tell him all about it.

"Mr. Devlin, I need to speak to you," she called out when she was still just passing the saloon.

"Certainly, Mrs. Gillespie," he replied, wondering what burr she had under her saddle this morning. He waited until she drew near, then said, "I'm at your service. What may I help you with this fine morning?" He watched as a hectic flush lit her pale cheeks, making her eyes look even bluer.

"May we speak inside?" she asked, indicating with a slight nod the curious faces of two women watching them from across the street.

"Of course. Ladies…" He opened the door to his office and indicated with a gesture that Livy and Jovita were to enter.

"Jovita, you said you had some things to get at the general store?" Olivia said to her housekeeper in a peremptory tone.

The Mexican woman looked anxious. "Oh, Señora Leevy—" she began, but Olivia raised a hand, cutting her off.

"We've already discussed this, Jovita, and my mind is made up. Go ahead, and I'll meet you at the general store after I've been to the bank."

Jovita Mendez flashed an apologetic look at Cal, then gathered her rebozo around her shoulders and retreated.

Olivia followed him inside, and after a glance at the two empty cells, accepted the chair by his desk. Alone with him, she seemed suddenly uneasy and uncertain where to begin.

"You look upset, Livy," he prompted her.

"Yes—n-no! That is," she stammered, "it's just come to my attention that you did something—with the best of intentions, I'm sure—that I cannot allow."

He stared at her, mystified. "And just what might that be, Olivia? I haven't even seen you for several days, so how could I have managed to offend you?"

"I'm not offended," she insisted in an affronted tone. "It's just that I've learned from Jovita that you've paid her through the next two months."

"Isn't she helping you? Is she lazy?" he asked.

"Of course she's helping me! She works *very* hard. In fact, I'm not sure how I ever did without her!" Olivia said, obviously startled by his questions.

"Then what's the problem?" he drawled. "You needed someone to help you, and I found her for you. I was just doing what a friend would do, Olivia," he said gently.

"But you *paid her wages,* not only for the first few days but for the next two months, and I cannot allow you to do that. As I've indicated, I'm sure you meant well, but I have money to pay my household help, and just as soon as I leave here, I'm going to go to the bank, where I intend to draw out enough to repay you. Now, if you'll just tell me how much you paid her…"

Something about the stubborn set of her mouth inspired him to mischief. "No," he said.

Her jaw dropped. "I beg your pardon? What do you mean, no?"

"Seems a clear-enough word to me, Livy. I said no—that means no, I won't tell you what I paid her, and even if you browbeat Jovita into telling you, I won't accept any money from you—so save your money to use on yourself. I figure you might need it. Livy, I just did you a favor, that's all—a kindness to an old friend," he insisted.

"Caleb, I assure you I'm grateful, but you don't seem to realize you've overstepped the bounds of friendship. I have enough trouble in this town, what with falsehoods that have spread about me, without you doing more to injure my reputation!"

"You don't *sound* very grateful!" he retorted, starting to feel annoyed at her prim, lecturing voice. "And who in Gillespie Springs knows that I paid Señora Mendez except you, me and her?"

"No one," she said stiffly. "But that's not the point, Caleb."

"Then what *is* the point you're all hot under the collar about, Miz Olivia? Forgive me, but if no one else *knows* I paid her wages for a couple of months, I don't think there's a problem unless *you* decide to go tellin' everyone about it. Señora Mendez doesn't seem like a chatterbox. I haven't seen you get all stiff-necked and haughty like this since the day before I went away to war."

"Stiff-necked?" she cried, jumping to her feet so hastily that the chair nearly toppled behind her. "Haughty? How *dare* you, Cal? I'm merely trying to preserve what little respectability I have left in this town, while you insist on compromising me by paying for things—the way a man would do for—for a mistress!''

He just stared at her, openmouthed, astonished that she would think such a thing, let alone voice it. "You seem real concerned about your respectability all of a sudden, Olivia, for someone who was braggin' about havin' a lover—'a Mexican lover,' I believe is how you put it, the last time I saw you...."

"B-bragging about having a lover?" she sputtered. "Why, I never said that!"

"Far be it from me to call a lady a liar, but yes, you did," he asserted, refusing to back away even though he was aware of the dangerous glint in her eyes.

The slap, when it came, was still a surprise.

"You—you're lower than a snake's belly, Caleb Devlin! You misunderstood me on purpose. I never said I *had* a lover, just that folks around here *assumed* I had and were treating me like I was fair game for anyone. I won't let you treat me like that, Caleb, is that clear?"

"Very clear, Miz Livy," he said, rubbing his stinging cheek. She might look frail, but Olivia Childress Gillespie packed a wallop in that tiny little hand of hers. "And I'd like to make something clear to you, too."

"And that is?" she asked warily, her eyes big and round as he took a step toward her. Yet he had to admire the way she refused to back up.

"That is—*this* is—how a man treats a mistress," he said, suddenly closing the distance between them, taking hold of both her arms at the elbow and forcing them down at her sides so that she was powerless to push him away. She went instantly rigid, but didn't turn her head quickly enough to evade the descent of his mouth upon hers.

He took advantage of her moment of shock to pin

her arms behind her, capturing both wrists in one hand, while his other hand rose to hold her chin while his lips lowered to hers. Then he kissed her deeply and thoroughly, his tongue parting her lips to ravage the sweetness of her mouth.

He felt her go even more rigid and try to pull out of his embrace, but he wouldn't allow it. Instead he went on kissing her until her resistance collapsed and she gave a soft moan. Then she was kissing him back, straining against him, her tongue dancing against his. After a moment he trusted her enough to let go of her wrists, and sure enough, her arms stole around his neck and she went on kissing him.

It was as if the years fell away and they were at the ball her father had given in honor of her eighteenth birthday. During one of the waltzes they had stolen out to the depths of the garden and he had asked her to marry him, and when she had agreed, he had kissed her with such passion—a man's passion even then—that she had opened her mouth to his for the first time. It had been the first time his hands had strayed to her breasts, too, which had felt so wonderful beneath the cloth of her bodice that he was still not sure how he had ended the embrace without pulling her deeper into the shadows and making her fully his.

He was feeling that same burning need to touch her now, and since she gave him every indication that she was burning for him, too, he gave in to the urge and raised one hand and closed it around a breast. She was wearing a corset, of course, but he stroked her and let his thumb circle where her nipple should be, and she moaned again against his mouth. At some time while he was kneading the soft globe beneath the confining corset, his other hand started undoing the line of buttons marching down her bodice, and in the far edges of his mind he heard one of them hit the floor with a tiny click.

Lord, if he didn't stop now he was going to throw the bolt on the door and take her right on the cot in one of the jail cells! And that wasn't at all what he'd set out to accomplish by kissing her, more's the pity. With difficulty he raised his head, fighting to catch his breath before he spoke.

"That's how a man treats his mistress," he said softly, his breath coming hard and ragged as he fought for control so that he wouldn't kiss her again. "Now, I hadn't done that to you, Livy, so you didn't have any call to accuse me of trying to destroy your respectability. Have *I* made *myself* clear, Miz Olivia?" he drawled, his face just inches from hers, his hand holding hers once more with a grip of iron. He had no wish to get slapped again, even though now he thoroughly deserved it.

He saw her eyes widen with hurt and shock, and shame clouded his male sense of triumph. He'd taken a memory that had been beautiful to both of them and cheapened it. He wanted to cry out, *No, wait, that's not what I meant,* but it was too late.

"Yes," she said through gritted teeth, her eyes blazing. "I think we've both made our positions very clear. *Now let me go, or I'll—*"

The sound of the door banging open caused them to spring apart.

"Hey, Sh-Sheriff!" began Georgie, his face red, his chest heaving as if he'd been running. "You gotta come—" He stopped, his mouth agape, as he caught sight of Olivia standing there, her face flushed, two or three of her top buttons undone, the black lace on her bodice rising and falling rapidly, almost as if she, too, had been running. "'S-scuse me fer interruptin', Miz G'lespie…" he stammered.

"You weren't interrupting anything, Georgie," Cal said, struggling to tame his own ragged breathing. His hands, which had just been touching her, still felt like they were on fire. "Mrs. Gillespie was just leaving. What's bothering you?"

Georgie tipped his hat elaborately to Olivia, who started to head for the doorway. She must have remembered her partially unbuttoned bodice, for she stopped, turned her back to both men and then, without looking at either man, headed for the door again.

"Y-you should hear the awful lies this man is tellin' about you in th' s-saloon, Sheriff! Y-you gotta come set 'im straight!"

Cal was aware of Olivia pausing in the doorway, but he didn't allow himself to look at her as he inquired, "What are they saying, Georgie?" But he figured he already knew.

"They're sayin'—they're sayin' you used to be a blue-bellied *Yankee!*" Georgie cried, his eyes wide with horror at the thought. "Y'gotta come say it ain't so!" he repeated.

"But it *is* so, Georgie," Cal informed him gently. "At least, it used to be." He laid a hand on the retarded man's shoulder and looked him in the eye. "It's true I fought on the Union side during the war—but the war has been over now for three years, and I'm happy that Texas is at peace. Do you understand, Georgie?"

Georgie looked flustered.

"Cal, I—I didn't tell anyone," Olivia said from the doorway.

He glanced in her direction and saw that the anger in

her face had been replaced with anxiety. Anxiety for him.

"I know you didn't, Livy. It was bound to come out," he said in an even voice. Then his gaze went back to the retarded man. "Georgie?"

"I—I guess I unnerstand, Sheriff," Georgie said haltingly. "Like you said, th' war's over. I—I reckon it only matters what y'are today, right?"

"That's the way I reckon it, Georgie. Don't let it worry you, hearin' things like that. But thanks for telling me." Cal heard a swish of skirts and creaking wood as Olivia shut the door quietly behind her, then he watched through the flyspecked window as she walked across the dusty street to the bank.

All at once, on the bank's steps, she paused as if she'd had a sudden thought. She looked back over her shoulder toward the jail, and he ducked, not wanting her to see him staring after her as if he couldn't get enough of the sight of her. Then, when he looked back again, she had changed course and was heading for the general store. He smiled, hoping that meant he'd convinced her not to try to press money on him for Jovita's wages. It didn't ensure that anything else was going to go smoothly between them, but it was something, anyway.

"I—I guess that means you ain't gonna put that cowboy in jail for sayin' it, huh, Sheriff?" Georgie said from behind him.

Cal had almost forgotten Georgie's presence, but recovered quickly. "Nope. Cain't hardly put a man behind bars for tellin' the truth," he said, extending his hand. "See you later, okay, Georgie?"

"Okay!" the retarded man said, reaching out to pump his hand with sweaty enthusiasm.

Cal sighed as Georgie ran back out, letting the door bang behind him. Now it would begin, he thought with a sigh. The whispers, the accusations...before long, the good people of Gillespie Springs who had invited him to be sheriff would find a way to uninvite him.

Lord, would he ever find a place that would welcome him? Was he going to have to move out to the unsettled territories before he found a welcome, or would he just encounter men there who hadn't learned to forgive and forget? You couldn't run from a problem any more than you could run from the Lord, he thought. He'd always found that troubles had a way of tracking a man no matter where he went.

He pulled out the blank copybook he'd purchased in the mercantile and began to write up a report about arresting the drunken cowboy. He'd scrawled only a couple of sentences before he put the pencil down.

Suddenly restless, he snatched his broad-brimmed hat and plopped it on his head. Now that his cells were empty, there was nothing that needed doing here. It was still a long time before the saloon would send over his dinner. Maybe he'd take a walk through town. As he'd told Georgie, he wasn't going to go in and confront his accuser in the saloon, but he wasn't going to cower in the jail as if he were ashamed to show his face, either.

He headed first to South Street, as he had when he'd first explored the town.

"Mornin', Miz Gray, ma'am," he said, touching his hat brim to the woman whose packages he'd carried the other day, then to another woman he hadn't met, though he knew she was the widow who owned the millinery shop. The two had been talking across the fence to each other as he approached.

"Good *morning*, Sheriff." Ada Gray beamed. "Have

you made the acquaintance of Mrs. Phoebe Stone? I imagine you've seen the little millinery shop on the other side of the hotel? That's Phoebe's," she informed him.

Cal supposed something more was called for now that he was being formally introduced, so he doffed his hat and bowed slightly. "Pleased to meet you, ma'am."

Phoebe, a faded blonde who still affected corkscrew side curls, blushed and dimpled prettily. "*I'm* pleased to meet *you*, Sheriff Devlin," she said archly, as if she were correcting him. "Actually, I feel as if I already know you, having seen your heroic actions of the other day," she informed him, her close-set eyes taking on an adoring glow.

Cal shifted uncomfortably. "Thank you, ma'am."

"Phoebe sings soprano in the church choir," Ada Gray announced.

It seemed Phoebe Stone had been given her cue. "Oh, I heard you've been a preacher, Mr. Devlin. I'll bet you know all the hymns, and I can just imagine you have a fine, deep voice. Could I interest you in joining the choir? We have the nicest party just before Christmas, and a picnic in the spring, and—"

"Aw, Miz Stone, I'm afraid I can't carry a tune in a bucket," he said with a rueful grin. "My old congregation sang loud just to drown me out." It was a lie, for he did have an excellent baritone voice, but he could almost see the plans taking shape in Phoebe Stone's busy mind—plans that included him.

"Well, don't let that stop you from dropping into the Wednesday night prayer meeting, then, or Sunday service," Mrs. Gray said, stepping into the breach when it seemed her friend didn't know what to say.

"I might just do that, ma'am, as my duties permit,"

Cal said politely, prior to removing himself from Phoebe Stone's overbright gaze.

"Phoebe's the one who makes those cunning little creations you see on all the *best*-dressed ladies of Gillespie Springs," Mrs. Gray told him, obviously loath to let him go so easily. "We'll be losing her to Paris one of these days, I just know it, unless someone gives her a reason to stay in Gillespie Springs...she's a *widow,* you know," she added, waggling an eyebrow at the end of her obvious hint.

"Creations..." Cal said, assuming a blank look. "Oh, you mean the *hats* she makes!"

The women's trilling laughter sounded like mockingbirds in the trees at home.

"Why, I think that would be mighty excitin' for a lady to go to Paris and make hats for those stylish Frenchwomen, yes indeed. You ought to do it if you want to, Miz Stone," he added, inwardly amused that his reaction was hardly the one these women had hoped for. "Ladies, have a nice afternoon," he said, plopping his hat back on his head and making good his escape down the street.

Reaching the doctor's house at the west end of South Street, which was just behind the doctor's office, he crossed Main Street and entered North Street.

He saw the same fat sow lolling in the sunshine, but the yards were once again empty of people; perhaps a blessing, he thought ruefully, after the way he'd been accosted by the matchmaking Mrs. Gray.

A shout down the street drew his attention from the pig. So that's where everyone was, he thought, seeing a half-dozen people gathered around two men arguing over a pile of junk that sat out in front of one tar-paper shack, though he was too far away to hear what they were yelling. As his eye narrowed against the glaring sunlight, something large was tossed on top of the heap, narrowly missing a child who had been fingering something in the pile.

Whatever it was that had been thrown, the object seemed to signify the last straw for the smaller of the two men, who flew at the other with clenched fists, screaming in some incomprehensible tongue. But the larger man repulsed the attack easily, and as he quickened his pace, Cal saw the smaller man thrown among the growing pile, which he could now see was furniture.

"Hey, hold up there a moment," Cal called as he approached, noticing that the small, swarthy man who had been thrown amid the wreckage of chairs, a table and what seemed to have been a bed, was gathering himself to spring back at the smirking, lanky cowboy who faced him from the front stoop of one of the houses.

His voice caused the participants in the scene to freeze, then look around. Of the onlookers, half seemed to be women and girls as dark featured as the man who'd been thrown into the furniture—the man's family, Cal guessed. The others, Cal supposed, lived in the other rude dwellings nearby.

"What's going on here?" Cal asked in an amiable tone as he stopped in front of the heap of furniture and extended a hand to the man on top of it, who was struggling to stand. Ignoring Cal's hand, the man picked up the handle of what had been an ornate, colored glass pitcher and let loose a spate of words in some foreign tongue in the direction of the smirking cowboy. Cal guessed it wasn't a blessing.

"Nothin' to worry about, Sheriff," drawled the cowboy from the front stoop. "Just roustin' out one of them furrin devils thet doesn't cotton t'payin' rent."

"And who are you?" Cal inquired of the cowboy, though he'd seen him heading into the saloon once or twice. "I thought Mr. Gillespie owned these, um, buildings," he added, nodding in the direction of the frame house, which unlike its neighbors was whitewashed, with shutters that hung straight. The small yard was free of rubbish, and though the grass was sparse, some attempt had been made to grow flowers instead of weeds next to the dwelling.

"I'm Mr. Gillespie's, uh...Mr. Gillespie's agent, Sheriff," the cowboy said, grinning. "Just followin' his orders to evict these no-'counts."

"Do you have a name?" Cal persisted.

The smile faded from the other's face and he straightened, letting his arms fall to his sides. "Leroy Scruggs."

"Cal Devlin," Cal replied, still in an amiable voice. "Leroy, I reckon I ought to hear his side of things, don't you think?" he said, inclining his head toward the small, dark man next to him, who was watching him warily.

"Aw, Sheriff, he ain't nothin' but a dirty Hunky," protested the cowboy. "Mr. Gillespie wants him outa his property so's he can rent it to some upstandin' *American* who'll pay his rent on time."

Cal ignored him. "Sir, I'm the sheriff. What's your side of things, here?"

"Side?" the man repeated, his brow furrowing in confusion. One of the older girls came forward and whispered something in his ear. "Oh! I see! I am Lazlo Kristof, and I pay my rent—on time," he added, shooting a murderous glare at the cowboy on the step. "See?

Here is paper they give me at bank,'' he said, holding
out a crumpled, blurred scrap of paper.

Cal peered at it, but he couldn't tell what it had been,
the ink was so smudged.

"Huh, that ain't no receipt," scoffed Scruggs. "I saw
it before I—before it got ruint, and it was full of furrin
symbols and such. Probably curses on Texas, if ya wuz
t'ask me.''

"I don't recall asking you," Cal retorted, though he
kept his tone mild. "Mr. Kristof, you're telling me you
paid your rent on time?"

The man nodded, tears streaming down his face. "I
pay rent—first of month, three months now. Never is
there question. Today he come and take from me my—
how do you call it, Dorika?" he asked, turning to his
daughter again. She murmured something in an incomprehensible language and then Lazlo continued, "My
proof I have paid. Forgive my—my stumbling, Mr.
Sheriff. I am Hungarian, but I try to learn the En-
glish…fast as I can, yes? This man, he pours water on
my proof, so now you can not read."

Cal, aware of the man's wife and daughters staring
at him with mingled fear and hope, looked back at
Scruggs, wishing he had an excuse to wipe that insolent
smirk off his face. "That so, Leroy?"

"Naw, you cain't trust nothin' no furriner says,"
Leroy insisted, his arms crossed over his chest.

"Why, Sheriff Devlin, you wouldn't be attempting
to interfere with my employee's lawful attempt to perform a legal eviction, would you?" said a voice behind
Cal.

Chapter Nine

"Nope. Not if it's legal, Mr. Gillespie," Cal said, before he even looked over his shoulder at the banker.

"Then why do you seem to be impeding Mr. Scruggs's efforts?" Gillespie inquired as he approached, his back rigid with indignation, a livid vein throbbing in his temple.

"Well…" said Cal, drawing out the syllable, "there seems to be some doubt as to whether it's a *legal* eviction." He resisted the urge to add "sir" simply because he knew Gillespie expected it—even if he'd once urged Cal to call him Bob. "Y'see, Mr. Lazlo Kristof here claims to have paid his rent on time and that this piece of soggy paper was a receipt for that same rent—until your employee there—" he gave a nod to indicate Scruggs, who still stood smugly on the front stoop of the disputed house "—ruined it by giving it a bath, according to Mr. Kristof." Cal held out the limp scrap of paper and waited, the thumb of his other hand hooked in his belt loop, which brought the hand suggestively close to his Colt.

Cal caught the look exchanged between the banker and Scruggs. Then Gillespie snatched the paper with his pudgy fingers, peered at it and crumpled it with an exclamation of disgust. "This could be anything!"

"Exactly," Cal said. "I'm sure that's what your *agent* was aimin' for when he wet it."

"No, no," Gillespie said, trying to sound patient but sounding contemptuous instead. "The damned foreigner's trying to bamboozle you, Sheriff."

"I don't think so," Cal said. Then he fixed his gaze on Kristof. "Mr. Kristof, are you telling the truth? Have you paid this month's rent and was this the receipt for that rent?"

"Now, just a minute, Devlin," Gillespie sputtered before the Hungarian could speak. "You're paid to enforce the law here, not to encourage foreigners to cheat me." His tone implied he was the one doing the paying.

"I tell you the truth, Sheriff! I pay the rent!" the small man cried, his black eyes glistening with entreaty.

"Yes, Mr. Gillespie, I am *paid* to enforce the law in Gillespie Springs—by the *town*. But the law is not just for one man. And it seems to me it's your word against his." Cal raised his head to scan the crowd. "Can anyone else here tell me anything about this?"

The inhabitants of North Street, other than Lazlo Kristof's family, seemed to shrink away, some of them stepping backward, their eyes downcast.

"They will tell you nothing," Dorika said, jerking her head toward the crowd. "They are afraid Mr. Gillespie will make them leave, too, if they tell. They all live in his...houses," she said, her hesitation indicating her scorn for the rude dwellings.

She was right about the crowd, Cal thought. A couple of the men he saw in the crowd were also bank tellers, and as Gillespie's employees, had twice as much to lose if they sided with Kristof.

Cal squared his shoulders. "Seems like we have a standoff." He waited.

Gillespie said nothing, just alternated his glaring between Cal and Kristof.

"How about a gesture of goodwill, Mr. Gillespie? How about saying you believe Mr. Kristof paid this month's rent, in exchange for his promise to pay next month's on time, just as he has been doing?" Cal suggested, though he already knew the answer.

Gillespie snorted. "Not on your life, Devlin. If he wants to stay he's got to pay up right now. Five dollars!"

Cal looked back at the ramshackle dwelling, his jaw dropping. "Five dollars a month for *that?* It looks like a good wind would knock it flat!"

The banker bristled. "Now see here, you upstart—"

Kristof laid an urgent hand upon Cal's wrist. "I have no more five dollars to pay him!"

"How do you earn your living, Mr. Kristof?" Cal asked, ignoring the indignant banker for the moment.

"I am blacksmith. I work from home, here, because rent too high to save for shop. But no one needs shoes for horses lately." He sighed, then seemed to give way to despair. "If he says we leave, we do not even have tent to live in!"

"Now, hold on, Lazlo," Cal said, clapping him bracingly on the shoulder. "I reckon my horse could use a new set of shoes. What would that run me, about five dollars?" He reached in his pocket and fished out the last half eagle he had between now and payday. Blue didn't need to be shod, of course. Cal reckoned he wouldn't starve, what with his meals being provided, but there'd be no whiskey or beer at the saloon for a while. That wouldn't hurt him, he supposed.

Kristof shook his head. "Oh, no sir, just two bits a shoe—one dollar for whole horse!"

"Well, then, I'll pay to have him shod for the next five times. You keep account of it for me, all right?"

The Hungarian began to cry, and all the women in his family with him. "Oh, yes, thank you, sir!" he said, shaking Cal's hand so vigorously Cal was afraid it might come off. Then he handed Gillespie the gold coin Cal had given him.

Gillespie accepted the coin with the grace of a man being compelled to hold a lump of horse droppings in his bare hand.

"I—I don't have to take this from you!" the banker sputtered, clenching a fist and waving it at Cal. "You—you're fired, Devlin! You're no longer the sheriff of Gillespie Springs. Get your gear out of the jail building and ride on out of here!"

There was a collective gasp of dismay from the Kristof family, and renewed weeping from the man's weary-looking wife.

Cal drew himself up. "You can't fire me, Mr. Gillespie. That's up to the mayor."

Gillespie gave a bark of laughter. "Long won't save you—especially not after what we've found out about you!" He nodded at the onlookers as if to include them. "The uniform you wore in the war was blue, not gray, and the last half of the war you hid out and didn't wear any uniform!"

"I wasn't hiding, and I never misrepresented myself when you and he insisted I take this job," Cal said evenly. "But I'll be glad to discuss that with Mr. Long at his convenience."

"Oh, his *convenience* will come very soon, I promise," Gillespie asserted. "But don't count on continuing as sheriff. I own Long, just as I own everyone and everything else in this town.'' Gillespie's nod included the tar-paper shacks and the sullen crowd watching him.

"Well then, you tell Mr. Long I'll be waitin' for him at the jail," Cal said, looking him in the eye. "Meanwhile, I think it would be a neighborly thing for your Mr. Scruggs to help the Kristof family carry their furniture back inside—what's left of it, that is. Don't you?"

Gillespie jerked his head in Scruggs's direction, then turned on his heel. But Kristof had moved in front of him and barred his retreat. "I will need receipt, please," he said with European dignity.

"I don't carry paper and pen around with me—"

"I will follow you to bank," the immigrant informed him, and fell in step beside him as the banker stalked off.

Cal watched them walk away for a moment before turning to the immigrant's daughter. "If he gives him any more trouble after I'm gone, you go see Mr. Whyte at the saloon, Miss Dorika. He used to be a lawyer, and maybe he can help."

The Hungarian girl regarded him somberly. "We thank you very much. We are sorry to make you trouble. He can do this, this 'firing'?"

Cal shrugged. "Probably. But don't worry about it. He and I were bound to tangle."

"You are good man, Mr. Devlin." To Cal's surprise, she kissed his hand, then fled into the rude dwelling.

Cal walked back to the jail, aware of the crowd's eyes on him. Again he'd done the right thing, but Lord, what was he going to do now? He hated the idea of riding back home with his tail tucked between his legs, but what else could he have done after he'd heard Kristof's side of the story?

Well, if he wasn't going to be the sheriff of Gillespie Springs anymore, at least he wasn't going to keep running into Livy, who plainly despised him.

Or did she? This morning, when he had kissed her, he hadn't just imagined that her mouth had softened and welcomed him, even if a moment or two later her blue eyes were blazing with outrage. She had been so passionate in her denial that the Mexican had ever been her lover. Later, she had wanted Cal to know she hadn't been gossiping about his Yankee past.... Was she just trying to preserve her sense of moral uprightness, or did she really care what he thought?

If only he hadn't had to tangle with that pompous bully Gillespie before he learned the answer to that question!

Well, there was no use crying over spilled milk. Maybe the saloon cook would have delivered dinner before the banker managed to get rid of Kristof and go give Long his orders, Cal consoled himself. It was always easier to retreat with a full stomach.

Cal was halfway through with the delicious dinner of ham, mashed potatoes and peas that the saloon had sent over when James Long entered the jail.

Cal laid down his fork and stood up. "Hello, Mayor. I reckon this is what you've come after, isn't it?" he said, reaching up to his vest and unpinning the silver star. He held it out to Long, forbidding himself to give the badge one last, wistful look.

Long made no move to take it. "I don't want that— at least, not yet."

"But—"

"Oh, Gillespie's been to see me already, just as he no doubt told you he would. May I?" he asked, indicating a stool in the corner of the small room.

"Here, take the chair—the mayor shouldn't have to perch on a stool," Cal said, starting to move the chair around in front of the desk.

"Don't be silly, Devlin. I've interrupted you at your dinner. The least I can do is not take your seat, too," Long said firmly, and went to fetch the stool.

"Help yourself to some ham, then. The Last Chance cook always fixes more than I can eat," Cal said, afraid to let himself hope. Perhaps the mayor just wanted to preserve the formality of hearing his side of things before telling him he was dismissed.

Long smiled and shook his head as he brought over the stool. "No thanks, Mrs. Long said dinner would be waiting for me when I got back, but you go right ahead."

Cal tried, but swallowing the forkful of mashed potatoes he'd put in his mouth was nearly impossible as he watched the mayor settle himself across the desk from him.

"Cal, as I indicated, Gillespie lost no time in coming to see me. I'm sure you know why."

Cal nodded. "He found out I served on the Union side in the war. Don't worry, I understand how folks might not want their sheriff to be an ex-Yankee. My hometown wasn't too happy to see me back again, either." He hoped his smile wasn't too bitter.

Long sighed and stared down at the knuckle he was rubbing. "I can't say his news made me too happy," he said. "Bein' as I was a captain in the Confederate army and all."

"I should have mentioned it that first day," Cal said,

feeling the distant drumbeat in his temples becoming a dull throbbing with each pulse. "I *did* say you folks didn't know anything about me, but I should've laid it all out in front of you."

Long shrugged. "Folks out West have always felt a man's past was his own business. I didn't think much about it at the time."

Cal forced himself to say the words. "Do you want me to resign? I will, if that's what you or the townspeople want."

Long sighed again, so gustily that a Wanted notice Cal had been meaning to tack up blew onto the floor.

"I expect it would be prudent of me to say yes," the mayor said, "seeing as how I face an election next spring."

Cal's heart sank.

"But I haven't always been the prudent type. What I'm proposing to do is to put you on a voluntary probation period—just between the two of us—until the first of the year. During that time, if I decide I don't like the way you're doing your job, or if enough of the people who elected me can't stomach your having been a Yankee, you ride on out of here with whatever pay is coming to you. Meanwhile, you keep on doing the excellent job of maintaining law and order in Gillespie Springs that you have been doing, and if there are no further objections, I'll see you get a year's contract on January 1. Does that sound fair?"

It was hard for Cal not to let his relief show, but somehow he kept a poker face. "More than fair. But why—"

"I got my reasons," Long said, with the expression of a man who didn't want to be asked further.

Cal was surprised Gillespie's objections hadn't been

enough to decide the matter already. Evidently the mayor was more independent-minded than he—or Gillespie—had thought.

"I imagine Gillespie gave you an earful about me sticking up for one of his tenants, too," Cal said, not wanting to leave anything hidden that the banker could use against him.

Long looked surprised, which surprised Cal in turn. "No, he didn't mention anything like that. What are you talking about?"

Briefly, Cal told him about the incident on North Street. "I believe Kristof paid the rent, and I can't tolerate a man pushing a weaker man around just because he can, Mayor. Sticks in my craw."

Long looked thoughtful.

"Does what I did change your mind about firing me?"

The other man shook his head. "If you're convinced the fellow was tellin' the truth, that's good enough for me," he said, then stood up. "I'll let you get on with your dinner now, and go home and have my own."

Cal rose, too, and extended his hand. "I'm obliged to you, Mayor."

Long took it. "I have a feeling I won't be sorry." He started for the door, as if suddenly reluctant for Cal to see too much in his eyes. Then he stopped. "Hmm, what's this?" he said, bending down and picking up something from the floor. He held it up for Cal's inspection.

It was a carved jet button, the kind that had been on the front of Livy Gillespie's bodice when she'd been in here this morning. Suddenly Cal remembered the tiny clicking sound that had barely penetrated his desire-fogged brain while he had been kissing her.

"I reckon this belongs to Miz Gillespie, doesn't it?" Long said, then grinned when Cal wasn't quick enough to hide his startled reaction. "Oh, don't look so spooked. I saw her come in here this morning."

Cal said nothing, concentrating on keeping his features impassive. He hoped Long wasn't about to say something disrespectful about Livy and destroy the fragile truce between them.

"Now, your being the sheriff is my business. Who you care about isn't my business," Long continued, and Cal stiffened.

The mayor held up a hand. "Hold on now. All I was going to say is that I think there's a good chance she's not at all the way she's been painted in this town. I reckon I'm just glad there's someone else who thinks she's a fine, decent woman, too."

Cal nodded, too surprised to say anything.

"Be seein' you around town, I expect," Long said with a breezy wave, and pushed open the door. Then he called back over his shoulder, "Don't forget to pin that badge back on, Sheriff."

James Long smiled as he walked over to his house on South Street. He knew Devlin had expected to be sent packing and had been mystified when it hadn't happened. Maybe someday he could explain to Cal how he had come to be little more than Gillespie's puppet, and how good it felt to be standing up to the banker at last.

Long chuckled aloud when he remembered how Cal had looked like a thunderstruck mustang when he had brought up Olivia Gillespie's name. It was obvious to the mayor that the woman had her brand on Cal's heart. Long had sensed Cal had been ready to knock him flat if he'd said anything negative about the Widow Gillespie.

If Devlin only knew I'm the last man on earth who'd ever assume a woman had loose morals just because someone said so. His own mother had been an outcast back in Springfield, Illinois, just because some fast-talking drummer had seduced her, then abandoned her, never knowing that he'd left her carrying his child. James had been that child, and he had known the shame of growing up as the visible reminder of his mother's "sin." When his mother had killed herself at the age of thirty-two, unable to face life anymore, he'd lit out for Texas and had never looked back. But that didn't mean he had forgotten.

Just one good man believing in his mother would have made all the difference, Long mused. He didn't know how it was between Cal and Mrs. Livy Gillespie, but he hoped Cal would make the difference in her life, just as he'd already made a difference in Gillespie Springs.

Just look at Davy Richardson, for instance. That boy reminded Long so much of the half-wild scamp he himself had been. He had heard how fair Cal had been to the lad when Tyler had caught him filching candy in the mercantile. And then there was Georgie, who was more than a little slow-headed. Cal had been kind to him when almost everyone else treated him like a nuisance.

And now, today, Cal had stood up to Gillespie over the matter of his immigrant tenant. The banker had been used to doing pretty much as he pleased in this town, and no one had been strong enough to tell him otherwise. Maybe things were about to change....

But things would change only if folks would consider

the kind of man Cal Devlin was now, rather than whatever he had been during the War between the States,
Long reminded himself.

Chapter Ten

Jovita had stayed in town to visit with her grown son, his wife and their baby, and while she was gone, Olivia had decided to whip up a surprise for the Mexican woman, to thank her for all her hard work and the pleasure of her company. Livy knew she had a sweet tooth. Using the sugar that she had sent Jovita to trade eggs for at the mercantile, and the pecans that rained down from the trees in her yard, Olivia had decided to whip up a pecan pie.

She was quite proud of herself. Imagining her house-keeper's delight while she shelled the pecans and mixed the ingredients, she flushed with pride as well as from the radiated heat of her oven as she pulled the finished product from it and set it on the table to cool.

Then Olivia heard footsteps on the back porch. Had Jovita returned already? Olivia had told the woman not to feel she had to rush back, but to have a good visit with her family. That she herself was feeling just fine and could surely do without her for several hours. But no, through the lacy curtains that shielded the kitchen from the late afternoon sun, she could see the outline of a man, just as he knocked.

Her heart gave a lurch. *Cal!* The audacity of the man, after she'd told him not to call on her, and especially after the way he'd treated her after she'd slapped his face this morning! She'd give him a piece of her mind, all right!

But what a fraud she was, she thought ruefully. In spite of the fact that he had deliberately tried to erase the passion that had always existed between them by cheapening it, by comparing it to the liberties a man would take with a mistress, she had been able to think of little else but him after she'd left the jail—how his mouth had felt on hers, how she'd thrilled to hear his ragged, hot breathing and know he wanted her, how deliciously wonderful his hand had felt on her breast. Her statement about not needing a man—*this* man, anyway—had been shown for the lie it was. When Cal touched her she couldn't remember that he'd been a traitor, couldn't remember his betrayal of everything a Southerner should hold dear. Which was why she must not let it happen again.

What on earth was she going to say to him? Why, she could hardly get her breath! Hurriedly smoothing her hair away from her flushed face, and hoping she did not have flour on her nose, she went to the door and opened it.

However, it was not Cal Devlin who stood on her back porch, but Robert Gillespie, and for a moment all she could feel was disappointment before the alarm bells started ringing in her mind.

"What do you want, Robert?" she said, closing the door until she could barely see his face. She felt suddenly very vulnerable and alone with Jovita in town.

But how could she have guessed he would come? Gillespie had never tried to see her in the weeks since

Dan had died, thank God. All their meetings had taken place in the bank or on the streets in town. In fact, he hadn't darkened her door since that day he'd found her standing at the open barn door, looking in at the bodies of Dan and Francisco Luna, screaming....

"Why, Miz Olivia, is that any way to talk to your brother-in-law? Business brings me here to see you, my dear, but what is that heavenly smell? You've been baking?"

"Yes," she said warily. "What do you want, Robert? I warn you, my housekeeper's within easy calling distance. Don't try anything."

Gillespie smirked. "No, she's not. I just saw her over on North Street, playing with her grandchild out in the yard."

She tried to keep the dismay from her face. "Oh? And what were you doing on that street full of the miserable hovels you rent as houses?"

He flushed as the barb went home. "Surveying my property, Olivia. And surely such an adversarial tone is not necessary with me, your brother-in-law. I'm certain it would be more polite and genteel of you to invite me in for a piece of that pecan pie I can smell from here. And very delicious it smells, I must say."

She felt her jaw drop. "Of all the nerve! You're the last person I'd invite in for so much as a cup of cool water, Robert Gillespie! I forgot all about polite and genteel the day you treated me like no brother-in-law should ever think of treating his brother's wife—or any other woman."

All the color that had just flooded his face drained as he heard the accusation, the same one old Sheriff Watts had ignored.

He arched an eyebrow. "I'm sure I don't have any idea what you're referring to, Olivia."

"And I'm sure you do. Now go away, Robert. I have a gun in my apron pocket, and I know how to use it." It was a lie, of course, for the only gun in the house had been the one Dan had used to kill himself and Luna, and the old sheriff had confiscated it as evidence. But Robert had no way of knowing if she'd obtained another or not.

He backed away, his palms raised. "Now hold on there, Olivia. There's no cause to talk like that. I just wanted to lay a business proposition in front of you, that's all. If you won't ask me in like a Christian, why don't we talk here on your porch?"

Gritting her teeth to keep from rising to his bait, she looked at her feet. It was obvious he was determined to talk to her, and if she didn't get it over with now he'd only embarrass her by importuning her in public.

"Very well, Robert. I'll be with you in a moment." She shut the door in his face and shot the bolt, knowing the sound would be further proof of her lack of trust in him. Waiting until he had sat down in one of the two cane-backed rockers, she looked desperately around her kitchen for something that would make her apron pocket sag as if she truly was carrying a pistol.

Her coffee cup? No, too obviously round. Her eyes searched the kitchen quickly, discarding objects. Ah! The iron handle! Going to the flatiron that sat on its side on the hearth, she detached the handle and dropped it into her pocket. The dark calico apron was of heavy cotton and couldn't be seen through, so in the pocket, the weight and shape of the iron handle would suggest a short-barreled pistol. She snatched up a butcher knife from a drawer so she'd have a real weapon, too.

"Land sakes, Olivia, I do believe you're the only woman in this town who locks her doors," Gillespie drawled as she stepped onto the porch.

"I'm probably the only one who has reason to," she said with ironic sweetness, and smiled as his eyes widened at the sight of the butcher knife held in her right hand.

"That's not necessary, Olivia."

"It's just insurance, Robert." She settled her skirts in the rocking chair next to him, then laid the knife casually in her lap, with her palm resting across the hilt. "Now, say what you've come to—but I warn you, I'm still not interested in selling this place."

He'd been staring at the knife across her knees like it was a rattler he expected to rise up hissing at him, but now his eyes flew to her face. "But why not, Olivia? You're a woman alone. You can't be thinking of farming, all by yourself. You have a milk cow in the barn and a few chickens. You're virtually an outcast in this town. Why are you so determined to stay on here?"

"My reasons for remaining are my own, Robert. But I might just as well ask why you're so determined to have it," she retorted.

"You might," he agreed, the soul of reasonableness. His pale eyes shifted away. "Call it sentimentality, if you will. But it was my brother's house, and before that it was my father's. I was born on this land, you know, just like Dan—though in those days, there was just a dogtrot cabin over yonder." He pointed near where the barn now stood. "Sometimes, my dear, I long for those simpler days."

"That's a load of horse droppings, Robert, and you know it," she snapped. "Dan told me you couldn't wait to leave this house, and you never looked back once you built your fine house on the hill. You looked down on both of them for still being farmers since you were a rich *banker*. What would you do with my land? It's not as if you just want to add to your grounds—my back property line doesn't even march with yours.''

''But, Olivia, my dear—''

She held up her left hand. ''I'm not your dear, and I don't want you calling me that. Be that as it may, though, Robert, I'll just say that perhaps *I'm* staying here for sentimental reasons. Dan brought me here as a bride, after all, and I still have some happy memories of our brief time together before he went away to the war and came back...*changed*....'' Her voice trailed away as she recalled those days.

He reached out a hand as if to comfort her, and she stiffened and pulled away.

''All right, I won't touch you. But I do sympathize, Olivia, I wish you could believe that.''

How easy it would be for a stranger to believe those earnestly entreating eyes, that kind tone, she marveled. But she knew him for the snake he was, and she wasn't about to let him lull her with that falsely compassionate voice.

''I'm not selling Dan's farm to you, Robert, so if that's all you want, you can leave,'' she managed to say.

''But you haven't heard my new offer.''

''And what might that be?'' she said with assumed boredom. She was glad he couldn't know how anxious she had become at the rapid disappearance of the money she and Dan had managed to save, despite the eggs, milk and preserves she sold and the other things she made to sell at the general store, and how tired she was of being Gillespie Springs's ''scarlet woman.'' She didn't want him to guess how close she was to giving up and letting him win.

What *was* she holding on for, anyway? Her initial reasons—a stubborn refusal to leave unless it was her idea, and a deep belief in her ability to survive anything, now that she had survived the suicide of her husband— no longer seemed valid. What was she trying to prove— and to whom?

"Well, Olivia, I've offered you a fair price for this property before, but I'm prepared to double it. I'll give you three thousand dollars, which is more than enough for you to go anywhere in these fine United States and live very comfortably."

She gasped. "Three thousand dollars?"

He nodded, his face smug. "It's yours on the day you agree to leave the county and never return to Gillespie Springs."

She was tempted for a brief moment, but there was something about his smirking self-satisfaction that ignited her temper. "Three thousand dollars," she repeated, shaking her head. "Most folks around here don't have even three hundred dollars in their savings, do they, Robert? What little they had was lost either trying to survive the war or pay the taxes afterward! But *you* have lots of money, don't you? You profiteered in cotton while better men—like your brother—were taking bullets for the Southern cause."

He jumped to his feet, his face darkening with anger. "How dare you talk to me like that, you impertinent...female! Why, I'm the only one who's kept you from being run out of town like the whore you are! All right, I'll assume your rudeness means you're throwing my generous offer in my face. But you'll be sorry, Olivia Childress Gil—"

Robert stopped speaking as a sudden rustle of dried pecan leaves warned them that someone was coming around to the back of the house.

Jovita, thank God! her mind screamed as she got to her feet, dropping the butcher knife out of sight into her apron pocket.

But it was Cal Devlin who came around the side of the house, stopping stock-still when he saw Robert Gillespie standing next to Olivia.

"I'm sorry...I didn't know you had company, Miss Olivia."

"Mr. Gillespie was just leaving, weren't you, Mr. Gillespie?" she said, trying to calm her features.

Robert Gillespie stood still on the porch, his eyes darting between Olivia and Devlin, measuring.

"I believe I've just guessed why you're so reluctant to take my offer of late, Miz Olivia," he said, tipping his hat elaborately at her, then clapping it firmly on his head. "Good day to you." He strode hurriedly past Cal without looking at him, and a moment later Olivia heard the front gate creak as he opened it.

She stood staring in the direction Gillespie had gone, feeling Cal gazing at her. How much had he heard? And what would he make of Gillespie's insinuation that she wouldn't take his offer because she was interested in Cal?

"Was he botherin' you, Olivia?" His voice, etched with concern, bathed her frayed nerves like a soothing caress.

"No more than usual," she said with a forced lightness. "Dan's brother and I have never gotten along very well. I'm afraid we're like oil and water."

He took a step closer to the porch. "What was that

offer he was talking about, if you don't mind my asking?''

She hesitated, not wanting him to see how unnerved she'd been by the encounter. ''Oh, it's nothing. Just his same old tiresome plea to buy this farm, and I don't wish to sell,'' she said, dismissing it with a breezy wave. ''I can't imagine why he wants it so much when he's got that big fancy house up on the hill. Have you been over there yet, Cal? It's got six bedrooms and a room big enough to hold a ball, can you imagine? Dan never did feel at ease there....''

She was aware of Cal watching her, his gray-blue eye searching her soul as she rattled on like the belle she once had been.

''No, I haven't been there, Livy,'' he said quietly. ''I suppose you could say I'm not exactly on the best terms with Gillespie, either.''

''Well, you certainly came along at the right time to get him to leave, Cal. Now, I was just about to start supper—was there something I could do for you?'' she said briskly, her tone hinting she had no more time for idle conversation, when she wanted nothing more than to hear him say he just had to see her in spite of what she had told him before, wanted nothing more than to invite him in for a piece of fresh-baked pecan pie.

''There's something more to it, isn't there—his coming here?'' Cal said, the look in his eye telling her he knew exactly what she was trying to do.

''Something more?'' she echoed, then laughed. ''Of course not! Don't be silly, Cal, he just can't bear that I'm refusing to sell, that's all. Now, you must have had a reason for calling?''

His hand went to the pocket of his shirt, inside his

leather vest, and drew out something. He held out his hand and opened his fingers.

Olivia looked, and there on his callused palm was the jet button she had noticed was missing when she had tried to rebutton her bodice inside the jail.

"I found this on the jail floor some time after you left," he said, the ghost of a smile playing about his lips. "I believe it's from your dress?"

His face suggested he knew exactly when the button had come loose—when he'd been trying his best to unfasten the front of her dress and cup her breast without the barrier of cloth between them. She felt her face flame at the remembered pressure of his mouth against hers, of his tongue....

"Thank you," she said with deliberate ungraciousness, and plucked the button off of his palm with as little contact between their flesh as possible. She tried to ignore the fact that it was still warm from being carried next to his body. "And I'll thank you also to wipe that complacent grin off your face. You more than made your point this morning, sir." She felt her skirts swirl around her ankles as she whirled and fled into the house, slamming the kitchen door behind her.

Stopping just inside the door, she could see him standing there for a long moment, staring after her, and then he shook his head and left.

Chapter Eleven

Lord, whiskey would taste good right now, Cal thought, walking back down the road into town. He had one of *those* headaches. Alcohol might quiet the thumping in his head that had started during his confrontation with Gillespie this morning in front of Kristof's shack, waned during his talk with Long, only to reappear with dull insistence when he'd seen the banker standing next to Livy on her back porch.

Well, he'd have to do without, Cal told himself, feeling in his pocket and coming up empty. He didn't have so much as two bits for a glass of whiskey, so he'd just have to wait the headache out. It'd go away. They always did, eventually.

And he wasn't going to take refuge in laudanum, either. He'd left the remains of the bottle back in his room on the Devlin farm and had resolved that he wasn't going to buy any more if he could help it, though he was pretty sure the mercantile carried the painkiller. Laudanum was available everywhere, but he wasn't going to rely on it. During the war he'd seen the drug grab on to a few soldiers and refuse to let go.

What had Gillespie been doing on Livy's porch? Was

she telling the truth that he just wouldn't take no for an answer about her land?

It was going to be hard to help her if she wouldn't confide in him, but Cal meant to keep an eye on that slippery snake Gillespie—at least as long as he was allowed to remain in Gillespie Springs. The townspeople might decree otherwise, once the poisonous news that he'd been a Yankee had festered a little.

Maybe he ought to check on that, and the best place was in the saloon, where Georgie had told him the fact had first been announced. Yeah, he'd go check in at the Last Chance, even if he couldn't have a drink.

"Afternoon, Miz Petree," he said, tipping his hat as he passed the woman who'd been sitting with her large brood of sore-throated children in Dr. Broughton's office that day he'd come to town. As before, the children stared, but Ginny Petree just sniffed and pulled her skirts aside. She must have heard the news already.

He found Hank Whyte's establishment empty except for the barkeep.

"Afternoon, Hank."

The barkeep looked up as Cal came through the batwing doors. The glare of the afternoon sunlight made it hard to read his expression. "Afternoon, Sheriff. What can I get you?"

"Nothing, thanks. Just passin' by on my rounds."

Hank grinned. "It's a long time till the end of the month, ain't it?"

Cal grinned ruefully, embarrassed that the man had seen right through his polite evasion. "It is for a fact."

"Well, have a drink anyway, Sheriff. It's on me for what you done today for ol' Lazlo. He's already told me. It was damned decent of you to lend him the rent money."

Cal shrugged. "I was just buying some shoes for my horse."

He watched as Whyte poured a measure of whiskey into a glass and passed it across the polished surface of the bar to him. "Thanks. Don't mind if I do," Cal said.

"This is on the house, like I said, but don't stay away. Your credit's good here," Whyte said with a wink.

Cal figured he might as well go for broke, since Whyte wasn't going to bring it up. "Sure you don't mind havin' a man drink here who once wore a blue uniform?"

Whyte had been washing a glass, and he finished that and picked up another and washed it. Cal had just begun to think he hadn't heard him, and was about to repeat the question, when the barkeep put the glass down and laid both hands on the top of the bar.

"Devlin, I lost a son at Shiloh, and for a while I hurt so bad I would have killed any Yankee on sight. But then a letter reached me, a letter my boy had written and sent off before the battle, and it made me think."

"What did it say?"

Whyte reached down under the counter for a cigar box and opened it, bringing out a wrinkled and much-folded sheet of paper.

"I won't read you the whole thing, just that one part. He wrote, 'Papa, our picket lines ain't so far apart. Sometimes when we're on sentry duty we share a chew or a mug of coffee with Billy Yank, and you know what? He's just like me, under that blue coat. He's young and scairt, but he's just as sure he's fighting for the right as I am. I ain't sure who's right no more. I only want it to be over.'" Whyte turned suspiciously bright eyes to Cal. "I guess you did what you thought was right, huh?"

Cal nodded silently.

"Well, I think my boy wouldn't want me to act hateful toward you, 'specially not when you've shown yourself to be a decent man. Yeah, I heard the talk in here—some hired man a' Gillespie's was in here spoutin' off yesterday about how you'd been a Yankee, and then deserted, and there was fellas in here this mornin' jawin' about it, but I don't intend to pay it no mind."

Cal's throat suddenly felt thick. "I'm much obliged to you."

"Just one question, though, if you don't mind my askin'—*did* you desert? It don't sound like you, somehow."

Cal shook his head. "No, I don't mind," he said, though he was weary of defending himself. "Here's what happened, and you feel free to set anyone straight if you feel like it."

After he had finished telling about those years when he hadn't known who he was or where he was from, Whyte whistled. "You're plumb lucky to be alive, and that's the truth. I figgered there had to be more to it. A man like you don't run away like that."

"I appreciate your saying that. Now I've got a question. Do you reckon the folks 'round here are ready to be as fair as you are? Are they going to let me stay on as sheriff?"

Whyte suddenly became busy with drying glasses. "Hard to say. They liked what they saw of you that first day, and there's folks that'd like to see Gillespie lose his stranglehold on this town. Half the families here either pay rent to Gillespie or borrowed money from him and are payin' it back at ruinous interest. But there's just as many are still bitter about the war, and maybe they're in debt up to their ears to Gillespie, too. It's hard to fight that combination. You just keep on walking tall, though, Cal. I reckon this is time for some of that faith of yours, isn't it?''

Cal smiled. "I reckon it is. Seems like that's about all I've got right now."

Robert Gillespie was still fuming as he sat over his supper that night, alone in the dining room in his big house on the hill. His cook and butler, who had once belonged to him but still worked for him after the war because of what he considered ridiculously high wages, had long ago served his dinner and left him in his solitary splendor, sitting at the long mahogany table in his ornately carved, high-backed chair. His *throne,* Junius the butler called it, much to Gillespie's amusement.

He was not amused now. In front of him was yet another letter from the president of the Houston and Texas Central Railroad, reiterating their eagerness to purchase the land that Gillespie had promised to them, a narrow strip some ten miles long that was key to the route they had chosen in the building of their new railroad between the coast and northern Texas. The president had promised him the line would stop in Gillespie Springs, bringing increased prosperity to the town and its people and a handsome profit to the man who could sell them that all-important right-of-way.

However, time was running out, the letter indicated. They were going to have to have his answer soon. If he couldn't deliver the entire stretch of land, they would have to deal with the individual property holders. Since that meant more work and waiting for them, they would not be able to pay him as much for what he could already sell them.

Gillespie had written them a few months ago, boasting that he would soon own all of that strip of land and would be interested in doing business with them. He was a fair man, he'd said, who only wanted to share prosperity with his neighbors. He knew the railway board of trustees would not be fooled, but that was unimportant. What *was* important, Gillespie knew, was that no one but himself realized the Houston and Central was interested in this part of Texas, and he already owned all but the middle twenty acres of the very land they wanted. Once he sold it to them, he would be truly wealthy—able to hobnob with the financial barons in the North—not just a moderately prosperous businessman in a backwater Texas town. His brother had just died, making that prize real estate as good as his. Or so he had thought.

Who'd have guessed Olivia Childress Gillespie would turn out to be so all-fired stubborn and want to hold on to her picayune farm, which just happened to be that all-important twenty acres? Who'd have thought she would be willing to stay in Gillespie Springs, even though it had meant enduring the scandal of being pregnant with a bastard child while her husband was fresh in his grave?

If Dan were still alive, Robert knew he could have talked him into selling. And if it hadn't been for the baby, Dan would still be alive.... Damnation, it was all such a tangle! And the beginning of the tangle was the emotion Robert had felt when he'd first met Olivia.

He'd lusted after his brother's wife from the moment he had first seen her, so dark haired and slender against Dan's bluff good looks and broad-shouldered build, her eyes the same hue as spring bluebonnets. But Olivia had never seemed to notice *him* in any but a superficial, sister-in-law sort of way.

The war had taken Robert to New Orleans, center of the cotton profiteering, away from the source of his temptation. But when it was over, and he'd returned to Texas, he found his feelings hadn't changed. Dan returned, too, and confided bitterly to his brother about the wound that had left him impotent.

Robert had been secretly, guiltily glad, sure Olivia would be disappointed and missing the joys of the marriage bed. He assumed now he'd be able to cuckold his brother with ease, at least once. Then she would cease to be such an obsession with him, for once he had had a taste of her he could go back to worshipping his real idol, money.

But Olivia had continued to treat him in her courteous, cool way, never seeming to notice the ardor-filled looks he gave her, and if she missed the intimate pleasures of married life, she gave no signals to him.

He hadn't exactly planned that day in the barn when Dan was over in Bryan selling some heifers, but by that time, Robert's lust had reached a fever pitch and if he didn't have her he thought he was going to die. What he'd *planned* to do was call unexpectedly on the lovely Olivia and try to seduce her, but when he'd seen her disappearing into the barn, and had spotted the empty feed sack lying on the ground just by the entrance, he couldn't seem to master the impulse that had made him steal inside, throw the sack over her head and take her in silence while she lay in the hay and fought him.

It had been so exciting, but over so quickly, and afterward, as he lay on top of her and heard her weeping, he only could taste ashes in his mouth. He'd bound her hands with a length of twine—not tightly enough to leave her captive until his brother returned, just firmly enough that he could run away before she could yank the sack off her head and discover that her violator was her brother-in-law.

He suspected she knew who had raped her, but once she had told Sheriff Olin Watts and he had disbelieved her—Robert had paid him well to do so—she had never even hinted about his reprehensible crime. Until today.

And Caleb Devlin had shown up just moments later. Even though the new sheriff acted stiff and formal toward Olivia, it couldn't be a coincidence. That had to be why she was suddenly brave enough to hint at the rape. She now fancied she had a protector.

Gillespie ground his teeth in frustration. If Long had only done as he'd been told, Devlin would probably have ridden sullenly out of town by now, unwilling to remain without that little tin star. But the mayor, damn him, had had an unexpected streak of independence and refused to fire Devlin—"at least until *I* see fit," the little bantam rooster had crowed. Hell—that just meant until the townspeople pitched a collective fit about their sheriff being an ex-Yankee. And they would. Scruggs had laid the groundwork in the saloon yesterday. Probably the men who'd been in the saloon had told their wives the news over dinner, and the swell of indignation was rising this very minute. Tomorrow was Sunday, and they'd all be getting their heads together at church. By suppertime they'd be demanding Devlin's resignation, and he'd be gone.

Then there'd be no one between him and Olivia Gillespie.

Now that his lust for Olivia had been satisfied, Robert had no difficulty with the idea of taking more extreme measures if she remained mulish about selling the farm to him. No one in town would lift a finger to protect the woman who had driven her husband to suicide—or shed a tear if anything happened to her.

Chapter Twelve

The church bell started to chime just as Cal was putting the finishing touches on his tie with the aid of the cracked mirror hung over the washbasin. He buttoned his waistcoat and straightened the watch chain that was attached to his father's old watch just as the bell finished its tenth sonorous note.

Ten o'clock. Time for church. Back in the days before the war, when he had been the rector of the Bryan Episcopal Church, he would have been in the vestry prior, getting ready to go out on the front steps to greet the members of his congregation.

He hadn't spent much time in church since those days. Sunday services in the army had been catch-as-catch-can, impromptu affairs. During the time when he'd lost his memory and was living on that farm with Lizabeth, they'd been too far from a town to go to church. And in wild Abilene, he had not been welcome at the services Mercy's father had conducted in his home, but that was before the Reverend Fairweather had really known Cal. After Sam had married Mercy, of course, things had been different, but by that time Cal was homesick for Texas.

The only Protestant church in this little town was the Baptist church, but he figured the Lord they worshipped was the same one. It would sure be different sitting among the congregation rather than standing in the pulpit, though.

He wanted to go to church, *needed* to worship his God among his fellow Christians now that he was trying to put down roots in a new town, but he wondered if Gillespie's poison would have spread so that he wouldn't even be welcome. There was a good chance of that. Cal had to remember that whatever hymns they sang and prayers they prayed, these were the same folks who had made Livy an outcast.

Well, there was one way to find out. Picking up his Bible, he opened the door and strode down the back steps to the street, then headed past the general store to the Gillespie Springs Baptist Church.

The white frame building was smaller than the stone church he'd pastored in Bryan. As he stepped inside, heads turned to face him and he had a vague impression of varnished pine pews, a bad painting on each of the side walls, dealing with the Garden of Gethsemane and the Feeding of the Five Thousand, and a large, gold-painted cross on the altar. The cross was taller than the preacher, a balding, red-cheeked man with a stiff, celluloid collar who had stepped up to begin the service.

Cal nodded at the Reverend Poole, to whom he'd already been introduced during his strolls around town, and looked for a seat. He was aware of the soft murmurs and neck cranings and whispers behind hands that had begun when he'd entered. He heard one old woman gasp and repeat, in the overloud voice of the nearly deaf, "You say he was a *Yankee?*" only to be shushed by her elderly husband, who avoided looking in Cal's direction.

He caught sight of James Long and a sweet-looking woman with graying hair who must be his wife, sitting toward the middle of the church. Long smiled and nodded his head, and Cal felt encouraged. There was Hank Whyte, the barkeep of the Last Chance Saloon, looking uncharacteristically formal in a frock coat and tie, sitting next to a plump gorgon of a woman who was expressing her indignation about something, or someone—most likely himself. Whyte managed to smile in a beleaguered fashion at him, though. Cal's gaze wandered to the front again and there, in the front pew, sat Robert Gillespie, his rigid back suggesting that he'd seen Cal come in and wasn't about to be caught looking.

He saw Phoebe Stone beaming and simpering at him from the center of the choir, as if she thought he had come just to see her there. Cal knew he was going to have to try to avoid her after the service. Then Ada Gray, standing next to her, murmured something into her ear, and Phoebe's mouth changed from a curved bow to a wide, horrified O.

Well, maybe his old blue uniform was going to protect him from the likes of Phoebe Stone, he thought in amusement.

The pews were nearly full. The only vacant space was in the very last row, next to Mrs. Petree and her squirming, fidgety brood. It was either sit by her or stand, and he'd heard Reverend Poole could be long-winded.

He gave Ginny Petree his most congenial smile as he stepped into the pew, but it didn't work. She glared at him, then made an elaborate production of shooing her children down to the far end of the pew, and moving with them so that not even the hem of her voluminous skirts would have a chance of contact with him. Once she'd achieved that, there was space for three of Cal.

She turned her face to the front, as if she wanted not even her eyes to be contaminated by the sight of him, but her children had no such compunction. They immediately began to stare and point at his eye patch.

At the altar, the preacher cleared his throat. "I'm sure we'd all like to bid Gillespie Springs's new sheriff welcome to our service," he said.

A few tentative smiles were sent his way, but from the stiff backs of about two-thirds of the congregation, Cal reckoned most were not at all sure. Probably a handful would sooner lynch him than welcome him.

"Now let's all stand and sing 'Bringing in the Sheaves.'"

Livy had awakened early that morning. Today was the day. She hadn't attended church since her husband's funeral service, and for a while that had been strictly self-preservation. She had had no desire to expose herself to the cruelty of the townspeople who were so sure she had caused his death. But she had missed the comfort of the hymns and the Scripture reading, and somehow it wasn't the same to sing hymns or read the Bible by herself. Besides, she wondered if she hadn't been cooperating with the formation of some sort of vicious circle; the townspeople shunned her, so she stayed in her house, except for necessary forays for supplies, and they continued to treat her as a pariah.

Maybe if she ended her voluntary isolation and showed them that she didn't see herself as an outcast, they would gradually stop seeing her as one, too. Still, she thought it was probably better that she come in just after the singing had started, at least this first time, so that there would be no chance for anyone to object to her presence before the service started—especially Robert Gillespie, who, as deacon, always held the pride of place in the front pew, the hypocrite! Once she had sat through a whole service, maybe they would treat her presence as irreversible and would not be bold enough to object the next time.

A desire to see Cal, if only from a distance of several pews, formed no part of her decision, she told herself as she donned her Sunday-best black wool challis dress and affixed the jet brooch—which matched her tiny black jet earbobs—amid the black lace at her neck. Even so, she found herself taking extraordinary care with the way she fixed her hair into a knot at the nape of her neck, taking a curling iron to the loose tendrils at her temples.

A touch of rosewater to her throat and wrists? No, of course not—someone would call it fast behavior for a widow whose husband was dead less than a year. Anyway, she wasn't trying to appeal to anyone, least of all Sheriff Cal Devlin, she argued with herself as she walked up the steps to the tune of "Bringing in the Sheaves."

The piano player, glancing up to see who the late-comer was, simply stopped playing to gape at Livy, an action that caused everyone in the pews to turn around and stare. Livy felt her face flame as the choir tried gamely to continue a cappella, and she tried to lift her eyes just enough to see where there was an empty space in a pew.

She'd identified Cal even before he'd turned around; no one else was so tall and lean, though his shoulders filled out the seams of the black, broadcloth frock coat admirably. Lord, there had to be a place for her to sit other than in the empty spot between him and Ginny Petree, who was looking daggers in her direction.

All was lost for him if she sat down next to him, Livy thought. The town already knew about what he'd done during the war, so any association with her would doom him for sure.

Besides, she had her own reasons for not sitting down next to him! She was still furious with him for kissing her yesterday, kissing her the way no gentleman kisses a lady, and then having the nerve to show up on her doorstep! He *had* been just in time to encourage Robert Gillespie to leave, but she told herself she hadn't needed his help then and she didn't need it now.

She saw him motion to the gap between him and Ginny. Didn't the man have the sense God gave a mule? Didn't he know that any open kindness shown toward her was poison for him?

It was foolish for her to have come, she thought, her vision blurring as she turned to head for the door. She'd just leave, even though it would sting to give the gossipy old cats the satisfaction.

"We shall come rejoicing, bringing in the sheaves...."

And then she heard the floorboards creak as he stood, felt his hand on her arm, and that deep, familiar voice said, just loudly enough to be audible in the rear pews, "Mrs. Gillespie, don't leave. See, there's room next to me." He added, in a whisper only she could hear, "Don't let them beat you, Livy. Show 'em what you're made of."

In an agony of embarrassment, she saw him standing aside, beckoning again toward the empty space in the pew as the rest of the congregation sank back in their seats and stared unashamedly. Ginny Petree's face would have turned Lot's wife into salt all over again.

Olivia had no choice but to comply, for to flee now might only compound Cal's problems. If the town's scarlet woman wouldn't even sit next to him, they would say, then he was indeed worthy of their disapproval. So she made her way into the pew and sat down, ignoring Ginny Petree's indignant face. Livy wouldn't talk to him, wouldn't take any notice of him, and maybe the two of them would come through this harrowing experience relatively unscathed.

But taking no notice of him was easier said than done. The pastor called for a responsive reading in the Psalms, and as the swishing sound of hymnal page-turning replaced the hissing whispers, she realized she had left her Bible at home.

"Here, you can share mine," he said next to her, placing the well-worn, leather-bound book on his thigh and flipping open to the right passage with the ease of familiarity. Then he handed it to her, and what could she do but pick it up? As it became the congregation's turn to read, Livy's ears were filled with the velvety baritone of his voice, and she could smell the faint scent of bay rum. Her skirts just barely had contact with the leg of his trousers, but she could feel him next to her as if that fabric had nerves just like her skin, as if they were pressed intimately hip to knee. Livy struggled to find her voice and read along, darting a glance upward from beneath her lowered lashes.

As she suspected, he was not looking at the book, he was reciting the Psalm by heart.

The reading done, Phoebe Snow stepped forward and commenced a reedy-voiced solo of "Rock of Ages." The milliner seemed to be singing to Cal alone, Livy noticed with a pang of resentment. She wished *she* had a big rock to hide behind about now. Hmmph, what was she doing worrying about Cal's acceptance among the townspeople? If Phoebe Stone had decided she wanted Cal to end her lonely widowhood, then he'd be all right, no matter that a few stubborn old men wanted to fight the war all over again.

However, Cal didn't seem to be taking note of Phoebe's earnest warbling in his direction, Livy saw with some surprise. Instead, he seemed to be studying her hands, which she had clasped together on top of his Bible.

This week she had felt strong enough to start sharing the chores with Jovita, and she knew her hands showed the results. Suddenly self-conscious about her work-roughened, chapped fingers, she unclasped them and thrust them under the thick book. Then, as his gaze didn't seem to waver, she suddenly remembered that the Bible was his, not hers—perhaps he was trying to discreetly hint that he'd like it back?

She shut it with more force than she'd intended, causing Ginny Petree's toddler, who'd been dozing in her lap, to wake with a start and begin to wail. Ginny clucked her tongue in exasperation before clasping the child to her bosom and trying to soothe it.

Livy could feel the woman's murderous glare boring a hole in her side as she handed the Bible back to Cal. "Sorry," she whispered, turning back to Ginny, but her apology only seemed to heighten the woman's ire.

"He kept me up all night, too," Ginny Petree muttered, under the cover of the child's crying. Her tone implied that that was also, somehow, Livy's fault.

She could still feel Cal looking at her, and when she

returned his gaze, he gave her a quick smile that was both rueful and conspiratorial at the same time.

The upward curve of his lips, underneath his mustache, transformed his face, erasing the tension around his mouth, making the lines at the corner of his eye crinkle in the most attractive way, despite the patch over the other eye and the scars that marked the lean planes of his face.

She felt her heart give a sudden skip, then accelerate, and looked away in confusion. Tarnation, but why did this man still have the power to make her feel like an excited girl again, to make her want—

But no, she dared not want anything from him. For even if she dared brave the disapproval of the town toward herself and him, wanting this man in her life would lead to one thing. Sooner or later, with or without marriage, kisses and caresses would progress to him expecting to bed her. And though it had been hard to remember in the midst of their heated embrace yesterday, after that day in the barn she wasn't sure she could ever allow a man to get that close—to have that power over her—ever again.

She steeled herself not to smile back, not to show any expression, and to turn her eyes to the pulpit, where the Reverend Poole was just commencing his sermon.

Chapter Thirteen

The preacher finally ran out of steam about noon, and they sang the closing hymn. What the Baptists missed in stately liturgy, Cal thought as they all rose to their feet, they more than made up for in spirited delivery.

Not that he could have given anyone a detailed account of Reverend Poole's sermon, he admitted to himself. He'd been much too conscious of the woman sitting on his left side. He'd studied her a time or two out of the corner of his eye, but she kept her eyes steadfastly to the front, seemingly unaware of him.

That was all right. He could enjoy the purity of her profile, the way her night black hair swooped gracefully over her ears into the knot at her nape, the sweet lushness of her lips. He could have sat like this all day, studying her surreptitiously, for he knew as soon as the closing prayer was said she would be lost to him. And who knew if circumstances would ever force them into an hour of togetherness again?

They stood for the final hymn, and when no one came to the front of the altar to be prayed over, the preacher asked Deacon Gillespie to say the final prayer.

"Excuse me, Sheriff Devlin," Olivia murmured,

while the "Amen" was still dying in the air, "but I'd best be going, before..."

She didn't have to say it. She meant before the rest of the congregation started to leave, too. He knew she'd like to avoid the open hostility that she as the town outcast might expect, especially with her former brother-in-law there to view it and gloat. Cal didn't know how regular her church attendance had been of late, but some of the Gillespie Springs churchgoers probably didn't like her stepping on sacred ground.

"Don't worry, Livy," he whispered back, "I'll walk with you."

A regretful look flashed in her eyes, then she lowered them to his chest and her mouth set in a stubborn line. "Don't be foolish, Cal," she whispered. "Now let me *out,* please."

There was nothing he could do but step out into the aisle so that she could get by. They were in the last row of pews, so it should have been possible for Livy to make a quick getaway—except that the preacher was now standing at the door, ready to greet each one who had attended. Basic courtesy forced Livy to stop and shake his hand.

"Good day to you, Mrs. Gillespie," Cal heard the preacher say in a guarded tone, and he relaxed somewhat. He'd have hated to have to punch Reverend Poole on such short acquaintance. The congregation surged behind him and little boys, Ginny Petree's among them, ducked under the minister's outstretched arm to make their escape down the steps and onto the lawn.

"Oh, Sheriff Devlin..." sang a female voice from behind Cal, over the chatter of the congregation.

He knew without looking that it was Phoebe Stone calling to him, and he did not want her to slow him down, not when he wanted to be sure that Livy got away from the church grounds all right. Perhaps if he just pretended he didn't hear her and kept going...

"Yoo-hoo, Sheriff Devlin!" she trilled again, more loudly, and there was no way Cal could have pretended to miss hearing her this time. With an inward sigh, he stopped and turned around, plastering a bland expression on his face as the crowd eddied around him.

Ada Gray was in front of Phoebe, glaring right at him. As she swept by him, her bustle under the choir robe making her look like a ship under full sail, she hissed, "I never in all my born days thought I'd see the day when a *Yankee* darkened our doors."

"Good day, Mrs. Gray," he said, having no desire to get into a war of words with her and be slowed down by two women instead of just one. She was content to fire her broadside and go on, however, and now a somewhat breathless Phoebe Stone reached his side.

"What did she say to you?" she asked without preamble, squinting after Ada Gray, her pale brow scrunched up in worried furrows, an expression that suggested she needed spectacles and out of vanity did not wear them. "I just know she said something hateful to you, didn't she? I'm so sorry, but Ada doesn't forget or forgive very easily, while I—"

"Oh, it wasn't anything, Miz Stone, don't you worry. There's bound to be folks who don't agree with what I did, but—"

"Damn blue belly, go back up North," an old man grunted as he went by.

"Oh, Mr. Devlin, that wasn't very charitable or Christian of either of them, I'm afraid," Phoebe said anxiously, laying a hand on his arm and peering up into his face.

"Don't pay them any mind. I don't. Uh...you were in fine voice this morning, Miz Stone," he said, when she kept her hand on his arm as if she expected something more from him. It was hard to keep from looking over his shoulder through the open door, to see if Livy was still in sight.

Phoebe dimpled and preened, her faded prettiness reviving somewhat. "Oh, if you aren't the kindest man..."

"Nope, I just have ears," he lied, as he wondered how to politely extricate himself. "Um, was there something I could help you with?"

She blushed and appeared flustered as a girl. "Why, yes, there *is*, but you're going to think I'm awfully forward...."

He waited, while every instinct in him warned him he needed to get outside and away from Phoebe Stone with her needy, lonely eyes.

"Why, I'm sure you couldn't be forward if you tried, Miz Stone," he said at last, when it seemed she would not speak again without encouragement.

She batted her eyelashes again and Cal was hard put to stand still. "Why, I was thinking last night about Sunday dinner, which is never very much fun to eat by myself, though sometimes my kind neighbors invite me to dine with them, but right now Ada and I aren't on the best of terms...." She rolled her eyes, and Cal caught the heavy-handed hint that the two neighbors had had a tiff about *him*. "But anyway, I just happened to think, there's Sheriff Devlin all by himself, too, and I'll bet no one's cooking Sunday dinner for him, either, so why shouldn't I just make some extra dumplings and invite him? That is, invite *you*," she finished with a girlish giggle. "Would you like to come have Sunday dinner at my house today, Mr. Devlin?"

Oh, Lord, how could he be polite without encouraging her? Clearing his throat, he said, "Miz Stone, you're more than kind, but I promised my mother I'd ride over to Bryan and have dinner with the family today. I'm so sorry." He hoped he'd be forgiven for the lie. Now he'd have to ride home and make it true, when he'd actually been looking forward to a good nap in his room above the jail. Wouldn't his mother be surprised to see him! At least *she'd* be pleased.

The light faded from Phoebe Stone's eyes. "Oh, that's too bad," she said, her tone still bright. "Another Sunday, perhaps."

"Yes." Courtesy forced him to answer, though he hoped he'd never have to make good on his word.

"Well, you have a long ride ahead of you, so I won't keep you," she said, and then Cal was next to greet the preacher.

"A fine sermon, Reverend Poole," Cal said, extending his hand.

The preacher hesitated for a second, then shook it. "Thank you, Sheriff," he said with that stiff nod that men use to acknowledge one another when they are not necessarily friends.

I did the right thing by coming, anyway. Perhaps in time they'll change their minds. Cal stepped past the preacher and out onto the steps, hearing Gillespie behind him greeting the minister and giving him a heavy-handed critique of the sermon. It seemed every church had a member like that—Cal certainly could remember the one who had bedeviled his Sundays at the Bryan Episcopal Church.

A number of boys were already intent on a game of

marbles in a bare patch on the lawn. He noticed that
the oldest Petree boy had been given custody of the
toddler, apparently to enable his mother, still somewhere behind Cal, to carry the baby. On a bench under
a live-oak tree, a trio of giggling girls chattered together, their gloved hands held to their faces as they
exchanged secrets. James Long and his wife stood talking to another couple on the lawn.

They fell silent as they saw Cal pause on the steps,
then he saw Long raise his hand in a greeting and gesture for him to join them. But Cal just nodded and
smiled in their general direction and kept scanning the
churchyard for Livy.

He saw her just as she opened the gate and stepped
into the street—and just as Ada Gray hailed her.

"Just a minute, Mrs. Gillespie," he heard the older
woman call out. "I want a word with you."

Livy paused, her hand still on the gate, and waited.

The woman's tone did not promise that it would be
a *friendly* word. Cal quickened his stride, wishing he
had insisted on walking out with Livy so the woman
wouldn't be so bold.

"I'd just like you to know that I think it took a tre-
mendous amount of gall for you to show your face in
our church this morning, you Jezebel," Ada Gray announced in her carrying voice.

Cal saw Livy go white and her hand clutch the gate-
post tighter. By this time he was close enough to hear
her quiet, dignified reply, "I'm sorry you feel that way,
Mrs. Gray."

He closed the remaining distance in a few strides. He
was not going to let Livy face this woman's spite alone.
"Mrs. Gray, surely the house of God welcomes *all* peo-

ple, not just saints." *Such as yourself,* he longed to add with blistering sarcasm.

"Cal, never mind, it's not necessary—" Livy began, her hand held up.

But it was too late. Ada Gray whirled, her face purpling above her lavender, high-necked gown. "And *you*—don't you have the audacity to speak to me, you—you wolf in sheep's clothing. Better men than you were dying in gray uniforms while you ran roughshod over your fellow Texans!" she cried dramatically.

The yard was suddenly silent, a frozen tableau of women and men, girls sitting on the bench under the tree and the three of them at the gate. Only the boys, crouched over their marble ring, seemed oblivious of the confrontation taking place.

"Come, Mrs. Gillespie," Cal said, taking her elbow gently but firmly, "I'll walk you home."

Livy's eyes were chips of blue ice in her pale face. Her gaze directed past Cal and Ada Gray into the churchyard, she said, "Mr. Devlin, that's very kind of you, but I assure you, it's not necess—"

A woman's sudden cry, from near the steps, interrupted Livy midword. "Billy? Billy? What's wrong with you? Help, someone! Something's happened to my child!"

Cal turned to see the boys gathered around something at the edge of their marble ring.

It was Ginny Petree, and her cry had changed to a scream as she swooped down on the boys, still clutching her infant. "Oh, my God, Billy's not breathing! He's turning blue! Freddy Petree, what did you do to your little brother?"

"Nothing, Mama, I *swear!*" cried one frightened

boy. "He was kneelin' down by me and I was shootin', an' alla sudden he started coughin' and chokin'—''

Cal ran to the spot as Ginny Petree blindly thrust her baby into her oldest boy's arms and scooped up her toddler, screaming hysterically and shaking the limp, dusky-faced child.

The yard, filled with deadly silence just a moment ago, was suddenly bedlam. Women were crying and clutching their handkerchiefs or their own children or their husbands. Reverend Poole had clasped his hands in prayer.

"Mrs. Petree, let me have him, perhaps there's something I can do!" Cal commanded, but the woman just stared at him, wild-eyed.

Suddenly Livy was at his side. "Hold on to her, Cal!" she cried, and reached for the toddler.

He didn't know what Livy planned, but certainly Ginny was doing the child no good by just clutching him and screaming. Cal took hold of the woman's waist and shoulders while Livy pried Billy, limp as a rag doll, out of his mother's frantic embrace. Ginny Petree fought like a wildcat to keep hold of her unconscious child, unaware of who was trying to take Billy, just knowing that someone was and that Billy was dying. But eventually she lost the battle.

Cal watched as Livy held the small child upside down by his heels and smacked him with the flat of her hand between his shoulder blades once, twice, three times.

"What are you doing?" Ginny screamed, struggling in his grasp and trying to kick him. "You're murdering my child! Let me go! Give him back to me, my Billy's *dying!*"

Livy was still smacking the child's back as if oblivious to Ginny Petree's frantic attempts to escape Cal.

All at once a round object flew from the child's mouth and plopped onto the hard-packed ground.

"Now *breathe*, Billy," Cal heard Livy cry as she laid the apparently lifeless child down on the ground and threw the marble he had just coughed up away from them. "Oh, God, please let him breathe!"

He added his prayers to hers as Ginny stopped struggling and began to cry helplessly in his arms.

And then the child blinked and coughed, and began to breathe, the color seeping back into his face as he took one breath, then another. His eyes widened as he seemed to recognize his mama standing near, and he began to wail.

"Oh, thank God, she saved him! She saved my baby!" cried Ginny Petree as Cal released her. She flew to Livy's side, laughing and sobbing simultaneously as she picked up the bawling toddler from the ground and held him to her.

Thank you, God, Cal rejoiced in silence. He watched as a white-faced, shaking Livy smiled tremulously and started backing away from the scene.

But Ginny wasn't ready to let her child's savior go. She cried, "Oh, I can't thank you enough, Miz Gillespie! You saved my child's life!"

"It was nothing," Livy murmured. "I just happened to look in his direction when he put the marble in his mouth, that's all...."

"My Billy would have choked to death if it weren't for you," Ginny cried. "Did y'all hear that—especially you, Ada Gray? Livy Gillespie saved my Billy! Y'all better be nice to her from now on, y'hear? Or y'all'll answer to *me!*"

Ada Gray harrumphed; the rest of the churchgoers

just stared, dumbstruck. After a moment James Long rose to the occasion.

"Mrs. Gillespie, you have my thanks, too. Thank God for your quick thinking."

"I—I'm glad I could help, Mayor," Livy said, her eyes huge in a face that was still much too pale for Cal's peace of mind.

"I think Mrs. Gillespie needs to go inside and sit down for a moment," Cal called to the preacher, stepping forward just as Livy began to sway. He took both of her elbows, steadying her.

"Oh! Uh...certainly! Of course!" Reverend Poole said, in a voice that was anything but certain.

"N-no..." she murmured, closing her eyes. "No, thank you. I—I just got a bit dizzy for a moment." She opened her eyes. "I'll be fine, thank you, Mr. Devlin. You needn't trouble yourself." Cal felt her trying to shake herself unobtrusively from his grasp, but he held her firmly, remembering that she had just lost a baby six days ago. He'd also wager a dollar she was wearing a corset that was laced too tight.

"I'm walking you home, and don't argue, Mrs. Gillespie. You're white as a shroud," he told her, aware that the eyes of the entire congregation were on them.

In silence, she let him steer her out of the churchyard and down the road.

"That was really fine, what you did, Livy," he said, once they were out of earshot. "Now Ginny Petree thinks you just about hung the moon. That ought to improve the way those old biddies treat you."

She shrugged. "Perhaps." They were just about to come to the jail. "Well, I won't keep you, Sheriff. I'm sure you have things to do."

"I said I was walking you home, Livy, and I am. You still look like a good wind would blow you away."

She stopped and faced him with her hands clenched into fists at her sides. "Caleb Devlin, you don't have any sense at all, you know that?" she said in an exasperated tone.

"Oh?"

"No, you don't. Not a lick. If you did you wouldn't be seen being friendly with *me,* the scarlet woman of Gillespie Springs."

"Perhaps you haven't noticed, but I'm not any too popular myself since someone spread the news that I fought for the Union."

"Oh, it didn't seem to bother the Widow Stone," she snapped. "I'm surprised she didn't ask you to have Sunday dinner with her."

He couldn't help but smile a little. "She did, as a matter of fact, but I...uh, had to decline. I—I'm riding home to see the family."

"Well, if that adoring, moonstruck gaze of hers was any indication, I'm certain she'll ask you again, so all is not lost," Olivia retorted.

His grin broadened; he couldn't help it. "Why, Miz Livy, could it be you're *jealous?*"

"Jealous?" she repeated incredulously, going pale again, and then her blue eyes blazed up at him. "Why, you have your nerve, you—you conceited polecat! If we weren't on a public street, I'd—I'd slap your face, Caleb Devlin!"

He raised an eyebrow and hooked his thumbs in his frock-coat pockets. "Again? My, you are becomin' a violent woman, aren't you, Livy?" he drawled. He saw her hands clench into fists at her sides. "Uh...if the urge is really overpowering, we could just duck in here, ma'am, so you could get it out of your system in private,'' he added, nodding toward the jail they were standing by.

He felt his grin widening. He'd heard it said some women were even more beautiful when they were angry. Livy was one of them. Her eyes became even bluer, her bosom rose and fell underneath the stiff black lace and her face was flushed—like a woman in the throes of passion. She really would slap his face if he told her *that*.

He saw her struggle for control, for the right words to deliver a crushing set-down to his effrontery, and then he knew the exact second when she remembered what *else* had taken place in the privacy of the jail office. He saw the crimson color flood upward from beneath the black lace at her collar.

"Damn you, Caleb Devlin," she breathed. "How dare you?" Her anger was gathering steam. "You used to be a gentleman before the war, but you aren't anymore."

"I used to be a lot of things, before the war," he said with a self-deprecating laugh.

"Well, don't think you can use that eye patch as an excuse to say whatever comes into your head," she retorted, and began to stalk away. "No, don't you even try to follow me," she warned, pointing a finger at him when he started to fall in step at her side. "I've had about enough of your patronizing ways, too. I'm no fragile belle anymore, so don't try and treat me like a hothouse flower. I may have felt dizzy for a moment back there, but getting angry at you has been the best tonic I could have found, thank you very much. You just leave me alone from now on, you hear?"

"Yes, ma'am."

She flounced on down the road toward her house on the edge of town.

There was nothing else to do but let her go. Cal went up and changed his clothes, then headed for the livery stable where he kept his horse. He'd better hit the saddle, or he would find nothing at the Devlin table but scraps for his trouble.

As he rode out of town, he took one last, longing look at the jail. An afternoon nap sure would have been pleasant…or better yet, he wished Livy had taken him up on his offer to step inside there. It would have been worth the slap, he decided with a grin, for once she had vented her ire, he could have stolen a kiss, as he had the day before.

At the thought of the way her lips had felt beneath his and the sensation of the tips of her breasts brushing against his chest, his groin tightened and he groaned to himself. He was a fool to let himself even think about that again. Why torment himself when it was clear she meant to avoid him every chance she could? He nudged Blue into an easy lope.

Oh Francisco, why can't there be more men like you in this world? Olivia thought as she stood beneath the big cottonwood once more. Simple, uncomplicated, never asking more of a woman than her friendship. She hadn't known he had had a sweetheart, of course, but she sensed Francisco Luna would have never trespassed beyond the bounds of propriety with her. He had too much honor, and she had been a married woman, and an Anglo one at that. Francisco had been a shrewd judge of character, too. He'd never said so much as a word of what he'd thought of Robert Gillespie, but she'd known by the way he hovered nearby when Dan's brother visited that he hadn't trusted the man.

He'd been gone—perhaps to visit his *novia,* Olivia realized now—that day she'd been attacked in the barn. And she'd never told him about it, not even when she'd discovered she was pregnant. Yet he seemed to sense what had happened, for the dark eyes he turned on her in the last weeks of his life were eloquent with sorrow and self-blame—as if he thought somehow he could have prevented what had happened.

God, if only she had guessed that Dan would need a scapegoat, and that her friendship with his Mexican employee would make him the likely target! *I could have warned you. You could have fled and taken Rosa with you!*

It was too late for warnings, of course. Livy noticed absently that the withered roses had been taken away and replaced by a bunch of marigolds. Soon the frosts would kill even those and the grave would lie bare beneath the cottonwood.

Francisco, what about Cal? What should I do about Cal? she silently pleaded. *I can't seem to forget what we once had. Does that mean I should trust him? Tell me!*

There was no sound but the gentle soughing of the wind through the cottonwood leaves.

Chapter Fourteen

"Land sakes, I don't know how I can be expected to feed all the riffraff that rides in here hungry," Sarah Devlin grumbled as she came out on the porch to greet her son.

"Aw, Mama, I know you don't mean it," he said, sweeping the silver-haired woman into a big bear hug. "Admit it—you're actually overjoyed to see me, aren't you?"

"I reckon so," she allowed grudgingly, but now there was a twinkle in her eye. "At least if you're here, you aren't in Gillespie Springs bein' shot at. Actually, I was just wishing you could be here, son. Come inside—Mercy's sister has come for a visit."

"Charity's here?"

"Arrived last night. Come on inside, son. We were just about to sit down to dinner. I'll lay another place."

"Good, then I'm not too late. I was worried I'd miss your Sunday chicken," he said, handing Blue's reins to Tad, the boy who helped out with the horses.

"You always did have good timing about when to show up for meals. I can't recollect you ever missin' any as a boy. Sam and Garrick would be off doing some fool thing, but not you,'' his mother teased.

Everyone was seated at the table when he went inside, but they all rose to greet him, except for Garrick, who made no move toward the crutches that lay propped against the table.

"Charity, good to see you," Cal said to the blond girl standing shyly next to Sam's wife, her sister. "Hello, Mercy, Annie, Sam, Garrick."

"Hello, Deac—uh, Caleb. I'm sorry, I'm afraid I still tend to think of you as Deacon Paxton, as we knew you back in Abilene," Charity told him.

"That's all right," he said, smiling. "There are still times *I* think of me that way, too. After all, that's who I was for five years, as far as I knew. How nice you could come and stay with us for a while. Your papa didn't come with you?"

"No, not this time. He sent me on the stage along with a lady from his congregation who was going to visit relatives in Austin. But I'm going to stay until next spring, when Mercy's baby arrives, and then he'll come to fetch me and see his first grandson," Charity replied, nudging her sister.

Mercy's belly had grown more prominent since his last visit, Cal noted, as he watched his sister-in-law roll her eyes.

"I don't know why he's so sure it's a boy," Mercy commented. "But I hope it is. I suspect he always wished one of us had been a son."

"I'm sure he wishes *I* had been," Charity said ruefully as Sarah Devlin brought in a plate and silverware for Cal and they all settled down at their respective places around the table. "A son would have been a whole lot less trouble than I was." The sisters exchanged a look, and Cal guessed they were thinking of all the scrapes Charity used to get into, particularly the one that had resulted in one of Sam's cowboys thinking she was a saloon girl and therefore fair game.

"I'm sure you've been a model of decorum since those days, though, haven't you?" Cal teased.

She laughed. "Yes, and I've even learned how to cook a lot better, and how *not* to burn Papa's meals," she told him.

Mercy raised her arms dramatically in the air. "It's a miracle!" she announced, and there was general laughter. Even Garrick cracked a smile.

"Cal, would you ask the blessing?"

They all bowed their heads and Cal said grace with the ease of long practice, and then conversation resumed again.

"I'll bet that Ned fella is going to be heartbroken while you're gone," Sam teased. "He was right sweet on you, as I recall."

"Hmmph!" Charity sniffed, "Ned Webster up and married Agnes Tackett over in Salinas just before I left! So much for him and those cow-eyed looks he used to give me!"

"It's his loss, Charity," Cal said gallantly, and her sister laid a consoling hand on Charity's wrist.

"Oh, I'm not pining, believe me," Charity asserted. "Marrying Ned would have meant being stuck in dusty old Abilene, Kansas, forever. I wouldn't have gotten to come visit here in Texas, for one thing! That reminds me, Sam—now that you're back home, do you ever hear from that cowboy who stayed in Abilene with you? Oh, what was his name…ah! Jase Lowry?"

Cal wasn't fooled by the apparently casual tone Charity Fairweather used, for the sparkle in her eyes and her heightened color as she said the man's name was anything but casual. A glance at Mercy's face showed she wasn't fooled, either, but other than giving a deep sigh, she was silent.

"Last I heard he was planning on wintering in San Antone," Sam said. "Shall I write and tell him you're here?" His question evidently earned him a small kick under the table from his wife, for a moment later Cal saw him wince. "What'd I say wrong?" he asked innocently.

"He's a *cowboy*," Mercy said, exasperated.

"So? *I'm* a cowboy," Sam retorted.

"That was different," Mercy insisted. "Charity doesn't need—"

"Charity doesn't need to hear you talking about her like she isn't here," Charity said. "I was just asking because he had been so kind to me, not because I was nurturing any…any grand *passion* for him or anything! Let's change the subject, shall we? Cal, they tell me you're a lawman now," she said, her eyes silently imploring him to help her lead the topic away from dangerous territory.

Cal obliged, telling her about his first days as the sheriff of Gillespie Springs and the colorful characters that made up the town. He finished up by telling about the Last Chance Saloon and those who frequented it.

"That reminds me, there was some saddle bum nosin' around in Bryan, especially in the saloon, askin' questions about you," Sam said, his normally carefree expression growing serious. "About who you fought for in the war an' all. Did he cause you any trouble?"

"Oh, he tried," Cal replied. "He came back and spread the tale. Some of the townsfolk would just as soon the mayor fired me now that they know it, but others seem willing to give me a chance. I reckon it'll all blow over," he said, praying it was true.

"You mean they want to get rid of you because you fought for the Union?" Charity said, her blue eyes wide. "Why, those silly rebels! *I* think you're a man of principle, and they're very lucky to have you!"

Cal cleared his throat, aware of Garrick's face growing morose and that Sam was looking down at his hands. "Um, thank you, Charity, but we've, uh, had to agree to disagree about that whole thing here at home, too."

Charity colored, her eyes flying to Garrick's crutches propped against his end of the table and then to Sam's face. "Oh! I'm sorry, Garrick, Sam! I—I forgot you both fought for the South," she said. "I've *got* to learn to think before I speak!"

"Don't give it a thought," Sam said in his usual conciliatory fashion. "*We* think Gillespie Springs is lucky to have our brother as their sheriff, too, don't we, Garrick?"

Garrick only harrumphed, but at least he didn't deny it. Then he said, "You seen any more of that woman? The Widow Gillespie?"

Cal felt every eye at the table on him. "It's a small town, Garrick. Naturally I—I see Olivia around town, from time to time." He hoped his older brother would be willing to let it go at that, but of course he wasn't.

"That isn't what I meant by *seein'* her, brother, an' you know it," Garrick told him.

"Garrick," his mother warned, "I'll thank you to remember there are ladies present—"

"I happened to sit by her in church today, brother, but I'm sorry to disappoint you, that's the most I can report," Cal said evenly.

"That woman dares to show her face in a *church?*" Garrick asked with a snort.

Cal felt his hands clench into fists in his lap. "'That woman' saved the life of a small child today, Garrick," he said, conquering the urge to knock his older brother off the chair. Really, he was becoming as violent-minded as he'd accused Livy of being, Cal decided! Instead, he told his family about the child choking on the marble and Livy's quick action, which had saved his life.

"Why, she's a heroine!" Charity said, obviously moved. "But what had she done to make them dislike her?" she asked curiously.

"Um, Charity, perhaps you could help Mother Devlin, Annie and me with the dishes?" Mercy said, rising with difficulty and plucking at her sister's sleeve.

"But—" Charity protested, looking at Cal.

"But nothing," Mercy insisted. "Come along, now."

"Sam, why don't you go out to the barn with me? I think I'd like to see how old Goliad is doing," Cal said, ignoring Garrick as he rose to his feet.

As they stepped out into the yard, Cal noticed that the temperature had dropped substantially since he'd arrived. "Brrr! Feels like a norther blowin' in. Who'd have guessed it after the pretty morning we had?"

Sam scanned the lowering skies overhead and nodded. "You better plan on spendin' the night, Cal. It isn't gonna be fit for man nor beast out there pretty soon."

Cal had to agree. There was an edge to the air that promised sleet, and he wouldn't want to subject Blue or himself to a long, miserable, slippery ride home. They reached the barn and pulled the door open.

"Sorry about what Garrick said," Sam muttered as they stepped inside the barn and the familiar odors of horses, leather and hay met their nostrils. "He can be meaner than eight acres of snakes sometimes. I don't think he means to be mean, but his wife leavin' him like she did sure hasn't sweetened him up any."

"He always did have foot-in-mouth disease," Cal commented wryly. "Ah, there he is, my old partner," he said as they reached Goliad's stall and the tall stallion poked his head out to greet him. Cal reached up and stroked the black's sleek neck and the edge of his muzzle, where white hairs were mixed with black. "Are they treatin' you right, fella? Givin' you lots of good oats and friendly mares to comfort you in your old age?"

Both men laughed as the horse tossed his head up and down as if agreeing.

"I can't wait to see his colts."

"Well, there's half a dozen mares in foal to him already—four around the county and two here on the farm," Sam told him.

"Goliad, you never had it so good in Abilene, did you? The only horses around there were cow ponies and plow horses." He chuckled as the stallion nuzzled him for treats. Cal didn't disappoint him, for he'd taken a few lumps of sugar from the bowl on the table and now he brought them out of his pocket.

"Mercy looks like she's feelin' well," Cal commented, as the horse went back to the hay in his manger.

"Yeah, she has the energy of ten women, now that the mornin' sickness is past," Sam said proudly. "I keep tellin' her to slow down, not to get herself so tired, but..." He cleared his throat. "Say, brother, I hope you don't mind me askin', but how *are* things with you and Olivia Gillespie? Is there more than what you wanted to let on in front of Garrick?"

Cal studied his younger brother, but there was nothing but genuine interest and concern in Sam's open face. Marriage had been good for him, Cal decided. Sam had always been a good man, but wedding Mercy had settled him, made him more careful and compassionate. For a moment Cal envied Sam the love that seemed to hum between him and Mercy, and the baby that would be born of that love in the spring.

"No, Sam, I don't mind you asking. But there really isn't much more to it than what I said." He thought that would be the end of the discussion, but it was not.

"Have you gone to see her, Cal? More than that first day when so much happened, I mean? Does she know you still care for her, or are you waiting for her to read your mind?"

Cal sighed and leaned his head back wearily. "She's made it pretty clear she doesn't want me or any other man around, Sam." Before he knew what was happening, it was all pouring out—about the day he'd gone to visit her while she was recovering from losing the baby and how pleased she'd looked to see him, but how coldly she had rebuffed him when he'd asked to come back again. The day she'd come in the jail office to complain about his paying Jovita's wages and the kiss they'd exchanged. About her jealous remarks regarding Phoebe Stone's attentions, after she'd saved the child in the churchyard.

"Sounds like there's hope, then," Sam commented with a grin. "A woman won't bother getting jealous if she doesn't care about a man."

"You think so? I don't know, Sam...."

"Cal, she loved you once, enough to agree to marry you. If the dang war hadn't come up, y'all'd probably be old married folks with half a dozen kids by now."

Cal sighed again and leaned on the stall door, scratching Goliad behind the ears as the stallion munched his hay. "She seems to have got it in her head that I think she's a loose woman and that I'm just lookin' for some dishonorable relationship with her. I don't think she's ever going to get over that idea."

Sam grinned. "Shoot, Sam, there's something to be said for 'dishonorable relationships,' I reckon. Mercy and I might never have met if I hadn't been lookin' for one of those and thought she was Mercedes LaFleche, the sportin' woman, instead of the preacher's daughter."

"But—"

Sam held his hands up and laughed. "I know, I know. The situations aren't the same, exactly. But don't give up, brother. Just keep usin' that Devlin charm—it worked on her once before, after all. Be helpful where you can. A widow's bound to have things that need doin' around the place that aren't easy for a woman. Just ignore the spines on the cactus and pretty soon that prickly woman'll blossom for you."

Cal had to smile at the comparison. "Well, all right, but if she ever does learn to tolerate me, I'm not gonna tell her you compared her to a prickly pear. And I appreciate your not talking about her like she was Jezebel and Salome combined, the way Garrick does."

"Well, I've done some thinkin', an' I figure there might be more to what happened than meets the eye. After all, if she *was* the kind of woman they say she is—if she had really had a Mexican lover who made her pregnant and if she hadn't cared about her husband's feelings or mourned when he killed himself—seems like she would've been tickled to death to see you come callin', no matter what your intentions were. She'd probably have encouraged you, don't you see?''

"I suppose that's true."

"Of course it's true. I don't know how she got in the family way, but if she's really a good woman, she's caught in a bind. If she takes up with you right away, it's gonna look like the town was right about her, no matter what she wants to do."

"Are you tellin' me I have to wait at least a year before I try to call on her again?" Cal asked. "When did her husband die, September?" It was now November, and the prospect of waiting until next autumn was totally unappealing.

His feelings must have shown on his face, for Sam commented, "Whoa there, Cal, you look as mournful as an old hound dog! I don't reckon you need to wait a whole year, but you know how folks talk. Go easy, that's all I'm sayin'. What are you afraid of—having to fend the lovesick ladies of Gillespie Springs off till then?"

"Aw, I don't reckon there's too many ladies that would want to wake up to a face like this," Cal said.

"You're too modest, brother," Sam said with a look that told Cal he didn't believe him for a minute.

Cal found himself telling Sam about Phoebe Stone's pursuit of him.

"She's a nice lady, and she's lonesome," he concluded, "but I don't want to give her any ideas." The thought of having to fend off Phoebe's Sunday dinner invitations until next fall was daunting indeed.

"Maybe you should bring her out to dinner here and introduce her to Garrick," Sam suggested with mischief dancing in his eyes. "Surely the prospect of having him as a relation would frighten off the eagerest of women."

The idea of Phoebe, with her hopeful, earnest face, meeting their crusty older brother made him laugh. "I believe in miracles, but Sam, you don't know Phoebe!"

He *did* believe in miracles, Cal reflected, but it would take a miracle of biblical proportions, apparently, for Livy to learn to love him again.

Go easy, Sam had said. Cal chuckled inwardly. For the impetuous Sam to have said such a thing must mean that Mercy had worked miracles on his youngest brother.

It seemed like the best way to follow Sam's advice was to leave Livy alone for a while—weeks...months, if need be. She'd told him to leave her be, hadn't she? A man had his pride, after all. And he had to face the possibility that she might never love him again.

Chapter Fifteen

"These are right fine, Miz Gillespie. I'll take any more you can bring me between now and Christmas," the proprietor of the mercantile told her as he took the half-dozen dolls Livy had brought him.

"Gracious, Mr. Tyler, Christmas Eve is only four days from now. I'm not sure how many more we can make between now and then. Are you sure you can sell that many?"

Tyler shrugged. "If not, I can always keep 'em stored away till next year. Little girls always want dolls."

The dolls had been a joint project between Livy and Jovita, for the Mexican woman had carved the wooden heads and bodies and Livy had cut up some of the dresses she hadn't worn since the war. Jovita had protested at the sacrifice of the beautiful gowns in their colorful hues, but Livy insisted they were hopelessly out of style, and in any case, the vivid colors didn't seem appropriate to her present state. Perhaps they would never be appropriate again, she thought.

"I'll pay you two dollars apiece—twelve dollars in all, all right?" Tyler said, opening his till.

Twelve dollars. Livy would insist Jovita take half, for

her effort in making the dolls. Her own six dollars would buy groceries, at least. She would be sure to purchase sugar, so she could make Jovita some fudge as a Christmas present. The Mexican woman had a sweet tooth.

"I—I'd take any more jelly or preserves you might happen to have, Miz Gillespie," the proprietor offered.

The man was practically standing on his head to be helpful to her, Livy noted, secretly amused. What a change from the way he'd been before the incident in the churchyard. Prior to her saving that little boy's life, he had been curt and cold, buying what she made to sell, but offering no pleasantries. Now it seemed he couldn't be kind enough.

"Oh, Mr. Tyler, you'd be welcome to them if I had any left, but I'm afraid I've brought you all I made. But perhaps you could use some butter, if my cow doesn't go dry?"

"Sure, anytime. Can I get something down for you?" he asked, as he saw her scanning the shelves behind him.

Her longing must have shown on her face, Livy thought, and she tried to sound carefree as she said, "No, not today, I'm afraid, though that rose-colored marquisette is lovely."

"Ah, you have an eye for fine cloth, I see," Tyler said approvingly. "Why don't I just take it down and measure you out a dress length? You won't be wearing black forever, so—"

"No thank you, Mr. Tyler, though I will take five pounds of sugar and the same of flour, some cornmeal and some bacon."

"Miz Gillespie, I'd be pleased to let you have that dress length at half off the price. Ginny Petree *is* my sister, after all, and I—I'd like to do something to thank you for what you done for my little nephew a few weeks ago.''

"You're very kind, Mr. Tyler, but not today, thank you," she said, hoping her smile didn't show the regret she felt. Once, she wouldn't have given a second thought to such a purchase, but would have waved an imperious finger and purchased the whole bolt. Her maid would have toted the fabric to the waiting carriage and a modiste would be summoned to the plantation to make up the gown in a style suitable for Miss Olivia Childress, the acknowledged belle of Brazos County and the apple of her daddy's eye.

Well, those carefree days were gone forever, she thought. Her father, a fiery supporter of the Confederates, had lauded her decision to break her engagement to "that traitor Caleb Devlin," but he'd been obviously disappointed when she'd chosen Dan Gillespie, a rebel captain, rather than his more prosperous brother Robert, the banker.

When reconstruction began and the ruinous taxes were levied on all "rebel" properties, her father had died of a heart seizure—a broken heart, Livy had always called it—almost as if he couldn't face the inevitable changes to their way of life. Her two brothers were lost to her. One had been killed in the war. The other had fled west after Appomattox and she had never heard from him again. Perhaps he was dead, too.

Mr. Tyler was done wrapping her purchases up in brown paper now, and as the bell over the door tinkled, announcing another customer's arrival, she thanked him and turned to go.

And ran right into the broad, waistcoated chest of her brother-in-law, Robert Gillespie.

"Buying frills and furbelows, Olivia?" he inquired silkily, as she recoiled.

"I think you know my bank balance better than that, Robert," she retorted dryly, glad that he could not have seen Tyler buying the dolls. She didn't want to give Dan's brother the satisfaction of knowing she was having to make things to sell for extra money. "No, just some necessities, Robert. Good day to you," she said, intending to go around him and make her escape.

He caught hold of her wrist in a way that could not be seen by Tyler on his side of the counter. "Oh, but Christmas is coming, and I haven't bought your present yet. Perhaps there was something here that caught your eye?"

You hypocrite, showing off your supposed generosity to your brother's widow for Mr. Tyler's sake.

And then she caught the speculative look in Tyler's eye and realized that Gillespie's offer had put her in an unenviable position. Now the mercantile proprietor was wondering if some deeper, clandestine relationship existed between the widow and her former brother-in-law.

But she didn't want to reveal the depths of her loathing for Gillespie in front of Tyler and give the town more to gossip about just when many of the inhabitants were starting to speak to her again, so she just said, "Oh, my needs are few, Robert, though it was a kind thought."

"Tut-tut, my dear sister-in-law, I believe you're being self-sacrificing to a fault. It doesn't have to be something practical. Tell me what would delight you."

It would delight me if you turned into a toad and hopped away, she thought, allowing her lips to curve into a smile while her eyes clashed with his. She stood her ground, determined not to so much as shrug to preserve appearances.

Gillespie turned to Tyler. "You see how selfless she is? Perhaps you'll help me out like a good fellow. Was there something Mrs. Gillespie here was interested in, that she denied herself?"

Clearly eager to please the banker, who held the mortgage on his store, Tyler said, "There sure was—a dress length a' that pink cloth up there. It's right costly, and that's a fact."

"Well, haul it down, my good man, and I'll buy it, the whole bolt."

"*No,* Robert," she whispered as the proprietor turned his back to comply. "I won't take anything from you! Tell him you've changed your mind."

Gillespie lounged against the counter, smirking.

"Mr. Tyler, put the bolt back up there," she said. "I don't wish to have Mr. Gillespie buying me presents."

Dead silence followed. She saw Tyler's jaw fall, making him look, she thought, for all the world like a bluegill that had just been hooked and hauled out onto dry land. She avoided glancing at Gillespie altogether. Gathering up her purchases, Olivia beat a deliberately unhurried retreat. Just as she reached the door, she heard Gillespie break the silence with a forced chuckle and then make some remark to Tyler.

Damn him, she cursed inwardly, knowing he had set up the encounter so that she would lose no matter which way she had reacted.

"What'cha doin', Sheriff?" Davy Richardson inquired, spying Cal sitting outside the door of the jail.

Georgie had been keeping his idol, the sheriff, company. "Why, he's whittlin'," Georgie informed the boy loftily. "Any durn fool kin see that."

The boy just grinned, unoffended by Georgie's words. "Is that all?"

"Why, actually I reckon I *am* doing more than that, Georgie," Cal informed him. "I'm enjoying the winter sunshine and your company. You're welcome to set a spell, too, Davy, if you aren't supposed to be doing something for your mama."

Cal really was glad of their company. As long as he had Georgie's and Davy's artless chatter to respond to, his mind wouldn't drift to Livy, as it always did when he had nothing else to think about. He'd been sticking to his resolve of leaving her alone, but Lord knows it wasn't getting any easier. He forced himself to make do with chance encounters on the street and glimpses of her from the jail window as she went about her business, but it wasn't enough.

"My chores're all done," Davy assured him as he took up a perch on the hitching post. "You comin' to the Christmas pageant at the schoolhouse on Christmas Eve? I get to be Joseph and wear a fake beard an' everything!"

Cal smiled, remembering Christmases when he was a boy, and he and his siblings had taken part in other such Christmas pageants. His mother had been sure the town of Bryan would never get over the Devlin brothers as the Three Wise Men. That had been the year Livy had played Mary, and he'd been so taken with the beauty of her in her blue robe and white veil that he'd totally forgotten his lines.

"I reckon I wouldn't miss it for the world, Davy," he told the boy.

"Great! Gee, I wish I had a knife. I asked Mama for

one for Christmas, but I'll probably just get a dumb ol' shirt or something.... Say, do you need the jail swept out or some errands run? If I could earn some more money before Christmas, I could buy Mama them earbobs I saw in the mercantile.''

''I reckon my jail needs to be swept out about every other day, Davy,'' he told the boy. ''Broom's on the other side of the door. Mind you don't listen to anything that desperado in the jail cell tells you, though, if he wakes up.''

The boy's eyes widened. ''You have a sure-'nough *outlaw* in your jail? Is he anybody famous, like Quantrill or the Reno Brothers?''

''You been readin' dime novels, Davy?'' Cal asked, amused.

''Only one or two, but I bought 'em fair an' square at the general store,'' Davy assured him.

''I see. Well, I was exaggerating a little to call him a desperado. Truth to tell, the fellow in there ain't anybody famous, not even anyone worth talkin' to.''

''I promise I won't talk to him. I might sneak a look or two, though, iffen he's asleep.''

Cal exchanged a grin with Georgie as the boy stepped inside. Actually, the whittling was just an excuse to be sitting outside. Cal had noticed a sudden, disturbing increase in the number of strangers loitering in town and he wanted to keep an eye on them.

Gillespie Springs had never been more than a wide spot in the road—a little town to water a man's horse and wet a man's whistle in, with a hotel to furnish him a good meal and a bed if he was too tired to go on. But no one lingered here. It wasn't big enough to be a wild, anything-goes town like Fort Worth or Abilene or San Antonio. Troublemakers looking for cheap whiskey and fast women didn't generally seek them in Gillespie Springs.

So why, all of a sudden, did all roads seem to lead to his little town, at least as far as every saddle tramp in Texas was concerned? As Cal had told Davy, he had one locked up in his jail now, whom he'd arrested just last night for getting liquored up and shooting a hole in the heart of the bull in the painting hanging over the bar of the Last Chance. And there was another pair, he observed, narrowing his gaze to observe two horsemen slowing their horses to a trot just down the street.

They had the look of hired guns, both of them—their faces hard under several days' growth of beard, their eyes constantly darting around, assessing. As Cal watched, one pointed at the bank and they halted their mounts in front of it.

"I wonder what them fellas want," Georgie murmured in his slow way, as he caught sight of them. "I wouldn't reckon they'd have any money to be puttin' in the bank."

"I wouldn't think so either, Georgie. I think I'll go check up on them. Here, you hold on to my knife and whittling stick."

"I—I'll c-come with ya, Sh-Sheriff," Georgie said, excitement making him stutter. "R-reckon they be *b-bank robbers?*"

Lord, Cal hoped not. "I don't think so," he lied. "But I want you to stay here and guard the prisoner, okay? And keep Davy here, understand?"

"O-okay, Sh-Sheriff," Georgie said, his reluctance obvious.

Cal stepped quickly into the jail office, ignoring the complaints made by the occupant of the cell and Davy's questioning look as he snatched up the rifle from the rack on the wall.

"What's up, Sheriff?" the boy asked, dropping the broom.

"You stay right here, Davy, you hear me? I'm putting Georgie in charge, and you're his deputy to guard the prisoner, okay?"

"Okay, but—"

Cal didn't wait for the rest of his question, but went back outside, glad he'd always kept the weapon loaded and ready.

With his heart hammering in his ears, and praying he wouldn't have to kill anyone, Cal crossed the street, which was a sea of mud from a recent rain. He made a wide circle so he could approach the bank from the side and peer into the window.

He expected to see the two saddle tramps transformed into bank robbers, their bandannas pulled over their faces. What he did see, however, were the two men talking with all apparent civility to a teller, who looked not the least alarmed. He pointed to his right, as if the two had been asking directions.

Perhaps they were just more brazen about letting their faces be seen and hadn't yet demanded—at gunpoint— that the teller open the safe. Cal strode into the bank, the rifle held low but ready.

He was just in time to meet the two sauntering out the door, apparently in no hurry to get anywhere. They saw his badge, stopped and then lowered their eyes to the rifle he carried.

"Afternoon, Sheriff. You expectin' trouble?" one of them drawled. The other snickered.

"Maybe."

Cal stood in the door as they went around him, then

watched as they strolled across the street toward the mercantile.

"What'd they want, John?" he asked the teller behind the bank window.

"They said they were looking for Mr. Gillespie, Sheriff," the teller said. "I told 'em he'd gone over to the mercantile for a minute. Coupla rough customers, eh?"

Cal nodded and went back outside, feeling vaguely foolish for jumping to a false conclusion. Just because there had been an attempted bank robbery once didn't mean that every dusty cowboy riding through was there to try a robbery again. But why were those two looking for Gillespie?

Then Cal saw Olivia fly out of the mercantile as if the devil was on her tail. He wondered what had her in such a lather, and he thought about hailing her and asking if anything were wrong, but then he saw her path blocked by the two saddle tramps heading into the store.

As Cal watched from the steps of the bank, he noticed both of them finger the brims of their hats in a gesture of courtesy that was entirely negated by their hemming her in so she couldn't leave. He could see them grinning down at her, moving to the side when she moved to the side, then back in front of her when she tried to escape that way.

Feeling the hair at the back of his neck rising and his gut clenching with a primitive, protective rage, he stepped down into the street and strode toward them.

"These men botherin' you, ma'am?" he inquired, not wanting to give them her name to sully.

A flustered-looking Livy looked up, and for a heartbeat he didn't have to guess at her relief at seeing him.

"Yes, Sheriff, I'd have to say they were," she replied coolly.

"Why, Sheriff, that's the second time we've encountered you in less than a minute," one of the two saddle tramps said with a derisive grin as he turned to Cal. "Don't you have anything else to do but follow us around?"

"Nope, my dance card's pretty free at the moment," Cal said. "Why don't you just let the lady by?"

The stranger who had spoken to Cal turned to his partner. "Why don't we just let the lady by, Clem?"

The other man made an elaborate production of shrugging his shoulders. "I dunno. Guess we could, since the sheriff asked so po-lite."

They moved aside and Livy swept by them, with a murmured, "Thank you, Sheriff," as she went.

"Much obliged, *gentlemen*," Cal said with heavy irony, and stood there as they went inside the mercantile. He wished he could have been a fly on the wall to hear what they said to Gillespie inside, but of course they wouldn't speak freely in front of him. It would be interesting to see if the three came out together, though Cal would have preferred to walk Livy home. She probably wouldn't have welcomed his company, though, he thought gloomily as he recrossed the street and took up his stool in front of the jail again.

Davy and Georgie, who had been watching from the window, poured out of the jail.

"Ain't ya gonna arrest anyone, Sheriff?" Georgie asked, clearly astonished.

"Didn't they rob the bank?" Davy asked.

"Sorry to disappoint you both, but there weren't any crimes being committed, so I couldn't arrest them," Cal said, amused. He kept his eye on the mercantile as he spoke.

"But...they was botherin' Miz Gillespie," Georgie said, his simple face troubled.

"Unfortunately, leering is not considered a crime in the state of Texas," Cal told him. "I'd have liked to wallop them, I have to admit, though."

A moment later, his vigilance was rewarded. Gillespie and the saddle tramps came out together, not from the front entrance of the mercantile, but the side door toward the rear of the building. The three appeared to be in earnest conversation and disappeared down the alley that went behind the bank. Had Cal not been sitting at the corner in front of the jail, where he could see up and down the two intersecting streets, he would have missed seeing them.

Had they gone into the back entrance of the bank, where Gillespie could talk to them further, unobserved? And why?

Suddenly restless, Cal went in to put his rifle back on the rack and to check on the prisoner.

"When ya gonna let me out of this place, Sheriff?" the bleary-eyed man demanded, as he had every time he saw Cal.

"Maybe tomorrow, if you behave yourself," Cal told him.

He'd let him go tomorrow, all right, after fining him the hefty sum of one dollar—the amount, coincidentally, that the cowboy had had in his pocket when he was arrested. Cal couldn't very well keep him until the circuit judge came around, just for shooting a hole in a saloon painting.

He wished he could go patrol the town and keep his eye on the strangers who suddenly seemed to find Gil-

lespie Springs such an attractive place to be. He wanted
to make sure none of them were hanging around Livy's
place, too. He wanted to stand guard over her, whether
she liked it or not!

But he couldn't just go off and leave the jail un-
tended. With so many potential troublemakers in town,
it was entirely likely that they'd all get liquored up and
decide to stage a jailbreak.

Tarnation, as long as he had anyone in a cell, he was
as much a prisoner as the prisoner was. He couldn't
even go upstairs and sleep in his own bed, but would
have to try to snatch a little sleep at his desk while
guarding the man behind bars.

Hadn't he planned to hire a deputy for times like this?
Cal had forgotten all about the idea when the story of
his past had traveled to Gillespie Springs and it looked
like he wouldn't be sheriff much longer. But weeks had
gone by, and so far it seemed he was still here....

As if in answer to his thoughts, he heard Georgie and
Davy greet the mayor outside, and a moment later
James Long breezed into the jail office.

"Howdy, your honor," Cal greeted Long. "Come to
see my prisoner?"

"You the mayor of this one-horse hole?" the prisoner demanded from his cell. "Get me outa this place!
I'm being imprisoned fer no reason a'tall! This poor
excuse of a lawman's starvin' me to death on moldy
bread and water!"

"Uh-uh, that's not bein' a good boy," Cal said, shaking an admonitory finger at the man in the cell. "Remember how I said I'd spring you tomorrow if you
behaved?" He turned back to Long. "Now, what can I
do for you, Mayor?"

"Aww, Sheriff..." the man whined.

Long ignored the prisoner. "Cal, is it my imagination or is every drifter in Texas suddenly roosting in Gillespie Springs?"

"So you noticed, too."

Long nodded. "Wonder why they're here."

Cal raked a hand through his hair. "Mayor, I wish I knew. But I saw something a few minutes ago that makes me even more curious." Briefly, his voice lowered so that the prisoner couldn't hear, he told Long about the two saddle tramps looking for Gillespie, and about seeing them talking to the banker as they left the mercantile.

"Hmm," murmured Long, stroking his handlebar mustache. "I wonder what he's up to...." He shrugged. "No way of knowin', I guess. But that doesn't solve the problem, does it? What do you suggest we do?"

Cal grinned. "Mayor, I reckon your question is an answer to my prayer. I think you oughta hire a deputy to give me a hand—nothin' permanent, maybe, just a man to help me when needed, at least until these drifters either show their hand or clear out. I can't be out keepin' an eye on the streets if I have to be in here watchin' the likes of him sleep."

"Yes...it makes sense. I'd volunteer my services, but I'm sure my missus wouldn't hear of it. She'd call me an old fool and remind me I can't shoot worth a damn, anyway," Long said with a rueful look. "Do you have anyone in mind?"

Cal thought a minute. "What about that Hungarian fellow, Kristof? He told me the other day he'd been an officer in the Hungarian army, so I imagine he knows his way around a gun. I'm certain he could use the money, and he sure doesn't owe any loyalty to Gillespie."

"The very man! I'll authorize it immediately. Why don't you go speak to him right now and I'll stand guard here till you get back? Set up some arrangement so he can spell you on guarding the jail when you have a prisoner. That'll free you up to patrol the town, with the added advantage of him bein' already sworn in if trouble breaks out. Tell him the town will pay him by the day, whenever you feel he's needed."

"Sounds good to me, Mayor," Cal said, grabbing his hat from its peg. "The rifle's right here on the wall if that yahoo gets out of line," he added, nodding in the direction of the drifter in the cell.

Chapter Sixteen

Olivia sat in her parlor the next afternoon, enjoying the sunshine streaming through the window on the unseasonably warm winter day as she put the final touches on a doll's dress. If she hurried, she would have time to take it and the other two dolls they had completed down to the mercantile while she went and tended to Rosie, the cow. Then she'd help Jovita make supper, though she doubted the Mexican woman needed her help. The truth was, Olivia wanted to learn how to make enchiladas the way Jovita did.

It was several minutes before the sound penetrated Olivia's consciousness, but as she tied off the final stitch in the hem of the doll's flounced skirt, she was aware of a repetitive thudding noise coming from somewhere outside the house, toward the back.

Apprehension filled her. Dear Lord, had some of the growing band of rowdies in town decided to fell her pecan trees so that they crashed onto her roof or the barn? She wouldn't be able to stop them herself.... Could she summon Cal in time to prevent any serious damage?

Dropping the doll on the horsehair couch, Olivia

dashed to the kitchen at the back of the house, where she found Jovita peeking out the lifted lace curtain over the back window. The little smile playing about the woman's lips, however, told Olivia that whatever the sound was, it was nothing to fear.

"Jovita, what's that racket out there?"

"Señora Oleevia, you are getting a beegger woodpile."

The remark made no sense. Olivia lifted the other corner of the curtain and peered out.

She gasped at the sight that met her eyes.

Cal stood in her backyard, bare to the waist, swinging an ax at the thick trunk of the old cottonwood that had fallen prey to the last big thunderstorm this summer. His shirt and vest were draped over a nearby lilac bush. As she watched, he succeeded in sundering a two-foot section of the trunk, and he set the log on its end and split it into firewood.

For a moment she could only stare at the beauty of the rippling, sweat-drenched muscles of his back while he swung the ax again as if the tree were the devil himself.

Sweet Lord, he was a fine figure of a man! The shirts and vest he normally wore were well filled out, but they had only hinted at the powerful shoulder muscles and trim, tapered waist she beheld now. All at once she felt as if a summer wind had suddenly blown into the kitchen, warming her all over.

"He ees *muy macho, sí?*" Jovita commented, her tone amused, causing Olivia to realize she'd been staring at him like a starving woman stares at a banquet.

She jumped back from the window as if it were ablaze.

"*Sí*—I mean, no! Did you ask him to do this?"

"No, Leevy," replied Jovita, still smiling.

Olivia couldn't resist looking again. "The presumption of the man! I didn't ask him to come chop my wood, and I mean to tell him so!" Grabbing up her shawl from its hook, she threw the door open.

"But Leevy, we *need* some wood—the woodpile was getting low," called Jovita, but Olivia barely heard as she stormed down the back steps and out into the yard.

"Cal Devlin, what do you think you're doing?" she demanded, just as he hefted the ax and swung down again, splitting another log neatly in two.

Still holding the ax, he turned around, a grin spreading over his sweaty face. "I would have thought it was obvious, Livy. I'm splitting some firewood," he drawled in that maddening, deep voice of his. "Stand clear now," he warned, and he swung the ax again.

"Thank you, but I didn't ask you to do that, and you can stop right now. I can very well afford to pay some boy in town to come and do that." In actual fact, she couldn't afford it—she or Jovita usually ended up chopping firewood, but he *didn't* have to know that.

"So this time you can save your money," he said, not looking at her as he bent to lay the split log on its end before cleaving it in half.

"Cal, I don't want to be beholden to you! Now stop that and get on back into town!"

"You're not beholden to me," he said reasonably. "Call it my Christmas present to you."

"Thank you very much, Cal Devlin, but I *will not* be accepting presents from you, do you understand that? I thought I'd already made myself clear that I want nothing—"

"Then call it my Christmas good deed, Livy," he said, and went back to swinging the ax.

"Don't you have some law to be upholding, or someone to put in jail?" she persisted, exasperated. "The town's overrun with drifters, if you hadn't noticed."

"Yes, Livy, I noticed," he said. "I've got a deputy now, Lazlo Kristof. He's keeping an eye on things till I get back."

"Well, you can go back right now."

He grinned at her again. "Hush up, Livy, so I can get on with this."

For a moment she just stared at him, her hands on her hips. He was ignoring her express command to leave! Not sure what to do next, she stormed back into the house, slamming the door.

Jovita was suspiciously busy gathering up the dolls.

"Jovita, go tell the sheriff he can leave," Livy commanded, pointing out the window. "He won't listen to me."

Jovita shrugged her shoulders elaborately. "Leevy, why would I do that? We need the wood, no?"

"No—yes! But not from him. Don't you understand that I can't have that man doing favors for me?"

"Why not, *señora?* If he wants to do thees for you, let heem."

"Oh, Jovita, don't you see? Then he'll—he'll start to expect…um, something in return."

Jovita shrugged again and said something in too-rapid Spanish.

"Well, I don't know what you said, but please, Jovita, go out there and ask him to quit. Tell him I thank him very much, but—"

"No, *señora,*" Jovita said, showing an unusual stubborn streak as she wrapped her rebozo around her shoulders and stuffed the dolls in a poke. "I must go take thees dolls to the store now."

"But I was going to do that," Livy said, desperate to escape herself if she could not get Cal to go away.

"I weel do eet," Jovita informed her. "You can do the meelking and gather the eggs," she added, as if Livy were suddenly the employee, not Jovita.

Livy could only watch as the determined woman strolled out the back door, calling a friendly greeting to Cal as she went around the side of the house.

Jovita was right, Livy supposed, staring out the kitchen window at the man who kept splitting logs as if there were nothing else in this world to do. The cow had to be milked and the eggs had to be gathered, but if she was going to do that, she'd have to walk right past Cal to get to the barn!

Well, was she afraid of Cal? Was she going to let his presence in her backyard keep her from doing what she knew had to be done? Not by a darned sight! She'd just ignore him. Snatching up the egg basket, she sailed down the steps and walked right past him, keeping her gaze straight ahead.

She paused at the entrance of the barn, however. Though she had to come in here nearly every day, it always took her a moment or two to calm the panicky fluttering of her heart that had plagued her ever since the attack. *No one is here but you and the animals,* she told herself, as she had told herself so many times before. *You can't spend the rest of your life avoiding the barn. Think of something else.*

She began to gather the eggs first. She'd done well to just march past Cal as if he weren't there, hadn't she? She'd kept her eyes straight ahead, looking neither to the right nor the left. She'd take her time, and perhaps the yard would be empty when she went back to the house.

"Ouch!" Her inattention had cost her a peck from an old broody hen that had taken exception to Olivia stealing her eggs.

Next she forked some fresh hay into the manger and opened the gate to let Rosie into her stall from the pasture, fetched her stool and the bucket, and sat down to milk the cow. It soothed her flustered spirits to lean against the cow's flank, listening to the *swish-swish* of the milk squirting into the pail and the steady crunching noise as Rosie dined on the hay in her manger. But why, when Livy closed her eyes and let her mind roam while her fingers squeezed the cow's teats in a rhythmic pattern, was her brain filled with the image of Cal's half-naked body?

Surely he'd be gone by now, she thought when she finished, straightening and giving the cow a last pat. She would just empty this milk into the jug in the springhouse and go get a head start on supper. She'd thank Cal politely for chopping the wood when she next ran into him in town, she decided as she left the stall and headed down the aisle in the shadowy twilight.

All at once she saw a figure loom up in front of her in the gloom, and she froze. Her pulse pounded in her ears.

No, not again...she couldn't allow it to happen again....

The figure took a step forward, still silent.

She shrieked and tossed the full pail of milk at him, then ran in the opposite direction. If she could only reach the pitchfork before her would-be attacker caught her, she wouldn't have to suffer that horrible shame again....

"Lord Christ, Livy, what's got into you?" Cal's voice pierced the gloom behind her just as she whirled with the pitchfork raised on high. "Now put that thing down. What made you think I was going to hurt you?" he demanded, his voice incredulous as he came closer.

The shirt he'd evidently just put back on was soaked. Milk formed white beads on his belt buckle and spread as a dark stain all over the front of his pants. The fabric squished as he walked.

"Livy, I swear, I was just coming to ask if you had an old towel I could use to wash up at the pump! Why on earth...sweet Jesus, honey, you're trembling!"

Olivia closed her eyes for a long moment and wished she could expire on the spot. What could she ever say that would explain away the momentary panic she had felt? She leaned the pitchfork against the wall again.

"Oh, Cal, you're drenched! I—I'm so sorry! I—I don't know who I thought you were, but I couldn't see your face, and you just appeared out of the shadows, and—" She was babbling, she knew, and it wasn't helping anything.

"Livy, has someone been hanging around, bothering you? Why did you think you were in danger?" he asked, coming close enough to put his hands soothingly on her shoulders. She had a sudden sense that if he hadn't been dripping wet, he would have pulled her into his embrace.

And she would have let him.

"N-no, of course not," she said, trying to still the shaking that rippled through her in the aftermath of fear. "I can't tell you how sorry I am, Cal. Come on up to the house. You can wash up, and I'll find some old clothes of Dan's that'll fit you. I'll launder your clothes, of course..." She was babbling again as she pulled on his wet sleeve to lead him out of the barn.

"Livy, I don't give a damn about the clothes. I want to know who you thought I was," he insisted.

"Why, no one.... I guess you just startled me, appearing like that, and I couldn't see your face. Why, I cannot tell you how silly I feel!" she said with a little, self-deprecating laugh as she picked up the egg basket she had left by the door. "And now I've not only soaked your clothes, but lost a whole pailful of Rosie's milk!"

"Livy, stop. You don't have to play the belle for me," he said, pausing and facing her as they reached the yard.

Olivia looked up into the scarred but still-handsome face and realized that was true. She didn't have to act the empty-headed, vivacious, chattering belle. But neither could she tell him the truth.

They stopped at the pump and filled a bucket of water, then Livy showed him into the little room off the kitchen that had towels and a ewer and basin on a stand for washing.

"I'll just go and get those clothes of Dan's," she said, suddenly self-conscious as he started unbuttoning his shirt. He was no taller than Dan had been, yet somehow Cal filled a room in a way that Dan never had.

When she came down moments later with the clothes, Cal was just drying his face.

"Here's those clothes," she said as she stopped in the entranceway. "I think he was a bit stockier than you."

"Thanks, Livy," he said, turning around.

And then she realized he had removed his patch before washing his face.

He stood stock-still, watching her reaction.

Olivia had imagined this moment, feared this moment, but there was no hideous empty socket on the right side, just an eye that was milky gray.

She'd been holding her breath. Letting it out, she smiled deliberately and said, "Well, try them on, and if they won't do, I'll find something that will. I'll be out in the kitchen getting things ready for Jovita."

She heard him exhale, too. Evidently he'd been just as afraid to breathe as he awaited her reaction. He'd been fearful that she'd flinch in disgust. The realization wrenched her heart.

By the time Jovita came up the front walk, Cal was dressed in a pair of Dan's old osnaburg trousers and a well-worn, patched shirt and was preparing to take his leave.

"I'll bring those clothes down to the jail in the morning, when I've had a chance to press them," Livy promised, after telling her maid laughingly about how Cal's clothes came to get soaked in the first place.

"No," announced Jovita, putting her hands on her ample hips. "Señor Devleen, you do not leave yet. Leevy, the least you can do after to trying to drown poor Señor Devleen een meelk ees invite heem to share our supper," she insisted, a glint both challenging and pleading in her liquid eyes. "By the time we are done the clothes weel be dry."

Livy stopped in the act of holding the door open. "But…"

To her surprise, she found the thought of Cal eating supper with them not at all as distressing and unsuitable as she had thought at first. She rather liked the idea, in fact.

She turned to Cal. "Jovita's right, Cal. Giving you supper is the least I can do after what happened. And she's going to make her special enchiladas, which are really a treat. Please say you'll stay, if you think your deputy can handle things just a little longer?''

He hesitated in the doorway, his gaze searching her face as if he feared this invitation, too, was merely her "acting the belle." Apparently he was satisfied it wasn't, for he smiled.

"All right, ladies. If you're sure it's no extra trouble, I'd love some good enchiladas. Kristof wasn't expecting me back till after supper, anyway, and I could use a change from the hotel food." But the look in his eye told Livy it was more than just the change in his usual fare that appealed to him.

Chapter Seventeen

"Jovita, those were the best enchiladas I think I ever had."

The Mexican woman's black eyes shone. "Thank you, Señor Devleen," she said.

"And Leevy, that pie—if it was any better, it'd be against the law—even if I didn't have any milk to wash it down with," he teased, grinning down at her.

She gave him a rueful smile. "Cal, I promise, the next time I see you, I won't throw a bucket of milk at you."

The next time. That sounded encouraging. Had an evening of reminiscing about old times before the war persuaded her to relax her guard around him? Emboldened, he asked, "Why don't I stop by and pick you up tomorrow evening and we'll go to the Christmas pageant at the schoolhouse together, Livy?" he said, looking down into her smiling, relaxed face as he put his vest back on over the now-dry shirt.

She looked away and the smile faded, to be replaced by a guarded, wary look. "Um, I don't know if I'll be able to, Cal...I have so much to do...."

"Livy, you can't mean to miss the pageant! Davy

Richardson says he'll be the best Joseph that ever was.
I think he has a crush on Dorika Kristof, who's playing
Mary, and Ginny Petree's baby is going to be Baby
Jesus. Please say you'll come,'' he pleaded, daringly
taking her hand in his.

She stared at their clasped hands, but did nothing to
remove hers. "Well, perhaps. If I get everything caught
up... In any case, you don't have to stop by for me.
Perhaps I'll see you there.''

*But I want to stop by and pick you up. I want it to
look like I'm courting you,* he started to insist. Then he
intercepted a wink from Jovita. Better to ease into things
as long as Livy was skittish.

"I'll count on it,'' he said. He wanted to ask her to
follow him outside, so he could kiss her, but he sensed
she would bolt if he tried to go beyond the progress
he'd made tonight. But if she showed up at the pageant
tomorrow night, and if he could get her to sit with him,
perhaps he could get her to attend the social hour that
would follow, with cookies and punch being served
while the pint-sized Wise Men, shepherds and Holy
Family ran around underfoot in a frenzy of Christmas
Eve excitement. And maybe there would be some mistletoe somewhere.... A lady couldn't blame a man for
putting mistletoe to good use, could she?

It *had* been fun talking about old times, he thought
as he strode back into town, grinning as he remembered
Livy telling Jovita about the time she and a handful of
young friends from the Bryan Young Ladies Academy
had hidden behind the bushes at the place where all the
boys went swimming in the Brazos. Once Cal, Garrick,
Sam and Livy's brothers, as well as a goodly portion
of the rest of the boys of Bryan, were all frolicking
naked in the river, she and her accomplices had run out

of the bushes, giggling and squealing as they snatched up the clothes and ran. He'd been the only one bold enough to go running out of the water in a vain attempt to retrieve his clothes before the girls escaped.

Getting the clothes back had required some delicate negotiations behind the scenes—and some hasty explanations when Livy's father had discovered what was going on.

Once he'd gone away to seminary and returned as the rector of the Bryan Episcopal Church, he'd been expected to put such frivolous behavior behind him, of course. But tonight he'd seen that Livy hadn't forgotten a time when their hearts had been so much more carefree.

The one-room schoolhouse was filled to capacity when Cal arrived. The walls were decorated with pine boughs festooned with strings of popcorn. Gilded pinecones interspersed with paper snowflakes hung from the ceiling. Up front where the schoolmarm's desk normally sat, Phoebe Stone was already leading the costumed children in a carol.

That was one problem solved, he thought, eyeing Phoebe's back as she energetically directed the children's off-key rendition of "Oh Come All Ye Faithful." If the widowed milliner was already occupied with the children's chorus, it would be easier to evade her and go sit with Livy.

Except Livy wasn't there. Cal scanned the rows of benches, occupied by the proud parents of Gillespie Springs. Robert Gillespie, he noted, sat up front in the schoolteacher's chair, as if it were a throne. Next to him sat Doc Broughton, who turned around to eye Cal as if he'd never seen him before.

Cal nodded, and the old sawbones nodded back, then turned to whisper something to Gillespie. Cal started looking around again to make sure he hadn't missed Livy, but he could feel the banker staring at him.

No, he'd not been mistaken; Livy wasn't there. Disappointed, but still hopeful she would steal in late, he joined the throng of men standing at the back of the schoolroom while the choir dissolved and Miss Pringle, the horse-faced, middle-aged schoolmarm, bustled importantly up to the front to begin directing the pageant.

"Your Dorika makes a right pretty Mary," Cal observed to Lazlo Kristof. His deputy was standing just in back of his wife, who was sitting in one of the last seats in the back row.

The Hungarian smiled proudly as he translated Cal's comment for his wife, who beamed when he had finished.

"I thank you. She's a beautiful girl, yes?" Kristof said, nodding toward his daughter, who was dressed in the traditional blue robe and a white "veil" that looked suspiciously like her mother's best tablecloth. Dorika sat on stage, serenely rocking the sleeping Petree baby as the shepherds led in bleating sheep and Davy, as Joseph, forced a braying burro up the middle aisle.

Cal was touched to see that Kristof was wearing his deputy's badge, incongruously pinned on the front of an embroidered vest he must have brought from the old country. Kristof wasn't even on duty, but he was obviously proud of his new status and wanted to show that he was ready even here.

"Your children all excited about Santa Claus, Lazlo?" Cal inquired, mostly to keep himself from searching the room in vain for Livy again.

"Ah, but they have already put out their shoes for

presents from Father Christmas," Kristof informed him. "In Hungary we do this on the sixth of December. Next year we will have to think about celebrating like Americans, yes?"

Cal was about to disagree, to say that bringing customs from the old country made American celebrations richer, but before he could, Phoebe Stone materialized at his side.

His heart sank. He'd successfully avoided any further invitations from her, and he still didn't want to encourage the lady to think he would ever court her, but he was running out of polite regrets. If she invited him for Christmas dinner, though, he already had a built-in excuse. He was expected at home tomorrow—assuming no one kicked up any fuss around town between now and then.

But her first words disabused him of the notion that she wanted to invite him anywhere, at least this time.

"Sheriff, you've got to be Santa Claus," she informed him, a desperate expression dominating her pinched features.

"I beg your pardon, Miz Stone?"

"I said you've got to be Santa Claus. Please? I had the mayor all lined up to do it, and his wife just sent me a message he's down with the grippe. Oh, please, Sheriff?" she entreated, clutching his arm.

"Miz Phoebe, I'm sure there are lots of fellows here who'd make a better Santa Claus than me," he protested. "Besides, who ever heard of a Santa Claus with an eye patch?"

"But all the other men here are the children's fathers, except for Hank Whyte over there, and he's too big for the costume," she told him, still clutching his arm.

"But they'll know who I am by this patch," he argued. "They won't think I'm Santa Claus."

Phoebe Stone's jaw set. "Sheriff, right now all that matters is that we have no one to wear the costume and yell 'Ho, ho, ho.' It doesn't matter that they'll know you're really the sheriff. Come on, now, you have to get into your costume while the Christmas story is being acted out!" she said, treating his acceptance as a fait accompli.

He was so relieved it wasn't a *personal* invitation that he gave in gracefully. "All right, but I'm gonna feel mighty silly if I have to go do some sheriffing in a Santa Claus suit," he said, meekly following Phoebe Stone to the cloakroom.

"*Feliz Navidad,* Jovita," Olivia said as the housekeeper gathered up her packages and the carpetbag in which her night things were packed. "Have a lovely Christmas with your family."

Jovita, who was going to her son and daughter-in-law's house on North Street, grinned from ear to ear as she always did whenever her employer used any Spanish.

"*Gracias,* Leevy. I am sure they weel enjoy the fudge you make. Merry Christmas to you. Now, should you not go on down to the schoolhouse? You weel meess all the pageant!"

Livy smiled in spite of herself. "Yes, I know I'm running late. I just want to make sure everything's in order for the supper...."

The stout woman held up a peremptory hand. "Everything ees perfectly ready. Would I leave you eef eet were not? All you must do ees warm up the roast chicken and rice een the oven, and have Señor Devleen uncork the wine. Leevy, eet makes my heart glad that you weel be brave and ask Señor Devleen to have a Christmas Eve supper weeth you.'' She winked, and added with a mischievous twinkle of her dark eyes, ''Maybe you weel even have breakfast together, yes?''

Olivia blushed and held her hands up. ''Now, slow down, Jovita! Just because I'm asking him to supper doesn't mean he'll still be here for breakfast! I hope he's not going to make that assumption, either! And how do I know he'll even want to come to supper here with me?'' She knew she was dithering, but somehow she couldn't seem to stop.

''Calm yourself, Leevy,'' Jovita said, catching Olivia's hands, which were twisting together. ''Do not be nervous. The *señor,* he weel come eef you ask. He weel stay only as long as he ees welcome. But not eef you do not get there unteel the pageant ees over and everyone has gone home to sleep. Now *andale, rapido!*''

Livy found herself laughing at her housekeeper's good-natured nagging. ''All right, all right!'' she cried, raising her hands again, this time in surrender. ''I promise I'll be out the door just as soon as I see you off and go upstairs and find my jet earrings. Hmm, this is strange,'' she commented, as they reached the back door and found it ajar. ''Jovita, you didn't leave it open, did you?''

The Mexican woman shook her head. ''Perhaps the weend blows eet open?''

Olivia shrugged. It *had* been windy. ''No matter, I'll just shut it after you.''

''And lock eet, before you leave the house and after, Leevy. I do not like the look of the hombres who have come to town.''

''All *right,*'' Livy insisted, chuckling with mock exasperation. "Now *andale* yourself. You're going to be late to hug your grandbabies! They'll break the piñata without you!"

Finally Jovita was gone, and Olivia hurried up the stairs to find her earbobs. She knew she had spent too long debating with herself in the hip bath about tonight, about whether she was doing the right thing to invite Cal to have a midnight Christmas feast with her.

After the supper they had shared the other night, she knew she wanted to begin again with him, to try to recapture the love they had lost in the turmoil of the war. But perhaps, she planned to suggest to Cal, it was best if they began their courtship discreetly. Only a few months had passed since her husband's tragic death, and though she had recently won some acceptance in town by saving the Petree boy's life, she still didn't think it wise to risk offending the townspeople's sensibilities all over again. Once she and Cal were together at the pageant, she hoped to communicate her invitation to supper without anyone else overhearing.

However innocent she planned the supper to be, they would have to leave separately, she ahead of him, so that no one would guess they had a rendezvous planned at her house. The thought made her chuckle. How delightfully naughty it all sounded!

And once he was here, and they were enjoying supper, if he mentioned a desire to see more of her, she could voice her feeling that the courtship needed to be discreet, at least until a little more time had passed.

But if he came here for a secret supper, might he not think she was inviting him to remain for breakfast, as Jovita had put it? And if Livy were honest with herself, wasn't there a part of her that secretly wanted him to stay, to woo her as she knew he could until neither of them wanted him to leave?

No, Olivia argued with herself as she climbed the stairs. She wanted their courtship to be slow and steady, so that they could build a relationship that would *last*. She didn't want him to think she was exactly the kind of woman she'd been denying she was ever since he'd come back into her life.

A sudden thought struck her, and Olivia stopped still, midway up the stairs. If even a part of her was tempted to make love with Cal, didn't that mean she had begun to conquer the terror that had been so much a part of her life ever since the attack? She smiled. If nothing else went right tonight, she would have at least won that victory.

In any case, she needed to stop worrying so far into the future and just concentrate on getting to the schoolhouse.

She reached the top of the stairs and pushed the door open. Yes, there were the jet earbobs, lying right on her dresser where she'd laid them before getting into her bath. And there was the long-fringed, black, twilled-silk shawl on the bed, too.

For a moment Olivia eyed the dark shawl with dismay. She was so tired of dressing in black! And all for a husband who had seemed to resent her as much as he resented life itself in the last few years....

Suddenly a shape, cast onto the wall by the candlestick she carried, emerged from behind the door and loomed up behind her.

Olivia whirled, a scream on her lips. It was cut off by the blow to her head that drove the light from her eyes with the swiftness of lightning. The candle guttered out on the floor beside her. The single, horrified thought she had time to formulate before all consciousness fled was that it was going to happen again, and she could do nothing to stop it.

"Didja get her, Grady? Took ya long enough," said one of the three men waiting out under the trees at the side of the house.

"Yeah," another chimed in. "We figgered you was in there so long, you probably had a poke at her fer yer trouble. Only thing we ain't figgered is whether ya poked her before ya knocked her out or not," he jeered, and the other two snickered.

"Real funny, Ike," the fourth man, who had just emerged from the back, retorted. "Naw, I didn't poke her, though it woulda been right pleasant to have that purty bitch thrashing around under me. But I thought them women'd never stop jawin' about what they was gonna do tonight. It seems Miz Gillespie made arrangements for a late supper with her fancy man," Grady announced. "Guess he'll hafta make other plans, won't he?" he added with a snigger. "Anyway, I had to wait for that Mex woman to leave before I knocked Miz Gillespie over the head, didn't I?"

"Not as far as I'm concerned, ya didn't. What's one less Mex in this world?"

"It woulda taken two of us in the house t'be shore of overpowerin' both of them women without takin' the chance that either of 'em might escape and bring the law down on us. I didn't hear *you* volunteerin' to go in!" the other retorted.

"Aw, you sissy britches! We'd a' taken care of any woman who made it out the door!"

The gibes were ignored as the leader of the group, Leroy Scruggs, went to the front yard and looked up and down the dark road, then came back. "I don't see no one. All right, stop argufyin'—let's get in there an' make this look like an accident."

The four men strode around the house in the darkness and let themselves in the back door. After stopping to light a lamp one of them spied on the table, they stomped up the stairs to the bedroom.

They stared down at the crumpled figure on the floor for a long moment.

"Gawd almighty, she is one purty woman," one of them said. "I cain't think why that bastard wants her dead."

"He ain't paying ya t'think," Scruggs reminded him curtly. "Now let's git on with this, an' then we kin go have a drink t'celebrate."

"The Last Chance is closed tonight," one of the others said. "I seen the sign on the door as we rode past."

"Shee-it, you cain't read, churnhead."

"I reckon I kin read Closed right enough, Scruggs," the man protested. "But simmer down, I happen to have a bottle stashed in my saddlebags."

"Waal, Ike, ya ain't as stupid as ya look," Scruggs said approvingly. "Now you pick up her head, and Fred, you take her feet, and carry her downstairs. Lay her down jest at the foot, so's it looks like she fell, accidental-like."

The two bent to do his bidding, and Scruggs and Grady preceded them down the stairs.

Scruggs watched as they arranged her limp body as he'd instructed, her legs still touching the stairs.

"Now, I'm gonna lay this candlestick she was carryin' right by her hand, but so it's touchin' this here rug, see?" Scruggs said. "That way it'll look like when she fell, her candle hit the rug and set it afire. The candlestick's metal, so it won't burn, and they'll find it here layin' on its side, right by what's left a' her.''

"But what if the rug don't burn? What if it just smolders and goes out?"

"You know what, Fred? You'd have to study up t'be a half-wit," Scruggs snapped. "We ain't gonna leave jest that one little fire—we're gonna light it in several places," he said, lighting the candle Olivia had held from the lantern and touching it to the kitchen curtains, setting them ablaze. Then he went to the parlor and let some of the oil spill out on the horsehair sofa. Touching the candle flame to it, he set it afire, too. He watched with a smug grin as a parlor curtain caught fire from the couch and went up in a quick flash that sent sparks shooting across the floor.

"The fire'll get goin' good here directly, but it'll look natural, like it all spread from Miz Gillespie droppin' her candle. Now let's get outa here," he said, gesturing toward the back door.

"Let's go tell the boss the job is as good as done and collect our money," one of them suggested as they reached the road again.

Scruggs snorted. "There ain't no use bein' in such an all-fired hurry. I been workin' fer him a mite longer'n you boys, an' I kin tell ya he ain't gonna pay us till the house is burnt to the ground an' they find the woman dead!"

"So should we stay here fer a spell an' make sure the house goes up?" one of them asked.

"Thet house'll burn jest fine," Scruggs snarled. "What's the matter, ain't you never seen a fire before?"

"Naw, it ain't that. I jest reckon we ought t'stay till there ain't no chance that woman is gonna wake up and escape," the other said. "If she does, we'd be right here to bash her over the head again and carry her back inside.''

"And be right here when the town comes investigatin'? Why don't ya jest put yer head in the noose an' be done with it?" Scruggs retorted. "If she wakes up at all it'll be too late."

Chapter Eighteen

Olivia awoke coughing, her head lower than her feet. The spasms made her head hurt so ferociously she was tempted to allow the black velvet curtain to cover her again, but when she tried to breathe, the choking foulness filled her lungs once more. The air was thick and hot....

Where was she? Her legs seemed to be resting on steps. Slowly, fighting the blinding pain, she crawled away from the steps so that her legs rested on the floor, too. She reached out with one hand and felt the smoothness of a puncheon floor beneath her. Was she still in her own house? It felt like the kitchen floor....

Instinctively, she tried to rise, but found the air even fouler off the floor, and the effort made her so dizzy that she was forced to sink back down. *If I could just open my eyes,* she thought, and then realized that they *were* open, and she was staring into darkness. Yet it was not an absolute darkness. Here and there the inky blackness was pierced by writhing, crackling, orange-red flashes of color—*flames!*

Even as her brain registered the horrifying sight, a spark fell on her cheek, stinging her, and she slapped it away with her hand. There was a sudden, illuminating flare of flame as her apron, hanging on a hook on the wall, caught fire, and Olivia realized that she was indeed in her own house. *And it was on fire*.

She had to get out.... It was just a few feet to the back door, which, if she had calculated properly, ought to be just a little over to the right.... She could crawl to it if she had to.

On her hands and knees, she turned in that direction, but ran smack into a wall. Aware of the panic rising within her, Olivia desperately felt ahead of her with her hand, but all she encountered was the solid barrier of the wall. The door had moved!

But no, that was silly—the door hadn't moved, she was just disoriented in the smoke. She had to calm down and get her bearings. If the stair was behind her, the door had to be just about there...but it wasn't, and the smoke was getting thicker...!

All right then, she'd escape out the front door, though she'd have farther to crawl. And crawl she must, even if her head had been clear enough to permit her to stand, for the only relatively clear air was found just a couple of inches off the floor.

But when she made it to the doorway that led from the kitchen into the dining room and parlor, she gasped. The dining room was a mass of flames, effectively blocking her from reaching the front door. The only way she could go was up the stairs, and Olivia was by no means sure she could find them again in the smothering, flame-lit blackness. And what if the upper floor was on fire, too?

A spark fell on her skirt and flared into a tiny flame. With a shriek of fear, she beat it out. She was going to have to do something fast or her clothes would catch on fire, long before the smoke could smother her to death.

The thought nearly made her hysterical, but panic would not help. She forced herself to be calm, though it was nearly impossible in the heated, thinning air on the floor. No, by God, she was not going to burn to death! She'd make her way to a window and get out onto the slanting tin roof. It might mean a broken bone or two if she lost her balance and fell, but even a broken neck was better than burning to death—at least it would be quick!

Cal! she screamed silently. Doubtless right now he was at the Christmas celebration, perhaps wondering what had happened to her. Did he think she'd merely changed her mind about attending, that she had gotten nervous about sitting with him in front of the entire population of Gillespie Springs? *Cal, I didn't change my mind! I was coming to you!* she cried inwardly. She imagined him finding her charred body in the ruins of her home. Oh, God, she had to get out!

Reversing direction, she crawled along the floor, praying she'd find the stairs the first time. As hard as it was to breathe, she might not get another opportunity.

There! She'd reached the stairs. But the effort had cost her, and she coughed, thick mucus in her throat strangling her. She had to pull herself up the stairs, had to reach the top and find the window....

Help me, God! She wasn't sure if she'd cried it aloud or if the prayer was echoing in her brain. *Surely, if you made me realize that I still love Cal, that I need to see if he could still love me, too, you don't want me to die like this before I even have the chance to try!*

There was no answer but the roar of the flames below her as she crawled upward, step by step.

Gillespie, she thought. He was behind this. She'd caught a quick glimpse of a bearded, unknown face before the darkness had closed over her—enough to know that her assailant wasn't her former brother-in-law. But he'd hired whoever had knocked her unconscious and set the fire. Who else hated her so much he would want to burn her house down—with her in it?

She'd reached the top of the stairs, but so had the smoke. It was even harder to breathe up here. Beneath her questing hands, the floor was getting hot. How long before the fire broke through the ceiling and turned the second floor into an inferno, too?

She found it was already too late to get into her bedroom—the floor was a sea of undulating flames. She would have to make it out through the spare bedroom, then, the one Jovita had been sleeping in. Once, she had hoped it would be her children's bedroom, her children and Dan's....

The room hadn't been used since Dan had gone away to war, and the window had become balky with disuse. Jovita had claimed she didn't care, that she didn't like the night air on her anyway, and Olivia had planned that they'd both sleep on the back porch during the worst of the summer's ovenlike heat.

She wrenched at the window, feeling the throbbing in her head intensify from the effort. The sash didn't budge. Behind her, below her, the flames crackled ever closer.

She was going to have to break the glass. Frantically, Olivia felt around her for something heavy enough, but encountered only the bed frame and a discarded nightdress. She couldn't breathe....

Snatching Jovita's nightdress from the bed, Livy wrapped it around her hand and, closing her eyes, struck repeatedly at the window, sending shards of glass rattling down the corrugated tin roof and into the yard below.

For a moment Olivia just knelt at the window, taking great gulps of the chill, fresh night air. But the draft also refreshed the hungry fire behind her, and it roared anew. The flames had reached the top of the stairs now, and beneath her the floor was getting too hot to touch. She had to get out *now*, if she were going to survive.

Careful to avoid the protruding spears of glass remaining in the window frame, Olivia raised a leg over the ledge and gingerly stretched it out to the slanting tin roof that overhung the back porch. The roof would be hot, but if she covered her legs with her skirt and scooted quickly down to the bottom, it wouldn't be much more than an ankle-wrenching jump to the ground....

The throbbing in her head was reaching a crescendo, accompanied by the dizziness she had been fighting all the way up the stairs. *Just a little farther,* she pleaded. *Just let me reach the ground....*

Suddenly the roof slanted crazily as the outside wall it was fastened to collapsed. There was no way she could hold on. Screaming, she felt herself falling....

Dressed in the white-trimmed, red suit with a scratchy, fake white beard stuck with spirit gum to his chin, Cal came out of the cloakroom dragging a toy-filled bag and bellowing, "Ho, ho, ho! Merry Christmas, boys and girls!"

The presents had been provided by the parents, in most cases, though Phoebe had informed him with a virtuous sniff that the Baptist church had purchased some for the poorer children who lived on North Street.

Cal had to admit it was fun handing out dolls, hoops, balls, oranges and net bags of penny candy. The children all recognized Cal, but they didn't seem to care that Santa was obviously Sheriff Devlin, and they lisped polite thank-yous to him as they accepted their gifts.

There were presents in his pack for the adults, too, and Cal found himself grinning as he watched ladies opening brown-paper-wrapped packages that turned out to hold such prizes as fascinators and manicure kits, while men, uncomfortable in their stiff celluloid collars and cuffs, grinned over gifts of shaving mugs and mustache cups. All the enmity he had felt after his past as a Yankee soldier had been announced seemed to have vanished in the flood of Christmas goodwill that pervaded the room.

His pack was now empty, and there had been no gift for Robert Gillespie, of course, even from his browbeaten bank employees. Cal felt a momentary twinge of pity for the man.

Gillespie seemed not to notice, though, sitting importantly in his chair as if he were a king, making desultory conversation with those of his subjects he deemed worthy of his attention. Cal wondered why the man had come. Perhaps the banker was afraid he'd be talked about at any gathering he didn't attend, Cal thought, then dismissed the idea as uncharitable.

"Santa—I mean, Sheriff, this is for you, from my family," a voice said, and he looked down to see Dorika Kristof, still in her Virgin Mary robes, standing shyly in front of him.

He unfastened the string that bound the small, paper-wrapped package to find a comb that had been carved out of pecan wood, with the words *Sheriff Caleb Devlin* and a star engraved in exquisite detail above the teeth.

"Why, thank you, Dorika," he said, touched, and he smiled at the entire Kristof family, who were grinning proudly nearby.

After their gift he received others—a bone-handled razor from Mayor and Mrs. Long, an embroidered bookmark for his Bible from Mrs. Whyte, and a wrapped package that looked suspiciously like a bottle of whiskey—"a little somethin' to help you *really* celebrate, Sheriff," Hank Whyte said with a wink.

In addition, Martha Long invited him to dinner on New Year's Day. "And feel free to bring a lady if you're of a mind," the mayor's wife added graciously.

Her remark only served to remind him that Livy had not come tonight. Suddenly lonely in the midst of the celebrating throng, he said his goodbyes to the townspeople who had been so kind and to all the children who hadn't yet finished talking to "Santa," and went to the cloakroom to transform himself back into plain old Cal Devlin, Sheriff, again.

Someone *had* hung some mistletoe over the schoolhouse door, he saw as he emerged minutes later. Already Davy Richardson, still dressed as Joseph, was trying to maneuver Dorika underneath it. Dorika was blushing prettily and trying to pretend she didn't understand, but Cal guessed Davy would enjoy success before Christmas Eve was over.

Remembering the first time he'd ever kissed Olivia Childress under the mistletoe, Cal went around the flirting youngsters and opened the door into the night.

Why hadn't Livy come? Had she suddenly become afraid of the prospect of getting closer to him, after the congenial supper they'd shared with Jovita? By thunder, he was going to walk down to her house and have it out with her! Maybe he could make her see that he'd go as slowly as she wished, but he wasn't going to take no for an answer.

He wasn't going to take any nonsense about how busy she was as a reason for her not coming tonight, either. He couldn't think of anything that would keep her so occupied that she could not have attended, since she was virtually alone in the world. Damn it, he was going to force her to admit her fears about their getting close again, and he'd never let her forget that what they once had, they could recapture again!

"Where's he goin' in such an all-fired hurry?" Broughton asked, poking the banker and pointing at Devlin, who was going out the door.

Robert Gillespie suppressed the sharp reprimand he wanted to snap out after the old doctor's elbow dug into his side. It wouldn't do to alienate the old fool.

"Probably off to sniff at my former sister-in-law's skirts," he sneered.

Broughton sniggered knowingly. "She's still a hot piece, eh? Even after your late brother killed the Mexican she'd been fornicatin' with! Some women never learn, do they?"

Gillespie gave him a sidelong glance. Perhaps Broughton would assist him if tonight's plan somehow failed to achieve his goal? But no, the plan would go through without a hitch—and it was always better not to involve men of his own social class. One couldn't just pay them off, knowing they would move on to other towns and other easy money, as would the handful of drifters he was currently employing.

"Yes, I'm quite sure the Widow Gillespie would lay down for almost any man," Gillespie said. "She never appealed to me, of course. I tried to talk my fool brother out of marrying her, you know. Told him she had a wandering eye. He wouldn't listen, though. He had to have Olivia Childress, the belle of Brazos County.''

Broughton *tsk-tsked* and went to get some punch. Gillespie knew he'd surreptitiously add some whiskey to it from the flask he carried in the inside pocket of his frock coat.

Devlin was going to be in for quite a shock when he reached Olivia's place, Gillespie thought with inner satisfaction. He wished he could be there when the sheriff found Olivia's body amid the ruins of the house she had once shared with his brother.

No matter, the banker told himself. How sweet it would be to witness Devlin's fresh grief. Soon his men would rid the town of Devlin, too—it would be sweeter still to collect the money he would receive from the sale of the critical tract of land that would bring the railroad to Gillespie Springs. The trustees of the Houston and Texas Central Railroad would view him as an important, influential man—perhaps they'd even invite him to join the board. Before long he would be its president, and from there might move into politics. He could see himself as a senator, or perhaps the governor of Texas!

But for the immediate future, he was going to be happy to be even richer than he was presently.

The night air was smoky as Cal strode past the general store. Was someone celebrating Christmas with a bonfire? Or was someone on North Street burning trash—on Christmas Eve, of all nights? He'd better check it out. Drifters had been settling in Gillespie Springs like flies on a picnic lunch lately, and he wouldn't put it past them to be frustrated that the Last Chance was closed tonight and get up to mischief.

All of a sudden a figure came running toward him out of the darkness at the end of the street, shouting like a demented creature, his hand raised to hold his ragged old Confederate forage cap on his head. His coat flew out behind him like the wings of some giant bat.

Cal waved in greeting as Georgie skidded to a halt in front of him and struggled to catch his breath.

"Georgie! So there you are! You missed seeing me being Santa Claus at the pageant!"

But then he saw that Georgie's face was fish-belly white, his eyes bulging with horror. Cal reached out a steadying hand. "What's wrong, Georgie? You look upset."

"Sh-Sh-Sheriff! M-Miz Gillespie's house—it's on fire!"

His words were too unbelievable, like something out of a bad dream. "What do you mean, on fire? It can't be!"

"It's burning down, Sheriff! You gotta come!"

Chapter Nineteen

Cal was already starting to run. "Georgie, where's Olivia Gillespie? Is she inside?" he demanded.

Georgie's eyes were full of tears. "I d-dunno!" He panted. "I—I din' see n-nobody! But the house is *all* on fire, Sheriff! Hurry!"

"Georgie, run back to the schoolhouse!" Cal shouted. "That's where everyone is! Tell them what you've told me, and tell them to come help!"

"But I wanna help *you*, Sh-Sheriff!"

"*Go!*" Cal ordered. "I'll go see if I can get her out, Georgie, but the best way you can help me *and* her is to get the volunteer fire brigade going! They'll be able to get water from the spring across the street!"

"They—they won't listen to *me*, Sheriff!" Georgie cried fearfully, but Cal was already sprinting down the road toward Olivia's house.

"Livy! Oh, God, Livy!"

Even from a distance, Cal had seen that it was already too late for anyone who had been inside Olivia Gillespie's house, but he kept running anyway, crying her name. Now he stood outside the picket fence that ran around the front yard, trying to catch his breath, staring through a tear-flooded eye at the inferno that had been the home of the woman he loved.

Both upper and lower floors were fully engulfed in flames and wreathed with smoke. *Lord, you better have let the smoke kill her before the flames did, or I swear by all that's holy you and I are no longer friends.*

What could have caused such a terrible conflagration? Had Livy been careless with an oil lamp? Had a spark escaped the stove while she was upstairs and, unnoticed, developed into a raging fire that trapped her there? But why wouldn't she have used an upstairs window to escape? Had there been some sort of explosion, so that she couldn't get out?

In the distance, he heard the frantic tolling of the church bell, the signal that summoned the members of the volunteer fire brigade. Someone ought to go and tell them not to bother, he thought dully, swiping at his good eye with the back of a knuckle. It was too late to save Livy, and her house was already a lost cause. He wondered if Jovita Mendez was lying dead among the ruins, too.

He walked a little to the side and saw that the barn was still intact. By some miracle, could Livy have been in the barn? *Please, God!*

Cal ran around one side of the burning house and through the backyard to throw open the barn door. Chickens, clucking in alarm, flapped past his head as he ran inside. He could hear Rosie mooing and stamping.

"Livy!" he shouted as he ran through the barn, trying to pierce the shadows within. If she was here, he had to find her and get her out. If the wind carried a spark to the barn roof, it might very well go up in flames, too, he knew.

But the only living creature he found was Rosie. Livy was not here.

At least he could let the cow out into the back pasture in case the barn did catch fire, he thought, and did so.

He could hear the fire wagon clanging down the street in the distance as he started around the other side of the house, and the shouts of the townspeople as they ran behind it, buckets in hand. He ought to go and tell them there was no use running....

He was so intent on that thought that he almost stepped on the crumpled figure lying prone among the clumps of dead grass, just beyond what was left of the tin roof over the back porch.

"What the—*Livy!*" he shouted, falling to his knees as he recognized the tangled mass of black hair.

There was a warning shudder in the wall of the burning house next to her, and suddenly he was scrambling to his feet again, pulling Livy's inert body by the shoulders. Mere heartbeats later, the wall collapsed, sending up a shower of sparks, with flaming timbers landing where Livy had just been.

Cal still didn't know if she was dead or alive, though, and he sank to his knees again beside her, gingerly turning her over and staring at the pale, still face. "Livy?" he begged.

The pulse that fluttered beneath the trembling fingers he pressed to her wrist was ever so faint, but it was there. "Thank you, Lord," Cal whispered, the wetness running down his cheeks as he gazed through his tears at his soot-smudged, unconscious Olivia. He could see charred spots and holes where sparks had landed on her clothes and a small, angry red stripe where her cheek

had been burned, but other than that she appeared unscathed. Had she struck her head when she'd jumped?

"Livy?" he murmured, praying she'd respond. He
shook her ever so slightly. "Livy?"

She went into a spasm of coughing that seemed to
rack her whole body, and suddenly she was fighting
him, striking out at him and struggling to sit up, all with
her eyes still squeezed shut.

"Livy! It's me, Cal. You're all right, you're safe.
Stop fighting me, honey. Open your eyes and tell me
you're all right!" he cried, as he strove to keep her from
hurting herself any worse.

Her eyes flickered open. She stared at him uncom-
prehendingly for a moment. "C-Cal? Wh-what..."

"It's all right, honey," he said, gathering her into his
arms and bending to kiss her soot-streaked forehead.
"You're safe, Livy. You got out of the fire and I'm not
going to let anything more happen to you...."

Her eyelids drifted shut again and she sagged against
him, unconscious once more.

Shouting voices and whinnying horses announced the
arrival of the fire wagon and the Gillespie Springs volunteers. James Long was the first to reach his side.
"Cal, what on earth happened? Good Lord, is she—is
she dead?"

Georgie came shambling up just then, panting and
out of breath. "I told 'em, Sheriff! I did just what you
said! And they believed me!"

"Thank you, Georgie, you did good," Cal told the
retarded man, and then turned back to Long. "No, she's
just fainted, I think, thank God." Cal laid Olivia gently
back down. "I think she must have jumped from the
roof there. Looks like it may have collapsed under her.
As to the house, I don't have any idea what happened.

It was completely engulfed when I got here. I—I've no idea if Señora Mendez was inside at the time, too...."

From somewhere in the crowd a blanket was produced and laid over Olivia. Long began to call out orders to get a line formed to bring up buckets of water from the spring across the road. He appointed Davy Richardson—still wearing his Joseph robes—to keep an eye on the barn, and directed some of the women to go with his wife to their home to get coffee and a hot meal started for the volunteers, who would need them once the fire was under control.

"Cal, we can handle this," Long announced. "There isn't much we can do but try to keep the fire from spreading to the barn. Why don't you get Mrs. Gillespie to shelter? She's had a nasty shock. Take her to the hotel and put her in the suite—at my expense, of course."

"Much obliged, Mayor—"

Just then he heard a shriek, and a flood of hysterical-sounding Spanish. *"Señora Oleevia! Ay di mi! Oh, mi pobre amiga!"* Jovita cried as she ran to them.

"Jovita! She's going to be all right," Cal reassured her quickly. "Thank God you're safe, too. I didn't know if you were in there," he added, jerking his head in the direction of the burning pile.

"Gracias à Dios! No, I went to my son's house just an hour or so past! She was fine, she was geetting ready to go to the pageant! How could thees have happened?"

Cal shrugged, feeling helpless. "I don't know. Perhaps she dropped a lamp? A spark from the stove?"

"I have never known Señora Leevy to be careless," Jovita said decisively. "Perhaps she can tell us when she wakes. But let me go to the hotel weeth you. I weel care for her. Ah, the poor *señora!* What weel she say when she learns her home ees gone?''

''Sheriff, you can use our buckboard,'' Long said.

''I'll help ya lift her, Sheriff!'' Georgie offered eagerly as Cal bent to scoop Livy up in his arms.

''Thanks, Georgie, but I think I can manage,'' he said. ''I wish you'd see if you could find Doc Broughton, though. He probably ought to have a look—''

''Just one minute, Sheriff,'' said a voice Cal had begun to detest. ''I think we're overlooking a very obvious cause to this mysterious fire here.''

Cal straightened. ''Oh, and what would that be, Mr. Gillespie?'' he asked, eyeing the banker.

Gillespie, his face lurid in the reflected glow of the flames, obviously hadn't run to the fire scene with the rest of the townspeople. He was breathing easily, his hands folded around his lapels. Broughton stood beside him.

''Not what, but *who* would be more correct, in my estimation, Sheriff.'' He nodded grimly at Georgie. ''This fire apparently got started while all the decent townsfolk were at the Christmas pageant,'' he said. ''Everyone was there—everyone but the town idiot, in fact.''

Cal heard the murmurs begin among those townspeople who weren't part of the bucket brigade. He saw the fingers begin to point at Georgie. Cal would have to talk fast or Gillespie would have a few men whipped up into a lynch mob.

''What're you tryin' to say, Gillespie?'' Cal asked, allowing the distaste to show in his voice. ''That *Georgie* started the fire? Why would he do that?''

Georgie, who had been lingering nearby, cried out in horror, ''I didn't do it, Sheriff! I *didn't!*''

Gillespie made his shrug an elaborate gesture. "Perhaps simply to see what a burning house looked like—who knows what goes on in his simple brain, Sheriff?"

"That's ridiculous, Gillespie. Georgie's harmless as a shadow, and you know it."

Gillespie gave a derisive snort. "I know no such thing. All I know is he is the only inhabitant of this town who wasn't at the pageant this evening. I say he was the one who started the fire, and you should charge him and hold him, at least until Livy Gillespie can be questioned as to the events leading up to the fire."

Georgie was practically gibbering with distress. "I didn't do it, Sheriff, I *didn't*, I *swear* I didn't!"

Cal felt his temper flaring like the nearby flames. He wanted to get Livy to shelter, and yet he was having to argue with the pompous, scapegoat-seeking bastard standing in front of him.

"I know you didn't, Georgie," he said, putting a reassuring arm on the trembling man's shoulder. "I can't charge a fellow with no more evidence than that," he informed Gillespie, "and I won't. And as for Georgie bein' the only resident not at the pageant for all the town to see, you're forgetting about those saddle tramps that have taken up residence in Gillespie Springs of late. I didn't see a one of them sittin' in the schoolhouse tonight."

He'd made a telling point. Cal could hear the murmurs beginning again, but now they were about the drifters.

"Very well, Sheriff, if you won't do your job—"

"I *am* doing my job!" Cal snapped. "But I won't put Georgie in jail without any evidence, is that clear?" He made sure he was looking the banker right in the eye when he added, "And when Mrs. Gillespie comes

to, you'd better hope she doesn't mention seeing those
two drifters—the ones I saw *you* with the other day—
anywhere around her house tonight.''

Even in the firelit darkness Cal could see Robert Gillespie pale. "I—I don't know what you're talking
about, Devlin," he sputtered. "That's nonsense! What
would I have in common with two ruffians?"

"That's just what I was wondering," Cal replied, satisfied that Long and several others were staring specu-
latively at the banker. "Now, if you don't have any
more damn fool ideas to spout, get out of my way."

Their gazes dueled for a long moment, but Gillespie
was the first to look away. Cal heard him mutter something under his breath, something that sounded vaguely
threatening, but he ignored it, for he wasn't willing to
spend any more time dealing with blowhards.

"Doc Broughton, please follow us to the hotel and
have a look at Mrs. Gillespie once we get her settled in
a room," Cal said. "I want to be sure we're not missin'
some injury."

After exchanging a look with Gillespie, Broughton
said, "I'll meet you there, Sheriff. Just let me go and
fetch my bag."

"Davy," Cal added, spying the boy in the crowd,
"I'd be obliged if you'd see to feeding Miss Olivia's
livestock for a day or two, all right?"

"Sure, Sheriff!"

Cal scooped up the still-unconscious Livy in his arms
and motioned for Georgie to follow him. Jovita brought
up the rear, alternately clucking and muttering prayers
in Spanish, and together Cal and Georgie gently lifted
Livy into the wagon bed. Jovita scrambled up onto the
wagon to ride beside her mistress.

Cal motioned for Georgie to join him up on the high

seat. "Georgie," he said in a low voice after clucking to the horses, "I want you to come with me to the hotel and help me get Mrs. Gillespie settled."

"Shore thing, Sheriff!" Georgie said, trembling with apparent relief that he was not to be clapped into jail tonight, after all.

"After you help me with that, I want you to make yourself scarce around town for a few days, all right? Do you have somewhere you can go tonight?"

Georgie's forehead furrowed and he blinked several times. "I guess so, Sheriff, but why? Are ya angry at me? I thought ya said ya didn't think I done nothin' wrong...."

"No, I'm not angry at you, Georgie. Quite the opposite, in fact. I'm proud of you. You did just what I asked you to do and you did it quickly, even though you were afraid," Cal said patiently. He struggled to find the right words to get the simple man to comply, but not frighten him into paralysis. "It's...it's just that I don't trust Mr. Gillespie. I think he has some bad friends, like that Leroy Scruggs, and I don't want him telling men like that to come and bother you, okay?"

Georgie blinked several more times at Cal and then rubbed his stubbled chin. "All right, Sheriff. Reckon I could go visit my sister. She lives on a farm not too far outa town. She said I should come fer Christmas, anyway."

Cal wondered fleetingly why Georgie's sister didn't let her simpleminded brother live with her all the time, but perhaps Georgie liked living on his own in town, even with all the bullying that came with it. "That'll be good, Georgie. Come back in about a week or so. By then I reckon Gillespie will have found some new fish to fry.'' He could tell the expression puzzled Georgie, but the man didn't ask him about it.

Broughton closed the door of the hotel room behind him as he came out into the hall and faced Cal, who'd been pacing up and down waiting for him. ''She should be all right, Sheriff. She woke up briefly, long enough that I could tell she was in her right mind—''

The words acted like a trigger. Cal immediately charged to the door, anxious to see for himself.

Broughton barred his way. ''Now, just hold your horses, Sheriff. I said she *was* awake, but she ain't now. She complained of a headache and I gave her a dose a' laudanum. She should sleep through till morning. After a good night's sleep I reckon she'll be right as rain.''

''Thank you, Doctor,'' Cal said. ''I'll take care of her bill.''

He knew it was a mistake to have said it; the old man raised an eyebrow and a smirk took over his face. ''Of course, Sheriff,'' he said smoothly, and headed for the stairs.

Cal clenched his fists and struggled with the urge to shove the leering old fool down the steps. *Turn the other cheek. Think of Livy. He may be an insufferable old goat but he's the only doctor for miles around.* With the doctor's footsteps echoing up the stairwell, Cal opened the door and stepped in.

The room might not have rated the term *suite* in a big city like Houston, but it was luxurious by Gillespie Springs standards. It boasted a large bed, a table big enough for four to dine at, an overstuffed wing chair, a flower-painted china ewer and basin on a washstand. For those who preferred more complete ablutions, a copper hip bath stood in the corner. Situated at the corner of the building, the room had windows that looked out over Main Street and the side street between the hotel and the bank.

Cal's gaze darted immediately to the figure lying on her back in the middle of the huge bed.

Jovita, a finger to her lips, rose from her chair by the bed where Olivia lay. "She sleeps, Señor Sheriff. I theenk she weel sleep the whole night, like *el medico* say. Do not worry, I weel stay weeth her."

Cal couldn't tear his gaze from the fragile-looking figure whose dark hair was spread out on the pillow behind her like a banner. Livy looked like a gentle breeze could blow her away and leave no trace. There was only a faint color in her cheeks. Her parted lips were pale. The sheet barely rose with her breathing—but she *was* breathing, and for that he said a quick, thankful prayer.

"I know you would, Jovita, but I took the liberty of getting a room for you down at the end of the hall."

Jovita's mouth fell open and she stared at Cal as if he'd surely lost his mind. "But *señor,* I dare not leave the *señora* alone! The doctor tells me tonight I must be weeth her *constantemente*, constantly! Eet would be loco to leave her alone—"

Cal cut her off with a gentle hand to her wrist. "I didn't say she would be alone, Jovita," he told her. "I plan to stay in here tonight."

If Jovita had looked startled before, she was downright alarmed now. "But no, Señor Devleen! I know you love her, but Señora Leevy—thees ees not the time to—"

He put a finger to the excited woman's lips. "Whoa up just a minute there, Jovita. I'm not suggesting any-thing...well, anything shady. I plan to sit up in that chair you just vacated. Fact is, I'm more than a little worried about Olivia myself—''

"But the doctor, he says she—" Jovita began.

"Will be all right, I know. And I think she will, too. But I think there's at least a possibility this fire didn't start by itself, or by Livy bein' careless. There might be someone who was tryin' to hurt her, and until I get a chance to talk to Livy about how it got started, I'm going to be worryin' about that possibility, *comprende?*"

Slowly, the woman nodded.

"So I aim to sit by her bedside just in case. If you're down the hall, I can come get you if Miz Livy needs some help I can't give her, but meanwhile you'll have a nice comfortable bed to sleep on, all right?"

Jovita Mendez stared at him for a long moment, then, before he knew what she was about to do, seized his hands and kissed them. "You are a good man, Señor Devleen! A good man! I know she weel be safe weeth you to watch over her!"

Chapter Twenty

Robert Gillespie watched the wagon pull away and rumble down the street toward the hotel, Broughton following in his shay. Like a dog trotting at Devlin's heels, the banker thought sourly. He'd been right not to trust the old sawbones with any part of the plot to do away with Olivia Gillespie.

He was so angry at the failure of his plan, and his subsequent humiliating confrontation with Devlin, that he wanted to hurt something—or someone. But with a handful of curious onlookers watching his every blink to see how he'd react now that the sheriff was out of earshot, he dared not relax his poker-faced control. And since Broughton had taken the shay in which both had ridden the mile from the schoolhouse, he, Robert Gillespie—the owner of the bank and the richest man in Gillespie Springs, maybe even Brazos County—was going to have to *walk* back to his house as if he was a no-account sharecropper. He'd be damned before he'd ask any of the curious throng staring at him for a ride.

The tolling of the church bell woke Livy.

"Who...wha—" she cried, sitting bolt upright

against the carved wooden headboard, her speech slurred by the laudanum, but her eyes wide with fright.

Cal had been getting drowsy as the night grew deeper and he had nothing to do but watch her sleep, but now he was instantly alert. He bent over the bed from the chair next to it. "It's all right, Livy, I'm here. You're safe, honey. Go back to sleep."

"H-heard bells…"

"It's midnight, Livy, honey. That makes it Christmas Day. That's why the church bell's ringing." He saw her blink and take in the news.

"M-mer' Chrissmass," she murmured, and the dark-lashed eyelids drifted shut again.

"Merry Christmas, sweetheart," he said, though he was pretty sure she had fallen asleep again before he did. But there'd be many other Christmases to come when she would hear him say it, for he never meant to let her go again.

Gillespie kept Scruggs cooling his heels on a bench in the vestibule until nearly dawn. And a good thing, too, he thought as he kicked the drifter awake and Scruggs opened bleary, red-veined eyes. While Gillespie had been upstairs enjoying a blowsy-haired whore, Scruggs had had at least some time to sleep off a drunk. Gillespie despised drunkards.

"Gawdamn ya, whaddya think yore doin'?" Scruggs demanded as he jumped to his feet. He reminded Gillespie of an owl, the way he blinked and tried to focus on his tormentor.

"Oh, it's you, boss. Sorry," mumbled Scruggs, and tried to stand up straighter. "I—I guess you wanted to pay us?"

"You're sorry, all right, sorry as a sack of manure,

you empty-headed ox! Pay you and your equally sorry
accomplices? For what? For burning my former sister-
in-law's house down, leaving her none the worse except
for a lump on the head?''

"B-but…but I saw her—she was knocked out cold!
We drug her down to the kitchen floor…then set a fire
at the back door and set the parlor on fire, too, so she
couldn't get out neither way! Sh-she couldn't be alive!''
Scruggs's ugly face had paled and his eyes were bug-
ging out with horror.

Gillespie snatched the cowboy's shirt and dragged
him up close, so that they were practically eyeball-to-
eyeball. "She got out somehow," he ground out. "And
you'll be lucky if she can't identify the man who attacked her. Why didn't you slit her throat for good measure, while you were at it, you idiot?'' He threw
Scruggs against the bench, watching warily while the
drifter glowered at him for a long moment. Then
Scruggs evidently remembered how much money Gillespie had promised him, for the angry glint in his eyes
died. He swiped a hand across his mouth before speaking.

"I—I warn't th' man who knocked her out, Mr. Gillespie. Thet wuz Grady, boss.''

"Well, Grady is a fool, isn't he?'' snarled Gillespie.
"And so are you for trusting him with the job I gave
you to do!'' he said, giving Scruggs a vicious back-
handed slap. "He's a fool, all right, but you're an idiot
for assigning him the most important part of the job.
And because you did, Olivia Gillespie is very much
alive.'' His voice gradually gathered volume. "Oh, I
imagine she has a headache, but at this very moment
she's ensconced in Long's hotel in its very best suite!''

Scruggs closed his eyes as if the shouting hurt his

head. No doubt he had a bad headache, the result of his night's consumption of rotgut.

"I—I'll sneak in there today and kill her myself," he promised, and started to get up.

"Sit down, I'm not finished with you!" Gillespie said, shoving the drifter back onto the bench. "You'll do no such thing. The sheriff will be guarding her, I'm sure of that, since he's lusting after her. And how were you going to get into the hotel without being seen?"

"There's a back stairway," Scruggs said, his face sullen.

"Well, forget it, because you'd only make a muddle of that, too."

Scruggs looked more than a little dazed, so that Gillespie wanted to kick him all over again. "Yes, boss," he said, straightening with a wince. "But what about Miz Gillespie? Don't you want her done away with no more?"

"Of course I do," purred Gillespie. "But it's clear to me we're going to have to take care of her stalwart protector, the sheriff, first. But never you mind about that. I'll have to think of a new plan to get rid of Devlin and my former sister-in-law. Now get out of here—but stay where I can find you."

Olivia awoke when the first rays of sunlight came stealing through the lace curtains and struck her in the face with their dazzling December brightness. For a moment she didn't know where she was, but then she saw Cal asleep in the chair next to the bed, his head tilted against the wall, and it all came back to her.

Someone had attacked her in her own bedroom last night. Had he then violated her, while she'd been unconscious? She shifted experimentally, but thank God, she could feel no soreness between her legs, as there had been when—

But no, she wouldn't think of the past now. There was trouble enough in the present! Evidently whoever had attacked her had wanted to render her insensible, not rape her, so that the fire he had set would end her life. But she had narrowly escaped, and when she had awoken, Cal had been bending over her in her yard. He'd had her brought here for the night because her house had been burned to the ground.

She now had nothing—nothing but her life. Every bit of her furniture, every article of clothing she owned, was in ashes. *Dear Lord, what am I going to do?* Panic rose thickly in her throat. The little bit of money she had in the bank certainly wouldn't pay for her to build a new house on her land, or keep the wolf from her door for very long. Eventually she'd be forced to sell the property to Gillespie, just as he'd been demanding. The idea made her dig her fingernails into the mattress. How smug he'd be, how falsely regretful that necessity forced her to do such a thing!

And then what? She couldn't live in the hotel forever, on the mayor's charity. If she sold her land, the wisest thing to do, of course, would be to take the stage and go elsewhere—anywhere—perhaps out West. But instinctively she shrank from leaving everything familiar—and Cal.

Cal. The very man who made it impossible for her to want to leave was the same man who made it difficult to stay. Livy knew he wanted her, cared for her. She could always enter into some arrangement with him. Perhaps, knowing her pride, he'd even offer her marriage. But she didn't want him to marry her merely because she was poor but proud. She didn't want to be his wife just because she had nowhere else to go.

She'd have to rent a room somewhere, find some means of earning a living. Perhaps Ginny Petree would give her room and board to help mind her ever-increasing brood of children?

Livy discarded the idea almost as soon as she thought of it. Ginny Petree probably had no spare room to offer her, and it was about all her husband could do to put food on the table for his wife and children, let alone another adult.

Maybe James Long needed another cook or a chambermaid for this hotel? *Something* would turn up, she told herself. One step at a time.

She remembered Jovita removing the ragged remainders of her dress and her corset last night, but for the life of her she couldn't remember what had happened next. The laudanum Doc Broughton had bullied her into swallowing must have taken effect. Dear Lord, was she lying here *naked,* with Cal just inches away? The thought brought a fiery blush rising to her cheeks.

Cautiously, without rustling the crisp linens, Livy raised the sheet a few inches and looked. She was wearing a white cotton nightgown she'd never seen before. Evidently its owner was bigger than she was, for its loose neckline dipped low over her breasts and exposed part of one shoulder. She sighed in relief.

Her cheek stung. Reaching up with one hand, Livy felt some sort of gooey ointment smeared over her right cheek, and tender flesh beneath. She felt other areas of tenderness as she stretched beneath the sheet and blanket—bruises and more tiny burns where cinders had landed on her. But all in all, she knew she was very fortunate to be alive.

She turned to gaze at Cal again. Dear God, how tired he looked. His face still bore smudges of ashes from last night, and the lines were etched deeper in his beard-shadowed face. Was it her imagination or was there more gray streaking his tousled dark hair? Dimly, she remembered him carrying her last night, and how strong and dependable he'd felt.

Studying him led to purely feminine qualms about her own appearance. Goodness, she must look a fright! Jovita must have taken her hair down when they had put her to bed last night, and now it must be a veritable rat's nest! Somehow Livy had to put herself to rights before Cal woke. She didn't want him to see her like this.

What a vain, silly creature you are, she thought, suppressing a giggle. *Last night you were fighting for your life, this morning you're worried about your appearance. He's seen you looking worse—remember the day of the miscarriage? But what I wouldn't give for a mirror right now!*

Then she noticed that there was a framed one over the washstand. Sliding to the far side of the mattress as quietly as she could, and frowning as the springs creaked, Livy eased herself out of bed. She winced as various sore muscles announced themselves when she put her weight on her feet for the first time. Dizziness made her sway slightly, then she righted herself and, shivering in the chill air, padded barefoot to the mirror.

She was dismayed by what she saw. The burn on her cheek looked like an angry red brand under whatever unguent had been smoothed over it. The rest of her face was pale as a lily, which was certainly fashionable enough, but there were dark shadows under her eyes.

And her hair! It spread over her shoulders like an unruly black cloud. She looked like a cantina dancer!

"You look beautiful," a voice behind her rasped, and she whirled around to see Cal gazing at her from the chair.

She gave a shriek of alarm and dived unsteadily into the bed, pulling the covers up to her chin. "I—I was trying not to wake you," she said, feeling the crimson flood steal up her neck as she realized what Cal must have seen. The borrowed nightgown was threadbare with age, and with the morning sunlight coming into the room, it must have been nearly transparent!

Cal chuckled. "It's all right, sugar. I wasn't supposed to be sleeping, anyway. I was supposed to be watching over you. Merry Christmas, Livy."

She heard the casual endearment, saw the care and concern shining in his gaze, and for a moment she could think of nothing to say but "Merry Christmas" in return.

Then, because the silence between them was suddenly thick with an unspoken tension, she blurted out, ridiculously, "Whose nightgown am I wearing, anyway?"

He grinned in amusement. "One of Mrs. Long's. You know she's a mite, ah, broader than you are."

"Beggars can't be choosers," she muttered.

"How's your headache?"

"Better, but my stomach feels like a cowboy's must after a week's worth of tanglefoot," she confessed.

He chuckled again. "That's laudanum for you," he drawled. "Do you think you could eat some breakfast? I'll go see if the cook is anywhere around, or I could rustle up some bacon and eggs myself," he offered.

She shuddered at the idea. "Right now the very

thought of putting anything in my stomach, even coffee, sounds revolting. I expect that's due to the laudanum, too?''

Cal nodded. "Probably." His face, so dear to her, turned serious. "Livy, I don't want to bring up anything frightening, but I have to know. Do you have any idea how that fire got started last night? Did you...drop a lamp or something?''

She shook her head vigorously, which set it swimming again. For a moment she had to close her eyes until the swirling, nausea-inducing pain subsided. "No, nothing like that," she assured him, and told him how she had planned to come to the pageant, but had been running late. She saw a quick flash of something that might have been happiness in Cal's face when she said she had been planning to meet him at the school, but then it vanished and he was all business again. "I had just gone upstairs to get my shawl and earbobs. Someone was waiting in my bedroom, Cal! He..." She shuddered, recalling that terrifying moment.

"Did you get a look at his face, Livy? Did you recognize him?" Cal asked quickly, leaning forward in his chair. She was conscious of a rising tension in him, like a spring being wound too tightly.

"No," she said, this time remembering not to shake her head. "That is, I caught a brief glimpse of the man's face, just enough to know I'd never seen him before."

"Then it wasn't Georgie," he said. "You do know Georgie, don't you?"

"Everyone knows Georgie. Of course it wasn't Georgie!" she cried. "What an extraordinary thing to say, Cal."

Then he told her how Gillespie had been at the scene of the fire last night, and how he had tried to railroad them into thinking it had been Georgie who had started the fire, and how Cal had refused to charge him without any evidence.

The news made her even surer that Gillespie had been behind her attack last night, though she didn't say so aloud. Robert Gillespie would have no interest in blaming an innocent man—unless he knew who was to blame.

"Livy, think carefully," Cal said. "Could the man who attacked you be one of the saddle bums that've been thick as fleas in town lately?"

Livy shrugged. "Cal, I can't rightly say. I—I haven't looked closely at any of them—a lady dares not, you know, or she risks being on the receiving end of unwelcome advances. Well, I must admit I did get a good look at those two who were bothering me in front of the general store the other day, and it wasn't either of them."

She saw Cal's fists clench, and there was a dangerous glint in his eye.

"If I ever find out who tried to hurt you, Livy..." He looked away, a muscle in his jaw working.

Just then a knock sounded at the door, and Livy was startled to see Cal leap to his feet, his hand at his gun belt. "Who is it?" he growled.

"Jovita," the lilting voice called. "Open the door, Señor Devleen. My hands, they are full."

Cal crossed the floor to the door and opened it, and Jovita entered, carrying a bundle of clothing. "I just came from my son's house, and my son's wife, she send you thees things of her own to wear unteel you have your own again," she told Livy. "See? She ees nearer to you een size, I theenk, than Señor Long's wife. There ees another *camisón de noche*—how do you say?—another nightgown, a wrapper, a skirt and a rebozo, and the things that go underneath, which I weel not mention," she said with a wink at Cal.

"Oh, Jovita, thank you," Livy breathed, touched that the Mexican woman had anticipated her needs. "And please thank your daughter-in-law. I'll return these things to her as soon as I can—"

"*De nada,* Leevy," Jovita said with a wave of her hand. "And now that I am here, Señor Devleen, you weel leave, *sí?* Go get something to eat. Leevy weel want to bathe and dress."

Cal looked more than a little reluctant. "Jovita, just before you came in we were discussing who might've started that fire. Livy told me there was a man hiding in her room who knocked her out. She'd never seen him before. I'll wait in the hall—I don't think I should leave the hotel, ladies, since we don't know who or why someone would do that to her."

Livy hid the flare of alarm she felt at the idea that whoever had meant her harm before might try again. "Oh, Cal, I don't think you need to worry about that. No one's going to be about at this hour," she protested with a calm she was far from feeling.

"Ees no problem anyway," Jovita said to Cal, pulling a pistol from her capacious skirt pocket. "My son, he send thees weeth me. And yes, I can use eet."

Cal studied them both for a long minute, then went to the window and peered out. Turning back around, he shrugged. "All right, I know when I'm licked. But I'll be back in an hour or so."

"That ees *bueno, señor.*" Jovita nodded in approval. "Breeng breakfast back weeth you, yes? Leevy weel be hungry once she has been up and around for a while," she told him.

"I'll see what I can rustle up," he promised. "And I think it's about time you started calling me Cal, Jovita."

Cal supposed Livy was correct—that the sidewinder who'd set her house ablaze last night was unlikely to be up and about so early in the morning. He knew he ought to check in with Lazlo and let him know, in case he was needed, that Cal planned to be guarding Livy at the hotel the rest of the day. And it wouldn't hurt to wash up a bit, too, and to shave, he thought, giving an experimental rub to one cheek. There wasn't any use frightening Livy further by his appearance, after what she'd been through last night.

On his way out of the hotel, he strolled into the kitchen, but found it dark and uninhabited. It was likely Long had given his cook the day off, for there had been no other guests registered at the hotel last night.

Before stopping in at the jail, Cal took a stroll through the streets, appreciating the Christmas-morning quiet. None of the businesses were open, though smoke rising from the Last Chance's chimney gave him confidence that he'd be able to obtain some breakfast there. Hank would open up for him if for no one else, and wouldn't mind cooking extra for Livy and Jovita.

Cal stopped in at the Kristofs', where the house was full of savory smells and the children stopped their gleeful romping long enough to greet him and ask if he'd used his new comb yet. He had to admit he hadn't even thought of it, and made them laugh by pulling it out and making a big show of dragging it through his wind-ruffled hair. Regretfully, he turned down an invitation to enjoy a traditional Hungarian Christmas dinner and explained to Lazlo where he could be found.

"I will patrol the streets several times today, Sheriff," the Hungarian said. "Do not worry."

"Thanks, I'll try," Cal pledged, "but it's going to be hard not to until I know what lower-than-a-snake's-belly scum did this to Mrs. Gillespie."

"The fire did not start by accident?" Kristof said, his eyes troubled.

Briefly, Cal told Kristof what Livy had told him about the stranger. Then he bid the Kristofs a merry Christmas and departed, anxious to finish his rounds and return to Livy.

Chapter Twenty-One

Despite the night of fitful sleep in the chair by Livy's bed, Cal felt almost like a new man after shaving, washing up and changing his clothes in his room over the jail. There was a spring in his step as he descended the steps again, humming a carol.

By this time the bells of the Gillespie Springs Baptist Church were calling the townspeople to come and celebrate the birth of the Christ Child, and he was greeted by Davy Richardson, his mother and Ginny Petree and her flock of children.

"Hey, Sheriff! Merry Christmas! You comin' t'church?" Davy hollered with the exuberance of youth.

He wished things had been different and he and Livy could go to church and sing hymns about the newborn Baby Jesus. Maybe next year. Livy wasn't up to what was apt to be a very long church service this morning, after fighting for her life and nearly dying last night. He didn't want her to go out in public until he found out who had been trying to kill her, either.

"Maybe," he replied, hating the need to lie. He didn't want anyone, even Davy Richardson, to know exactly where he'd be and when. "I've got some busi-

ness to attend to that'll probably make me late. Sing a
carol for me if I don't make it, will you? Merry Christmas, folks.''

"Sure thing, Sheriff!''

There was no sign of the drifters who had flocked to
Gillespie Springs of late, and for a moment Cal wondered where they were holed up. He wouldn't put it
past Gillespie to have put them up in some of the cabins
that had once been slave quarters at the back of his
mansion. Perhaps Cal would have to find some excuse
to visit the property some morning when Gillespie was
at his bank.

Cal crossed the street to the Last Chance, and minutes
later left the saloon's kitchen laden with covered dishes
full of delicious-smelling bacon, eggs and fried potatoes, and a pot of hot coffee.

Luck was with him, and no one saw him, for by this
time the faithful had gone to church. Nevertheless, Cal
used the covered stairs at the back of the hotel to reach
Livy's room. No sense giving anyone anything to gossip
about. Once he reached the hallway on the second floor,
though, he set the food and coffeepot down and locked
the door to the outside stair.

Apparently Jovita had heard him, for the door opened
and she stepped out into the hall.

"I hope y'all are hungry, Jovita, 'cause Hank Whyte
cooked enough for an army,'' he told her with a grin.

"I theenk Leevy has recovered her appetite,'' Jovita
said, her black eyes dancing. "Me, I go to my son's,
now that you are back.''

"Why, Jovita, you don't have to rush off,'' he said,
surprised. "Who's going to eat all this food? It's way
too much for just Livy and me!''

"Oh, I theenk you weel manage," she said mysteriously. *"El amor se despierto el hombre."*

Cal's Spanish was a little rusty, but he could swear that she had said something very much like "Love makes people hungry."

"Also, my daughter-in-law weel not know how to make the *molé* sauce for the turkey, or how to rub the turkey with rosemary and make the stuffing of raisins and chestnuts the way my son likes eet," Jovita added, helping Cal to gather up the covered dishes again. Then she arranged her rebozo around her shoulders. "I weel be there tonight, eef you should need me."

Bemused at her departure, Cal entered the hotel room. A fire burned in the fireplace opposite the bed, and the room was pleasantly warm. He caught sight of the copper hip bath sitting in the corner of the room, with rumpled towels lying around its base.

"I hope you're hungry, Livy, 'cause with Jovita leaving we're going to have to eat this all ourse—" he began, and then he saw her, straightening from where she had been combing out her hair near the fire.

In the hour since he'd seen her last, Olivia Childress Gillespie had been transformed. Gone was the tousle-haired, sleepy-faced woman in a slumber-creased night-gown too big for her, a woman whose eyes still revealed traces of pain and fear.

All the smudges of soot had been washed away; all the odor of wood smoke that had lingered about her even this morning was gone, replaced by the delicate scent of lilacs.

Her hair hung in damp strands on her shoulders and down her back, raven dark, though midnight wisps already curled about her forehead.

"I—I'd hoped to get my hair dry before you returned,

Cal,'' she said, as if she found it embarrassing to be caught with her hair down like a young girl. ''It's...just so thick....''

''It's beautiful,'' he said, his voice suddenly raspy, as if the satin fall of her hair had wrapped itself around his heart.

The long-sleeved, embroidered white *camisa* that Livy wore was loosely gathered at the neckline with a scarlet satin ribbon. It rode low, revealing lovely white shoulders and the first hint of her breasts. He could see that she wore a chemise underneath, but apparently Jovita had not provided a corset—thank God, he thought, since the last thing Livy needed was something restricting her breathing after all the smoke she'd inhaled. And she looked softer, more approachable. A red-and-green calico skirt emphasized her narrow waist above curving, womanly hips.

He could still see the burn on one pale cheek, but it was insignificant next to the blueness of her eyes. She was smiling—a little uncertainly.

''You make a very pretty *señora*,'' he told her, sensing her uneasiness and wanting to banish it. ''I hope you're a hungry one.''

That gave her something to reply to, at least. ''Did I hear you say Mr. Whyte cooked all that?'' she asked, nodding at what Cal carried as she came forward to relieve him of some of his burden. ''That certainly is enough for an army, Cal! But I'm glad he did. Jovita was right—by the time she helped me get all cleaned up, I *did* get hungry. Mmm, if it tastes as good as it smells, I'm afraid I'm liable to embarrass myself with the size of my appetite. You'll be disgusted, Cal,'' she said with a little laugh.

''Never,'' he said with a gallant bow after he had set

down the dishes on the table. He was afraid the shoe was very much on the other foot. If Livy knew how delicious *she* looked, and how very much he wanted her at this moment, she was the one who was apt to be disgusted.

He busied himself with helping her arrange the plates and silverware on the table, pouring the coffee, anything to avoid revealing to Livy how he felt about being alone with her.

For a while neither spoke, concentrating on the food. Cal didn't want to bring up anything about last night's events for fear of destroying Livy's appetite. Yet what else could he talk to her about? How much he desired her? She'd told him in no uncertain terms once before how she felt about that!

After her hunger was satisfied, Livy was also having difficulty knowing what to say. She should be making conversation; a lady did not just wolf down her food silently, she told herself. But she didn't want to talk about the fire, or the fact that someone out there was trying to kill her, either. Nor did she want to speak of what she was going to do now that her home was gone. She was too afraid she'd cry, and she didn't want to sound self-pitying. After all, she was lucky just to be alive.

"My, I can't remember when I've eaten so much," she said at last, as Cal poured more coffee in both of their cups. "My late mother would be quite ashamed of me—she'd say I was eating like a field hand."

"Livy, I don't think you need to apologize. It has to have been at least what, sixteen hours since you ate your supper?" Something on her face must have alerted him, for he persisted. "You didn't eat supper?"

She shook her head. "I—I was so busy making supper for us...."

"*Us?*" He looked as if he was almost afraid to hope that the pronoun included *him*.

"For you and me, Cal. I was going to invite you to come back for a late supper with me, at my house." Now she found herself stumbling. "You've, um... indicated a desire to spend time in my company...." She shrugged. "But it's so difficult for us to, uh, get to know one another again...what with the whole town watching, probably judging me for—for even caring about a man just a few months after my husband's death. Judging you, too, for wanting to be around a woman like me...." She hid her face in her spread hand, unable to go on.

She heard him put down his cup; a moment later he was kneeling in front of her chair, one hand touching her cheek in time to catch the tears as they began to well over.

She sniffed. "That's why I was running late, Cal," she told him. "I wanted to cook you supper, and now I can never fix you supper there, ever, because my house is burned to the ground!"

She couldn't hold back the sobs any longer. She felt him pull her ever so gently off the chair and into his arms, then he let her weep against his chest. Her sobs came like a torrential rain; she wept, she raged, she trembled like a child. He held her through all of that, rocking her, enfolding her in his strong arms, and when she had cried herself out, he gave her his handkerchief and watched as she wiped her eyes.

"I'm sorry, Cal. I didn't mean to drown you," she said with a shaky laugh, reaching out to touch his soggy shirtfront.

He grinned down at her. "I'm not so sweet I'll melt," he told her. "Lord, Livy, I reckon you earned yourself a good cry if anyone has."

"I look so awful when I cry," she muttered, knowing her eyes would be red and puffy, hating that he was seeing her like that.

"Shh," he whispered, a finger to her lips. "You're the most beautiful woman in the world to me. I love you." And then, before she could tell him she loved him, too, his lips met hers in a kiss so sweet, so comforting, that all thoughts of tears and regret and fear dissolved.

It was Cal—the same Cal she had known and loved since she was a girl, though he was older now, as she was, and scarred, certainly. He was not the handsome, perfect Adonis he had been in his youth, when every belle in Brazos County had wanted to become the young rector's bride, and Olivia was the envy of all because she was his choice.

How could she have been so foolish as to throw all of that away because of the color of uniform he had chosen? Cal was worth more to her than all of the rest of those handsome boys in gray combined—she knew that now. She was getting a second chance, and by all that was sacred to her, she wasn't going to let him go ever again.

She wasn't the same person she had been, either. Life had changed the carefree belle of Brazos County. She'd been married and widowed...and raped. How she wished she could turn the clock back and come to Caleb Devlin as an unsullied girl! They could have avoided so much heartache.

She felt the exact moment the subtle change occurred, when his kiss altered, when it became not one of comfort and assurance but one driven by desire. There was less certainty in that kiss and more persuasion, as if he had known she needed and would accept his comfort, but was less sure that she would accept his passion.

Olivia hesitated for a moment and went still in his arms. She had had no intimacy with a man since Dan had gone away to war, for that brutal violation in the barn could surely not be called intimacy.

But then she made up her mind. No matter what happened between them as a result, she wanted it to be Cal who removed, by his lovemaking, the awful stain of the rape. Now she wanted to reassure *him,* to let him know that not only did she intend to agree to his desire, she intended to meet him kiss for kiss, caress for caress, hunger for hunger. So it was Olivia who deepened the kiss, Olivia who allowed her lips to part and who threw her arms around his neck, drawing him closer so that the softness of her breasts met the hard planes of his chest. She felt his tongue sweep inside her mouth as his embrace tightened fiercely, felt the evidence of his desire as the cradle of her hips was molded against him.

"Livy, I—" he began, when both of them had to breathe at last. She felt him try to pull away, try to do the honorable thing, and she felt she would die if she let him go.

"Shh," she whispered, her finger on his lips. She kissed him again, moving closer into his arms, her own tongue teasing his until he groaned and let her in. Then his hands were everywhere, stroking her breasts through the thin cotton of the Mexican blouse and her shimmy underneath, cupping her bottom....

Livy drifted backward, onto the floor, pulling him with her. She felt him tug the bow at the neckline of her *camisa* and push back the fabric of her shimmy so that one of her breasts was exposed to his gaze, and then his head lowered and he was suckling on it. The silky texture of his mustache rubbing over the sensitive flesh nearly drove her mad. She felt his mouth leave the nipple, and the cool air on the wet, aroused nub tormented her until his hand found it and consoled it. By then he had uncovered the other breast and his mouth on it wreaked havoc with her senses.

Her breath escaped in a moan. His lips went back to hers as his hand left her breast to begin inching up her skirt. Even with her decision made, this new action caused her to grow still for a moment. The last man who had pushed up her skirt had been possessed by the violence of his lust. Would Cal be brutal in his passion, too?

But her doubts lasted less than a moment. This was *Cal*, not the merciless beast who had violated her. He would give her pleasure, not pain.

She opened her eyes to find him watching her, a questioning look on his face. Clearly he was giving her room to stop even now, warning her that before long he would not be able to call a halt himself.

She had no wish to stop; indeed, she felt she might die if they did. In answer, she murmured, "I love you too, Cal," then pulled him more closely against her and moved against him in a way that was unmistakably encouraging.

"Oh, Livy," he breathed, against her neck. "Oh, honey..." And he moved against her, thrusting against her soft center once, twice, until she felt something curl within her and grow hot and demanding....

"No..." she heard him mutter, and she opened her eyes, thinking she was going to lose this moment, after all.

"Cal?" she questioned, searching his face, the face that was so dear to her. "Please?"

"I've waited years for you, sweetheart," he murmured, struggling to his knees and pulling her with him. "I reckon I can wait a few more seconds and make love to you in a bed. That is…if you're sure you don't want to wait until we're married?" he said uncertainly, as both of them struggled to their feet, their breathing ragged. "We *can* wait, if you want to, Livy. We *are* going to be married, you know, just as soon as you think we decently can."

"Yes," she agreed, answering the last question first. Since they had begun kissing minutes ago, Livy had not thought a moment beyond each caress, but was thrilled to know that *he* had, and that he wanted to live the rest of his life as her husband. "That is, yes, we *will* be married, Cal, but no, I don't want to wait. I don't think I *could* wait a moment longer than it'll take you to get me to that bed over there."

He laughed exultantly and scooped her into his arms, and she smiled up at him as he carried her to the bed.

Jovita had left the coverlet and sheet turned down invitingly when she had made the bed. Now Olivia knew why. The wise woman had known this would happen if she left; it was probably *why* she had left, for as much as she liked spending time with her son and his family, she had never expressed any doubt before as to her daughter-in-law's cooking ability.

Olivia didn't mention Jovita, though, as Cal swept the turned-down covers aside with one hand while lowering her to the bed and following her down. She was too busy trying to unbutton his shirt at the same time as he was trying to shrug out of his vest.

She was grateful for the simple clothes that enabled

Cal to pull the loosened blouse over her head, then unfasten the button that held the gathered skirt snug at her waist and draw it down over her hips and legs. Now she was sitting there in the thin cotton shimmy, feeling him tug at the few bows that tied it across her breasts. Then it was gone, sliding as easily as a cloud down her arms, and he had turned his attention to the pantalettes' tie at her waist.

In a moment, they were gone and she was naked and waiting while he impatiently stripped off the rest of his own clothes. She knew she should feel self-conscious and anxious now, as she had on her wedding night, when she had been waiting for Dan Gillespie to initiate her into the mysteries of married life. But she felt anything but reticent, and the only regret she felt was that it had not been Cal on that night. She sensed she would not have had those pangs of fear, but would have felt as she did now, filled with anticipation of pleasure to come and glorying in the sight of the play of his powerful muscles as he shrugged out of the shirt.

Cal stood to remove his trousers, his back to her, and she heard the clunk of his belt buckle as it joined the shirt on the floor. She caught a glimpse of tight buttocks and sinewy thighs as he removed the union suit, the last barrier between them.

He returned to the bed and her open arms.

Chapter Twenty-Two

The first head-to-toe contact of his bare skin touching hers gave her such a delicious jolt that she gasped out loud.

"I know," Cal breathed, as he moved against her, the hairs on his chest against her bare breasts causing delicious shivers to race up and down her spine. "Am I dreaming? Am I really about to make love to the woman who's owned my heart ever since I was a boy? Lord, if this is a dream, don't let me wake up, ever!"

This boyish eagerness—from a man whose hair had gray mixed in with the black—warmed her heart. "Oh, Cal, really? It's been as long as that for you, too?" she marveled. "I never forgot, ever, even when—"

He stopped her words with his kiss, and she was grateful. She didn't want to talk about anything or anyone else, just the two of them. When he kissed her like that, she didn't want to talk at all.

"I swear it has, ever since you stole my clothes at the swimmin' hole, sweetheart," he said, his hands stroking over her belly, making her muscles go taut with anticipation. "And now we're going to make up for lost time, aren't we?"

Olivia let her kiss be her answer.

She could feel him, hard and ready against her thigh, and she was aware of an answering excitement in her, knowing how pleasurable it would be to feel him filling her with himself. She shifted restlessly, but he was not to be hurried.

"No, Livy. I haven't touched you yet," he murmured, grinning maddeningly down at her. With that black patch over his eye and the rakish mustache over his lip, he looked like a pirate, she thought, not for the first time.

"You...haven't *touched* me?" she asked, incredulous, for just then his thumb and forefinger were pleasuring her nipple in a way that made her breath come in short, ragged pants.

"Not everywhere," he breathed, as he bent to take her breast in his mouth again. And then his fingers strayed down over her tense belly to the one place he hadn't touched her, the sensitive center between her legs, and he started stroking, parting the short curls and reaching inside with a finger while still caressing the bud on the outside.

She went wild, writhing and moaning softly and calling his name, begging him to end her torment, but he just went on stroking, telling her her skin was like satin and she was beautiful, the most beautiful woman in Texas—no, the most beautiful woman surely in all the world, and she was his, just his, forever. When she could stand it no more and thought she would die of ecstasy, and be the most beautiful dead woman in Texas, he parted her legs with his knee and entered her.

She nearly screamed with the joy of it, but just in time she remembered they were in a hotel and anyone in the world could come up those stairs and hear the

Widow Gillespie moaning with carnal pleasure, so she put her knuckles against her teeth and tried to smother her cries as he began to move inside her.

He stilled for a moment and smiled encouragingly down at her, apparently guessing her thoughts. "Let it out, honey. Don't try to be quiet. There's not another soul in this building and it does my heart good to hear how wonderful I'm making you feel. Of course, it's not a patch on how you're making *me* feel...." Then he began thrusting again, faster and faster, harder and harder, until she found his pace and joined it, until all at once the knot exploded within her and she cried his name out loud. He seemed to have been waiting for that, for his groan joined her cries and he spent himself inside her.

They slept in each other's arms. Even when Olivia woke, she continued to hold Cal in her arms while he slept. She watched while the sunlight streaming in the window faded into shadows. He needed the sleep, she thought tenderly, for he couldn't have slept but a few restless hours in that chair last night.

Robert Gillespie was sated from his Christmas dinner of rare roast beef, washed down with a fine imported burgundy. It had been difficult teaching his black cook, Junius's wife, how to cook his beef only until it was pink inside, but the results had been well worth it. Ignoring Scruggs, who had just been shown into the palatial dining room, Gillespie used his golden toothpick to prise a piece of beef from between his teeth.

Scruggs cleared his throat and scratched his stubbled chin. "So, uh....boss...how soon do you want us to kill the woman?"

Irritated, Gillespie set down his glass of wine so hard

that the liquid splashed onto the immaculate white linen tablecloth. The spreading stain looked like flowing blood.

"You idiot, didn't you hear what I said yesterday? Much as I want her dead, you're not going to be able to get to her with Sir Galahad guarding her."

Scruggs looked blank. "Sir who? I thought the sheriff wuz guardin' her."

Gillespie smacked the table in exasperation "I always forget that you've got the intelligence of hanging beef," he snapped. "I meant the sheriff, of course. I've realized we're going to have to get rid of Devlin before we can safely eliminate Olivia Gillespie."

"So you want the sheriff killed first."

The banker nodded. "I've decided to pay a bonus of five hundred dollars to the man who does it."

Scruggs felt his pulse quicken. "I'll do it, boss, the very next time he sticks his head outside Miz Gillespie's room."

Gillespie snorted, and when he spoke, his tone was derisive. "Fool, you're known to be my employee. You can't do it, not without tying the crime to me. And I wouldn't appreciate that."

"I could do it if no one saw me."

"Yes..." Gillespie lit a cigar and puffed on it, blowing a neat smoke ring above him. "But I'm convinced your talent lies more in...ah, being my right-hand man, my enforcer, Scruggs. I was thinking of giving you a permanent salary...and perhaps giving you the old overseer's cottage out back. You'd earn more than five hundred in a year and have your own quarters besides."

Scruggs's lips spread into a grin. "Sounds good, boss."

Gillespie guessed he was picturing himself buying fancy duds and carrying a gold-topped cane. "Very well. Tell Grady and the other two about the bonus, and any other gunslingers you think could get the drop on that uppity Devlin. They'd better be good, you know—the man proved he's a dead shot the very first day he came to town. But you tell those boys if anyone talks about my bonus, I'll deny it."

Cal lifted his head suddenly from Olivia's soft breast, all his senses alert.

"I'm sorry about my stomach rumbling, Cal," Olivia murmured. "I can't believe I'm hungry again after that big breakfast, but it must be suppertime by now and—"

"Shh!" he hissed, startling her as he sat up and grabbed for his union suit. "Someone's out there," he added in explanation, nodding toward the hallway. Keeping his eye on the door, he quickly thrust his legs into the garment, and then his arms. There was a soft knock at the door. Then he heard a muffled sound, as if one person was whispering to another.

Alarmed, Livy grabbed the sheet and pulled it up to her chin. He caught a glimpse of huge eyes in a face gone pale as he reached for his gun, but there was no time to reassure Livy—or put on the rest of his clothes. He was convinced whoever had tried to kill Livy last night had just come back and was relying on their curiosity to obtain another chance.

Whoever it was, he'd meet him with a hail of lead, Cal decided grimly. "Get under the bed, Livy, and don't come out till I tell you," he commanded in a whisper. Then he tiptoed to the door, his gun cocked and ready.

"Who is it?" he demanded curtly from behind the

door, then moved quickly and soundlessly to the other side of the door and listened. He wished he'd had the foresight to bar the front door of the hotel. What a fool he'd been—of course the would-be killer would want another chance! Pent up in the hotel room, they were like mice in a box. Olivia was in danger again, and it was all his fault.

Cal strained his ears, but all he heard was footsteps going down the front stairway. Bold as brass, going out the front door, Cal thought, but then he thought again. He wasn't so green he was going to fall for that old trick. The killer must have a couple of accomplices, and he must have motioned for them to make plenty of noise leaving, while he himself stayed in place, ready to shoot whoever opened the door.

"Cal..."

He whirled around to motion Olivia to silence, only to see that she was not under the bed, but standing at the window.

Of all the fool things! "Livy, get down!" he ordered, and crouched to dive at her, expecting any moment that a bullet would come whizzing up through the glass.

"Cal, look, it's the Longs," she said, pointing at the street below as she stood there with nothing but the sheet wrapped around her. "I think it was them at the door, because they were laughing at each other and pointing up at our window."

By the time he had joined her at the window that looked out over Main Street, the couple was just turning the corner to walk down the side street that led to South Street and their residence. He couldn't see them very well now because of the deepening shadows of evening, but he could tell from the short, stocky stature that the man was James Long, and he was arm-in-arm with a woman.

"But why..." Cal muttered in disbelief. If it had been Mr. and Mrs. Long calling to check on Livy, why wouldn't they have identified themselves? Maybe they just happened to be passing by. Convinced there was still a man with a gun on the other side of the door, Cal crept back across the room and suddenly threw it open, ready to put a hole into anyone revealed.

There was no one there, either in front of the door or waiting in the shadows down the hall. Instead, what was there was an enormous round, covered tray, a bottle of champagne and two glasses.

"It's all right, Livy," he called over his shoulder. "Come look what they brought."

Still clad only in the sheet, she did so, peering over his shoulder as Cal lifted the tray. The savory smell of roast goose wafted up to their noses. The Longs had also provided baked potatoes, gravy, biscuits and butter, baked apples and pieces of cake with white icing. Cal unfolded a note nestling among the dishes and read it out loud: "'Hope you both enjoy this Christmas dinner—James and Martha Long.' I guess they knew you were hungry, sweetheart," he added, secretly weak with relief that his fears had been groundless.

"Cal, how sweet of them! But you don't suppose they guessed that we..." She stopped as a fierce blush spread over her face.

Cal couldn't help grinning. "I'd have to say they either guessed or they want us to be *very* merry celebratin' Christmas," he said. "I don't know which, but I'm going to go bar the doors so we don't have any more visitors, well-wishing or otherwise."

* * *

After devouring the feast, they drank the champagne in bed, nestling in each other's arms.

"Cal, can you bear to tell me about the time when you were gone?" Olivia asked, putting down her glass to look at him. "Sam told me a little, that day in Bryan, but there's so much I don't know...a whole big chunk of time when I thought you were dead. But don't feel you have to if it's too painful," she added quickly, her face anxious.

He ran a hand down her cheek. "It hurts a bit, but I guess this is a good time.... There are so many lost years between us, aren't there, sweetheart?"

Cal told her about the horrors of war; of the shell exploding right next to him and Goliad; of waking up at the widow's farmhouse, miles from the battlefield, with no memory of who he was or how he'd come to be there. The only clue had been the tattered remains of the blue uniform he was wearing. He discovered he couldn't see out of his right eye, even when Lizabeth, the widow woman, changed the bandage. He'd stayed at Lizabeth's farm while he mended, but his memory didn't return, except that he knew his first name was Caleb.

Gradually he'd begun helping the widow with the farm chores, and the desire to rejoin the Union army and rediscover his identity—and reexperience war and all its terror—faded. He and Lizabeth grew close, and after a year, married. Needing a last name, he'd assumed Lizabeth's maiden name, Paxton.

Lizabeth had died in childbirth the same day as the Confederacy surrendered at Appomattox, he told Livy, staring down into his half-empty wineglass. The baby, a boy, died, too.

"Did you...love her very much?" he heard Olivia ask, her voice tremulous.

He turned to look at her and saw that there were tears standing in her blue eyes. He kissed them away.

"I loved her, Livy, but not like I love you. I was always aware there was something...*missing*.... Lord, I was half-afraid I'd forgotten I had another wife somewhere, wherever I came from."

"And you didn't remember anything until Sam found you tending bar when he drove those cattle to Abilene?"

"I'd get...*glimmers* of memory...every now and then," Cal said. "But that's all they were, just flashes. I knew I'd had something to do with religion, 'cause I knew the Good Book like the back of my hand, and I found comfort reading Lizabeth's old family Bible. The cowhands in the saloon teased me, called me 'Deacon,' and after a while I forgot all about being Caleb. And then Sam came, and he didn't even know me, what with this patch and all. It took a while, but when I finally remembered who I was, I remembered about you, and I was bound and determined to come home to Texas and find out what had happened to you."

"And you came home to find out I was married and my husband had killed himself after killing my lover, the man who'd made me pregnant when my husband couldn't," Livy said bitterly. "Lord, what you must have thought of me."

He nodded, his face sober. "For a while. But then I realized there had to be more to it...than the gossip. I wanted to find out for myself, anyway."

"I made that pretty difficult, didn't I?" she asked with a mirthless laugh.

"You were about as prickly as a cactus," he agreed

gently. "Livy, did you....did you love this Mexican man your husband killed?"

Her eyes filled with tears again. "His name was Francisco Luna, and no, I didn't love him, not like that. But when Dan came home from the war so broken and bitter, and told me about his injury, how he couldn't...that he couldn't ever give me a baby..."

Cal held her as she struggled for words.

"...And he wouldn't even kiss me or hold me.... Francisco was Dan's helper around the farm, but one day he found me crying out in the pasture, and we talked. I found I could tell him things and he would listen.... But no, he never touched me, he wouldn't have. I was his boss's wife. Francisco was an honorable man, Cal."

"I believe you, Livy," he said, looking her in the eye, waiting. He knew there was more. Livy radiated the misery of her long-kept secret.

She faced him, eyes full of sadness. "But now you want to know that if Francisco didn't father the baby I lost, *who did?*"

Chapter Twenty-Three

He nodded. "Livy, honey, if I thought you'd had a love affair, that some man had made you happy—even for a little while—when Dan Gillespie couldn't or wouldn't…well, I could accept that, I reckon. What right have I to judge?" He shrugged. "It's just that I don't think that's the way it was."

He took her chin gently between his thumb and forefinger and forced her to meet his gaze. "It wasn't that way, was it, Livy? Some man forced you, didn't he?"

She wrenched herself away, trembling. She wouldn't cry again, she *wouldn't!* But she had kept silence about this matter for too long, and the tears escaped around the fingers she held pressed to her eyes.

"Yes…I felt so…*dirty!*" she sobbed, sinking down on the bed. "Oh, Cal, I'm so sorry. I'd give anything to be able to have come to you without—without that stain.…"

Gently, Cal pulled her into his arms again, kissing her cheeks, her ears, her nose. "Hush, none of that. There is no 'stain.' You have no reason to apologize, not to me, not to anyone. It wasn't your fault. The only one who should feel dirty was the low-down polecat that did this to you, Livy, you have to believe that. You *do* believe it, don't you?''

Livy stared at him, knowing he meant it, feeling a measure of peace seeping into her soul from his words, and from having admitted that she had been raped. Cal said she wasn't responsible. Surely in time she'd believe that God forgave her, too. Slowly, she nodded, then saw that he was waiting, knowing there was more.

Cal wanted to know *who* had raped her.

No, she couldn't tell him that. She saw the steel underneath the gentle tone, saw the tightening of his jaw and the dangerous glint in his eye. If she told him she knew the rapist had been her brother-in-law, Cal would go after Gillespie.

Cal clenched and unclenched his fists. "The man deserves to be punished, Livy. Surely you know that."

She turned back to him. "Yes, and he will be. By God, someday."

"I'm afraid that isn't soon enough to suit me, Livy," Cal growled. "God can have him, all right, after I'm done with him." He hesitated for a moment, and when he spoke again, his tone was gentler. "You think I mean to kill him, don't you? No, honey. I admit, the thought *is* attractive, but I'd be satisfied just to beat him until he was a greasy spot in the dirt."

Olivia sighed, not reassured. Cal might intend only bare-knuckles punishment of her rapist, but Robert Gillespie would never let it end that way. Once openly challenged, he would have to either kill or be killed...not that he would try to do the dirty work himself. Gillespie had surrounded himself with the sort of unsavory characters who would do such things for him.

Olivia had no doubt Cal could kill Gillespie, no matter how many hired guns the banker surrounded himself

with. But she couldn't let it come to that. Cal was a
lawman, sworn to stand for law and order, and by killing Gillespie he'd violate the very honor he lived by.
He'd worked too hard to begin his life over again here
to let Gillespie spoil that, too.

What had been done was done. It was over. The innocent life that had resulted had been tragically lost, but
they had to go on.

"I don't know who it was, Cal," she insisted. "He
threw a sack over my head before I saw him, and held
me down, and when he was…done…he struck me hard
on the head. When I woke, I was alone in the barn."

Cal didn't believe her for a second. It was obvious
she was lying by the way she had looked him in the
eye and then looked away, twisting a corner of the
sheet. She knew who had raped her that day in the barn,
sack or no sack.

Why would she protect such a man? It couldn't be
that she had any tender feelings for the bastard. No, she
wasn't protecting her violator, she was protecting *him*.

And that could only mean the man was someone
powerful, someone who'd be able to harm him in some
way. And in a town as small as Gillespie Springs, that
could only mean Robert Gillespie. Gillespie had lusted
after his brother's wife, and when he'd forced himself
on her, she'd become pregnant. And he'd feared the
resultant scandal would destroy not only his reputation
in the community but his relationship with his brother,
so he'd let his brother believe Olivia was cuckolding
him with his Mexican hired hand. The result had been
an innocent man murdered by a wronged husband. Then
Dan Gillespie had killed himself, providing a tidy end-

ing—at least tidy as far as Robert Gillespie was concerned.

The *bastard,* Cal raged inwardly, careful not to let his feelings show by so much as a flicker of an eyelash as he gazed at Olivia. She was right—the banker would pay for his crime in the hereafter. But it wasn't right that Gillespie had allowed Olivia to face shame that was none of her own making, while he remained a respected pillar of the community. There had to be a way to make him pay *now,* to reveal himself for the sidewinder he was.

"All right, honey," he said to Olivia. "We'll leave it at that. Let's have a little more of the champagne, all right? I love the way your nose wrinkles when the bubbles tickle it," he told her, kissing that part of her face.

The next morning, Cal and Olivia had breakfast together in the hotel dining room. They had made love again before leaving the suite upstairs, and Cal, watching her across the table as she sipped her coffee, thought Livy had the radiance of a woman in love. A well-satisfied woman in love, he decided as she looked up and smiled at him.

It was early, and they were alone in the dining room, the cook having retreated back to her kitchen as soon as she had brought their bacon and eggs. Maybe now was a good time to find out how soon he could get Olivia to marry him.

All at once the door opened, and Cal heard the *jinkle-clunk* of spurred boots making their way across the floor. So much for being alone here. Cal's eyes didn't leave Olivia. With any luck the cowboy would be seeking breakfast, not a conversation with the sheriff, and would take a seat clear across the room.

"I thought I might find you here, since you weren't in your office."

"Why, Sam! What a nice surprise!" he heard Olivia exclaim, before he looked up and saw his younger brother standing in front of their table, grinning down at them.

"Mornin', Miz Olivia," Sam said, plopping his hat down on a nearby chair and taking a seat without waiting to be asked. "Nice to see you, ma'am," he added, grinning first at Olivia and then Cal.

"Please join us," Cal said wryly.

"Don't mind if I do, brother," Sam said with a wink, motioning to the cook, who had stuck her head out the swinging kitchen door to see who the newcomer was.

"To what do I owe the honor of this visit—apart from fraternal regard, of course?" Cal inquired with a raised eyebrow, aware that Olivia was blushing under his brother's cheerful scrutiny.

The amused look Sam shot back told Cal he was well aware that Cal would have preferred to be alone with Olivia. "Well, the family jest thought someone ought to check and see if you were all right, seein' as how we were expectin' you for Christmas dinner yesterday, and you never showed up. Mama was havin' visions of you shot dead and layin' in your coffin, but I told her that was nonsense, of course. I said you probably had other things you had to do."

Olivia choked on her coffee just then and grabbed her napkin.

Cal covered his face with his spread fingers. "Oh, Lord, I forgot all about coming for Christmas dinner like I promised. You might as well shoot me now," he said ruefully, "and spare me the agony of Mama's tongue-lashing. Sam, you wouldn't believe what's gone on in the last day or so here.''

''I reckon that's right,'' Sam said, his grin growing even more wicked as his eyes darted from a crimson-faced Olivia back to Cal.

''Sam, be serious,'' Cal said, setting his coffee down. Quickly he told his brother about Olivia's narrow escape from the fire and his suspicion that the blaze had been set.

''Well, I sure can see why Christmas dinner slipped your mind,'' Sam said when Cal had finished. ''I guess Mama will have to let you live, after all, brother.''

''How about if I promise to come Sunday, and bring the lady who's agreed to become my wife?'' Cal inquired, grinning himself as he saw Sam's surprise.

''Is that the truth? You're gonna marry Cal?'' he asked Olivia, who blushingly acknowledged she was. ''Why, that's the best news I ever heard the day after Christmas!'' he said, clapping his brother on the back. ''Congratulations! When's the happy day?''

''Umm, we haven't figured out a date yet,'' Cal said awkwardly, ''what with Olivia bein' widowed fairly recently and all....''

''Of course,'' Sam said quickly. ''Well, there'll be time to think about that. But what about now? Where are you gonna live, Miz Olivia, now that your place is burned to the ground? Why don't you come home to Mama's with me? I'm sure she'd want me to offer you a room.''

Cal was torn, unwilling to have Livy so far away from him just when he could barely stand to keep his hands off of her, but knowing it was the right thing for her to do.

Livy's face was stricken and she seemed to be struggling for words. "Oh, Sam, that's so kind of you, but I couldn't impose—"

"It's not an imposition, seein' as how you're going to be my brother's wife and all," Sam said cheerfully.

"Livy, I think you ought to do it," Cal said, his heart heavy as a stone. "You'd be safe there, don't you see?"

"But I'd never see you, Cal. Your responsibility is *here*. You couldn't be riding over to Bryan all the time to see me."

He was silent, knowing it was true, especially now, with all the drifters converging on the town he was sworn to serve.

"I could surely get over there every Sunday," Cal said, hating the idea of seeing her only once a week equally as much as he loved the idea that she would be safe with his family.

"It's not enough, Cal. And there's no guarantee I wouldn't draw the danger to your family. I'm sorry, Sam, but I can't accept your kind offer."

Cal sighed. A part of him rejoiced that she was so unwilling to be parted from him. In addition, he didn't want Olivia being around Garrick much until Cal was sure his brother had either changed his mind about Olivia's character or had promised to be polite to her. And there was the smallest chance, after all, that she was right about drawing the danger to the Devlin farm.

"The lady has spoken, Sam," he said at last. "But Livy, honey, we *are* going to have to figure out something about where you're going to live until your house can be rebuilt...." He could tell Livy was dismayed at the thought of their idyll in the suite upstairs coming to an end, but what else could they do, since she was determined not to scandalize the town by marrying him right away?

Seeing she was struggling with the idea, he turned to his brother to give her time to think. "How's Mercy feeling?"

Sam's face looked comical. "Oh, I reckon she feels better, but she's a mite cranky now that her waist is gettin' bigger and none of her clothes fit. She an' Charity are sewin' up a storm. By the way, speakin' of Charity makes me remember to tell you, we had a letter from my old ramrod Jase Lowry, and he's gonna come visit after New Year's."

"Oh? How is Jase?" inquired Cal, remembering the man who had helped protect Sam and Mercy while Sam had been recovering from his wounds. "He must be bored wintering in San Antone waitin' for the next drive."

"Yeah, I reckon he is. And his coming might have something to do with the fact that when he last visited, Mercy told him her sister was gonna come for a spell. I think he was kinda sweet on Miss Charity back in Abilene."

"Is that a fact?" Cal inquired, tickled at the idea of Reverend Fairchild's other daughter being involved with a Texas cowboy after he'd been so opposed at first to Mercy marrying one.

"Yep—"

Just then the mayor and Mrs. Long swept into the dining room. "Mornin', folks," James Long called. "We were hoping we'd find you in here, Miz Gillespie. Fact is, we have a proposition for you."

"I wish I could just stay here," Livy murmured a few minutes later, as Cal helped her gather up her few remaining belongings in the suite. "Oh, Cal, I know it's scandalous of me to say this, but how will I ever alone with you if I'm staying at the Longs' home? It's so kind of them to offer me a place to stay, but I couldn't bear to wait until we can be married to have you make love to me again!'' she confessed. ''It'll be months!''

''I know, sugar,'' he said, taking her in his arms one more time. ''But you know it's necessary—''

''To keep up appearances,'' she said heavily, her face rebellious.

He raised her chin so she could meet his gaze. ''To preserve the good name you have every right to have,'' he corrected her, feeling as sad as she looked. ''Oh, honey, don't you think I'll wish you could be in my arms every night we're apart? We only have to be patient for a little while longer, and then I can court you openly. And maybe,'' he drawled, doing his best to look rakish, ''if we're very careful, I could sneak you up to my room without anyone seeing you.''

She brightened. ''Oh, I could be *very* careful, Sheriff.''

''That's the spirit. Now, we better get on downstairs. Sam's probably talking the mayor's ears off about our horses, and it sounds like Mrs. Long can't wait to take you shopping at the general store so y'all can sew up some new dresses and what goes under 'em,'' he said, grinning. ''While you're doing that, I'll see Sam off, then go down and make sure your stock's all right.''

''All right, brother, we'll count on seein' the two of you Sunday for dinner, then,'' Sam said later as he bent to untie Goliad's reins from the hitching post in front of the hotel. ''Don't you dare forget, or as happy as she'll be to hear you're gettin' hitched, Mama will have [y]ur hide.''

Cal had just seen Olivia disappear into the mercantile with Mrs. Long. "I won't forget," he assured Sam. "But you get Garrick aside and have a talk with him, will you? Tell him I won't brook any mean—"

"Hey, Sheriff!" someone yelled from down the street, in the direction of Doc Broughton's office.

Cal looked up to see one of the drifters who'd been recently hanging around Gillespie Springs standing in the street facing him, his gun belt low on his hips, his feet spread apart.

Beside Cal, Sam stopped untying the reins. Cal motioned for him to be still.

"What can I do for you?" Cal called back, straightening. He thought he knew the answer already, unfortunately. The man stood with a gunslinger's cocky posture, apparently relaxed, yet ready to go off like dynamite if Cal made the right move.

"Y'kin settle a bet between me an' my pard," the drifter called back, an insolent grin spreading across his face.

"Oh? What would that be about?" Cal called, keeping his voice even, while he prayed he wouldn't have to draw on the smirking fool.

"Well, *he* said you was the fastest gun in Brazos County and *I* said that time ya killed the bank robbers was a fluke. Y'made a coupla lucky shots, thass all. Y'got just one good eye, Sheriff. Y'couldn't possibly be as fast as me."

His heart sinking at the inevitability of it all, Cal stepped into the street, motioning for Sam to stay by his horse.

"Now, you don't want to draw on me just to settle a wager," Cal said reasonably. "There's no stakes worth losin' your life over."

"Oh, I don't think I'm in any danger, Sheriff," the drifter retorted. "I reckon I got me a sure bet," he added, and went for his gun.

What happened next seemed to take less time than a heartbeat. Cal's gun cleared leather and he fired, shooting the gun out of the other man's hand. The drifter screamed as the bullet ripped into his hand and the Colt went flying into the dirt. Cal said a small prayer of thanks, as the acrid smell of gunsmoke filled his nostrils, that he wouldn't have to kill the man.

As he stepped forward to arrest the man, he hoped Olivia wouldn't get hysterical. She was bound to have heard the shots from inside the general store.

But the drifter wasn't willing to lose the bet, it seemed, because he made a dive for the gun and came up shooting.

The bullet whistled by Cal's head. He fired, hitting the drifter right in the center of his chest.

Sick at heart, he walked over to the body, aware of the people starting to come out of the buildings, of women screaming. He'd dropped the man almost in the exact same spot as the bank robber had fallen that day, right in front of the bank.

He bent down to study the face of the man he'd just been forced to kill, and just then, without warning, another shot rang out, from the other end of the street, missing him by a hair's breadth.

Cal whirled, still in his crouched position, his brain registering the fact that there was another man shooting at him from down by the barbershop, even as his finger moved to squeeze the trigger. But before he could fire, another shot rang out from in front of the hotel, and the man went down, clutching his chest.

Sam had just saved Cal's life.

Shaken, Cal looked around, uncertain that it was over, but he saw no one except the horrified townspeople. "Thanks, brother," he said, hearing that his voice was steady even if his pulse wasn't, aware that down the street, Mrs. Long was holding Olivia, and both were sobbing. But he couldn't go to her now, not while his would-be assassin was writhing in the street.

With rapid strides he reached the wounded man, Sam following behind, his gun still cocked and ready.

The drifter's face was pasty gray, and there were beads of sweat on his forehead. A stream of blood trickled from his mouth. But his eyes were open and staring at Cal.

"Why?" Cal demanded, looking down at him. It was obvious the man hadn't long to tell him. "Why was it so important to kill me? You're about to meet your God, mister, and you know it, so don't hand me that nonsense about a bet, either."

"N-naw...no bet. It wuz...Gil—" There was a rasping sound and the man's mouth fell open. He was dead.

Gil— Had the man been about to say "Gillespie"? Cal was sure of it as he stood up, his gaze finding Robert Gillespie, who stood on the steps of his bank.

The two men's eyes met and locked. There was a defiant, furious quality to Gillespie's eyes. It put Cal in mind of a cougar at bay, like one he'd seen treed by a pack of coon hounds once when he was a boy. That cougar had been the death of three dogs before a bullet had ended its life.

Cal nodded, a motion so slight that no one but Robert Gillespie saw it, as Cal intended. It was both an acknowledgment and a promise.

Chapter Twenty-Four

"Someone get the undertaker."

How calm he sounded, as if nothing at all serious had happened, marveled Olivia as she stared at Cal through her tears. He stood there in the middle of the dusty street, a solid, unshakable rock, surrounded by townspeople who had stepped down off the plank walkways to gape at the dead men.

Yet a closer look revealed a jaw tightly clenched and lips set in a firm line beneath the dark mustache as he looked down again at the two who had just tried to kill him. He shook his head, and when he turned to look at her she could see the anguish that tore at him.

Olivia could tell he wanted to come to her no less than she wanted to run to him and throw herself into his arms, to sob out the terror that she had experienced in the last few moments. It might have been *him* lying there in the street, *his* blood mingling with the dirt! She might have lost him, just after they had found each other again!

But she couldn't run to him, she told herself. She had to be strong. Cal was the focus of all eyes at the moment, for many townspeople had heard the shots and were now standing between the sheriff and herself. They had to be discreet. They had to be careful not to offend anyone's sensibilities. Hadn't it been she who'd vowed that very thing, just before the fire?

Olivia saw the same struggle taking place in Cal's face. She saw him glance at the crowd, then back at her. He seemed to set his shoulders, as if a decision had been made, and then he started striding toward her.

And then she was in his arms, and he was holding her as if he never wanted to let her go.

"I'm all right, Livy," she heard him say against her hair. "I'm all right."

She couldn't seem to say anything at all, she could only cling to him, for her knees seemed suddenly no more substantial than snowballs in July. She was barely conscious of the shocked silence that slowly turned into a faint hum as the inhabitants of Gillespie Springs watched their sheriff embracing the town's most notorious widow—and she couldn't find it in herself to care.

"Mrs. Long, Mrs. Gillespie has had a nasty shock, seein' all that so soon after the tragic fire an' all," Olivia heard Cal say over her head to the mayor's wife, who had been hovering uncertainly nearby. "Perhaps today isn't the best day for y'all's shopping expedition. Since you've been so kind to offer her a place to stay, I think it'd be better if you take her over there and get her settled in."

"But Cal," Olivia protested softly, so that only he and Martha Long could hear, "I'm fine, really I am. After all, it wasn't me they were shooting at."

"Now don't argue, Livy, honey," he said in a low voice, a voice that wrapped itself around her like a warm, soothing quilt, "you're white as a sheet. You go with Mrs. Long. I'll be by later to check on you, I promise."

"Come on, Livy dear," Mrs. Long said in her soothing way. "I'll brew you a nice bracing cup of my comfrey tea. Tomorrow's soon enough to get started on your new clothes."

By this time Sam had joined his brother, and before Olivia was led away, she heard Cal say in an undertone, "Now, there'll be no need to speak of what went on here to Mama, all right?"

"You think the news won't travel to Bryan?" Sam's response was skeptical. "I'll be lucky if I make it home before the word travels, brother."

Olivia heard Cal sigh. "Well, all right, go ahead and tell her, but play it down as much as you can, okay? Tell her I'll be bringing Livy out for dinner next Sunday and that I have some news for her. That ought t'distract her from frettin' too much."

She saw Sam's grin nearly split his face. "That'll work, all right."

"Let's get away and talk some while I'm there, okay? I have an idea I want to pass by you—about what to do about the trouble in this town."

"I can see you're plottin' something," Olivia heard Sam say before she was out of earshot.

Cal spent the afternoon patroling the streets, but all seemed quiet. Stopping in once at the Last Chance, he accepted a drink from Hank Whyte, then had to politely fend off offers of more drinks from one after another back-slapping fellow. It seemed everyone wanted to celebrate his fine shooting today. It didn't seem right to Cal to toast the deaths of two men, even two gunslingers.

Leroy Scruggs was in the Last Chance, too, Cal noticed—sitting in the corner with a bottle and a pair of shifty-eyed strangers. They grew silent when he came in, studying him, then resumed a low-voiced conversation. But he could feel their eyes boring a hole in his back the whole time he was there.

After supper, Cal made his way over to the Longs' house on South Street. He'd forced himself to wait as long as he could stand it, knowing that Livy really needed the rest, as much as he wanted to be with her.

James Long greeted him at the door. "Cal, glad you're here. We were just thinking of going to prayer meeting as we usually do of a Wednesday night, but we didn't feel right going off and leaving Olivia by herself, and the missus didn't think she ought to tire herself out by going with us."

"I'll be glad to stay with her while you're gone," Cal told him, seeing Olivia sitting in the parlor smiling at him. She was wearing a flowered challis dress that must have been a relic of Mrs. Long's youth, and looked pretty as a picture.

"Evening, Sheriff," called Mrs. Long as she descended the stairs, throwing a paisley shawl around her shoulders. "You'll have time for a real good visit," she said with a wink. "You know how Reverend Poole likes to pray."

If it was anything like the prayer meetings he'd held at his church before the war, Cal knew the preacher would have his job cut out for him just getting the ladies to cease gossiping and get down to the business of prayer. And he imagined after today he and Olivia would be the prime topic, at least of the gossip.

"Yes, ma'am, I do," he replied, trying not to look too sheepish after that wink. He didn't dare look at

Olivia just then. "Say a prayer for me if you wouldn't mind."

As soon as Cal, peering through the front window, saw the mayor and his wife reach the end of their walk, he shot the bolt on the door and turned to Olivia, opening his arms.

"Oh, Cal, they knew how much we wanted to be alone together, didn't they?" she asked moments later, after he'd kissed her till they were both breathless.

"I'll bet they couldn't keep their hands off one another when they first fell in love either, Livy," he said, smiling down at her.

"Oh, I can tell they're still very much in love. Martha Long's eyes light up the minute James comes into a room. He's the same way about her. Cal, I hope we're always that way."

"We will be," he promised her. "How are you feeling, Livy? You look wonderful."

Her eyes sparkled at the compliment. "Cal, they're spoiling me to death! They won't let me lift a finger. I'm all fidgety from just sitting around resting."

He gave her a wolfish grin. "Well, sugar, is there anything you can think of we could do to work off those fidgets?" Cal asked with apparent innocence, though his lips were inches from hers. "I reckon they're going to be gone at least an hour and a half. But I wouldn't want to tire you out," he drawled.

Olivia's hands dropped from around his neck to take his hands. "Come upstairs, Cal," she said. "I reckon I could think of something."

Afterward, while they dressed, Cal said, "Livy, I want you to promise me something."

"Anything, as long as you'll do what you just did to

me every night,'' she purred, holding up her hair and presenting her back to him, where a vertical row of twenty tiny buttons needed to be fastened.

"And twice on Sunday, sugar,'' he said, surrendering to the irresistible opportunity to kiss the bared back of her neck.

She shivered from the delightful sensation of his silky mustache brushing her skin, then stood at the cheval glass and quickly began coiling her hair into the same demure knot it had been in when the Longs had left. Even though the Longs had probably guessed exactly what she and Cal would be up to while they were gone, it wouldn't do for them to return and see it loose and tousled from their passion.

"What did you want me to promise you, Cal?'' she prompted, seeing in the mirror that he looked mesmerized at the sight of her arranging her hair.

He looked mildly startled, as if she'd awakened him from a dream, then his face grew serious. "I want you to promise me that until I tell you otherwise, you won't go anywhere alone. And if both the Longs go anywhere and leave you here, you lock the door.''

She stuck the last hairpin into place and turned around. "But Cal, surely that's not necessary! No one's going to try anything in broad daylight in this tiny little town! And I've got so much to do. Why, I've got to go down and tend to Rosie and the chickens, and speak with Jovita, and consult with Jack Gray—he builds houses, you know—about the cost of rebuilding my home—though I really don't think the little I have left in savings is going to cover it....''

He held up a hand. "Whoa, there! You're getting way ahead of yourself, Livy. Let's go back to my asking you not to go out alone. It *is* necessary, honey. Just for a while. Have you forgotten that someone tried to kill you just two nights ago? I don't want them to have another chance.''

"But...but it'd be like being a prisoner here," she fretted. "It'd seem like whoever attacked me won, don't you see?"

"You can still go to the store with Mrs. Long—I don't think anyone would try anything in town, as long as someone's with you. If you want to go out and check on your stock, I'll go with you, but Davy Richardson's feeding them for you and keeping Rosie milked, so don't worry about them. This won't be forever," Cal soothed. "I believe whoever's behind your attack is going to show his true colors pretty soon."

Troubled, Olivia watched him making the bed. "I'd like to know what makes you think so." She wanted to ask him about what he'd suggested to Sam—that the two of them go off alone to talk when Cal and she visited the Devlin farm—but she figured he'd sidestep the question.

He smoothed the pillows, erasing the evidence that Olivia's head had recently lain there, then spread the coverlet over them. "Just a feeling I have," he murmured, and she could tell that was all he was going to say about the matter. "I'll ask Jovita to come visit you here, and Jack Gray too, for that matter, but is it all right if I'm there when he comes, since we're going to be married and live there together, honey?"

"Oh, Cal," she said, feeling the warmth of a blush spread over her cheeks. "Of course I want to involve you in planning the new house, but wouldn't that be rather, um, brazen of us, to be talking to Mr. Gray about a house as a couple, just yet?"

He stroked her cheek. "I reckon our secret's out, after what happened today, sugar. I guess I'm not very good at pretending not to love you and need you, so we might as well put a bold face on it. I imagine the town'd rather we married a bit sooner than live in sin.''

"Oh, Cal," she said with a little laugh, rising on tiptoe to kiss him on one cheek. "I'm not very good at it, either.''

She realized that they hadn't spoken of how they were going to afford a new house. In the normal course of things, they would apply for a loan at the bank. But there was no way she could bring herself to ask any favors from Robert Gillespie, and how could she ever explain that to Cal?

One step at a time, Olivia, she told herself. For now it was enough to know that Cal loved her, and wanted her safe.

Cal had barely sat down with his coffee the next morning when Reverend Poole entered.

"Good mornin', Reverend," Cal greeted him. "Hope you had a nice Christmas.''

The minister snorted by way of an answer. "I'm here to speak to you on quite another matter, Sheriff.''

Cal had a feeling he knew what it was. "Have a seat, Reverend. I'm listening," he said, hoping the sermon he was about to get wouldn't take too long.

Reverend Poole took out a handkerchief and wiped at the beads of sweat that had popped out on his forehead. "You came perilously close to death yesterday," he began. "God be thanked you were spared.''

"Amen," drawled Cal.

The preacher cleared his throat, looking everywhere but at Cal. "Yes. Well. I must tell you that several of the congregation have already spoken to me about what happened next, about the, um...scandalous embrace you shared afterward with the Widow Gillespie. I told them perhaps your judgment was, um, momentarily clouded by the peril you had just been in.''

Cal leaned back in his chair, fighting the urge to tell the minister to go to blazes. ''Nope.''

''Ah, um...excuse me?'' the minister said, mopping his brow again.

''No, my judgment wasn't *clouded* by my 'brush with death,' Reverend. If anything, I could see clearer after it than I have in years. I love Olivia Gillespie, and just then I didn't feel like pretendin' it wasn't so. In fact, I don't intend to pretend it isn't so anymore at all.''

''But—but...'' the minister sputtered. ''It isn't decent. She was just widowed a few months ago. It isn't right.''

Cal stood up on the other side of the desk. ''No, what isn't right is that I lost this woman back in 1861, Reverend. It's going to be 1869 in a few more days, and since I still love her, and she loves me, I don't intend to live without her much longer. Now, since you obviously don't relish the idea, I suppose I'll have to ask my sister-in-law's father in Kansas to come marry us. It'll take a little longer to get him here, and he'll be dismayed, I'm sure, to hear a fellow man of the cloth wouldn't marry us.... Nonetheless, we *will* be married just as soon as we can be, Reverend, and I'll expect everyone to give my intended wife every ounce of the respect she deserves, is that clear?''

Cal watched as pride struggled with sanctimoniousness on the preacher's face, and pride won.

''Sheriff, I...'' Poole struggled to his feet. ''You mistake me, sir. Perhaps I spoke too precipitately. I was merely, um, trying to ascertain that your intentions were honorable, that's all. Never let it be said I would not bless a union of two of my flock who love one another. If you intend matrimony, I'd be happy to marry you."

Cal couldn't help but feel sorry for Poole. He reminded Cal of a big rabbit who'd been trapped by a cougar. "Oh, I intend matrimony, all right," he replied, softening his tone somewhat. "Now, if you'll excuse me, Reverend, I need to go confer with my deputy."

Chapter Twenty-Five

Señor Cal and Livy's embrace in the street after the gunfight was the talk of the town, Jovita Mendez said when she came two days later. She was here to help Olivia and Mrs. Long cut out the fabric, fit and sew the first of Olivia's new clothes.

"I can tell," Livy said with a wry look. "When we went to the general store yesterday to buy this cloth, Ada Gray and Phoebe Stone and a handful of other ladies were in there talking, and when I walked inside, suddenly you could have heard a pin drop. Then they went on talking, but you could tell they must have changed the subject. And they were so *interested* in what sort of fabric I was buying, what sort of dresses I was planning. I wonder what they think of me for buying something besides black."

"It's not as if either of these fabrics are gaudy colors, though," Martha Long said comfortably, pointing at the pieces of muted lavender brilliantine and gray flowered cassimere. "And under the circumstances," she added with a meaningful smile, "it wouldn't be appropriate for you to wear mourning anymore. I heard Reverend

Poole's already planning to make this the best wedding he ever officiated.''

"Goodness," Olivia said with a laugh, "Cal and I haven't even set a date yet!"

"They say eet weel not be long, after seeing the way he keesses you," Jovita said, kneeling at Olivia's feet to baste the hem of the pinned-together dress of gray cassimere. "Señor Cal, he ees *muy macho,* no?"

"No! I mean, yes!" Livy laughed in helpless confusion, feeling herself blush as the two women chuckled at her embarrassment. "Not to change the subject or anything, but are we really going to be able to finish this dress in time for me to wear it tomorrow, when Cal and I go and visit his family?"

"*Sí, sin duda,* of course," Jovita said. "We must have you looking your best for your future *suegra,* your mother-een-law, no?"

"Yes. Though I've known her as long as I've known Cal, of course. I hope she'll really be as pleased as Cal says she will."

"Once she sees how happy her son looks, she's bound to be."

"It'll be good for Cal to get away from town for the day," Livy said. "He's so worried about the number of drifters that have showed up around here lately."

"There's two less than there were, thank God," Martha Long reminded her.

"Yes," agreed Olivia, shuddering as she remembered the sight of the two gunslingers lying dead in the street. "But there's half a dozen more prowling around town like wolves. They're up to all kinds of shenanigans, as if they're *trying* to provoke him. Why, he's got one in his jail right now who was shooting the glasses off the bar of the Last Chance. If Cal hadn't gotten the advan-

tage of him by sneaking in the back way and shooting
the gun out of his hand, I'm sure he would have tried
to provoke Cal into a gunfight. And I know Cal
wouldn't have told me, but I saw a bullet hole next to
the jail door—it seems someone took a shot at him as
he was passing the front of the jail the other night after
he left here. He went looking, but never found anyone.
He heard a horse galloping away, though.''

"*Madre de Dios,*" murmured Jovita, crossing herself. "*Jesús* protect him!"

"We're going to leave at dawn tomorrow for his
mother's farm, rather than go after church, just so
there's less chance of any of those drifters being up and
around to see us go. I declare, I won't draw an easy
breath until we reach the Devlin farm!''

"Gracious, Livy, I hate to see you having to worry
like that—you've been through so much lately," Martha Long sympathized.

Olivia sighed. "Yes, I wish we could just relax and
look forward to being married, but Cal seems to think
all this trouble is going to be over someday. It's as if
he knows something I don't...."

"Men!" snorted Martha Long. "I hope he didn't tell
you not to worry your pretty little head about men's
business?"

Olivia smiled at that. "No, he wouldn't talk that way.
He just...keeps his own counsel, you know?"

"Well, I'm sure you know my husband has the ut-
most confidence in him, just as the town does," Martha
Long said, as if that settled the matter.

It was late by the time they neared Gillespie Springs
the next night after their visit to the Devlin farm. A

light rain had just begun to fall, but they were sheltered under the calash top of the rented shay.

"Oh, Cal, I'm so relieved that your mother seems happy about our upcoming marriage," Livy said. "I was so afraid she'd be shocked that we're not waiting a year and all."

"Honey, my mother has always liked you," Cal said, giving her a hug as the horse trotted along.

"Even after I was so mean to you when you were going away to war?"

"Does that mean you've repented your righteous anger at me for wearing blue?" Cal could not resist teasing.

Livy sighed deeply. "Oh, Cal, it was all so long ago...I think there was right on both sides, but neither side had all of the right. But I wish I'd never lost sight of the most important thing—our love."

Cal hugged her closer. "Well, we'll never lose sight of it again, will we? And as for my mother, she thought *you* were right, that I should have fought for the South."

"Well, I don't think Garrick will ever approve," she said. "He was always a serious boy, but it's sad how... gloomy and disapproving he is about everything."

"Oh, I wouldn't worry about Garrick putting a stick in our spokes," Cal said. "He's going to have his hands full deciding what to do about that letter he got."

"Indeed! Just imagine getting a letter from the wife who deserted him, after all this time, saying she's coming back! Is Garrick going to accept her, do you think?"

"I don't think even Garrick knows the answer to that," Cal mused.

"And isn't Mercy's sister pretty as she can be? But so different from Mercy! And she seems quite excited about Mr. Lowry's upcoming visit," Livy continued. Cal had told her about the attraction that had sprung up between Jase and Charity back in Abilene.

She and Cal were getting close to town, and Olivia steeled herself to ask the question that had been plaguing her. "Cal, what did you and Sam go off in the barn to discuss?"

"Oh, horses and old times in Abilene and such," Cal said, keeping his eye on the horse trotting steadily in front of him.

"Caleb Devlin, I don't believe that for a minute!" she said, impatient at the evasion. "I hate it when I know something's being kept from me, and I know you're worried about the drifters in Gillespie Springs lately. Your going off to talk to Sam has something to do with them, doesn't it?"

"I don't know why you'd think that."

"Let's just call it women's intuition," she said.

His gaze was serious in the shadows of the covered vehicle. "Livy, I'm going to have to ask you to just trust me on this for a while. I can't talk about everything that's on my mind right now, for your own safety, honey. Please, just trust me?"

Olivia sat back, frustrated.

"Please, honey?" he said, his free hand taking hold of hers. "I promise you one of these days soon you'll understand, but for now..."

Olivia stared at his shadowy face. She thought of insisting that he tell her what was going on, but then she felt guilty about adding to the pressures he faced as sheriff. And she had her own secrets, didn't she? Surely it wasn't right to plague him for answers he wasn't willing to give yet when she was also unable to tell him the identity of the man who had raped her?

They were passing the charred ruins of her house by this time. The stone chimney, all that remained standing, shone like a giant tombstone. She averted her eyes until they were past.

Main Street was deserted and dark except for the light and the tinny piano music coming from the Last Chance.

"Oh, Cal, we don't have to say good-night yet, do we?" she asked wistfully. "The Longs don't know when we're getting back, though they knew it'd be late."

"Livy, honey, what're you saying?" he asked, turning to her, surprise evident on his lean face.

She looked down at her hands, suddenly feeling foolish at the unladylike obviousness of what she had said. She sounded like a shameless hussy, didn't she? Was he sorry that his passion had awakened that side of her? Did he long for her to be a lady again, even if it meant she just lie passive beneath him when he took his pleasure?

He tipped her chin up and she could see the smile playing about his lips. "Now, don't go gettin' all shy, honey. I love it when you let me know you want to be with me. Why don't we steal up to my room above the jail? We'll have to put Blue and the shay away first, and I'll go into the jail for a moment so Kristof knows he can go on home. Can you wait that long?"

Her pulse began to race. "If you hurry," she said with a little laugh.

Cal's horse was handed over to the sleepy liveryman, and minutes later they were tiptoeing up the wooden stairs behind the jail that led to Cal's room.

"I'll just be a minute," he said, turning the key in the lock. "Go on in."

While she waited for him, she busied herself with lighting the lamp beside the bed, then looking around the small room. There was little in the spartan bachelor's quarters besides the narrow bed, a table and a chair, but all was neatly arranged. There was none of the usual masculine clutter—the plugs of chewing tobacco, wadded-up clothing and half-consumed bottles of whiskey—left lying about as there had been in the spare bedroom Dan had taken over when he'd returned from the war. The worst thing she saw was a folded-up newspaper from yesterday on the table.

"Well, Kristof says the prisoner's been behaving," Cal said as he entered a few minutes later, taking off his hat, hanging his coat on its hook and unstrapping the gun belt he'd donned for the trip. "I sure wish I could get him to say why he picked Gillespie Springs to drift into...."

His voice trailed off as she came to him, smiling that winsome smile that made him ache for want of her.

"I don't want to talk about him, do you, Cal?" she murmured, beginning to unbutton the stiffly starched shirt that was his Sunday best.

He grinned. "Who? I've already forgotten," he said hoarsely, trying not to groan as her fingers finished the shirt buttons and went on to the buttons of his trousers. He was already hard and ready, but he was determined to delay his own satisfaction until he'd shown her another way to pleasure.

"Wait, honey, wait," he murmured in her ear, holding on to her with one hand as he bent to turn down the lamp until it was just a soft glow in the room. "You're making me so hot I want to toss you on the bed and throw up your skirts and bury myself inside you,'' he confessed, returning to lay his forehead against her cool one.

"Would that be so bad?" she whispered with a little laugh, pulling him into the cradle of her hips.

"Yes, because then I would be too spent to do what I had in mind," he murmured, undoing the buttons on the back of her dress.

"Oh? And what did you have in mind, Cal?" she asked, her breath warm in his ear as she strained to be closer to him. Why did women use so many darned tiny buttons, he wondered, feeling his hands shake as he struggled to free the woman he loved from her clothing. After the dress came the petticoats, layers of them, then the corset cover, followed by the blasted corset itself...

When at last they were naked, he pulled her to the bed and sank down on it with her. "Lord, honey, I never dreamed when I came to this town I'd be making love to you on this bed one night."

"Me, either," she whispered back. "Mmm, Cal, that feels so good. Cal...Cal?" her voice took on an uncertain note as he knelt before her and spread her legs, then lowered his mouth to kiss her in that most intimate of places. "Cal, just a minute! What are you—are you sure you should—Cal?"

"Shh," he whispered, reaching up to put a finger gently on her lips. "Yes, I'm quite sure I should, Livy...just enjoy it...."

He felt her gasp as his tongue stroked her. She bucked and tried to pull away. "Oh, Cal!" she cried raggedly, burying her fingers in his hair, clutching his shoulders as he continued to please her—and himself. She writhed and moaned as he continued to love her with his lips and tongue, his hands holding her hips to him.

He smiled as she gave a little shriek and went still, then collapsed into the softness of the bed. Stretching out beside her, Cal pulled her limp body into his arms and waited until she came back to her senses.

"Cal, I never—I mean, how would a preacher like you were—" She broke off in confusion, burying her face in his shoulder. "Never mind, I don't want to know how you learned to do that..." she paused and sighed "...as long as you promise to do it again sometime."

"Sweetheart, in future all you have to do is ask. There isn't anything I wouldn't do to make you feel as good as you make me feel," he promised her, rising above her and parting her legs gently with his knee. "And now I'm going to see if we can make that happen for you again, while it's happening for me...."

"It's safe," Cal called up the stairs some time later.

Olivia blew out the lamp, then cautiously opened the door and crept down the shadowy outside staircase. The rain had stopped, and there was a fresh, crisp smell to the midnight air.

"Honey, I'd have given anything just to go on to sleep with you in my arms," Cal said, putting his arm around her waist as they walked up the darkened side street in the direction of the mayor's house. "I love being with you in any way, but I want to be *married* to you, Livy, not worryin' about who might see us and what they might think."

"Oh, Cal..." she began.

"And if you're still worried about what people will say, what're they going to say if our baby's born seven months after the wedding, hmm?"

Olivia stopped stock-still in the quiet street. The fact that she might already be carrying his child was something she hadn't allowed herself to think about—much, anyway.

Pressing his advantage, he said, "Let's go ahead and get married, honey. As soon as possible."

She could hear the frustration and longing in his voice. "Oh, Cal, do we dare? What about your job?"

"They got used to the fact that I fought for the Yankees during the war and I believe they'll accept this, too, if they know I won't back down on it. Wearin' this badge is a lot less important than you are to me. If they can't accept that, I'll give 'em back the badge and we'll go elsewhere! I hear California's mighty pretty."

"Oh, Cal, how could you stand to leave Texas and move so far away from your family? I hope we don't have to do that," she said. "All right, we'll go ahead and get married. But Cal," she said, just as they reached Main Street, "could you give me a couple of weeks to make a wedding dress? I've dreamed of this day, the day I'll become Mrs. Caleb Devlin. I want to have time to make a really beautiful, special dress, please?"

She looked up at him entreatingly, but she was walking on his right side, the side with the patched eye, and he had his profile to her, so she couldn't tell what he was thinking. She stopped him in the middle of the street. "Cal, *please?*"

"Okay," he said, giving her waist a loving squeeze. "I'd marry you if you were wearin' a feed sack, honey, but I guess I can wait a couple of weeks. But no more," he added teasingly. "Let's set a definite date for...the second Saturday of the month, all right? Let's see, that would be what—the eleventh of January? I'll go see Reverend Poole tomorrow."

If she hadn't happened to glance down the street past

the jail just then, she wouldn't have seen it—a quick red glow that faded as quickly as it had appeared.

"Cal, there's someone down there," she said nervously, knowing he wouldn't have seen it because of his blind eye. "I saw a light...like someone inhaling on a cigarette...."

Olivia felt him stiffen and withdraw his arm, and saw his right hand fall to the Colt on his right hip as he turned to look. The glow was gone. She could see no one in the shadows that shrouded the fronts of the buildings.

"Who's there?" Cal challenged, stepping in front of her, but only silence answered him.

She felt the hairs on the back of her neck stand up.

A click sounded clearly in the night air, the sound of a pistol being cocked.

"Damnation!" Cal exclaimed. Olivia felt him give her a shove with his left hand while he drew his Colt with his right. She went down heavily on her shoulder, landing just at the corner of the bank building. But she had no thought for the stinging pain and twisted in time to see a red flash as the man in the shadows fired. Cal returned fire, and she heard a grunted curse from the direction of the livery stable, then the sound of running footsteps.

Stunned by what had just happened, Livy scrambled to her feet and huddled against the side of the building, peering around it, expecting to see Cal get shot down at any moment. *"Cal!"*

He ran to her side and ducked behind the building, flattening himself against it and looking around it in the direction the shot had come from. "Are you all right?" he asked over his shoulder.

"I—I think so, Cal. How about you?"

"I hit the bastard," he hissed, "but there may be more of them in the shadows. Come on, we've got to get you to cover!"

Hugging the side of the building, they ran through the darkness to South Street, not stopping till they had reached the mayor's house, where Cal covered her while she fumbled with the key Mrs. Long had loaned her.

The Longs had left a lamp burning in the vestibule.

"Cal, are you all right?" Livy demanded as she stared at him in the flickering lamplight.

His face was grim. "Yeah, though we might both be dead if you hadn't seen that light. Sorry I had to knock you down, honey, but you were an easy target in that light-colored dress. Are you sure you're okay?"

Olivia eyed the torn, muddy sleeve of her new dress and gingerly felt her shoulder. "I'm just scraped," she said, but that wasn't important now.

"I've got to get back out there," he told her. "I winged whoever shot at us, and he may be lying wounded by the livery or close by. I'll be back, Livy," he said, and then the door slammed behind him.

A moment later, she heard the creak of floorboards above her. "What's going on?" demanded a voice from the top of the stairs. James Long stood there in his dressing gown, with his wife behind him, clutching a shawl fearfully around her.

Chapter Twenty-Six

It was an hour before Cal, who'd been joined by James Long as soon as he had thrown some clothes on, returned to the house.

Livy and Martha jumped up from their chairs by the hearth, leaving their cups of tea on the side table as they rushed to greet Cal and James.

"We didn't find him, though there's some spots of blood between the jail and the livery stable," Cal told them, hating to see Livy's face so white and frightened. "Kristof came and said someone galloped down North Street going east, but he couldn't see who it was. I sent him to check on the prisoner till I could get back. Half the town's out in the street demanding to know what's going on, but apparently the shooter managed to get away before anyone got to a window."

He saw Livy's back become a little less rigid, but her eyes remained troubled.

"Well, thank God neither of you was hit," Martha Long said practically. "I imagine you men could use some coffee," she said. "Come help me, James," she said, and bustled in the direction of the kitchen.

As soon as they were alone, Cal turned to Olivia.

"That settles it, Livy. You're going to my mother's till all this dies down."

Her jaw dropped. "Or until you're killed? I'm not leaving, Cal, unless you leave with me," she retorted, her hands on her hips.

He slammed a hand against the side table in frustration. "Livy, you might have been killed tonight!" he shouted at her, his fear for her transforming itself into anger—and helpless rage that he had not found the would-be assassin.

He saw her flinch at his loudness, then she drew herself up to her full height. "So might you have!" she shouted back, her eyes blazing blue fire at him.

Already dangerously frustrated, he felt his temper start to boil. "Livy, damn it, you're going to go where I know you're safe if I have to bind you and gag you to get you there!"

"That's a fine way for someone who used to be a preacher to talk!" she retorted. "And don't try ordering me around in that high-handed way, Caleb Devlin. I'm not leaving!"

He started to shout back at her, then caught himself. "Livy, please," he murmured. "Honey, I just have to know you're safe. Please say you'll go."

"I'm staying right here in Gillespie Springs and starting on my wedding dress, *if* you still want to marry me," she said.

"If?" he echoed, his gut clenching.

"If you still want to marry someone who isn't meek and mealymouthed," she explained. "Cal, I'll stay right here at the Longs' house, except when we go to the general store to buy my wedding-dress material and trim and such, but I'm not leaving town."

He stared at her, loving her for her determination and spirit even while his heart raced with fear for her.

Robert Gillespie felt angry as a teased rattlesnake when Leroy Scruggs was announced the following evening.

"I sent Junius for you an hour ago," he informed his enforcer in a frigid voice from his wing chair beside the fire. "Where have you been?"

"I was down at the Last Chance when he found me," Scruggs said. "Boss, I know ya ain't happy with how things've been going, but—"

"No, Scruggs, I 'ain't happy,' as you so succinctly put it," he mocked. "Two of your 'associates' are dead, and last night, I'm informed, someone tried to gun Devlin down in the dark when he was walking his paramour home. Couldn't even ambush a one-eyed man, damn him! And now the news is all around town that the sheriff is going to wed that bitch Olivia in a fortnight! The whole town's planning to come to the wedding. Do you have any idea how that makes me feel, when I gave you the simple task of ensuring that both of them were killed? *Do you*, Scruggs?"

"Yessir, I reckon so. But boss—"

"Where is the miserable son of a bitch?" Gillespie interrupted. "The one who shot at Devlin last night?"

"Grady? He hightailed it outa town with his arm still bleedin'. Said he'd go find a sawbones in some other town," Scruggs replied, eyeing Gillespie as if he guessed that his boss wanted to draw the gun he kept hidden in his smoking-jacket pocket and shoot *him*. "But boss," Scruggs went on quickly, "a new fella came to town today—I met him in the saloon this eve-

nin'. I think he's gonna be the answer to yer prayers."
Scruggs's face was eager now.

"Is that right? And who might he be?"

"He says his name is Johnny Santone—I guess he's
from San Antonio," Scruggs added unnecessarily.
"And he's a gunslinger, all right. The best. He'll gun
down the sheriff for ya, right enough."

"Oh? And what makes you so sure, when all the
others have failed so abysmally?" Gillespie inquired,
letting acid drip in his voice. He knew from Scruggs's
blank expression that he didn't know what *abysmal*
meant, and for a moment Gillespie was so disgusted that
he began to finger the derringer in his pocket. It would
be so enjoyable to kill the useless idiot who stood before him, if it weren't for the bother of getting rid of
his body afterward.

"I could tell just by lookin' at him, even if it wasn't
fer the notches on the butt of his gun, boss. But I figgered ya'd like t'see fer yoreself," Scruggs said. "All
right if I show him in? He's waitin' 'round back."

"He is? How very enterprising of you, Scruggs."

Scruggs left as if he couldn't get out of the room fast
enough. A moment later, Gillespie heard the *clink-clink*
of spurs as the gunslinger was shown in through the
kitchen in the back and down the hall to the room where
he waited.

The man entering the room was dressed all in black
except for the silver *concha*s on his belt and decorating
the band around his hat, and he was whipcord lean. It
was hard to place his age—maybe thirty? There was a
Colt strapped to each hip, and sure enough, a score or
so of vertical marks notched the polished wood grip of
the gun on the right side. His eyes were shadowed under
the brim of his hat; a couple of days' growth of beard

shaded lean jaws. The gunslinger clinked to a stop at a respectful distance from Gillespie's chair and pulled off his hat, revealing collar-length black hair and the coldest dark eyes Gillespie had ever seen.

"I'm Johnny Santone, Mr. Gillespie," he said in a voice that was neither awed nor insolent. "I heard you needed a man killed."

"Yes," Gillespie said, still looking him up and down. "Did you really kill that many men?" he asked, pointing to the notches cut into the butt of the Colt.

A half smile played about the other man's lips, as if he found it a foolish question but was too polite to say so. "Yes."

"Then how come I haven't heard of you? Seen a Wanted poster?"

"I've been over in the Arizona Territory," Johnny Santone said. "I just came back to Texas last month, and happened to be ridin' through when I heard that you needed a gunfighter."

In spite of himself, Gillespie felt a stirring of excitement. This man could get the job done; he knew it.

"I'm offering five hundred dollars if you can kill Caleb Devlin, the sheriff."

"That's a lot of money," the stranger drawled.

"I can afford it, and I want him dead. And if you aren't too squeamish to kill a woman, I want his fiancée killed, too—Olivia Gillespie. I'll throw in another two hundred for her."

"Gillespie?" the man said, looking intrigued. "Kin?"

"My former sister-in-law, the conniving bitch. You aren't too squeamish to contemplate killin' a woman, are you?"

Santone's smile never reached his eyes. "The first person I ever killed was a woman."

Gillespie made himself smile back, though he found it difficult to meet those cold eyes. "Then we have a deal," he said, extending his hand. "Scruggs, go tell the servants to get that empty cabin ready for Mr. Santone. You're to discuss his reason for staying there with no one—*no one,* do you understand? Then I want you to go tell the saddle tramps hanging around town to hit the trail. Tell them I've abandoned the plan, that I don't need them anymore."

"But boss—" Scruggs began, blinking in confusion.

"Do as I say," Gillespie snapped.

He was silent while the man shuffled out of the room. Maybe he could think of a way to have Santone kill Scruggs, too, Gillespie realized. The "enforcer" had proven himself intolerably incompetent, but he knew too much, and Gillespie would have to get rid of him. "Now here's what I'd like you to do," he said, as soon as Scruggs shut the door behind him. "I want you to remain out of sight, Santone, until I give you the word. Your meals will be brought to you three times a day. I don't want you seen in town. I want Devlin to think his troubles are over, you understand?"

Again, the stranger flashed that cold smile. "I understand."

"I'll let you know a few hours before you are to act. It might be as long as a fortnight, is that clear? You'll be given your instructions regarding Devlin and his bride at that time—and half the money. I'll have wired the other half to a bank on the Mexican border. You'll need a fast horse after you carry out your orders—"

"I have a fast horse." He paused, clearly waiting on Gillespie. "I'll go get settled in, if that's all."

The banker waved a hand in dismissal, watching the gunslinger close the door behind him, then he smiled to himself. He wasn't foolish enough to tell Johnny Santone all the details until he needed to know them. Gillespie had considered just telling Santone to come back the night of the tenth, but he'd thought better of it. He wanted him here where he could keep an eye on him. Gunslingers were always getting in drunken brawls and landing in jail, or worse, getting killed. No, he wanted Johnny Santone right here, getting edgy and bored and spoiling for a fight.

This plan was pure poetry. "That smug fool," Gillespie murmured aloud, thinking of Devlin. "Just when he least expects it—" he held up his fingers as if they were a gun, suddenly flexing his thumb "—*Blam!* How perfect to have Devlin and his fiancée murdered on their wedding day by a gunman who then escapes."

The railroad trustees had given Gillespie a deadline— the middle of the month. If he couldn't turn over the property in its entirety by that time, they'd have to consider another route. He'd go to Bryan tomorrow and send a telegram to the trustees, letting them know he'd won Olivia's agreement to sell him the last portion of the needed property, and invite them to come and view their new holdings on the thirteenth—even earlier than they'd specified, which would make him look even more competent. By then he'd be wearing a black band of mourning for the tragic murder of his former sister-in-law and her husband-to-be, the sheriff, but the trustees wouldn't know how false his grief was.

When they came he'd have the bill of sale ready in the safe, complete with Olivia's graceful copperplate signature, which he'd copy from an old letter she'd sent Dan when he was fighting with the Confederate army.

How tragic that she hadn't lived to enjoy the profits from her sale, he'd say. But of course, as the only living relative of her dead husband, that money would come back to him, too.

Leaving his wing chair and going over to the sideboard, he poured himself a brandy from the cut-glass decanter and stared into the fire as he thought of Dan's wife.

Olivia. If only she hadn't repulsed his earlier advances and had married him instead of his brother. Then he wouldn't have had to do what he had done. She had forced him to it.

Jealousy he thought long conquered made his insides writhe like serpents inside him at the thought of her arching in passion under Caleb Devlin. *It should have been me.*

Suddenly Gillespie threw the delicate snifter into the fire, watching in grim satisfaction as the glass shattered and the alcohol made the fire flare up in green-blue flames.

It seemed like the plague of drifters and saddle tramps afflicting Gillespie Springs was over as quickly as it had begun. They'd come for no apparent reason and, like locusts, had inflicted the town, loitering in front of the saloon, leering at the ladies who passed by, getting arrested for the mischief they got into out of boredom. And then, just as suddenly, they were gone. Why? Even the rowdy cowboy Cal had arrested for shooting up the Last Chance hadn't lingered any longer than it took to collect his horse from the livery stable and saddle up.

"I know I should just be thankful that they've drifted somewhere else," Cal was saying a few evenings before the wedding day, after he, Olivia and the Longs had just finished a fine supper at the hotel. Cal and Olivia had insisted on treating the mayor and his wife, as a way of thanking them for giving Olivia a home until she married Cal.

"Yes, you should," Martha Long said in her decided way. "It's an answer to everybody's prayers, I say! Let's talk some more about the house! When does Jack Gray think he can start, Olivia dear?"

"The first of February, if the weather is good. And it's so wonderful to think that the men in town are all going to help build the house, while the women cook dinner and supper, too! They must really appreciate their sheriff!"

"I think they've learned to appreciate the woman I love, too," Cal replied gallantly, giving the hand he held on the top of the table a squeeze.

"I never would have imagined that, a few months ago," she admitted with a wry smile. "Only fancy, Phoebe Stone offering to sing a solo at our wedding, when it was obvious she'd set her cap for you when you first came to town."

The mayor and his wife chuckled at Cal's discomfiture.

"I think you're imaginin' that, honey."

"Oh, no, I'm not—I saw the gleam in her eye!" Olivia retorted tartly.

"It sounds as if your new home is going to be even nicer than the old one," James Long interjected, rescuing Cal.

"Yes, it's going to be bigger, with plenty of room for the family we hope to have," Livy told him, blushing slightly, as befitted a woman about to be married.

"And of course, we shall have to have new furniture made...."

Livy was radiant with joy, just as a bride-to-be should be, Cal thought, drinking in the loveliness of her face. He wished he could join wholeheartedly in it and just savor the peace that the sudden disappearance of the drifters had provided.

He wished that he knew exactly what Gillespie was planning. Even the man who had come secretly to his room over the jail in the middle of the night a week ago had to admit he didn't know the details of when and how. It made Cal feel damned uneasy, like a man forced to walk blindfolded and barefoot through a room in which he knew there was a loose rattlesnake.

"None of this would be possible, of course, without the bank loan we were able to get in Bryan. I guess they've decided to 'forgive' Cal," Livy was saying. "Of course, Robert offered us money, too, but we didn't feel right about taking it, even though it was almost no interest."

"Perhaps your former brother-in-law has had a change of heart," Martha Long suggested. "For his brother's sake. Oh, dear, I didn't mean—"

"No, it's all right," Olivia said, smoothing over the awkward moment. She shrugged, saying, "I suppose miracles do still happen—after all, Cal and I have found each other again after so many years."

Everyone smiled.

"Cal, your family will be in town the day before the wedding?" James Long inquired. "Good. We'll have their rooms all ready. Sure you won't mind spending your wedding night in the same hotel?"

"I reckon we'll be just fine." Cal grinned. "They'll be going on home the next morning. And we're much obliged, not only for you puttin' them up but for letting me and Livy stay there until our house can be built. My room above the jail would be intimate, but even newlyweds shouldn't have such close quarters as that tiny room.''

Long beamed. "I just want to keep the best sheriff this town ever had happy enough to remain here with his lovely bride. I congratulate myself every day when I remember it was I who asked you to pin on that star."

"I can't thank you enough, Mayor." Cal was touched by the man's warmth, which reflected that of the rest of the town—most of the people, anyway, he thought, remembering Gillespie perched in his grand house like a coiled rattlesnake—a snake that had once struck at the woman Cal loved.

Lord knew he and Livy hadn't had much private time of late, but even if they had, he doubted she would have confided in him that Gillespie had been the man who had once raped her, causing the death of an innocent man and his own brother's suicide. And yet Cal sensed the event festered in her soul. Please God, let him find a way to make Gillespie confess.

"And speaking of lovely brides," Martha Long piped up in the silence, "I can't *wait* for you to get a glimpse of Olivia in her wedding dress, Cal! She'll be like a vision from heaven, I promise you! We plan to add the finishing touches of the lace flounces tomorrow, and don't you dare try to peek when she tries it on, Sheriff— it's bad luck, you know!" she admonished him with a wagging finger.

Cal held up his hands in mock surrender. "I promise, I won't even try."

Chapter Twenty-Seven

"I wonder how Garrick's doing about now?" Sam muttered on the morning of the wedding as he wiggled his neck against the unfamiliar starched collar.

Garrick had received another letter from Cecelia, this one telling him she was due to arrive in Bryan on the stage today. Cal regretted that his eldest brother wouldn't be present to see him take his vows, but he knew Garrick had wanted privacy for his first meeting with the woman who had once deserted him, so perhaps things had worked out for the best.

"Lord, I hope he decides to bend his stubborn pride a little," Sam continued. "His wife wasn't such a *bad* woman, as I recall, just a little flighty. And who wouldn't have found Garrick hard to be around when he first stumped in on those crutches, mean as a maddened bull?"

"Neither of them is perfect," Cal agreed absently, though his mind wasn't really on the reunion taking place in Bryan. He was going to be married in less than an hour.

"You about ready to go get hitched, Cal? I reckon you're about as pretty as you're gonna get," Sam said as Cal checked his appearance in the cracked mirror over the sink for the hundredth time.

"Fortunately Livy's pretty enough for both of us," Cal retorted, giving a rueful nod toward the image in the glass.

"Well, come on then, you don't want to leave your bride waiting for you at the church," Sam said, heading for the door.

Just then they heard a knock. "James, that you?" Cal called, thinking the mayor had come to collect him instead of waiting in front of the hotel as he'd said he was going to do.

"No, it's me—Jase. Hurry up and let me in," a low voice said.

Cal's heart sank as Sam opened the door and Jase Lowry stepped in.

"I don't think anyone saw me," he said with a glance over his shoulder as he kicked the door shut with his boot heel. "Everyone's either at the church or out on the street waiting for the bride and groom to go by."

It was Jase Lowry, the man who'd been Sam's trail-driving ramrod. Beneath the floppy brim of his hat, Jase had several days' growth of beard shadowing his cheeks. He looked dangerous.

"Hello, Jase. Long time no see. Please tell me you're not here for the reason I think you are," he said. "Not today."

"Yeah, I'm afraid so. Sorry, Cal. I didn't find out until a couple of hours ago, and then I had the devil of a time sneaking here to warn you."

"On our wedding day. *Damn him*," Cal growled. "Our wedding day! Damn it to hell, he's got the devil's own sense of timing, doesn't he?"

"I'm afraid he couldn't resist the idea of having you

gunned down today of all days. Guess he figured you wouldn't be armed.''

"He'd be wrong," Cal said, lifting the frock coat to show the pistol stuck in the waistband of his pants. "When?"

Jase told him.

"Will there be anyone else?" Sam asked.

Jase Lowry shook his head. "Nope. Guess he was pretty disgusted when all those other hired guns failed to get the job done. He's putting all his eggs in one basket. Well, I'd better be goin'. Oh, and Cal—" Lowry hesitated at the door "—he means for me to gun down your bride, too."

Cal stared at Sam after the door had closed behind Jase. He swallowed. His throat felt thick with the rage that threatened to swallow him. "Damn him! It's bad enough he wants to have *me* killed on our wedding day, but he thinks he's going to have Livy murdered, too? Maybe I'll kill him twice."

Sam met his gaze steadily, not trying to calm him down, not arguing. Then his eyes focused on something behind Cal. "I know you'll do the right thing, Cal," he said at last.

Cal turned around to see that Sam had been staring at the big, black, leather-bound Bible that was sitting on the small table where Cal had been reading it only this morning.

"Vengeance is mine, I will repay, saith the Lord," echoed in Cal's mind, along with "Blessed are the peacemakers."

Well, Lord, you sure made it hard to be a peacemaker and leave the vengeance to you when you sent a snake like Robert Gillespie into my life—and Livy's. I believe

*you want me to keep Livy safe. Show me what you want
me to do.*

Aloud he said, "I'll do what I have to do." He
pinned the star on his waistcoat, then let the folds of
the black frock coat fall back over it.

"My dear, I'm sure you're the most beautiful bride
this town ever saw," Sarah Devlin said to Olivia,
straightening the flounced train of her daughter-to-be's
wedding dress. "That color is just perfect with your
dark hair and blue eyes."

"Thank you, Mother Devlin," Olivia murmured, using the name Cal's mother had suggested. It sounded
strange on her tongue as yet, but she thought she would
get used to it. It would be nice to have a mother again,
she decided, smiling at the gray-haired woman before
her. It had been so many years since her own mother
had died.

"That's called 'mauveine,'" announced Martha
Long, referring to the delicate shade of lavender of
Olivia's gown. "It said so in the *Harper's Bazaar* we
looked in at the general store."

"And that yoke bodice with the satin-ribbon lattice
is just exquisite," Mrs. Devlin gushed. "Your handi-
work, Señora Mendez?"

Jovita, dressed in her Sunday-best skirt, blouse and
black mantilla, had been hovering nearby. "*Sí*, Señora
Devleen, I deed the needlework, but Mrs. Long gave
her the freshwater pearls between the reebbons."

"Oh, pshaw, they were from a broken necklace and
were just lying in a dish. I'd always meant to have it
restrung, but then I decided it was just the thing to dec-
orate Livy's dress."

"And here's something borrowed," Mercy said,

coming forward and holding out a gold necklace with a cross pendant. She went behind Olivia, careful to avoid the lace flounces of her train, and fastened it.

"And here's your something blue," Charity said, pulling a tissue-wrapped object from her reticule. She removed the paper, revealing a garter of garish royal blue satin with an ostrich-feather trim.

"Charity, where on earth did you get that?" Mercy asked her.

"From Mercedes LaFleche," Charity said with an impish giggle. "She said since I was coming to Texas, where all the handsomest men were from, I was sure to come back married, and I'd need something blue."

The women all chuckled, familiar with story of how Mercy's husband, Sam, had taken Mercy to be the notorious sporting woman Mercedes LaFleche when he'd first met her in the infamous Alamo Saloon—the very same saloon in which Cal had been working as a bartender before he'd regained his memory.

"Good Lord, Charity, you never change, do you? If Papa knew you'd been talking to that woman he'd have an apoplexy," Mercy groaned.

"Thank you for doing my hair, Annie," Olivia said to Cal's widowed sister, who was watching her from over by the window with a wistful expression on her face. Was she remembering the day she'd married her husband, who had been killed in the war? "You've done wonders with that curling iron." Livy was pleased that the style looked neither overly virginal nor matronly.

"Your hair was a pleasure to work with, as thick and shiny as it is," Annie replied.

"Thank you. Thank you all," Livy said, staring almost disbelievingly at the beautiful image in the cheval glass. "I feel like a queen."

"Well, your majesty," quipped Charity, "when would you like to leave for the church? I'll make sure your royal train doesn't drag in the dirt."

"I'd say we could go pretty soon," commented Annie. "There go the men now."

With a rustle of taffeta petticoats, the other women rushed to the window that looked out over Main Street.

"Lord, why do men always look like they're goin' to a hangin' when they're goin' to a wedding?" Sarah Devlin said aloud.

Livy looked, and there they were, walking abreast— Cal, and Sam, resplendent in black frock coats and starched white shirts and ties.

Cal looked serious. Solemn. Maybe even a little stern, she decided as they turned onto Main Street and were joined by the mayor. She could see Georgie, newly returned from his sister's ranch, capering and cheering from the plank walk in front of the saloon.

Did Cal's pale, set face indicate he was regretting asking her to marry him? *Foolish woman,* she chided herself. The man never did anything on impulse, and once he decided on something he was as immovable as a rock.

"I think men look that way because they're mourning what they call the 'loss of their freedom,'" Annie said cynically from her position at the window. "But if you ask me, women are the ones who should look mournful. The men lose the freedom of having to cook their own meals and see to their own laundry, while the brides take on responsibilities that last from sunup to sundown."

"But there are compensations," Mercy interjected, laying a hand on her thickening waistline.

Leroy Scruggs showed the three well-dressed men into Robert Gillespie's office.

Tense as an overwound watch spring, Gillespie peered over the sheaf of papers he'd snatched up when he'd heard his employee's footsteps.

"What is it now, Scruggs?" he snapped. "I told you I was not to be disturbed this morning. If you can't follow dir—" His jaw dropped as he beheld the trio behind the sheepish Scruggs.

The broadest of the three, a man with a huge, graying mustache and muttonchop side-whiskers, came forward with his hand outstretched. "Robert Gillespie, I believe? I'm Louis Montgomery, president of the Houston and Texas Central Railroad, and these gentlemen behind me are Andrew Daniel and Henry Prestwick, two of the trustees."

Feeling as if a yawning chasm had suddenly opened in front of him, Gillespie rose and automatically shook the hands that were proffered.

"I trust it's no inconvenience that we've come a couple of days early," Montgomery was saying. "We have another property to look over just north of here, so it seemed foolish to wait until Monday, since you indicated you would have all the necessary paperwork in order well in advance."

A bell began tolling just down the street, signaling that Olivia Gillespie had just become Olivia Devlin.

"What's going on?" inquired Montgomery, nodding his head in the direction of the sound. "We noticed people in their Sunday best thronging into the church as the carriage went past. A wedding, perhaps?"

"Yes, the town's sheriff is getting married to a local widow," Gillespie replied with feigned disinterest, as he thought fast. He had the forged paper ready and waiting in the safe. It could still work.

He glanced at the grandfather clock in the corner of the room. By this time, Johnny Santone would be in place at the side of the bank, waiting for the bridal procession to come down the street. The president and trustees might have to be witnesses to Devlin and his new bride being gunned down, but that would make no great difference. The all-important paper would be in their hands by that time, and the tragedy would no doubt cause them to hasten their departure—hopefully before they had a chance to converse with any of the inhabitants of Gillespie Springs. It wouldn't do for these gentlemen to hear that the bride and bridegroom were about to rebuild on the critical strip of property that Gillespie claimed to own.

"Of course, a day or two one way or the other makes no difference," he replied. "I'll just go over to my safe, here, and get you the bill of sale." Walking to the small wall safe on feet that seemed to have no connection to the ground, he turned the lock, using his secret combination, and felt the tumblers click into place. A moment later he handed them the crucial paper.

"Excellent, excellent," Montgomery said as he accepted it, and behind him the trustees cooed their agreement.

Through the window he had left open a crack, Gillespie heard the noise and hullabaloo of a crowd coming down the street. The wedding party and guests must be exiting the churchyard. He glanced at the clock again. "I assume you would like to view the property, since

ou've come all this way. Shall we take your carriage
and go out to see it?''

But it was the noon hour, Montgomery protested.
Perhaps they should seek some refreshment at the local
hotel, assuming it served dinner? They could drive out
to see the property following an enjoyable meal, during
which they could discuss the coming of the railroad and
what it would mean to the town.

"I'm afraid the hotel is closed for business today,
since they're serving dinner to the wedding party," Gillespie explained, as the sounds of the crowd came
nearer. "But if we could stop at my home on the next
street over and let me give instructions to my cook, I'd
be pleased to offer you dinner there after we look at the
property." He doubted he'd have to go through with
the offer, after what was about to happen in the street
outside took place. The officers of the Houston and
Texas Central would be horrified by the tragedy and
make all speed leaving town.

His suggestion was very agreeable to the three gentlemen. "That would be quite satisfactory," Montgomery said, following him to the bank entrance. "I must
say, Mr. Gillespie, it's a pleasure to find a capable businessman like yourself in such an out-of-the-way place."

The banker allowed himself a gracious nod. "Thank
you, sir, but I don't intend that Gillespie Springs remain
'out-of-the-way.' The coming of the Houston and Texas
Central to my town will ensure that."

Yes, there they were, Gillespie thought as he stepped
out into the noonday sun on the front steps of the bank.

"Ah, the happy bride and groom," remarked Montgomery behind him. "Look, gentlemen, does it take you
back to the day you vowed to love and cherish?"

Till death do you part, Robert Gillespie added inwardly, staring as Devlin and his bride approached.

Chapter Twenty-Eight

Lord, where *was* Jase? When was it going to happen? Cal wondered as he emerged from the church with Livy on his arm. He smiled down at his beautiful bride, though he was as edgy as if he was watching for a real gunfighter to suddenly spring out and challenge him. Not that that wasn't possible, he thought as Livy beamed back up at him. Gillespie could have lied to Jase and have half a dozen hired guns ready. But Cal didn't think he had. The town had been free of aimless shifty-looking drifters of late, and he hadn't seen any sign of strangers newly arrived in town as he'd walked to the church.

He just wanted it to be over.

He nodded and smiled at the well-wishers crowding around the bridal party in the churchyard, thanking those who had come to see him wed Livy. Behind them, the Devlins, the Longs, Jovita Mendez, the Whytes and Lazlo Kristof and his family formed a procession, with Georgie bringing up the rear.

"Lead the way to the hotel, Mr. and Mrs. Devlin," commanded James Long, flushed with festive good spirits—and a little celebratory whiskey he'd imbibed from a flask Hank Whyte was carrying. "My cook at the hotel has promised us a bridal dinner fit for a king— and his queen, of course!"

"'Mr. and Mrs. Devlin'—how wonderful that sounds," Livy murmured, her blue eyes shining up at Cal as she gave his arm a little squeeze. "I don't think I've ever been this happy in my life, Cal! I love you so much!"

"And I love you, *wife*," Cal said, wishing he could forget all about Gillespie and his plots for a moment and just drown in the blue pools of Olivia's eyes. *Lord, let this all work out as we discussed it*, he prayed. *Let the man who threatens us be defeated, and let the shame he inflicted on Olivia be washed away forever*.

They had just passed Doc Broughton's office and were coming to the bank when the voice rang out. "Sheriff Devlin! Sorry t'intrude on such a happy day an' all, but I reckon I'm a faster gun than you, an' I reckon this is as good a day as any for you to die!"

Beside him, Olivia gasped—a gasp that was echoed by several behind her—and clutched Cal's arm as the man, dressed all in black except for the silver *conchas* on his hatband and his belt, stepped around the side of the bank and out into the street, his hands hovering just over his gun belt.

Cal halted, aware that Jovita and his sister, Annie, were hurriedly shepherding the rest of the women in the wedding party off the street—all but Livy, who was clinging to his arm as if a sudden norther had frozen her in place there. He heard her muffle a sob as he drawled, "Are you sure we can't put this off until another time? I've just gotten married. I'd purely hate to spoil my wedding day by killing you."

Cal pretended to look at his challenger, but his gaze

went beyond him to the man he'd guessed would be taking advantage of a front-row seat to the drama about to unfold. Sure enough, Robert Gillespie was standing on the steps in front of the bank, flanked by Scruggs and a trio of city gents Cal had never seen before. Cal gave Scruggs and the well-dressed strangers no more than a glance, however, for he was fascinated by the hot, avid gleam in Robert Gillespie's eyes.

There were gasps from the onlookers, then the rustle of cloth and the thudding of feet as everyone who could took cover, scurrying into the doctor's office, the jail and the general store.

"Oh, I don't think you'll be killing me. My name's Johnny Santone and no man who's drawn against me lived to tell about it. You gonna send your bride over there outa the way, Sheriff, or are you gonna hide behind her skirts?" the gunslinger demanded insolently.

"You sound pretty sure of yourself."

"I am. Real sure. Your bride's gonna be a widow before she's a wife."

"*No!*" Livy shrieked, letting go of Cal's arm and launching herself toward the gunman. "No! I won't let you take him from me! I won't let you do this to us!"

Cal caught up with Livy in two strides, wondering if she'd intended to claw the gunslinger's eyes out. "Livy! Stop! It'll be all right, I promise you!" he said, wrapping his arms around her and holding her with fierce intensity until she stopped struggling. Then, in a softer voice, hating the necessity of frightening her like this on their wedding day, he said, "Trust me. Nothing's going to happen to me, honey. I'm going to make it through this just fine."

She was not convinced. Cal could tell as much from the frightened, tear-filled eyes she focused on him. She thought his reassuring words were sheer male bravado, just something to calm the little lady long enough to get her off the street so he and his challenger could begin their deadly duel. He hated it, but she'd have to go on thinking that for a little while longer. If she knew the truth it would show on her face and Gillespie would guess something was up.

"Livy, honey, there's no way out of this—you know that, don't you?" he said.

"You could refuse to fight, Cal! You *could!*"

"Not and be able to hold my head up in this town or anywhere else."

"Damn your male pride!" she cried. "Is this what our life is going to be like—one gunfight after another until at last I'm wearing black again? Give them back their badge, Cal! I want *you,* not the sheriff!"

He took hold of her hands and stared intently into her tear-filled eyes, willing her to believe him. "Livy, you've been a very courageous lady and I love you for it. Just be brave for a couple more minutes, okay, honey? Have a little faith in me, as well as God. He's brought us through those other incidents, hasn't he? I know He'll see me safely through this one."

She stared at him in stony silence.

"Now go on inside the jail, honey, where I know you'll be safe. This'll all be over in a couple of minutes, I promise."

For a moment he thought she would refuse, then she flashed him one last pleading look and with a small cry whirled around and ran over to the jail. He saw out of the corner of his eye that she went no farther than the bench outside of it, but he made no attempt to insist she go inside. He looked back to the waiting gunman.

"I reckon you're gonna have t'borrow a pistol, Sheriff,'' called the man in black, as the noon sun glinted over the silver trim on his hat. "I figure a man who just got married ain't armed, right?"

"Wrong," Cal said, pushing the front of his frock coat aside and revealing the gun in the waistband of his trousers. "Shall I borrow a gun belt, so the odds will be as even as possible?"

"Naw, I reckon it don't make no difference. You're still gonna end up dead," the man calling himself Johnny Santone retorted.

Cal darted another glance at Gillespie, who was still standing there watching like a man who knew he'd just bet on the winning rooster at a cockfight. The gentlemen behind him had expressions of horror on their shock-paled faces, but Gillespie was gloating.

Cal shrugged out of his frock coat and tossed it to Sam, who caught it before it could fall in the dust. Cal nodded to Lazlo Kristof, his anxious-faced deputy, wishing there had been time to let him in on the plan.

Then Cal's gaze locked with that of the man opposite him in the street, and he shifted his position so that he was directly opposite the gunslinger and about twenty paces from him.

"Whenever you're ready," he murmured.

"Now!" the other man cried, and brought his gun out of the holster and up to fire. Cal did likewise, a fraction of a heartbeat later.

But "Johnny Santone" swiveled, and suddenly his Colt was aimed directly at Robert Gillespie—as was Cal's.

"Wha-what's the meaning of this, Santone?" gasped Gillespie, his eyes bulging with surprise as they darted from the gunslinger to the sheriff and back again. "Why are you pointing that thing at me?" Behind him,

Scruggs and the three businessmen scattered, diving to either side, the businessmen careless of their fine frock coats as they rolled in the dust of the street.

Scruggs struggled to his feet and ran down the side street between the hotel and the bank. Instantly Sam and Lazlo Kristof were in hot pursuit, their guns drawn.

"Get your hands up, Gillespie, you damned scheming bastard," growled the gunslinger.

"B-but—what do you mean? Y-you s-said you came here to kill the sheriff!" sputtered Gillespie.

"There ain't no Johnny Santone, you gullible fool. I'm Jase Lowry," the man in black told the banker. "And I happen to take exception to people killin' friends of mine, like Cal Devlin, and plotting to kill the lady he's just married."

Behind him, Cal heard Livy's sharp intake of breath, the shuffling of feet on the plank walks and the opening of doors and windows as the witnesses began to believe there was not to be a gunfight, after all.

"I—I don't know what you're talking about," Gillespie huffed, his face going beet red as he desperately tried to transform horrified surprise into indignation.

"I'm talking about the fact that you hired me to kill Sheriff Devlin here, when all the other guns you'd hired failed to do it. I'm talking about the fact that your toughs set fire to Olivia Gillespie's house and damn near killed her. You wanted her dead, didn't you?"

There were cries of outrage from the townsfolk within earshot—and the men who'd traveled from Houston to accept the deed from Robert Gillespie.

"You're a liar—or insane!" cried Gillespie. "I didn't hire anyone! I'm a law-abiding man, a pillar of this community!"

"Now, I don't take kindly to being called a liar,"

Jase Lowry said with deadly intensity. "Or crazy. I reckon I'm going to have to show you how much I don't like that."

He cocked his pistol and fired, the shot sending splinters of wood flying from the door frame just above Gillespie's right ear.

"Stop that! Sheriff, you've got to stop him!" demanded Gillespie, frozen in place by the threat implicit in the Colt Jase had trained at his belly.

"Oh? Does that mean you'll confess?" Cal inquired in a lazy drawl, his own pistol leveled at Gillespie's chest.

"Confess?" Gillespie demanded, as if the word were in Hindustani. "How *dare* you, Sheriff? I have nothing to confess!"

"Oh, I think you do, Gillespie. Go ahead, we're waiting."

Just then a red-faced, panting Scruggs came plodding around the corner, his hands up in the air, the barrel of Kristof's pistol prodding him from behind.

"Your employee's been tellin' us all kinds of interestin' information, Gillespie, by way of tryin' to bargain with us," Sam announced grimly.

"Oh?" the banker said with an air of icy boredom. "I can't imagine anything that wouldn't be a lie. I'm not in the habit of entrusting anything more challenging than rent collection to Mr. Scruggs."

"Thet's a durn lie, boss, an' you know it!" Scruggs cried.

"He told us you had him and some other fellas set that fire that nearly killed Miz Olivia," Sam said.

"Well, Gillespie? What do you say?" When the banker remained stubbornly, defiantly silent, Cal lowered his gun and shot a spot just a hair away from the banker's left foot.

With an indignant squawk, the banker jumped to the right—only to have another shot fired by Jase Lowry a second later cause him to jump to the left again.

"That's right, dance, you son of a bitch," growled Jase, and he fired just in front of Gillespie's foot, forcing the banker to jump up in the air with a fearful yelp.

Jase and Cal alternated firing, and there were jeers from the crowd as Gillespie capered from one foot to the other. "What—what do you want of me?" he finally cried. "What do you want me to do?"

"Cal? Was there something you wanted him to do?" Jase called over his shoulder.

Cal eyed Gillespie. "I think you could start by admitting you hired this man to kill me today, thinking he was a gunslinger."

"Sheriff, I can testify that's true! I was there when them two met!" hollered Scruggs from behind Gillespie, causing the banker to round on him.

"Shut up, you fool!" he snarled. "They have no proof of anything!"

"Now, I wouldn't say that's true, especially when Mr. Scruggs knows the judge will go easier on him for telling the truth about *you*," Cal told him.

Jase turned back to Gillespie. "Well?" He cocked the gun suggestively.

The banker remained silent, his face purple with frustrated fury.

Jase fired, his shot coming so close to the banker's cheek that a flying wood splinter cut it.

Gillespie wiped at it angrily with his sleeve. "Damn you!" he shouted, the curse meant for Cal. "All right! I hired this—this counterfeit gunfighter to kill you!"

"Why?" Cal couldn't help asking.

"Because I regretted hiring you as sheriff, you righteous fool!"

"Because you couldn't control me, could you?" Cal retorted. "But there's more, isn't there? You had to kill me before you could kill Olivia, isn't that right? The fire you ordered set didn't kill her as you were so sure it would, did it? But why did you want her dead, I wonder?"

"I don't know what you're talking about, Devlin," Gillespie muttered.

"I think you do," Cal retorted silkily. "Now spill it." When Gillespie remained silent again, he deliberately cocked the gun and fired it—just above Gillespie's head.

The man flinched and hunched over, then slowly straightened.

"I'll kill you where you stand, Gillespie," Cal told him.

"No, you wouldn't. It would be murder, in front of plenty of witnesses."

"But you'd be just as dead, wouldn't you?" Cal demanded, his gaze boring into Gillespie's. "I don't think you realize how much I want you dead, or how much this town hates you for the iron fist you've ruled it with. I reckon no one would breathe a word if I just shot you here and now."

There was a buzz of conversation in back of them, and even a cry of "Go ahead and plug him, Sheriff!" from somewhere in the crowd.

Gillespie hesitated, then muttered, "All right. I wanted my sister-in-law's property, but she refused to sell it to me. I had to get rid of her. But Scruggs set the fire!"

The buzz rose to a roar. Cal held his left hand up for silence. "And why did you want that property, when you practically own the whole town?"

Gillespie's expression was sullen as he darted a glance at the railroad trustees, whose faces were aghast. "Because the Houston and Texas Railroad wants to run track through here. Being able to sell them the entire right-of-way would've made me even richer."

"Mrs. Gillespie—uh, Mrs. Devlin," one of the businessmen called from the sidelines, "then you did not sell your property to your former brother-in-law?"

"No, indeed I did not, sir!" Livy answered clearly from the jail steps.

The businessman made a grimace of disgust and yanked a folded paper from inside his waistcoat. "Then Mr. Gillespie, you can consider our negotiations null and void, since the signature on this bill of sale must be a forgery."

Gillespie's fists clenched at his sides and he glared at Cal and the rest of the onlookers. "You fools! You've just lost me the deal that would have brought wealth and prosperity to this town!"

"I don't think we want it bad enough to make a deal with the devil," James Long called out.

"But there's more to confess, isn't there, Gillespie?" Cal inquired, his gun still aimed at the banker. "About what you did to Olivia, my wife?"

"Wh-what do you m-mean?" stammered Gillespie, the blood fading from his face, leaving him sickly pale.

"Cal?" Olivia's voice quavered behind him. "Cal, *no*..."

"Surely your memory isn't so dim, Gillespie." Cal's voice was a menacing purr. "Surely you remember lusting after your brother's wife, so much so that one day you attacked Olivia Gillespie.... In the barn, wasn't it? I'd guess you came at her from behind and threw something over her head so she couldn't identify you, you snake. And then you violated her, and when she became pregnant by you, and your brother knew it couldn't be his child because of his war injury, you told him she'd cuckolded you with his employee, Francisco Luna, knowing all the time that Olivia had never betrayed her husband. And Dan Gillespie became so enraged that he killed Francisco Luna, and then himself. Isn't that the way it was?" Cal demanded like an avenging Fury. "You might as well confess it all, Gillespie. You're already being charged with attempted murder." He was dimly aware of Olivia walking quietly into the street to stand at his side, facing her defiler with her head held high.

Gillespie smiled bitterly. "You think you have it all figured out, don't you, Devlin? Yes, I raped my brother's wife, and the child was mine."

Cal put his free hand mockingly to his ear. "Can't quite hear you. Are you saying that Olivia Gillespie was *innocent* of the shame you allowed her to face?"

"Yes, damn you!" Gillespie's face was a mocking mask. "But my brother, Dan, didn't kill the man he thought cuckolded him—he didn't have the guts for it, the lily-livered coward. I had to do it. And then I killed my useless, spineless brother."

Cal's jaw dropped. Even he hadn't guessed so much. "Raise your hands, Gillespie. You're under arrest for the murder of your brother and Francisco Luna, and for conspiracy to commit murder. You'll hang, I reckon, and may God have mercy on your twisted soul."

Gillespie smirked. "You like that image, don't you, the idea of me climbing the gallows with the crowd barking like jackals below? Well, it isn't going to happen. I believe you two are out of bullets," he said to Cal and Jase. "See you in hell, Sheriff." With that he shoved his hand inside his pocket and pulled out a pistol, aimed and fired.

Simultaneously, Livy screamed and threw herself in front of Cal, shrieking when the bullet struck her. A flower of scarlet suddenly bloomed on the bodice of her wedding dress.

"Livy!" Cal caught her in his arms and lowered her to the dusty street, kneeling down with her, staring helplessly at his beloved's pain-filled eyes and ivory face.

"Such a loving sacrifice," Gillespie sneered. "Well, it seems I must go first and be in hell to welcome *you*, Devlin." In a movement almost too quick for the eye to follow, he raised the gun to his own head and cocked it.

Jase Lowry was quicker, though. Leaping at the banker, he tackled him and knocked him off his feet. There was a swift, deadly wrestle for the gun, and then Jase seized it, throwing it safely out of reach. A moment later Lazlo Kristof had it in his possession and aimed it at Gillespie, while Sam maintained a hold on Scruggs.

"Lettin' you blow your own brains out is way too easy," Jase told the banker, keeping him restrained until Sam handed him the handcuffs, which Cal had given him earlier for just such a moment.

Now every eye was on Cal and his wounded bride. Livy had closed her eyes, though her face was drawn with pain. And the scarlet stain kept spreading ominously over the bodice of the wedding gown.

"Livy, please don't die," Cal whispered hoarsely.

From somewhere in the crowd Doc Broughton lumbered forward, his face looking a great deal less florid and sour than it usually did. Obviously he, too, was shaken by what had just taken place.

"Lemme have a look," he ordered Cal gruffly, and Cal obediently shifted his position so that he could get at the wound.

The doctor took out a pocketknife, and with a muttered, "'Fraid I'm gonna have to cut this," inserted it into the bloodstained shoulder of the dress and slashed it downward. Freshwater pearls plopped into the dust, but all Cal heeded was the rise and fall of Olivia's chest. He prayed as he had never prayed before during the endless moments while Broughton peered at the wound.

At last the doctor struggled to his feet. "Just a deep graze, Sheriff. Carry her on down to my office, won't you, and we'll get this properly cleaned up. You oughta put off the weddin' festivities for a day or so, but your bride ain't gonna die."

Later that afternoon, Olivia, her shoulder bandaged, sat propped up on pillows against the headboard of the bed in the grand suite of the Gillespie Springs Hotel. She was wearing the embroidered nightgown that had been Jovita's wedding present and had just finished the bowl of soup that the doctor deemed suitable fare for a wounded lady.

"Stop staring at me like you expect me to expire after every spoonful, Cal," she admonished the man who sat watching her anxiously from the side of the bed. "You heard the doctor—I 'ain't gonna die.'"

The corners of his mouth turned up somewhat, but his gaze remained somber. "I had my doubts for a moment there," he admitted. He got up and started to pace in front of the window.

"Is everyone in your family all right, Cal? That had

to have been frightening for your mother, even though she'd met Jase before—and for poor Mercy, who's with child!''

"Everyone's fine, honey. Long insisted they come and have dinner anyway, as soon as I carried you down to the doctor's. I checked on them a few minutes ago. Jase Lowry's getting treated like the conquering hero," he said wryly.

"He made quite a convincing gunfighter, didn't he? Cal, stop pacing and come tell me what's still bothering you!''

He did as she asked. "I—I reckon I'm still worried about how you feel about me, Livy," he said when he had settled himself in the chair again. "Are you sorry you married me, after what I made Gillespie admit to? Was I wrong to make him confess in front of the whole town?''

"You knew all along, didn't you?" she asked him. "That he was the one who...who raped me, I mean."

"I guessed," he said, looking down at his hands, "after we made love the first time. And I felt you'd never know any real peace until everyone knew who'd done that to you, Livy, and that you'd done nothing wrong.''

"Oh, Cal, I wanted to tell you," she said, wincing at the pain as she leaned forward and stroked her hand through his hair. "But I was too afraid—for you. I thought he'd kill you," she told him.

"I had no idea he'd killed Luna and Dan, though."

"Nor did I. It's comforting, in a way...." Livy mused. "That poor man...I'm glad to know that, bitter and changed as Dan was after the war, he wasn't a murderer, or a man who could take his own life."

Cal said nothing for a few moments, then raised his

head. "Livy, now that Gillespie's been arrested, I don't
think there's going to be a parade of gunslingers comin'
through here, trying to outdraw the sheriff, but do you
want me to resign and try my hand at something else?
I'll do it, honey, if that's what you really want. You're
more important to me than any badge—I want you to
know that."

She was astonished. "Cal, I was scared out of my
wits when I said that about you giving them back the
badge. I'm proud to be the wife of the best sheriff this
town's ever had, you hear me? You wear that badge as
long as you want to."

He gazed at her, smiling now. "I reckon I'll do that,
Mrs. Devlin."

"A kiss to seal the bargain, Mr. Devlin? I think I'm
up to that much, at least. Maybe more—we'll see."

Obligingly he leaned forward and covered her lips
with his.

Epilogue

True to their word, the railway trustees did not bring the Houston and Texas Central through Gillespie Springs. But the line came close enough that the town nevertheless grew and prospered.

Robert Gillespie was sentenced to hang for the murders of Dan Gillespie and Francisco Luna. Sentence was carried out at Huntsville Prison on June 4, 1869. Leroy Scruggs was sentenced to life imprisonment after he turned state's evidence on his former employer.

Caleb Devlin served for many years as the sheriff of Gillespie Springs, and then as its mayor. Olivia, as Gillespie's former sister-in-law, inherited Gillespie's mansion and lands. She transformed the mansion into a home for old soldiers of both the Confederate *and* Union armies.

* * * * *

HE SAID

SHE SAID

Explore the mystery of male/female communication in this extraordinary new book from two of your favorite Harlequin authors.

Jasmine Cresswell and Margaret St. George bring you the exciting story of two romantic adversaries—each from their own point of view!

DEV'S STORY. CATHY'S STORY.
As he sees it. As she sees it.
Both sides of the story!

The heat is definitely on, and these two can't stay out of the kitchen!

Don't miss **HE SAID, SHE SAID.**
Available in July wherever Harlequin books are sold.

◆ HARLEQUIN®

Harlequin® Historical

Coming this summer from
Award-winning author
Theresa Michaels

The Merry Widows
A heartwarming new Western series

"Michaels at her poignantly moving best."
—*Affaire de Coeur*

"Pure magic!" —*The Literary Times*

"A true gem…" —*Rawhide and Lace*

"Will hold you spellbound." —*Rendezvous*

"Emotionally charged…" —*Romantic Times*

**That's what reviewers are saying about
Mary the first book in the Merry Widows trilogy**

Coming in June to a store near you.
Keep your eyes peeled!

Harlequin® Historical

If your tastes run to
terrific Medieval Romance,
don't miss

The
Bride
Thief

by Susan Spencer Paul

The exciting conclusion to her
Medieval Bride Trilogy

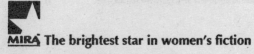